# SWORD OF VENGEANCE

Natassja smiled and ran a finger gently down the hand-maiden's scarred cheek. 'Do not be fooled by her current state. When given the proper command, she will change.' Natassja looked at her tenderly, like a proud mother. 'For now, she only has her own private world of pain. That can be altered by giving her a name.'

'A name.'

'A name is a mystical thing, Heinz-Mark. It has resonance in the aethyr. They can use it to find their prey. When they are ready, I will give it to them.'

'She's not ready?'

'Not yet,' said Natassja, stroking the handmaiden's remaining hair. 'There will be three of them, at least to begin with. Their creation is long and difficult. Then I will send them out. They will sweep across Averland like crows, never pausing, never resting.'

She looked back at Grosslich, and her eyes were shining. 'All they need is the name. *Helborg.*'

# WARHAMMER

## · WARHAMMER HEROES ·

SWORD OF JUSTICE
Chris Wraight

WULFRIK
C L Werner

SWORD OF VENGEANCE
Chris Wraight

SIGVALD (July 2011)
Darius Hinks

## ⫷ TIME OF LEGENDS ⫸

### · THE LEGEND OF SIGMAR ·
*Graham McNeill*

Book 1 – HELDENHAMMER
Book 2 – EMPIRE
Book 3 – GOD KING

### · THE RISE OF NAGASH ·
*Mike Lee*

Book 1 – NAGASH THE SORCERER
Book 2 – NAGASH THE UNBROKEN
Book 3 – NAGASH IMMORTAL (August 2011)

### · THE SUNDERING ·
*Gav Thorpe*

Book 1 – MALEKITH
Book 2 – SHADOW KING
Book 3 – CALEDOR (May 2011)

A WARHAMMER NOVEL

WARHAMMER HEROES

# SWORD OF VENGEANCE

## CHRIS WRAIGHT

BLACK LIBRARY

*To Alex at BL, for sterling work in steering this to print. You'll be sorely missed!*

**A BLACK LIBRARY PUBLICATION**

First published in Great Britain in 2011 by
The Black Library,
Games Workshop Ltd.,
Willow Road, Nottingham,
NG7 2WS, UK.

10 9 8 7 6 5 4 3 2 1

Cover illustration by Cheoljoo Lee.
Map by Nuala Kinrade.

UK ISBN13: 978 1 84970 020 7
US ISBN13: 978 1 84970 021 4

See the Black Library on the internet at
**blacklibrary.com**

Find out more about Games Workshop
and the world of Warhammer 40,000 at
**www.games-workshop.com**

Printed and bound in the UK.

THIS IS A dark age, a bloody age, an age of daemons
and of sorcery. It is an age of battle and death, and of the world's
ending. Amidst all of the fire, flame and fury
it is a time, too, of mighty heroes, of bold deeds
and great courage.

AT THE HEART of the Old World sprawls the Empire, the largest
and most powerful of the human realms. Known for its engineers,
sorcerers, traders and soldiers, it is
a land of great mountains, mighty rivers, dark forests
and vast cities. And from his throne in Altdorf reigns
the Emperor Karl Franz, sacred descendant of the
founder of these lands, Sigmar, and wielder
of his magical warhammer.

BUT THESE ARE far from civilised times. Across the length and
breadth of the Old World, from the knightly palaces of Bretonnia
to ice-bound Kislev in the far north, come rumblings of war. In
the towering Worlds Edge Mountains, the orc tribes are gathering
for another assault. Bandits and renegades harry the wild southern
lands of the Border Princes. There are rumours of rat-things, the
skaven, emerging from the sewers and swamps across the land.
And from the northern wildernesses there is the ever-present
threat of Chaos, of daemons and beastmen corrupted by the
foul powers of the Dark Gods. As the time of battle draws
ever nearer, the Empire needs heroes
like never before.

# What Has Gone Before

The first part of this story was told in
*Sword of Justice*.

THE SUMMER OF the year 2523. The province of Averland has been without an elector since the death of the mad Count Marius Leitdorf. Wearying of the long process of selection, Emperor Karl Franz dispatches his Champion Ludwig Schwarzhelm to Averheim to expedite matters, accompanied by his personal spy, Pieter Verstohlen, and an army of Reikland halberdiers.

The electorship is contested by two men: Rufus Leitdorf, second son of the old elector, and Heinz-Mark Grosslich, a relative unknown. During the long months of conflict between them, Averland has drifted into misrule. Reports arrive of orcs massing in the east, and most of Schwarzhelm's forces are sent to secure the distant marches. Back in Averheim, Schwarzhelm is subject to severe pressure. When reports reach him that his commander in the east has been killed, he immediately rides out to avenge him.

Meanwhile, Verstohlen investigates the origins of the narcotic traffic in joyroot, and stumbles across Leitdorf's wife Natassja at the centre of a Chaos cult. Barely escaping with his life, Verstohlen flees to the safety of Grosslich's forces. Promising him the elector-ship if he will declare war on the Leitdorfs, Verstohlen instigates open conflict between the two camps, and prompts the city Steward to send messages to the gar-rison of Reiksguard in Nuln. These are commanded by Schwarzhelm's great rival, Kurt Helborg.

Schwarzhelm is swiftly victorious over the orcs and rides west back to Averheim. On the way to the city, Schwarzhelm discovers the bodies of messengers and half-burned orders which seem to implicate Leitdorf in their murder. Nuln is referred to as well, fanning the flames of Schwarzhelm's already heightened sus-picion of Helborg.

In Averheim, Grosslich and Verstohlen drive Leit-dorf's forces to the edge of the city. As Helborg and his Reiksguard arrive, they see Averheim in flames and Grosslich's men running rampant. Helborg moves to quell the fighting, takes Leitdorf into custody and begins to orchestrate the capture of Grosslich.

Schwarzhelm arrives just as the fighting reaches its climax. Seeing Helborg riding against Grosslich, he leaps to the conclusion that the Reiksguard have turned traitor. Schwarzhelm's anger, stoked by days of fatigue, breaks. He fells Helborg with a terrible blow. Before he can kill him, the Reiksguard manage to pull their leader from danger. Taking Leitdorf with them, they flee the city, pursued by Grosslich's forces.

In the aftermath of the battle, Schwarzhelm fulfils Verstohlen's pledge and crowns Grosslich Elector of

Averland. He returns to Altdorf, and is removed from active duty by a devastated Emperor. Disconsolate, Schwarzhelm confides in his old mentor, the swordmaster Heinrich Lassus. During the conversation, Lassus unwittingly betrays the truth: that Helborg and Leitdorf are innocent, and Grosslich given over to Chaos, together with Natassja. The two devotees of Slaanesh begin to enact their terrible plan for Averland with all the resources of the elector's office at their disposal.

Working alone now, Schwarzhelm vows to return. Leitdorf and Helborg are hunted by Grosslich's troops, moving from safe house to safe house in an effort to evade detection. As Helborg fights for his life, surrounded by enemies, the Sword of Vengeance lies in the vaults of the Imperial Palace, far from its owner's hands.

# Chapter One

RUNNING DIDN'T HELP. They were faster, unnaturally faster, and they didn't give up. Anna-Helena tore round the corner of the old bakery, dragging snatched breaths into her overworked lungs, her fingers scratching against the stone as she grabbed at it. The alley beyond was dark, far darker than it should have been. She couldn't see the end of it. Panicked, she started to twist back around.

Then they were on her. Three of them, wheezing like animals. She broke free of the first grasp, hearing the fabric of her dress rip and come away in shreds. There was nowhere to go but further down into the shadows, away from the horror, deeper into the cool valley between the silent buildings.

'Mercy of Sigmar!' came a voice, her own, shrill and panicked, on the edge of hysteria. The sound sank deep into the uncaring stone. There was no one awake to hear her, no one to come to her aid. It had been foolish, *stupid*, to cross the river after dark. She'd heard the stories. Everyone had. But the woman with the deep eyes had whispered such kind words, and she'd promised root.

11

Her bare feet, criss-crossed with lacerations, made no sound as she sprinted across the filthy cobbles. Her fear made her fast, even as her tattered dress hugged at her thighs.

Not fast enough. She felt the first grip dig in deep, talons sinking into the flesh of her shoulder. She was pulled up, dragged back. She whirled round, ignoring the pain, trying to shake them off. Her heart raced out of control, flooding her body with hot, terrified blood.

'Get off me!' Her voice was almost bestial with horror, the cry of a prey animal.

Another of them seized her other shoulder, pinning her down. Their weight was crushing, forcing her to her knees. She fought back, panting and ineffectual. A blank helmet gazed down at her, distended into a muzzle. Broken wheezing came from behind the closed grille.

'What are you?' she sobbed, slumping in defeat as the grip tightened. They towered over her, the three of them, saying nothing, holding her down. 'Love of Sigmar, what *are* you?'

A fourth man appeared then, walking between them. She'd not seen him earlier. He was short, hunched-over with age. He had the grey skin of a scholar and black rings around his deep-set eyes. He pushed one of her pursuers aside and grabbed her chin, holding her face up to the scant moonlight. She gazed, trembling, into a cold and pitiless face.

'Let me *be*...' she protested, feeling hot tears run down her cheeks.

The man ignored her, pinching her flesh and rocking her face from side to side. He was looking at her like a housewife buying fruit, assessing suitability.

'She'll do,' he said at last. He had a thin, scraping voice. 'At last, we have three of them.'

She was dragged to her feet by the helmeted warriors. They started to haul her back down the alley, back the way they'd come, back to the building site and its hidden workings.

'Where are you taking me?' she screamed, jerking pointlessly against their iron-hard clutches.

The hunched man smiled sadly at her. It had been spirited of her, to run, but not much more than that. None of them got far.

'Into another world, my child,' he whispered, watching her disappear back into the night. 'Into another world.'

AVERLAND HAD SWELTERED under the beating sun for too long, and the weather had turned at last. Cold air tumbled down from the peaks of the Worlds Edge Mountains, ruffling the long grass of the plains and stirring the waters of the rivers. The herds of cattle felt it as they grazed, as did the peasants in their hovels. The wind had changed.

Averheim looked perfectly serene in the golden light of the afternoon. The recent battles in its alleyways and squares had done little to dent the facades of the elegant streets. More damage had been caused by the months of dereliction beforehand, during which men had lain in the streets half-sensible, their mouths open and drooling from joyroot. Back then thoroughfares had succumbed to piles of filth, and sewage had been left to gather in the heat, crawling with flies. Now discipline had returned, and the drift of the past was being expunged.

After his coronation, Heinz-Mark Grosslich had

moved his seat of power from the ancestral Alptraum castle to the Averburg, the ancient citadel that dominated the east bank of the river. Now the gold-rimmed device of the boar's head hung from every battlement. Signs of conflict, most notably in the Vormeisterplatz, had been scrubbed clean by an army of drudges. The fires had gone. Companies of armed men walked the streets at night, the merchant guilds had come back, and trade along the river had returned.

Dagobert Tochfel, Steward of the Averburg, walked down the wide avenue from the citadel to the Griffon Bridge, the oldest crossing over the river. He could smell the water as he drew near, dank and cool. The worst of the scum on its surface had been cleared away and the barges had come back. As he went along the quayside, he could see at least a dozen of them, jostling and bumping as they jockeyed for position by the warehouses.

He allowed himself a smile of satisfaction. The days had been hard, and the memories bad. Like everyone else, he needed to believe the worst of it was over. Every sign of renewal was seized upon, welcomed and documented. Averheimers wanted their city back. They wanted their lives back.

Tochfel's skin was now a shade less grey, his eyelids a little less red, but he still had the hunched look of a scholar. His life before the affair with Schwarzhelm had been dominated by parchment ledgers and legal depositions. It was much the same now. Rulers might come and go, but the real business of governing changed little.

Ahead of him, dressed in the crimson and gold of the Grosslich hierarchy, Captain Erasmus Euler was busy overseeing the unloading. A dozen of his men lounged nearby, their halberds casually leaning against the warehouse walls. The scene was relaxed. Merchants haggled in small groups around them, exchanging bills of lading.

Tochfel walked up to the nearest barge, the *Rosalinde*. She was ugly, dark and low in the water. Most of her crew were ashore. The cargo was obvious – building materials, and lots of them. Every day brought a fresh consignment from somewhere. Granite from the mines in the east, marble from Sartosa, iron from Nuln. Averheim was sucking it in, and Tochfel didn't even want to think about how much it was costing. It wasn't on his ledger, and that was the important thing.

'Good day, Herr Euler,' he said, waving to the captain.

Tochfel thought he caught a flash of irritation on the man's face.

'Good day to you, Steward,' Euler said, handing a sheaf of documents to one of his men. 'What can I do for you?'

'Thought I'd take a look at how the project's coming on. Even I feel stale eventually, cooped up in the citadel.'

'It's going fine.' Euler's voice was semi-hostile, but Tochfel was prepared to cut him a good deal of slack. Before Grosslich's elevation, the man had barely commanded more than a dozen men. Now he was in charge of hundreds.

The Steward looked out across the river. Behind the *Rosalinde* there were two more barges in line for the berth. More were visible under the wide arches of the Griffon Bridge. The queuing had become a problem. 'How many more are we expecting this week?'

'Couldn't say. Get used to it, Steward. They'll be coming in for weeks.'

Tochfel gave a rueful look. 'Oh, I am used to it, captain. Though I can't pretend I don't have my concerns.' He checked to see if Euler was in a tolerant mood. He'd heard the man had developed a temper. 'These landings are used for more than building materials. There are supplies for the citadel that are now two weeks late.'

'Then land them further down.'

'I would do so, Herr Euler, if you could show me one clear berth. The elector's project – important as it no doubt is – seems to have taken things over somewhat.'

He tried to keep his voice deliberately light – there was no point in provoking a fight over this. Euler ran his fingers through his hair. He looked tired.

'Things have changed,' he said. 'There's business you're not in command of any more. You'll have to talk to the elector yourself.'

'You think I haven't tried that? I can't get near him. I can't even get near to Herr Alptraum, whom I've now not seen for over two weeks. I thought perhaps this might be best coming from you.'

For a moment, just a moment, there was a flicker of fear in Euler's eyes. Tochfel could see the hollowness in his cheeks, the tightness around his mouth.

'The elector's busy. If you want to bother him with this, then feel free. I've got more important things to see to.'

Tochfel decided to take that as a warning. It was a troubling thought. If even men like Euler disliked bringing things to Grosslich's attention, then dealing with the elector would be difficult. For all the stories they told about Marius Leitdorf, he'd at least known how to keep trade flowing along the river.

'I see,' was all he said. He turned to look across the water. Half a mile distant, peeping over the crowded roofs of the poor quarter, was the object of all this work. With astonishing speed, Grosslich's grand project was going ahead. The wooden scaffolding was already higher than the buildings around it. Beneath the cages of oak, the frame was starting to take shape.

Tochfel couldn't suppress a shudder of distaste. Of course, he didn't know what it would look like when complete, but the early signs weren't promising. What kind of an architect came up with a tower made entirely of iron? Perhaps it would all become clear later. Perhaps he'd be surprised by it.

He hoped so. Just for once, it would be nice for the surprises to be good ones.

HEINZ-MARK GROSSLICH SAT on the electoral throne in the audience chamber of the Averburg. He was draped in crimson and the crown of his office sat heavily on his brow. The late afternoon sun slanted through the narrow windows, bathing the dark wood of the walls. As with every part of the citadel, banners with the Grosslich device hung along the room's flanks. The more traditional emblems of Averland and Solland were nowhere to be seen.

There were two other men present with him. At his side sat Schwarzhelm's aide, the spy Pieter Verstohlen. He was dressed in his habitual garb – a long leather coat, waistcoat and breeches, linen shirt, all beautifully tailored. His slender, handsome face gave little away.

Grosslich avoided making eye contact with him. The

man's continuing presence was an irritation. Schwarzhelm's leftovers would have to be dealt with at some stage, but for now the need for a respectable front remained acute. The eyes of Altdorf were on him. The eyes of the Empire were on him.

That fact was demonstrated by the presence of the second man. A messenger from the Imperial Palace, kneeling on the stone not five yards from him. It had taken longer than Grosslich had expected, but had been bound to happen eventually. This was the beginning, the start of the tussle between elector and elected. Even if he'd been an ordinary provincial governor with ordinary provincial aspirations, the balance of power between Altdorf and Averheim was always fraught.

But he was no ordinary governor, and his ambitions went beyond anything the Emperor was capable of imagining. Soon even Karl Franz would realise it.

'Rise,' he drawled.

The messenger clambered to his feet. He was armoured and wore the red and white Palace livery. His tunic was emblazoned with the Imperial griffon, and he carried a heavy sword at his belt. The man's grey hair was cropped close to the grizzled scalp, his shoulders were broad, and he looked like he knew how to use his weapon. A knight, then, seconded to the Palace's messenger corps. When he looked at Grosslich, there was no fear in his seasoned eyes.

'I bring word from His Most Imperial Highness, Emperor Karl Franz I von Holswig-Schliestein, Grand Prince of Altdorf, Count of the Reikland, Protector of the Empire.'

'That's nice,' said Grosslich. He felt Verstohlen stiffen slightly at his side. Perhaps he should resist the temptation to mock. The vermin around him needed humouring for a little while longer, as tedious as it was to do so.

'The Emperor has instructed me to congratulate your lordship on the succession to the throne, achieved though it was at such a high price. As war has conspired to prevent an assemblage of the Estates in recent months, his highness begs me to enquire of your lordship when your entourage intends to travel to the Palace, so that his highness may pay his respects in person.'

The stilted language was that of Imperial diplomacy, and to the untrained ear might have sounded like a gentle request. Grosslich was worldly enough to know what it really conveyed: he was being summoned to Altdorf. Karl Franz wanted to see if his intervention in Averland had brought him what he wanted.

'Convey to his highness my profound thanks for his gracious concern,' replied Grosslich. 'He'll be aware of the difficult circumstances of my inauguration. The traitors who conspired to ruin this province remain free from capture. There is work to be done on the city, and need for more men under arms. I trust he'll understand that I cannot leave the city for the foreseeable future. When all is placed in order, I'll be honoured to accept his magnanimous invitation.'

The messenger remained stony-faced. He could interpret the response as well as any of them. Grosslich might as well have told the Emperor to run along back to his stinking Palace and wait for him to turn up in his own sweet time. Grosslich allowed himself to enjoy the moment.

'May I ask your lordship if there might be a more... precise indication of how long the work will take?

You'll appreciate that the Emperor has many and pressing concerns of his own, and his highness has a personal interest in bringing this to a satisfactory conclusion.'

The translation being: think carefully what you're doing. Karl Franz doesn't tolerate insolence from anyone. He helped put you here, he can help remove you too.

The naïveté was almost touching.

'When Helborg is dead and the Leitdorfs are on the rack,' said Grosslich, speaking deliberately, 'then I will come.'

For the first time, a shade of disapproval coloured the messenger's face.

'No doubt you remember the order made by his highness concerning the Lord Helborg. He is to be recovered alive.'

'Yes, I noted the request. If it falls within my power, Helborg shall be preserved.' He gave the messenger a sly look. 'If it falls within my power,' he repeated.

There was a pause.

'I understand. This shall be conveyed.'

Grosslich didn't reply, and his silence concluded the appointment. The messenger bowed and backed down the length of the audience chamber, never turning his face away from the dais. As he reached the heavy double doors at the far end, they opened soundlessly and he withdrew.

'So what did you make of that?' asked Grosslich, turning to Verstohlen with a satisfied smile.

The spy didn't look amused. 'A dangerous game to play. I don't see the advantage in goading Karl Franz.'

Grosslich laughed. 'Ever cautious, Verstohlen,' he said. 'That's good. It's what I employ you for.'

'You don't employ me.'

'Ah. Sometimes I forget. Perhaps you'd better remind me what your intentions are here. I get used to having you around.'

'As soon as I hear from Schwarzhelm, I'll let you know,' said Verstohlen. 'I find it odd that I haven't had word already.'

Grosslich kept his impatience well concealed. Verstohlen's usefulness had long since expired. If he didn't find a reason to leave the city soon, then something might have to be done.

'Until then, your counsel will be invaluable,' he said.

'Any news of Leitdorf?'

'Which one?'

'Either.'

'There have been reports of Rufus from the east,' said Grosslich. 'I have men on his trail, but the country is wild and we can't cover everything. Don't worry. It's only a matter of time. Their power is broken.'

Verstohlen shot him an irritated look. 'So you evidently believe. But time has passed, and evil seeds will spring up anew.'

Grosslich found himself getting bored of the man's piety. Verstohlen had no idea about the potential of evil seeds. No idea at all.

'We'll redouble our efforts,' he said, looking as earnest about it as he could. 'The traitors will be found, and justice will be done. Believe me – no one wants the Leitdorf line terminated more than I, and it *will* happen.'

MARKUS BLOCH LEANED on his halberd and shaded his eyes against the harsh sun. He was high in the passes of the Worlds Edge Mountains, far from the warmth of

Averheim. Around him the granite pinnacles reared high into the empty airs, heaped on top of one another like the ramparts of some ancient citadel of giants. To the north and south, the summits soared even higher, crowned with snow the whole year round, glistening and sparkling under the open sky. The passes were clear, though the air was still bitter. It didn't matter how balmy the summers were in the land below; here, it was always winter.

The army he'd brought to the mountains with such labour was installed a few miles away in one of the scattered way-forts that lined the road to Black Fire Pass. Even though the way-forts were capacious, many of the lower ranks had been forced to camp in the shadow of its walls. He had over two thousand men under his command, the kind of force that only Black Fire Keep could accommodate with ease.

The place where he stood was far from the road and the way-forts. It was a desolate spot, a patch of wind-blasted stone in the heart of the peaks. A wide flat area, perhaps four hundred yards across, was bounded on three sides by sheer cliffs, cracked with age and flecked with mottled lichens. The piercing sun made little impression on it, and there was a dark aspect to the rocks.

Bloch didn't speak for a long time. This was the third such site he'd been shown. It never got any better.

He turned to his companion, the mountain guard commander Helmut Drassler. The man was tall and rangy, and like all his kind wore a beard and was dressed in furs. Drassler looked over the site with a kind of blank distaste. After seeing so many of them, perhaps there was little other reaction.

Aside from Bloch and Drassler, only Kraus, Schwarzhelm's honour guard captain, was present. His expression was as hard, cold and unreadable as his master's.

'This one's the worst,' muttered Bloch. Drassler nodded, saying nothing.

The site was a natural killing place. The cliffs on all sides turned it into a cauldron of death. For any forces out in the middle of it, there was only one escape – back through the narrow gap where the three of them stood. If that route were blocked, then there could be no hope for any trapped within.

So it had proved for the men lying on the stone in front of them. They had been dead for a long time. Their skin had been dried and bleached by the wind and hung in tatters from exposed bone. Their eyes had long gone, taken by the scavengers of the high places. Even now, carrion crows circled in the icy airs, waiting to feast again. The banner of Averland, crested with the golden sun of Solland, hung limply against the far cliff. The standard was surrounded by heaps of bodies, as if that was where they'd made their last stand.

It hadn't done them much good. Obscene images had been daubed across the precious fabric, obscuring the proud record of past conflicts. The figure of the sun had been transformed into the leering face of a corrupted moon.

Bloch couldn't tell how many bodies lay there. Hundreds, certainly. Probably far more. The way they lay atop one another, rammed together in death as they had been in their final hours, made it hard to tell.

'They took plenty with them,' said Kraus.

That they had. For every man who lay on the stone, there was an orc too. The greenskins' flesh had weathered better. The two armies were intertwined with one another, locked in an embrace that had lasted far longer than the fighting.

Despite the numbers of dead greenskins, it was clear who had won. The human bodies had been despoiled and their armour plundered. There were signs that goblins had crawled down the cliffs like swarming insects, no doubt raining barbs down on top of the defenders. One goblin corpse still hung forty feet up, its hand trapped in a crack, its lifeless body twisting in the wind.

It would have been a massacre. The soldiers must have known they were going to die. They would have fought for pride, but nothing else.

Bloch felt sickened. Just like the other sites Drassler had shown them. They'd come up here to be killed.

'*Why?*' he said, bitterly, not expecting any better answers than last time. 'Why leave the forts? These places are murder-traps.'

'I told you,' said Drassler. 'We had orders. You'll see it all at the Keep.'

Bloch shook his head despairingly. He hadn't been a commander long, but he'd fought in the Emperor's armies all his adult life and knew how they worked. There were some orders you didn't follow.

He crouched down and took a closer look at the bodies near his feet. The corpses of the Black Fire Keep garrison stretched away across the site, their clothes torn and flesh rent. Empty eye-sockets gazed up at the sky, laced with dry, crusted blood.

He wasn't interested in them. He was interested in the orcs. Before him lay one of the smaller breeds. Perhaps a large goblin – it had the hook nose and long yellow fangs of the kind. It had been skewered on the tip of a sword and the blade still stood, lodged in its scrawny chest. Dead claws clutched at the air, locked in the final throes of agony.

Bloch studied its armour. Like all the greenskins it was wearing close-fitting mail. It had been carrying a short sword of its own rather than a gouge or a flail. The workmanship was good. Just as with the orcs he'd encountered in Averland while serving under Grunwald, the greenskins had excellent wargear. Imperial wargear.

He shuffled forwards and took a closer look at the creature's face. Even in death it had a horrifying aspect. A long black tongue lolled from its cruel mouth, and its thin face was set into a scream of rage. The expression was so vivid, so locked in malice, it was hard to believe that some flicker of life didn't still exist within it.

The sun flashed from something shiny. Dangling from the goblin's earlobe was a coin. Bloch pulled it from the flesh and it popped free. An Imperial schilling, embossed with the image of Karl Franz and stamped with the date and place of manufacture. It was new, minted in Altdorf that year. Coins like that were rare – they took time to come into circulation. All the ones he'd seen in the death-sites were the same. Somehow, this horde of orcs had come across Imperial armour and a batch of newly-minted coins.

He stood up again, keeping the schilling in his hand.

'Same as before?' asked Kraus.

'Same as before.'

Bloch turned to Drassler. 'I've seen enough of this. We'll head to the Keep.'

'They're still camped in there,' warned Drassler. 'I don't know how many.'

'I don't care how many,' growled Bloch, clenching his fist around the coin and squeezing it tight. 'We'll kill 'em all.'

# Chapter Two

THE IRON TOWER was not the only building being raised in Averheim, but it was by far the largest. A whole district of the poor quarter had been scoured to allow its creation. Some of the demolished houses and streets had dated back to the time of the first Emperors, before the city had grown large enough to reach over the river and absorb the villages along the western bank. They were gone now, mere whispers in the long march of Imperial history.

The building work had taken place quickly. So quickly that men marvelled at it as far afield as Streissen and Nuln. Though the Leitdorfs and the Alptraums between them had erected plenty of follies in their long years of rule, each had taken years to complete. In a matter of weeks, the Iron Tower's foundations had been laid and the skeleton metal frame had shot up into the sky.

Despite the wonders of engineering, the Tower was not popular. Soon after work had started, ordinary folk of the poor quarter had learned to give it a wide berth. Few willingly walked under the shadow of the great iron spurs that marked out its future outline. Any who had to pass close by scratched the sign of the comet on their chests. It had an evil rumour, and in private many started to call it Grosslich's Folly.

No one knew for certain *why* the Tower was so hated. After all, the new elector was wildly popular. Order had been restored to the city, and the gold was flowing again through the merchants' coffers. It was even hissed in quiet corners that joyroot could be found again, though its trade had been heavily curtailed.

Still, the stories kept coming. A baby had been born in sight of the Tower with three arms and no eyes. Milk curdled across the city when the foundation stone had been laid. No birds would fly within a mile of it, they said, turning Averheim silent at dawn and dusk. All fanciful tales, no doubt. All unreliable, plucked from the gossipy lips of old wives with nothing better to do.

But the world was a strange place, and old wives weren't always wrong. What no one could deny was that, from time to time, attractive youths were still going missing. Not many – just one or two, here and there – but enough to attract attention. That had been going on even before the days of the Tower, and folk had put it down to the evil times with no elector. Grosslich had even issued an edict on the matter, promising death for any found engaged in the grisly removal of Averland's next generation.

It didn't stop the disappearances. Like the slow drip of a tap, they carried on. It was worse around the Tower, some said. Many believed the rumours, even though there was no proof. It was all hearsay, conjecture and idle talk.

Heinz-Mark Grosslich, still dressed in the robes he'd

worn to receive the Imperial messenger, found himself enjoying the irony of it all as he headed towards the Tower. The foolish, the ignorant and the savage were quite capable of seeing what was going on under their noses. Only the wise were blind to the horror that lurked around them. Blind, that is, until it was far too late.

Night had fallen. The Tower building site was heavily guarded by men of the elector's inner circle, loyal soldiers who'd seen the fight against Leitdorf through from the beginning. As he approached the perimeter of the works, Grosslich saw half a dozen of them leap to attention. They looked surprised to see him walking on his own. They shouldn't have been. He'd been back and forth between the Tower and the Averburg several times a day for the past couple of weeks. When the work was completed it would become the new seat of power in Averland. The Averburg would have to go. The city needed a fresh start, a new way of doing things.

He nodded to the guards as he passed their cordon and entered the site. None of them would ever go further inside – their job was to patrol the fences. That didn't mean the interior was unguarded, just that the guards there were of a more specialised type.

Once past the fences, the building came into view properly. It had the appearance of an upturned claw. Huge iron shafts had been sunk into the earth, on top of which the structure was now being raised. When finished, the Tower would resemble a giant dark needle, soaring up into the high airs and dominating the land around it. There would be a turret at the very pinnacle sending six spikes out over the cityscape, each twenty feet long. At the centre of those spikes would be his sanctum, far above the rolling plains. That would be the heart of it all, the fulcrum about which the realm would be moulded to his will.

There was still so much to do. The lower levels of the Tower were little more than a tangle of naked metal. Piles of beams, trusses, stone blocks, nails, rods and other paraphernalia littered the churned-up earth. The disarray offended Grosslich's refined senses, and he made a mental note to order the workers to take more care.

As he neared the centre of the works, a door loomed up out of the darkness. It was imposing – over twelve feet tall and nearly as wide – and decorated with friezes of pure, dark iron. Here and there, a face of tortured agony could be made out in the night air, lost in a morass of limbs and torsos. The iron doors themselves were covered in a filigree of sigils and unholy icons, all traced with formidable skill and delicacy. Grosslich had no idea what they all signified, but he knew he would soon. His abilities increased with every passing day.

The wall behind the door was barely started and rose no more than a few feet above the iron frame. Beyond it, the bone-like scaffolding was obvious. It was a door that seemingly led nowhere. And yet, for all that, it was guarded by two heavily-armoured soldiers. They wore strange armour, quite unlike the standard gear his men in the citadel were given. Each was clad in a suit of segmented plates, glossy and polished. The soldiers carried double-bladed halberds, though the steel had been replaced with what looked like polished crystal. Both were short and stocky and stood strangely, as if their legs bent the wrong way and their shoulders had been dragged out of place. Most disconcertingly, their closed-face helmets had long snouts, carved in the shape of snarling dog's muzzles. No unaltered human could have fitted into those helms. These were Natassja's creatures, the product of her endless experimentation.

As he gazed on her progeny, Grosslich felt a surge of love for Natassja bloom up within him. She was everything to him, the one who had taken him from a minor landowner in the border country with Stirland and turned him into the most powerful man in the province. Her imagination and beauty were beyond those of anyone he had ever met. Particularly her imagination.

'Open the doors,' he said. The soldiers complied without speaking, though there was a strained wheezing from their helmets. So many of them died after having the alterations made. That was a shame, but a small price to pay for art.

The iron doors swung inwards, revealing a staircase that plunged down into the foundations of the Tower. The smell of jasmine, Natassja's smell, rose up from the opening. There were other delights too, such as the pleasing chorus of screams, just on the edge of hearing. Things were so much better now that she had the time and freedom to truly give rein to her inclinations. This was just a foretaste of what was to come. Soon, the screams would be ringing out across all Averland.

Grosslich smiled and descended into the depths of the Tower. Behind him, the doors clanged closed.

LUDWIG SCHWARZHELM FINISHED writing and placed the quill next to the parchment. He sat back in his chair, rolled his massive shoulders to relieve the ache, and looked up from his desk.

The walls of his study in Altdorf looked alien in the candlelight. He'd hardly visited it in the past decade of constant campaigning. Now they were an indictment of him. He'd been ordered to stay in them, to keep out of Imperial affairs for as long as it took the Emperor to forgive him for what had happened. However long that might be.

The rooms were minimally furnished. Most men of his rank would have lived in opulent state chambers, attended to by scores of servants and surrounded by priceless treasures from across the known world. That had never been his way. His dwellings were close to the Palace, but they were simple. He had a single manservant to keep an eye on the place when he was on campaign and employed the services of an aged charwoman, the mother of one of the many men who'd died serving under his command. They were both devoted to him, but since coming back from Averland he'd found he could hardly look them in the eye. He was diminished, and felt the shame of it keenly.

Night air gusted through the shutters. The fire had burned low in the grate. The rain continued to plague the city, and he could hear the constant drum of it outside. He'd been working for hours, and was not an eloquent scribe. Composing the letter to the Emperor had taken him the best part of the day and all of the evening. Even now he wasn't sure everything was ordered correctly. He found himself wishing Verstohlen was around. He'd have been able to advise. He'd always been able to advise.

Schwarzhelm brushed sand over the parchment and folded it up. He slipped it into an envelope, reached for the candle of sealing wax and tipped a gobbet of it on the join. As the wax hardened he pulled his personal seal from the drawer at his side. That too was hard to look at. The Sword of Justice entwined with the Imperial seal atop the initials L.S. Once it had been a source of pride to him. Now, like everything else, it had been sullied.

He pressed the seal onto the wax, watching as the red fluid solidified, then placed the letter on the desk in front of him. Beside it was the key he'd taken from Heinrich Lassus's house. It had taken a while for him to discover which lock it opened, but he still had friends in the city. The old traitor had been careful, but not careful enough. He'd trusted in his reputation, and that alone had been sufficient to fool everyone. Even now, only Schwarzhelm himself knew of the man's treachery. The fire had concealed evidence of his transformation, and men assumed that the old general had suffered from a terrible accident. For the time being, that was how Schwarzhelm wanted it. The truth would emerge in good time.

He took up the key and ran it over his fingers. Iron glinted in the candlelight. Even after much time had passed, he still had no idea why Lassus had done it. As far as he knew, the old swordmaster had no connections in Averland and no interest in the succession. He'd never had any concern with matters of rank or promotion. That was precisely why he'd been so admired. *I've been granted the grace to retire from the field and see out the rest of my days in peace.* That's what he'd told Schwarzhelm, back before he'd ridden to Averheim. Such an effortless, professional lie, so smoothly delivered.

With an effort of will, Schwarzhelm turned his mind back to the present. The longer he lingered on his many failures, the less useful he could be. Deep down, the tidings of Verstohlen nagged away at him. The spy had seen the mark of Chaos in the city, and his reports had been vindicated by the horrific manner of Lassus's death. Schwarzhelm had to assume that Natassja was still alive. Perhaps Rufus Leitdorf was too. In any event, for as long as Verstohlen remained in Averheim, the counsellor was in terrible danger. Schwarzhelm had sent coded messages by secret courier, but had little hope of them getting through. The only course left to him was to return there himself. Amends had to be made, debts settled, secrets uncovered.

He'd tried to seek an audience with the Emperor to explain his worries, but that had proved impossible. Never before had any request of his to meet Karl Franz been turned down. That hurt him more than anything else that had happened. Perhaps the Emperor was still angry. Perhaps he was trying to protect Schwarzhelm from any further involvement, thinking it best that he recovered from his trials. Or perhaps there was corruption even in the heart of the Palace, blocking his missives from reaching their target.

In any case, it didn't matter now. His mind was made up. He would leave for Averheim as soon as his work in Altdorf was done. There were only three things he needed to do first.

He rose from the table, taking the key and the letter with him and placing them in his jerkin pocket. He took a dark cloak from the hook in the wall beside him and wrapped himself up in it. At his side he felt the cool presence of the Rechtstahl. He hadn't drawn it since returning from Averland, and he dreaded seeing the rune-carved steel again. The spirit of the weapon was sullen and accusatory. Like all dwarf-forged master swords, it cared about the nature of the blood it spilt.

Schwarzhelm turned to leave the room. Three simple tasks. To leave the letter where the Emperor would find it. To enter Lassus's private archives in the Palace vaults. To retrieve the Sword of Vengeance, ready to return it to its master if he still lived.

Simple to list, difficult to do. With a final look around his study, Schwarzhelm blew out the candles and left to break in to the most heavily guarded fortress in the Empire.

GROSSLICH REACHED THE bottom of the staircase. The echoing screams had now become a gorgeous cacophony, rising from the depths of the crypt and snaking through the many passages and antechambers of the whole foundation layer. For a moment, Grosslich paused to take in the sound. He could almost smell it. That wonderful mix of fear, desperation and utter hopelessness. They had no idea how lucky they were to be shown such exquisite varieties of sensation. Their minds were being expanded. Involuntarily, it was true, but expanded nonetheless. Sometimes literally.

At the bottom of the stairs, a long gallery ran ahead for two hundred yards. Far below the surface of the city, Natassja had been able to indulge her peerless sense of design. The floor was glassy and smooth. A gentle lilac light rose from it, picking out the detail of the baroque walls, each carved with the same care and intricacy as the doors above. The themes were the ones she loved – lissom youths of both sexes, locked in what looked like a ballet of agony. The artistry was such that the iron figures could almost have passed for real bodies, locked into eternal stasis and bound into the foundations of the Tower.

At regular intervals along the gallery, archways had been cut into the walls. Each of these was decorated in the same fashion, with sigils dedicated to Pleasure engraved over the keystone. The noises came from beyond these arches. Grosslich hadn't had time to explore all the rooms in person, but he knew they were where Natassja carried out her works of artistry. On the rare occasions when he'd felt able to peer within their confines, he'd found the experience difficult. He knew that a part of him was still mired in human weaknesses. Even now, after so much transformation, to see some of those... *scenes* made his flesh shiver. He'd have to work on that. The weakness in him, small as it was, was the last remaining impediment to glory.

At the far end of the gallery a large octagonal chamber had been hewn from the earth. When the Tower was completed, the chamber would sit directly beneath the centre of the mighty shaft. For now, all that stood above it was an iron cat's cradle.

Grosslich walked across the glass floor, enjoying the echoing click of his boots. The sound produced a pleasing counterpoint to the sobbing whimpers coming from door number four. As he passed it, he was pleased to see Natassja already waiting for him in the octagon.

'My love,' he said, marvelling as he always did at her splendour.

Natassja sat on an obsidian throne at the centre of the chamber. Her skin, once ivory, was now a shimmering pale blue. Her eyes had lost their pupils and become pure black jewels in her flawless face. Her teeth still shone as white as they'd ever done, even if the incisors looked a little longer. She wore a sheer gown of nightshade silk, and a necklace of ithilmar spikes now graced her neckline. Her hair, black as pitch, hung loose around her shoulders.

At Grosslich's approach, she rose from the throne.

'What word from Altdorf?' she asked, descending from the dais to meet him. Her voice was cool, though a sibilant undertone had been added to it.

'The Emperor summoned me. I played for time.'

Natassja looked thoughtful. 'He won't remain patient forever,' she said. 'Schwarzhelm will tell him the truth soon, if he hasn't already.'

Grosslich frowned at that. Everyone was always so worried. It was inexplicable, given the position of strength they were in.

'You're *sure* Lassus gave much away?'

'He was weak,' spat Natassja. 'Even now his soul is shriven. I have seen it. A thousand years of torment to ponder a slip of the tongue.' Vehemence made her voice shake. 'And yes, he did give much away. His presence in this has given us all away. Schwarzhelm is damaged, but he's still powerful.'

'Then I've no doubt you've plans in place.'

'We still have agents in the Palace,' she said. 'For as long as possible we must maintain the illusion that Rufus was the traitor here. In the meantime, there are two men we have to kill. One is Schwarzhelm, though that will be difficult at such a range. The other is closer to hand.'

'Verstohlen.'

'Quite. See to it.'

'Of course,' said Grosslich. That would be a singular pleasure – the man's bleating had become insufferable.

'And then there's the pursuit of Rufus. That troubles me.'

Natassja spoke quickly but clearly. There was no trace of mania in her eyes. Back when he'd been a normal man, Grosslich had assumed all cultists were raving fanatics. Natassja had her moments, but her demeanour habitually remained as smooth as onyx. Perhaps that shouldn't have surprised him. She'd been active in this, after all, for centuries.

'Any more news from your men?' she asked. 'How goes the hunt?'

'It's difficult, my goddess,' said Grosslich, not bothering to hide the truth. 'He's in his own country, protected by his own people. I send more men east every day, but we can't search every house.'

Natassja shook her head. 'Not quick enough. Come with me. I have something to show you.'

She led him back into the long gallery. With a faint shudder, Grosslich realised they were heading for one of the antechambers. Number one. He'd never been allowed in that one.

'The one uncertain factor in this is Helborg,' said Natassja as she walked. 'He was not part of the original plan, though we were able to make use of him. My senses tell me he still lives.' She turned to face Grosslich before entering the chamber, and her expression was intense. 'I fear his presence. He was not foreseen from the beginning. It might have been better if he had never come.'

She ducked under the archway. As Grosslich followed into the darkness his eyes took a moment to adjust.

'I thought you used him? To goad Schwarzhelm further?'

Natassja nodded. 'We did. Lassus and I had discussed the contingency. At every stage, we made it appear as if Helborg and Rufus were working in tandem. But that was always in addition to the main objective. I was never sure it was the right decision.'

Grosslich's vision began to clarify. The antechamber retreated far back into the darkness of the earth. He couldn't see the far wall for shadow. On either side of him were long wooden tables with leather restraining straps. There were vials of a lilac-coloured liquid and gut tubes leading from them. Surgical instruments had been placed on a separate table, and they glistened in the low light. Across every surface, parchment made of human skin had been draped, painstakingly inscribed with tight-curled script. There were diagrams, etched in blood so old it had turned black. The floor, hidden in the gloom, was sticky. In the darkness beyond, he could faintly make out a rattling sound. Something was moving.

'I saw the blow that felled him,' said Grosslich, trying to concentrate on the task at hand. 'He may yet die from it.'

'Possibly. But we have to be sure. Come forwards.'

The last command hadn't been directed at him. The rattling grew louder. Something was shuffling into the light.

'What is this, my goddess?' asked Grosslich. He was nervous. Despite all his training, all his immersion in the world of the Dark Prince, he was still nervous. He still had some way to go.

'A new toy,' she replied, eyes fixed on the approaching shape. 'A refinement of the creatures I was working on before. I call them my handmaidens. What do you think?'

The figure that emerged had been a woman. She had once been beautiful, perhaps. She was slim, pale-skinned, with mouse-brown hair arranged in long plaits. Maybe in the past she had moved with an easy grace, laughing in the sun and trying to catch the eye of the troopers marching to war.

Now she moved silently. Her once flawless skin was covered in incisions and sutures. Her eyes were gone, replaced with blank brass plates. Black rags had been draped over her naked shoulders, but they did little to obscure the surgery that had scored her body. Exposed bone glinted from her hips, her knees, her neck. Most strikingly of all, her fingers had been replaced with long curved talons. They shone coldly in the dark. What was left of her face was contorted into a silent, frozen howl of agony. It was unclear if she could still speak. It looked like she could barely walk.

'Impressive,' said Grosslich, trying not to imagine the full horror of the transformation. 'What can she do?'

'There has been extensive replacement,' said Natassja coolly. 'At her heart there burns an iron casket containing a shard of the Stone. That keeps her alive, despite the removal of the spine. Once given an instruction, she will never stop. These ones no longer need to be near me to retain their power.'

The handmaiden shuffled closer. It seemed blind as well as crippled. Every movement it made was tight with pain.

'It doesn't move fast.'

Natassja smiled and ran a finger gently down the handmaiden's scarred cheek. 'Do not be fooled by her current state. When given the proper command, she will change.' Natassja looked at her tenderly, like a proud mother. 'For now, she only has her own private world of pain. That can be altered by giving her a name.'

'A name.'

'A name is a mystical thing, Heinz-Mark. It has resonance in the aethyr. They can use it to find their prey. When they are ready, I will give it to them.'

'She's not ready?'

'Not yet,' said Natassja, stroking the handmaiden's remaining hair. 'There will be three of them, at least to begin with. Their creation is long and difficult. Then I will send them out. They will sweep across Averland like crows, never pausing, never resting.'

She looked back at Grosslich, and her eyes were shining. 'All they need is the name. *Helborg.*'

RUFUS LEITDORF LOOKED down on the stricken face of Kurt Helborg. The Marshal slept still, propped up on bolsters of duckfeather. The two men were alone in the bedchamber of one of his father's houses, far out in the eastern reaches of Averland. The room was typically grand, with a high plastered ceiling and heavy wooden furniture against all four walls. The bed itself was larger than some peasants' hovels, with fanciful images of dragons and crested eagles carved into the headboard.

The night was old. Candlelight made Helborg's face look even paler. The craggy features, so admired and feared across the Empire, were now haggard, and the proud moustache hung in lank strands across his cheeks. His breathing was shallow, and a thick layer of sweat lay on his skin.

Leitdorf took up another towel and began to dab the moisture away. Only a few months ago he'd never have stooped to minister to another man's discomfort, even a man as famed as Helborg, but things had changed. He was now a fugitive in his own land, hunted by men he had once aspired to command. There seemed little point in retaining old pretensions of grandeur.

He replaced the towel on the low table by the bed. Leitdorf sat for a while, watching the man's breast rise and fall under the coverlet. Helborg fought with death. The wound in his shoulder had closed, but some profound struggle was still going on within him.

There was a knock at the door. Leitdorf rose from the bed, smoothing the sheets from where he'd been sitting.

'Come.'

Leofric von Skarr, preceptor of the Reiksguard, entered. He was still in full battle armour and looked as grim and wolfish as ever. His dark hair hung around his face, criss-crossed with the scars that so suited his name.

'Any change?'

'None.'

'He hasn't woken?'

'Not while I've been with him.'

Skarr nodded. Around his neck hung the shard taken from Helborg's sword. It had become something of a totem for the depleted Reiksguard company who still guarded their master, the emblem of his future recovery.

'There was another patrol out there, beyond the line of the hills,' said Skarr. 'We killed them all, but they were getting close. They're going to find us.'

'Then we move again.'

'You haven't run out of houses?'

Leitdorf gave a superior smile. 'My father owned more houses in Averland than there are whores in Wurtbad.'

Skarr snorted.

'It's no solution, this endless fleeing,' he said dismissively, leaning against a fabulously expensive Breugsletter sideboard as if it were a country gate. 'They'll catch up with us eventually, and we don't have the men to fight them all.'

'I've been thinking about that.' Leitdorf walked over to a writing desk by the window. Across it lay a vellum map of Averland, lit by more candles. It bore the crest of Marius Leitdorf in the corner and was obviously a private commission. Each of the old count's many manor houses and fortified places was marked. 'Look at this.'

Skarr joined him.

'We're here,' said Leitdorf, pointing to a country mansion several days' ride from Averheim. 'Far, but not far enough. We should be aiming *here*.'

He indicated a blank spot on the map. The nearest landmark was a patch of scratchily-drawn highland called Drakenmoor.

'I don't see anything.'

'I know,' said Leitdorf. 'This is one of my father's own maps, and it isn't even displayed here. That's how secret he kept it. His last retreat. The place he went to in order to escape the dreams.'

Skarr looked sceptical. 'A hideaway.'

'Something like that.'

'How do you know of it?'

'There were *some* family secrets to which I was privy,' said Leitdorf, affronted. The Reiksguard treated him like a spoiled, feckless dandy.

Skarr continued to frown. 'You can't hide a castle.'

'Of course not. Those who live locally know of its existence. But there are few villages in the region, and fewer staff in the retreat. My father set great store by having somewhere no one could find him.'

'How far is it?'

Leitdorf pursed his lips. 'In the Marshal's condition, maybe three days across country. Once we get there, we'll be isolated. Even if Grosslich sends his men after us, we'll see them coming from miles off. In any case, he's sure to send his men to the houses he knows about first.'

Skarr hesitated, studying the map carefully, weighing up various options. Leitdorf began to get frustrated. There *were* no other options.

'Come on, man!' he snapped. 'Surely you can see the sense of it?'

Skarr whirled back to face him, his eyes bright with anger. Leitdorf recoiled. The preceptor had a quick temper.

'*Never* give me orders,' hissed Skarr. There was a dark expression on his face, drawn from years of expert killing. 'It's down to you and your games that we're in this damned mess.'

Leitdorf felt the blood rush to his cheeks. 'Remember your station, master kni–'

'Remember yours! It is *nothing*. You may think you're the elector of this blighted province, but to me you're just the man who's brought this whole thing down on us.' Spittle collected at the corner of Skarr's mouth. He was consumed by rage. Leitdorf backed away from him.

'Maybe I should leave you to Grosslich's men,' Skarr

muttered, turning away in scorn. 'What they want with the Marshal is still a mystery to me.'

Leitdorf, for once, found himself lost for words. His mouth opened, but nothing came out. He stood still, heart pounding, trying to think of a response.

'Skarr,' came a croak from the bed.

The preceptor turned quickly, wild hope kindling across his face. Helborg's eyes were open. They were rheumy and ill-focussed, but they were open.

'My lord!'

'I heard enough,' rasped Helborg. His voice sounded as if it had been dragged over rusted iron. 'Do as Leitdorf says.'

'Yes, my lord,' replied Skarr, suddenly chastened. For his part, Leitdorf didn't know whether to feel relieved or not. His position was still precarious.

'And we take him with us,' continued Helborg. The effort of speaking produced fresh sweat on his brow. 'We need him.'

'Yes, though I–'

Skarr didn't finish. Helborg, exhausted by the effort, drifted back into sleep. His head sank deep into the bolster, his breathing ragged.

Leitdorf turned to Skarr in triumph.

'I think that's given us our answer.'

Skarr shot him a poisonous look.

'We'll do as the Marshal says. For some reason, he seems disposed to be charitable towards you.' The Reiksguard glared at Leitdorf, every sinew of his body radiating menace. 'But I warn you, Herr Leitdorf, my only task is to safeguard Helborg's life. If you do anything – *anything* – to put it in danger, then so help me I will throw you to the wolves.'

\* \* \*

NIGHT LAY HEAVILY on Altdorf. The turgid waters of the Reik flowed fast, swollen by weeks of rain. Fires still burned across the city, sending acrid peat-smoke curling into the air. Lights glimmered in the darkness and at the pinnacles of the many towers. As ever, the turrets of the Celestial College retained their thin sheen of blue, glowing eerily far above the compass of its rivals. Any men abroad at that quiet hour avoided looking at the unnatural lights and kept an eye on their surroundings.

Schwarzhelm stole along the Prinz Michael Strasse, keeping his cloak wrapped tight around him and hugging the shadows. He feared no street urchin or cutpurse – the rats of the street went for easier pickings than him. Even stripped of his plate armour and helmet, Schwarzhelm was still a formidable-looking target.

Mannslieb was full, throwing a cool silver light across the cobbled streets through broken rainclouds. Schwarzhelm reached the end of the street and paused, checking his bearings. The southern wall of the Palace complex lay ahead. From his long acquaintance with the sprawling site he knew it was the least watched. There was nothing much of value at the southern end of the estates – just scholars' dens, storerooms, stables, fodder yards for the menagerie, and other semi-maintained buildings. Despite that, the walls were high and heavy, crowned with battlements and cut from unwearing granite. Along the top of them ran a wide parapet, ceaselessly patrolled by the Palace guards.

Schwarzhelm stepped out from the shelter of the street and turned left, walking close to the curve of the wall. He let his gaze slip over the stone as he did so.

There were no gates, no windows, not even a grille or arrow-slit. The surface glared back at him, unbroken and smooth.

He kept walking. From time to time he heard noises ahead of or behind him. Footsteps padding away in the dark, the distant cackle of a cheap strumpet, the barking of a chained dog. He ignored them all.

He reached his goal. A culvert placed at the base of the wall, barred against entry and guarding the outflow of a drain. The slops from the Palace ran straight out into the street, gurgling down the edges of the roads and off into the maze of buildings beyond. The stench was marginally worse than Altdorf's habitual fug of filth. The rains had made all drains in the city overflow, and a torrent of grey water surged from the outlet, filmy and dotted with floating refuse.

Schwarzhelm looked back, watching to see if he'd been observed. The street was empty, and there were no guards on the rampart above. He drew a huge ring of keys from his belt, wrapped in cloth to ward against clinking. There were some advantages to being so high in the Emperor's trust.

But, of course, that was no longer true.

He selected a long iron key. The arch of the culvert rose less than three feet above the surface of the street. Reaching down into the foaming water, he felt around for the lock. It was there, rusted closed. He tried the key.

No luck. He reached for another and repeated his groping. On the fourth attempt, he found the one that fitted. It was not an exact match – he had to force it into the lock and then wrench it round. With a grinding sound, the mechanism snapped open. Schwarzhelm grasped the bottom of the barred gate and lifted it. The heavy iron grille took some shifting, and as he laboured foul water splattered up into his chest and face.

Beyond the entrance, the drain ran into darkness, never more than a few feet high and dripping with noisome fluid. There was enough space between the surface of the water and the roof to breathe, though he'd be half-submerged in the stink. Schwarzhelm lay face-down on the street and began to worm himself into the gap. It was hard work – the grille had to be kept open while he snaked under it. Eventually he made it inside and the door slammed back down behind him. There was no way of locking it from the inside, and it was all he could do to keep his mouth and nose out of the drainwater. Like a beetle burrowing in manure, Schwarzhelm hauled himself along the cramped way, feeling his muscles bunch against the sides.

Darkness pressed against him like swaddling. The uneven stone jagged on his clothes, his sword-belt, his boots. He shuffled forwards, mouth closed against the noxious effluent around him. After just a few feet he felt like gagging and stopped in his tracks, working to control himself. He was hemmed in, crushed by the tons of rock above him. A flicker of panic flared up in his stomach.

He quelled it and pressed on. Working slowly, powerfully, he edged through the narrow space. Progress was slow, and he was almost wedged tight as the drain took a sharp dog-leg right before running onwards. As he hauled himself round the angle, he felt his heart thud rhythmically, his hands scrabbling at the cold stone.

Then, ahead of him, he saw the far end of the culvert

coming into view. A faint semicircle of open air, barred by a similar grille. He shuffled towards it, keeping a tight grip on the bunch of keys. Beyond was a small courtyard. Through the bars it looked like the rear area of a kitchen, or maybe a wash-house. There were barrels littering the space, some open and on their sides revealing their contents of rank-smelling refuse and spoiled food.

There was no movement in the square, and no light save that of the moon. Schwarzhelm fumbled with the lock. The key worked as before, and the grille clicked open. He shoved it up and pushed his way under it. As he rose, he made sure it was gently lowered back into position. He looked about him warily.

He was alone. His cloak, jerkin and breeches were covered in slurry. He stank worse than an ogre's jock-strap, and looked nearly as bad.

So this was what he'd been reduced to. The last time he'd entered the Palace precincts he'd been wearing ceremonial armour and had been accorded a full guard of honour. Now he looked like the lowest common street thief.

No matter. He was in. Now he had to find what he was looking for.

THE FEVERED NIGHTS over Averheim had given way to a more seasonal warmth. Cool airs ruffled the Grosslich standards as they hung from the walls of the Averburg, lit by the full face of Mannslieb.

Tochfel sat in his chamber high in the citadel wanting nothing more than to sleep. The day had been long, and his run-in with Euler had been an inauspicious start. The demands of the new elector were legion. Even though Grosslich was almost impossible to track down in person, his orders, delivered by messenger, just kept coming.

Most of them concerned the new building. Requisitions were coming in at nearly a dozen a day for everything from masonry and metalwork to wine and silverware. The proud home of the Averlander electors, the seat of the Alptraum and Leitdorf dynasties, was being emptied. Soon it would be nothing more than a cold stone shell, a faint reminder of the glories of the past.

But it was not the tide of paperwork that kept the Steward awake. He had a visitor sitting before him, a thin-faced man with receding hair and a wild look in his eyes. Odo Heidegger, the witch hunter in charge of the purgation of Averheim. He sat before Tochfel, his thin fingers clasped on his lap. He'd eschewed the leather coat and breeches worn by most of his order, and instead wore the ceremonial robes of his office – dark red lined with black. They were coloured that way, no doubt, to hide the blood.

'I do not understand,' Heidegger said again in his reedy, mellifluous voice. 'There was no objection to these names when they were first submitted to your office.'

Tochfel ran his hand through his thinning hair. He was strung out. He really needed to sleep. 'And as I told *you*, Herr Heidegger, I've not seen this list until now. I had no idea there were so many.'

In his hands he held the offending list. At the top was the stamp of the Temple of Sigmar in Averheim. Heidegger had been promoted to the pinnacle of the local hierarchy shortly after Grosslich had been installed. Since then it had been his solemn duty to oversee the remaining interrogations and to arrange suitable punishment for those found to have aided the traitors.

'Yes, it is sad, is it not, that so many chose to fall into darkness,' said Heidegger. He looked genuinely mournful. 'But they all confessed. You can see the signatures.'

Tochfel swallowed as he looked at the series of scrawled names from the literate victims and crosses from those who weren't. All of them were shaky, as if the owners' hands had barely functioned by the time they were called into action. Several were half-obscured by dark-brown smudges.

'Some of these names are known to me,' protested Tochfel. 'Here is Morven, my aide. What possible reason could you have for–'

'He confessed, Steward. What more do you want? It is there, all on the list.'

Tochfel could read it for himself. *Wantonly held the Averburg against the forces of the rightful elector, thus delaying the campaign against the Traitor Leitdorf. Sentence: Death by flame.* That was a travesty. Tochfel had passed those orders himself. At that stage in the campaign, no one knew the scale of Leitdorf's treachery, nor that Grosslich had the blessing of Schwarzhelm. For that matter, he himself could be liable to...

He shuddered.

'I will not sign these,' he said, putting the papers down. 'I need more time. There's been no scrutiny, no examination.'

Heidegger retained his sorrowful expression. There wasn't a hint of anger there. He looked a little like one of those otherworldly Jade magisters, lost in a reverie of gentle regret. And yet Tochfel was judge enough to see the fragility of the man's mind. Most witch hunters went mad sooner or later, and this one would not be long.

'That is regrettable, Steward,' Heidegger said. 'I will have to report it. The elector will not be happy to hear that his quest for justice has been impeded.'

'I don't care,' snapped Tochfel, his fatigue making him unwary. 'There are men on this list innocent of any crime. Why has the court of inquiry not included Templars from other cities? I've not been present at any of your interrogations.'

'You're welcome to join me. Some people find them... distasteful.'

Tochfel shook his head. Going up against the Temple of Sigmar was dangerous, even more so since Achendorfer had gone missing. He was running short of allies.

'I did not say I would block these sentences,' said Tochfel, speaking carefully. 'I merely wish for more time to study them. Give me until the end of the week.'

Heidegger thought before replying. 'I do not like it,' he said. 'Justice must be seen to be done.'

'There've been enough burnings already,' muttered Tochfel. 'A hiatus will do you good, give you time to buy in more firewood.'

Heidegger shrugged. 'As you wish. I shall inform the elector of your views.'

He rose, brushing at his robes as he did so. His fingers were forever fidgeting, as if they longed to grasp the instruments.

'Goodnight, Steward.'

'Goodnight, Herr Heidegger.'

The door closed, leaving Tochfel alone in the chamber. For a moment, he thought about climbing on to his narrow bed. Then he saw the pile of papers on his desk, and realised just how much more work he had to get through.

'This is getting beyond my control,' he mused, speaking to himself in his fatigue. 'I will speak to Verstohlen. He will know what to do.'

SCHWARZHELM MOVED EVER closer to his quarry. He went slowly, keeping to the darkness, watchful for the teams of sentries. He'd cleaned the worst of the muck from his clothes. The rain had started again. It might have been sent from blessed Shallya herself, as it damped down his stench and made the guards unwilling to patrol too zealously out in the open.

The interior of the Palace complex was a vast morass of interconnected corridors and buildings. No living man knew them all, though Schwarzhelm was as familiar with them as anyone. He'd never penetrated so far into the southern wings of the mammoth structure, but he knew that Lassus had had his private chambers there. They were modest, less than would normally have been offered to a general of Lassus's stature. Until recently, Schwarzhelm had been pained by the lack of respect shown to his old master. Now he cursed the fact that he even *had* chambers within such hallowed precincts.

From the courtyard, he'd moved quickly towards the collection of apartments given to distinguished retired officers. Most were housed in a heavy sandstone monstrosity covered in eroded gargoyles and overworked copies of the Imperial coat of arms. In an attempt to mask the grotesque devices, huge stretches of ivy had been allowed to creep across the stone, obscuring all but the steep tiled roof with its iron guttering. Originally the building had been set amid a pleasant ornamental lawn, though the demands of the Imperial bureaucracy had ensured that it was now surrounded by three gothic scriptoria and a gloomy vaulted archive.

Schwarzhelm paused, taking in his surroundings. The regular Palace guards were issued with crossbows, and without his armour he was vulnerable. If he was unlucky enough to stumble across Reiksguard, his situation would be far graver. For once in his life, stealth would have to take precedence over ostentatious bravery.

He crouched tight against the wall of one of the scriptoria. The rain splattered down from the leaky roof, bouncing from his hunched shoulders on to the uneven stone flags beneath him. Ahead, maybe thirty yards away, two sentries walked lazily around the perimeter of the apartments. They had hoods cast over their faces to ward against the rain and said nothing. By their manner, Schwarzhelm could see they weren't the Emperor's finest. They moved off, heading in the direction of the walls. Schwarzhelm waited until there was complete silence, then moved.

He crept across the open space quickly, lingering in the pools of shadow. Zigzagging from doorway to doorway, he reached the porch of the first set of apartments. The twin oak doors were flanked by crude sandstone columns, wrapped in ivy and surmounted by the coat-of-arms of some long-dead military commander.

He looked back the way he'd come. Nothing. He withdrew the keys from his belt and tried several in the lock. None of them worked. That was unsurprising – there were a thousand keys for different parts of the

Palace and most were jealously guarded by their own-ers.

Schwarzhelm stowed them. There was a time and a place for finesse, and this wasn't it. He pulled back, gathering his strength, and barged into the doors. They buckled against his massive frame, but held. He slammed into them again, sending a dull thud out into the night. On the third attempt, they caved in, swinging back violently and cracking against the walls. He went in quickly, pulling them behind him.

Inside all was dark. The place was deserted, as were most of the buildings in the outer reaches of the Palace at night. A central corridor ran back into the gloom, marked by regular doorways leading off on either side. Two high windows at either end let in the scant starlight, but little was illuminated. Schwarzhelm reached into his jerkin and retrieved a flint and a fist-sized lantern. The metal frame of the lantern was carved in swirling lines and the clear win-dows were crystal – the gift of a grateful elven prince after a battle over a decade ago.

He lit the wick of the candle and closed the lantern. The light glowed softly from the crystal, throwing dif-fuse shadows down the corridor. At the far end of it Schwarzhelm could see a stairway leading to the next floor.

He went quietly and quickly, padding like a great bear on the threadbare carpet. The doorways passed silently, each inscribed with the initials of the official to whom the room within was devoted. Chancellor Julius Rumpelskagg, Magister F. H. Heilstaff, Egbertus Schumann, Under-Scribe of the Fifth Archives. Schwarzhelm knew where it would be, and knew just what he was looking for.

Just before he reached the stairs he saw the name-plate glinting in the flame, its brass old and tarnished. Eryniem Hoche-Hattenberg, Master of the Keys. No official of that outlandish name had ever existed, though Schwarzhelm knew the room had been well used. He slid the key from Lassus's chambers into the door and turned it. The lock clicked open.

Inside, all was orderly and neat. The light of the lantern swept across a spartan chamber. Rows of books lined the walls. Most were treatises on warfare and military training. Schwarzhelm doubted Lassus had read many of them; the man had known all there was to know about war through experience.

There was a single, draped window at the far end of the room. In front of the window stood the desk, a heavy construction in an archaic style with a polished surface and no drawers. The surface was almost empty, save for an inkwell, a penknife, a blotter and a tray of sand. A few used quills had been discarded in a basket next to the writer's chair. No parchment remained, and there was no sign of any papers stacked up against the bookcases.

For a moment, Schwarzhelm began to doubt his intuition. Perhaps Lassus had been too careful. He knelt down beneath the desktop, running his fingers under the wood. He groped further back, feeling for the tell-tale switch that would hide a compartment. Just as he was about to withdraw his hand, he felt the slightest variation in texture. He pressed hard. From deep within the desk there came a *thunk*, as if a brass mechanism had shifted into place.

Schwarzhelm clambered to his feet. The right pedestal of the desk had opened, and a narrow door hung ajar on almost invisible hinges. The workmanship was perfect. When closed, the join would have been invisible even in full daylight.

Schwarzhelm shone the light against the cavity, looking for needle traps. Seeing none, he reached inside carefully and pulled out a roll of parchment, tightly bound with leather straps. Without unwrapping the bundle, he could see what they were – letters written in some kind of cipher. Schwarzhelm was familiar with most of the battle codes used in the Empire, but this one looked strange and he could make no sense of it.

He stowed the bundle in his jerkin and closed the door to the pedestal again. The first task on his list had been completed. He left the chamber, locking the door behind him. The corridor was as silent as before. He looked up at the window at the far end of the building. The clouds had parted again, and a feeble moonlight had returned. That would make things more difficult. He knew where the sword was being held, and taking that with him would be far more difficult than stealing letters.

Extinguishing the lantern, Schwarzhelm headed back to the main door. The Chapel of the Fallen, right in the heart of the ancient Palace, awaited him.

PIETER VERSTOHLEN WATCHED the moon ride clear over Averheim. For a change, he wasn't in his tower room in the Averburg. His guest lived several streets away and had kindly offered him the use of her bedchamber for the night. Of course, he'd had to pay for the privilege. Or, to be more accurate, for her company within it.

Visiting courtesans was not something he was proud of. He was careful, of course, and made sure only to procure the services of the higher class of courtesan. His stipend from Schwarzhelm, together with a history of cautious investments, had made him a man of comfortable means. He enjoyed the more exclusive things in life: good food, expensive wine, sophisticated women. Though the notion always seemed trite to him, it was true nevertheless – he valued them for their minds as much as their more regular services. Like many of his kind, solitude became a kind of mania after a while. It needed to be broken, even if that meant giving in to appetites that he'd rather not have had.

He pushed himself up higher against the bolsters, trying to get a better view of the moonlit rooftops through the open window. On his shoulder, Elisabeth stirred. Her flame-red hair fell across her face as her head rose.

'What is it?' she mumbled, brushing it free.

Verstohlen stroked the tresses absently. She had a striking face. Ivory-white skin, dusted with freckles, deep green eyes.

'Nothing. Just looking at the moon.'

Elisabeth frowned. 'Like a madman.'

'Indeed.'

The vista across the city calmed him. Despite all the difficulties, he felt a certain pride in what he and Schwarzhelm had accomplished. The streets were quiet. Averheim felt like a different place from the febrile mess they'd arrived in at the start of the summer. And yet it was strange that he hadn't heard from him. Nothing had come out of Altdorf since the man had left. That wasn't like him. Amid all the contentment he felt at a job well done, that made him anxious.

'You look worried, my love,' said Elisabeth with the astuteness of her profession.

Verstohlen tensed. That was the only thing he ever asked them, not to use the word 'love'. There was only one love for him, and it had been the purest, most sacred thing in his whole life. He made a mental note not to use this one again. She'd provided an acceptable diversion, but he needed companions who could be careful.

'Just expecting a message,' he said. 'Nothing important.'

'Anything I can do to help? I know many influential men in this city.'

'I don't doubt it. Are you this helpful to all your clients?'

'Only the ones I really like.'

'I'm gratified,' said Verstohlen, though he wasn't. It made it more difficult if they liked him.

'I mean it. You know how to treat a lady,' Elisabeth said, seemingly oblivious to the irony. 'There are some brutes out there, believe me.'

'I'm sure.'

'I had one last week. Stinking of root. Almost sent him away.'

'Joyroot?' asked Verstohlen, his interest piqued.

Elisabeth smiled. 'You sound surprised. I had you for a man of the world.'

Verstohlen didn't return the smile. 'I thought Grosslich had outlawed it.'

'That's what he said he'd do. That's what the last one said too. But you can still get it. Even I could get it, if you wanted.'

'No,' said Verstohlen. 'I do not.'

Elisabeth laughed, a girlish, babbling sound. 'So serious! There's no harm to it.'

Verstohlen said nothing. A dark thought had entered his mind. The Leitdorfs had controlled the trade. If it was still coming in, then there could only be two possibilities: they were still active in Averheim, or someone else had taken it over. Neither was an attractive proposition.

'Look, I'm awake now, love,' continued Elisabeth, a mischievous sparkle in her eyes. 'What do you suppose we might do about that?'

Verstohlen ignored her. His mind was now occupied with other things. He needed advice. With Schwarzhelm out of the city and Bloch engaged in the east, he was running short of allies. He determined to speak to Tochfel. He would know what to do.

SCHWARZHELM CROUCHED DOWN low, making sure his cloak was close around him. He'd moved towards the heart of the Palace complex. The shabby buildings had been replaced by grand structures of marble and gilt, and the patrols had increased proportionally. Though no one really cared about the half-forgotten cells of a few scholars in the semi-derelict southern wing, the core of the Palace complex contained treasures beyond the dreams of Ranald, and the defences were formidable.

It helped that Schwarzhelm was privy to the secrets of the inner circles. He could take routes that few knew existed, could circumvent places where he knew the guards would congregate, could open hidden doors and slip past traps designed to catch the unwary. There were wards engraved across the many gateways against the powers of Chaos, but he knew what they were and what they were looking for. He passed under them silently, feeling the blank scrutiny of the occluded sigils on his shoulders. It felt as if the arcane magicks could sense the guilt burning in his soul, and he didn't linger by them for longer than he needed to.

He couldn't avoid all the many layers of watchfulness by knowledge and stealth. Three times since leaving Lassus's old chambers he'd been forced to spring from the shadows to silence an unwary patrol. He'd held himself back from killing, even though the risk of one of his victims coming round made his position ever more precarious. There'd been enough slaying of loyal troops, and he planned to keep the Rechtstahl sheathed unless the need was desperate. It was a mean, dishonourable way of fighting, and with every blow of his mighty fists he felt the shame of it.

In the distance, he heard the eerie call of some fabulous creature. Unearthly shrieks rang out across the deserted courtyards of the Palace. The Imperial Menagerie wasn't far away, and the beasts within were disturbed.

Ahead of his current position, the man-made mountain of the Holswig-Schliestein Hofburg soared into the night sky, a confection of twisted columns and graven images. To his left, the mighty banqueting halls, all eleven of them, had been piled on top of one another, each vying with its companions for tasteless splendour. When one of the many Imperial receptions was in session they were filled with light and laughter, sparkling from the diamond chandeliers and from the crystal necklaces of the noble ladies. Now they were empty and sullen, brooding in the dark like jilted lovers.

Ahead of him lay the vast bulk of the Imperial

Chapel, a sprawling cornucopia of heavy plasterwork and staring gargoyles. That was where the daily procession of warrior priests ended up, all hollering their praises to Sigmar and swinging incense-loaded warhammers as they swayed towards the high altar. Within those mighty transepts benedictions were offered and penitent prayers issued on behalf of the wayward citizens of the Empire. Beasts were slaughtered before the eternal flames of the inner sanctum, their blood running down iron channels in the marble floor. Massive censers of brass revolved endlessly from chains set into the distant roof, powered by devices from Nuln and Tilea. Gold-plated cherubs poured a ceaseless torrent of pungent smoke from goblets of bronze, obscuring the tombs of the worthy and turning the stone coal-black.

The holy transepts of the Cult of Sigmar were not Schwarzhelm's destination, though. At the southern end of the soaring Chapel, a smaller building had been raised. Here there was no gold plate or churning machinery. The stone was blank and unadorned, and pairs of iron eagles gazed darkly out from the guttering. Even during the day the place was kept quiet and dark. Obsidian columns stood sentinel in the gloom, watching over the rows of graves within.

This was the Chapel of the Fallen, the resting place of the honoured protectors of the Empire. The guards were drawn from the priesthood of Morr, as were the attendants of the ranks of tombs. No hymns of praise were sung in that place, only a low dirge of remembrance. Few came to visit it, and fewer stayed to pray there. The heavy pall of death hung over the altars.

Schwarzhelm was close to it, and could make out the blank eyes of the eagles as they stared out across the jumbled squares and courtyards. There was a doorway opposite him, barred with metal and surmounted with a death's head, no more than thirty yards across a cobbled space overlooked on all sides. The low hum of the turning censers in the larger chapel masked his footfalls, and there were plenty of shadows to keep to.

He waited, checking for patrols. Instinctively his fingers crept to the pommel of his sword. The square was quiet. The dawn was still hours away, and none of the priests would be out of their cells for some time yet.

Moving more softly than his bulk suggested possible, Schwarzhelm crept out from the lee of the near wall and headed for the door. He heard his breathing grow quicker as he neared, and brought it under control. The death's head loomed up at him from the night, its hollow eye-sockets like wells of ink. As with all doors in the Palace, it was locked at night. Schwarzhelm drew the ring of keys from his belt and began to try them, one by one. Finally, he found one that fitted. The lock rasped open and the door began to swing back.

'What are you doing there?'

Schwarzhelm's heart froze. The voice came from behind him, close on his right shoulder. He'd been sloppy. He felt the tip of a sword press into his back, hard against the fabric of his cloak. Slowly, he raised his hands, showing he had no weapon drawn. He'd need to pick his moment.

'I could ask you the same thing, soldier,' he said, his voice assuming the habitual tone of command.

He turned as casually as he was able, neither seeking to evade the sword at his back nor getting any closer to its bearer. When he moved, he'd have to be quick.

Two men were facing him, both in the red and white of the Reiksguard. Both had their blades drawn, gleaming dully in the fractured moonlight. The nearest had the grizzled look of a sergeant. His companion, standing further back, was younger. For once, experience proved to be a liability. The sergeant recognised Schwarzhelm's features, and his sword-tip wavered.

'My lor–' he began.

He never finished. Schwarzhelm swung a fist into his face, smashing into the man's temple and sending him staggering to the ground. The youngster rushed forwards, sword poised to plunge into Schwarzhelm's torso. He evaded the stab easily, drawing his own weapon as he stepped away from the strike. The Sword of Justice flickered with an icy fire as it was released. The younger Reiksguard brought his blade up again, this time in a cutting arc. Schwarzhelm parried, and the metal met metal with a shuddering clang.

The sergeant leapt back to his feet. Schwarzhelm worked his sword quickly and carefully, mindful of the quality of his foes. They pressed home the attack expertly, swords working in concert, stabbing and retreating like ghosts.

Schwarzhelm had his back to the door, penned in by the onslaught. With a sick lurch of dread, he knew he'd have to kill them. If one or both escaped to raise the alarm, he'd never escape the Palace. He'd have to spill their blood, and two more good men would die.

Schwarzhelm brought the Rechtstahl round in a crushing parabola. The younger Reiksguard parried, but the blow was too powerful. It drove through his defence, sending him sprawling. The sergeant pressed the attack, raising his blade in the orthodox position.

Schwarzhelm knew the moves all too well – he'd coached his own honour guard in the same techniques. The Rechtstahl glimmered as it cut back sharply, meeting the sergeant's blow and knocking the sword upwards. Schwarzhelm punched out with his left hand, catching the sergeant in the torso before swinging back with the sword-tip.

The blades clashed once, twice, three times. The sergeant was good, quicker than he looked and as strong as a carthorse, but few men could withstand a prolonged assault from Schwarzhelm. As his companion struggled to his feet, Schwarzhelm saw the opening and the Sword of Justice flew into the gap. The blade bit between plates of armour, deep into the armpit. Blood spurted out, and the man crumpled heavily.

Schwarzhelm pulled his sword free, ready for the assault from the other man. He wasn't quick enough. With a cry of rage, the young Reiksguard leapt at him, sword swinging wildly, eyes lit with anger.

Schwarzhelm got his blade up just in time, but the force of the blow sent him reeling. He crashed heavily against the unlocked door. It gave way behind him, forcing him into the chapel beyond.

The Reiksguard plunged in after him, whirling his sword in a series of heavy, ill-aimed blows. The boy had been driven into a fury by the felling of his commander, and the rage was making him dangerous.

Schwarzhelm parried and countered, meeting the ferocity head-on and waiting for it to ebb. He withdrew step by step, containing the threat and drawing the Reiksguard deeper into the chapel. The interior was silent, cold and bleak. The heavy sword-clashes echoed down the long aisles, bouncing from the stone and rebounding like mocking imitations. Schwarzhelm could smell the pungent aroma of myrrh, could hear the clink of metal-tipped boots against the polished marble floor.

As the blades turned and thrust, effigies of the heroes of the past gazed down from dark altars. It was never going to last long. The knight was capable, but limited. He tried too hard to finish it, and his sword overextended. Schwarzhelm swung heavily at the moving blade, knocking it from the boy's hands and sending it skittering across the floor. Before the lad could react he hauled the Rechtstahl back, driving the metal of his right pauldron in and shattering the shoulder blade. The Reiksguard slumped to his knees, his cry of pain echoing down the transept. Schwarzhelm plunged the blade down a third time, finishing the task cleanly. The knight's lifeless body fell heavily to the marble. Almost immediately a pool of blood began to creep across the pristine surface.

Schwarzhelm gazed down coldly at the scene, waiting for his heartbeats to return to normal. He felt nothing but disgust within him. He half expected the commotion to bring a flurry of Morr priests coming to see what was happening. Part of him even hoped they'd come – that would at least have given some meaning to the Reiksguard's actions.

But there was nothing, no sound, no response. The chapel, lit only by narrow, heavily barred windows, remained cold and unmoving. The last of the echoes died away.

Schwarzhelm stirred into action again. The bodies needed to be hidden.

He looked up. There in front of him, either by

chance or some more capricious fate, was the object of his quest. The Magnus Memorial – a vast statue of the greatest Emperor after Sigmar – soared up into the vaulted roof, black as smog. The severe face of that puritan warrior was fixed in an attitude of grim piety, just as it had been, so all the records attested, in life. At its huge armoured feet was the Altar of Remembrance, carved from stone taken from Praag after the great siege and sanctified by a hundred Amethyst magisters at the very dawn of their order.

Above the altar, laid on a chaplet of black silk, was the sword. It was naked, and a notch had been taken from the blade halfway along its length. So Karl Franz had ordered it to lie until Helborg either returned to claim it, or was killed, or was proved to be a traitor beyond the doubt of the Theogonist.

Schwarzhelm took it up in his left hand. For a moment he held the two blades together, the Swords of Justice and Vengeance, just as he had in the Vormeisterplatz in Averheim, when madness had stirred in the air and his mind had been locked into a fury that wasn't his own.

The metal of the Klingerach was sullen, its runes barely visible in the gloom. Something about it spoke of betrayal, of anger, of death. He sheathed the Rechtstahl and took Helborg's weapon himself. Reaching inside his jerkin, he withdrew the letter he'd worked so hard to compose and left it on the altar in its place.

'It is done,' he breathed.

Then Schwarzhelm turned, unable to look up at the stern visage of Magnus, unwilling to gaze back on the bodies of the men he'd killed even as he dragged them into the gloom of the chapel recesses and hid the evidence of the brief, sordid combat.

Moving quickly and quietly, he left. He'd done what he'd come for. His business in the Palace was over, and Averheim beckoned once again.

# Chapter Three

NIGHT MADE THE air of the Worlds Edge Mountains even more bitter. Though not as bone-jarringly cold as it was in winter, the passes were still harsh at the end of the summer, and the rock underfoot was shrouded in a cloak of frost.

Bloch, Kraus, Drassler and the senior officers sat around a rough oak table high up in the tower of the last way-fort before Black Fire Keep. Most of the army were sleeping below them, either rammed up against one another in the hard stone halls of the fort or shivering in tents clustered close to the gates. The huge fires they'd built to ward off the cold burned still, denting the worst of the chill. Bloch had ordered that they be kept stoked, even though it would give away their presence in the mountains for miles around. They hadn't come to creep around like thieves.

At dawn they would march again. They knew where the enemy was, and thanks to Drassler's scouts knew the rough strength of the forces that remained to them. The back of the orc army had been broken by Schwarzhelm on the plains of Averland, but enough greenskins had survived to make the Keep a difficult target. Bloch had two thousand men at his command, including the remnants of the mountain guard that had survived the first days of the incursion. Drassler reckoned a similar number of orcs had made it back to the Keep, but they had the advantage of stone to hide behind.

'We'll need to draw them into the open,' Bloch said, looking over the plans of attack his men had been discussing. 'If they stay behind those walls, we'll never prise them out.'

'Why'd they come out?' asked Drassler. 'They've got supplies, and they've got protection.'

Kraus grinned.

'They'll come out,' he said. 'Give an orc a reason to fight and it'll take it.'

Drassler shook his head. 'Not these ones. They had a plan, and they stuck to it.'

'Just like the ones on the plains,' mused Bloch, remembering the artful way Grunwald had been drawn further and further east.

'It's like I said,' insisted Drassler. 'They've been armed by men, and given their orders by men.'

Bloch had heard this said many times since leaving Grenzstadt. He didn't want to believe it, but the evidence was there. The orcs wore close-fitting amour and carried straight swords. They'd not attempted a wild rampage through the east of the province, but had acted as if explicitly commanded to draw Schwarzhelm from the city. And there were the coins. An orc had little use for gold, but there was plenty of it on their corpses. They'd made the schillings into earrings and pendants, or stuffed them into the throats of their victims for fun. Someone in the Empire had planned it all.

'Tell me again,' he said to Drassler, his chin leaning heavily on his crossed fingers. 'How did you let them get at you?'

Drassler looked irritated. No one liked to recount the story of their failure.

'What more do you want?' he asked. 'We got our orders, just as we always did. Captain Neumann did as he was told. We were told there were four bands of greenskins coming over the passes, none of them more than a hundred strong. The orders from the Averburg were to destroy them before they defiled the memorial sites.'

Bloch knew all of this. He knew that the roving bands of orcs had turned out to be made up of thousands, that they'd worked in concert, and that once the defenders had emerged from the walls they'd been slaughtered. The memory of those killing grounds was still vivid in his mind.

'And who gave you those orders?' he asked, still searching for some clue. Schwarzhelm had told him that one of the contenders for the electorship, Rufus Leitdorf, had been a traitor. If he'd orchestrated all of this, then he deserved everything that the big man had no doubt dished up to him in Averheim.

'They came as they always did. A courier from Averheim, dressed in the livery of the citadel, carrying the scrolls in a locked casket. He had a guard of warriors, two dozen, all wearing the colours of the Averburg garrison. Everything was in the standard cipher, signed off by the Steward. I saw them myself. Nothing was different.'

'And you didn't think *anything* was strange?' asked Bloch, trying to keep the incredulity from his voice. 'Four incursions, all at once, all moving in different directions? What of the defence of the Keep?'

Drassler stiffened. 'Fighting is a way of life up here, commander. We're not like the rest of our kinsmen. When the order comes, we follow it.'

Kraus shook his head. 'You were played for fools,' he muttered.

Drassler slammed his fist on the table. 'How *dare* you?' he hissed. He looked tired. They all looked tired. 'We were doing our duty.'

'Your duty was to defend the Keep,' said Kraus, and his face showed his disdain.

'Enough,' said Bloch, unwilling to see the tension spill over into pointless bickering. He privately shared Kraus's assessment, but nothing would be gained by raking over past failures. 'This isn't helping.'

He held his head in his hands, trying to think. There was so much he didn't know. The idea of Averlanders deliberately sabotaging their own defences was disgusting enough, but perhaps the rot went deeper. The money, after all, had come from Altdorf. Maybe they were still being played for fools. Maybe all of this had been anticipated.

That didn't alter the bare facts. He'd been ordered to retake the Keep. He had a mixed army of Averlanders and Reiklanders, most of them seasoned by weeks of near-constant fighting, no siege engines and little artillery. There had been no news from Averheim since Schwarzhelm's departure for the city, and his supply lines were extended and precarious. A cautious commander might have withdrawn, pulled back to Grenzstadt until the situation in the province had become clear and reinforcements were received. Grunwald's failure weighed heavily on Bloch's mind. There was no sense in fighting a battle that couldn't be won.

'We have a few hours until dawn,' he said. He looked at the officers one by one, gauging from their response how ready they were for the fight. They all met his gaze. 'We'll stay awake until we've hammered out a plan to get the Keep back and the pass secure.'

His eyes rested on Drassler, who stared back at him defiantly. Despite everything, the mountain guard were keen to avenge their defeat.

'I want ideas,' he growled, feeling impatient for action again. 'We need to get them out of the Keep. One way or another, when the sun goes down tomorrow we'll have paid those bastards back twice what they handed out to us. I don't care how we do it, but the passes *will* be back in our hands, and the last of those scum choking on their traitor's gold.'

THE GRAND THEOGONIST Volkmar was an imposing sight even when bereft of his immense battle-armour. His skin was thick and leathery, tanned tight by a lifetime on the battlefield. Dark, direct eyes peered out from under feathered eyebrows. Like Schwarzhelm, he was not known for his humour. His mouth rarely smiled beneath its drooping Kislevite moustache, and his burly arms remained crossed across his chest when not kept busy swinging a warhammer. His shaven head and forearm tattoos completed the savage picture. He looked properly terrifying, as if he struggled himself to contain raging forces of anarchy within him. Even when at rest, he inspired trepidation. When unleashed on to the battlefield, that trepidation turned to awe.

Those who knew him well had even more reason to be fearful. This was a man who had come back from the dead, who'd passed beyond the barrier between the mortal world and that of Chaos. The pain of it still marked his every word, scored his every movement. No one knew the terror of the great enemy quite as intimately as Volkmar, and the experience had marked him out even more than he had been before. With each gesture, each glance, he gave it away. Under the skein of savage piety, a cold furnace of frenzy forever lurked, waiting for the kindling. Once he had been a warrior. Now he was a weapon.

The head of the Cult of Sigmar bowed to few men, but he did towards the figure before him. His ochre robes fell across his broad shoulders as he stooped, his right hand nearly touching the floor.

'Enough of that,' came a familiar voice. 'Sit. We need to talk.'

The Emperor Karl Franz sat in the same chair he'd used when commissioning Schwarzhelm for the Averland mission. Then, he'd looked at ease with the world, confident and self-assured. Now his skin had taken on a pale sheen and his eyes were ringed with grey. His hair, normally glossy, looked dull. The most powerful mortal man in the Old World was troubled, and he hadn't laboured to hide the fact.

Volkmar rose to his full height, grunting as he did so. The wounds that had ravaged his body during his escape from the daemon Be'lakor had been slow to close.

He sat beside the Emperor, saying nothing. The two men were alone. The fine furniture around them looked heavy and lumpen. Outside, a fine rain still spat against the glass windows, and the morning light was grey and filthy. In the corner of the room, the old engineer's clock ticked methodically.

Karl Franz looked down at some sheets of

parchment in his lap. They looked like they'd been read many times.

'Why didn't he come here himself?' the Emperor mused.

'My liege?' asked Volkmar.

'Schwarzhelm. He could have spoken to me. I was angry, but not beyond reason. Now I've lost both of them.'

Helborg. If the Reiksmarshal were found, then Volkmar would be the one priest senior enough to interrogate him. Though hardened by the fires of war and the poisons of Chaos, that was a task he wouldn't relish.

'Perhaps he tried,' said Volkmar.

'What are you saying?'

'That not all your servants are as loyal as he.'

Karl Franz frowned, displeased by the implication. He looked down at the parchment again. 'What do you know of this matter?' he asked.

'A little. Averland is now governed by Heinz-Mark Grosslich. Leitdorf's son is a traitor, and Helborg with him.'

'And do you believe it? What they say of Helborg?'

Volkmar gave a snort of disgust that said all there was to be said.

'Schwarzhelm has erred,' agreed the Emperor, 'and he knows it. Whatever forces were ranged against him have achieved what they set out to do.'

He looked up, and a little of the familiar resolve shone in his eyes.

'We've been granted a second chance,' he said. 'They made a single slip. You know of Heinrich Lassus? He was the man behind them. He betrayed himself. Schwarzhelm has killed him, taken back Helborg's sword, and no doubt seeks to return it to him. Perhaps he is already on the road.'

'So how stands Averland?'

'We don't know. All is clouded. The only thing we can be certain of is that the great enemy is active. They've used this succession to gain a foothold. Nothing has been purged. The stain remains, and it is growing.'

Volkmar let the implications of that sink in. Averland had always been the most placid of provinces, the one furthest from the strife that ravaged the rest of the Empire.

He should have seen this coming. Only in war was there purity; where there was peace there was disease.

'Can Grosslich handle it?'

The Emperor shrugged. 'Who knows? He doesn't answer my summons. That may be pride, or it may be worse. In any event, our response must be the same.'

Here it came. The Emperor's orders. Volkmar didn't need his fine-grained knowledge of statecraft to know what they would be.

'I have tried to manage the affairs of Averland by diplomacy. That has failed. Whether or not Grosslich is a part of this, he cannot be allowed to preside over treachery. It will be rooted out and destroyed.' The Emperor crumpled the parchment in his fist and the knuckles went white. 'You will take my armies, Volkmar. Empty the Reikland if you have to. The gold in the reserves is yours. Take warrior priests and the holiest devotees of Sigmar. Take magisters from the colleges, war engines and artillery. Take veteran regiments and a core of knights. This is no routine suppression of a minor rebellion. This is a new war and needs a new army.'

The Emperor looked into Volkmar's eyes, and his expression was desolate.

'Find out what's happening there,' he growled, his fists still clenched. 'Show the traitors no mercy. Crush them, burn them and grind them into the ground. I would rather see Averland turned into a blasted waste than see it harbour a second front against the enemy. You know what to do. You know it more than anyone else. Can I trust you, Volkmar? Can you succeed where both my generals have failed?'

Volkmar felt a surge of enthusiasm quicken within him, tempered with the fear that had never quite left him. Not since the horrors of Middenheim had he commanded men against the enemy. Now he was being asked to ride again, to take up arms and show his devotion to Sigmar in the way the warrior-god had always intended. He'd failed against Archaon. He'd failed completely. He might do so again, just like the others.

'Yes, my liege,' he replied, his thoughts racing. 'Yes, you can.'

DEEP IN THE heart of Averheim's exclusive jewellery quarter, the merchants had been quick to replenish their stocks. Averland was a province blessed with mines on its borders and Averheim sat squarely on the trade routes between Karak Angazhar and the heart of the Empire. There was money in the place too, and every fat merchant who'd made his fortune shunting cattle from the pasture to the slaughter-house had wives and daughters who needed draping in lines of pearls or traceries of silver, so the jewellery business had prospered with them.

Some of the craftsmen were Averland-bred, plucked

from the rural heartland and put to work at the forges or with the hammer. Over the centuries, the fame of the jewellery quarter had grown and artisans from further afield had settled there. Most came from Nuln, bringing new devices with them and a penchant for mechanical innovation, but there were also dwarfs, drawn as ever by the prospect of making money through the manipulation of the things they loved: steel, iron, gold and gromril. The stunted folk kept themselves to themselves, shunning the company of their human counterparts unless some deal needed to be struck or supplies of stones were running low. So it was that they formed a community within a community in Averheim, locked in their own arcane world of contracts and grudges, tolerated by their hosts but seldom interfered with.

Such isolation brought certain advantages. The dwarfs didn't involve themselves in human affairs, and were as happy serving under a Leitdorf or an Alptraum as they would have been under a Raukov or a Todbringer. Happy, that is, as long as they weren't over-taxed and were given free rein to market their creations.

That made the dwarf-smiths of Averland useful contacts for men of a certain profession. If the gold flowed, then they would be more discreet than a corpse. Of course, getting them to trust anyone but a member of their own clan was hard. It took persistence, patience, a working knowledge of the simpler forms of Khazalid, plenty of money and a formidable power of persuasion. Not many humans could boast all of those. Pieter Verstohlen, on the other hand, could.

So it was that the spy sat, knees up almost against

his chest, sitting on a three-legged stool in the forge of the master jewelsmith Rossik Valgrind. Before him the fire glowed angrily, throwing red light across the dark interior. Around the hearth hung metal objects of various kinds. Some were familiar – tongs, clamps, bellows and fine-headed hammers. Others looked like nothing Verstohlen had seen before, and their uses could only be guessed at.

The owner of the forge himself worked at the back of the chamber, ignoring Verstohlen and tapping away at a ring of gromril. His gnarled hands worked with astonishing speed and precision, caressing and moulding the metal as if it were a child's forelock. His naked arms were like corded leather, wound about with brass wire and latticed with tattoos. He smelled of scorched flesh, hot metal and charred oil, and his beard was wiry and truncated from a thousand singes.

He didn't speak, and the only sound to escape his bearded lips was the occasional grunt of satisfaction as the jewellery gradually took shape under his hammers. The deal he'd made with Verstohlen had been for a place to meet only. There'd been no payment for conversation, so he didn't provide any.

There was a tap on the door leading out from the forge and onto the street. Valgrind kept working, ignoring everything but his art. Verstohlen clambered up from the low stool and reached for the latch. Outside, wrapped in a long cloak, stood Tochfel. Verstohlen beckoned him in and closed the door behind him. The afternoon light stung his eyes after the occlusion of the forge.

'Glad you could make it, Steward,' said Verstohlen, pulling up a stool. The two of them sat before the hearth. In the background, Valgrind worked away as if nothing had happened.

'Safe to talk?' whispered Tochfel, casting anxious looks in the dwarf's direction.

'Absolutely,' said Verstohlen, speaking normally. 'Maybe the safest place to talk in the city.'

Tochfel nodded. 'Good. I'm glad my message got to you.'

'Your concerns and mine may be similar.'

'Maybe. How are things with the elector?'

Verstohlen shrugged.

'I see less of him every day. I suspect my services are no longer of much use.'

'But how does he seem to you?'

'His mood changes. Some days, I see the qualities I saw in him when Schwarzhelm and I first arrived. On others, things are less... clear cut.'

Tochfel nodded. 'That's right. That's what others say. It's harder to get to him. I've not spoken with him for days. He's becoming erratic.'

Verstohlen felt a qualm of recognition. That's what they'd said about Schwarzhelm. Was there something corrupting about the city? He immediately thought of Natassja. The witch had still not been found.

'So what are you saying to me, Steward?' asked Verstohlen. 'I can't believe you've come here to moan about your master's moods.'

Tochfel's hands fidgeted on his knees. By the glow of the hearth, his face looked distorted.

'Something's wrong here, Herr Verstohlen,' he said, his voice audibly shaking. 'I tried to warn you of it before Grosslich's coronation. No one's seen Ferenc Alptraum since the battle for the city. No one's seen Achendorfer. There are other disappearances.'

'Such things are normal when power shifts,' said Verstohlen, watching Tochfel carefully, looking for the signs of dishonesty. The Steward was not a master player of the game, but he could still have been subverted.

Tochfel looked hurt. 'I may not have your skill in such matters,' he said, 'but I'm not entirely naïve. Do you know how many men have been burned at the stake? *Two hundred*. They're not all done in public. I've seen the lists. That's beyond reason.'

'Are there trials?'

'Supposedly.' Tochfel snorted. 'The witch hunter Heidegger has his talons into everything. He even wants my own aides dragged to the stake. None of us are safe.'

At the mention of witch hunters, Verstohlen had to work to suppress a grunt of contempt. The cult members who'd taken Leonora had been Templars of Sigmar. He regarded even the uncorrupted ones as little better than butchers and sadists, and the fact he was frequently mistaken for one of them was a considerable irritation.

Tochfel leaned forwards, his fingers twitching with agitation. 'Can't you *see* it?' he implored. 'We've picked the wrong man.'

Verstohlen shook his head. 'Impossible. I saw Leitdorf's corruption for myself.'

'Now who's being naïve, counsellor? So much has turned on that, and yet you always say that the great enemy is ever more cunning than it seems. Could you not have been *allowed* to see what you did?'

Verstohlen froze.

'Natassja's still not been found,' he said. 'She may be

in the city. Her powers are formidable, and while she lives none of us should feel safe.'

Tochfel let slip a bitter laugh. 'You're obsessed with Natassja. Can't you see that *Grosslich* is the enemy? He's duped us all. You've seen that monstrosity he's building in the poor quarter. What sane man builds a tower of iron?'

Verstohlen didn't reply. The more Tochfel spoke, the more anxiety started to crowd around him. He'd been so *sure*. He'd convinced everyone of Leitdorf's guilt. Even Schwarzhelm.

For that matter, where *was* Schwarzhelm? Why hadn't there been any word from Altdorf? Why hadn't there been word of anything from outside the province?

'I won't deny there's something wrong here,' he said, 'but Natassja is the witch, and she's Leitdorf's woman. We need to find her, and her whelp of a husband.'

'What can I do to prove it to you?' asked Tochfel, sounding miserable. 'You won't accept the evidence of your eyes. No one will. I feel like I'm the only man left who can see it.'

'I'll speak to Grosslich,' said Verstohlen, placing a reassuring hand on the Steward's shoulder. 'There are things I'd like cleared up myself. Trust me – if the man has been tainted by anything here, I'll be able to tell. I'm not proud, Herr Tochfel. If I'm wrong, then I'll be the first to come to you to admit it. Then we'll decide what to do next.'

Tochfel didn't look reassured. 'He'll get stronger, the longer we leave it.'

'And what could we do, even if you were right?' asked Verstohlen. 'Could the two of us overthrow an elector? We need information. The Empire will not leave Averheim alone for long. This thing requires subtlety, and outside help.'

For a moment, Tochfel looked as if he'd protest further, but the words never came. He looked slumped and fearful.

'Take heart, Steward,' said Verstohlen, trying to improve both their moods. 'We have already saved Averheim from certain damnation. What corruption remains will be uncovered in time.'

Tochfel gave him a piteous look.

'If you really think that, counsellor,' he said, 'then I do not understand your reputation for wisdom.'

BLACK FIRE KEEP dominated the land around it, just as its architects had intended. The pass was under a mile wide at the point where it had been constructed. It had been raised on a hill of granite in the centre of the otherwise flat and featureless rock around it. The pinnacle of the fortress commanded long views both east and west, and in normal times the standards of the Emperor and of Averland rustled proudly from twenty-foot-high flagpoles.

The bare rock stretching away from the Keep on all sides was not there by accident of nature. After the second battle of Black Fire Pass, an army of men and dwarfs had worked for months to clear the land. Piles of stone were levelled in back-breaking labour, and the few clumps of foliage capable of surviving the blinding snows of winter were cut down and burned. Approaching the Keep undetected was now all but impossible, and bitter experience had taught the defenders to remain vigilant at all times.

The massive walls rose a hundred feet into the clear sky and were as thick as a man's height. Their stone was black from the many sieges levelled against them, and the signs of historical devastation were impossible to remove. For all the blood shed over the wind-scoured stone, it would never be left undefended as long as the Empire stood. Black Fire Pass was more than a trading route, more than a strategic foothold in the mountains. It was the place where the Empire had been born. There was never a shortage of volunteers willing to man the ramparts of the way-forts and Keep, despite the appalling casualties and near-certainty of attack. Indeed, the mountain guard commanders had to pick their men carefully, rooting out the genuine soldiers from the fanatic and deranged.

The cycle of fighting never ended here. Incursions would be followed by a bitter fightback, which would be followed by fresh incursions. The humans would never rid the world of the greenskin scourge, and the orcs would never be allowed to hold the passes. As Bloch looked up at the distant walls, now daubed with the blood of their last human defenders, he knew he was just the latest to contest the site. Whatever the result of his actions, the game would be played out for centuries after he was gone.

He found the thought reassuring. All he'd ever known was war. The idea of a world where it didn't exist felt as wrong as being bought a drink by a dwarf. Both were feasibly possible, but he didn't expect to see either in his lifetime.

He stood with his troops half a mile west of the fortress, in view of the ramparts but far enough away to be untroubled by them. At his side, as ever, were Drassler and Kraus. Behind him, the army stood silently. They were arrayed for battle, divided into companies and standing in well-ordered ranks. They'd held together well. Averlander companies still carried their standards proudly, both those which Schwarzhelm had raised in Averheim and the men of Grenzstadt and Heideck who'd been drafted into action. Amongst them were the Reikland detachments that had marched from Altdorf. They were tougher men, hardened by years of ceaseless combat, proudly wearing the white and grey of the richest Imperial province. The tall staves of the halberds glinted in the severe light.

At the front was Bloch's own detachment. To a man, they were survivors of Grunwald's army. All of them were Reiklanders, tempered in the fiercest of fighting, as unyielding and hard-bitten as any regular troops in the Emperor's armies. No fear showed in their grizzled faces, just a grim determination to see the campaign through. Many of their comrades lay in the rich earth of the pastures below, and the deaths required vengeance.

Bloch looked over the heads of the massed troops to the baggage train at the rear. Reserve companies stood ready, as silent as the main body of the army. Teams of horses stamped nervously, steam snorting from their nostrils as they shook their heads against the chill. Behind them were the few artillery pieces of any size that he'd been able to commandeer. Not much, and little danger to the Keep.

Finally, there were Drassler's mountain guard. No more than two hundred or so remained, the others having been killed or harried into the high peaks by the tide of orcs. The survivors looked as hard-edged as Bloch's own men, their beards ragged and their faces unsmiling. This was their chance for revenge, and perhaps for some measure of atonement.

All were watching him, waiting for the words of command. As they stood unmoving, the harsh wind rippled across the army.

Bloch turned away from them, back to the fortress. He couldn't make out much from that distance. There was no movement on the plain. The Keep rose tall and stark from the stone, a block of solid rock thrust from the core of the earth. Though there was no sign of the infestation, he knew that the place was swarming with greenskins. Schwarzhelm's orders, given so lightly after the rout on the grasslands of Averland, would not be easily fulfilled. That mattered not. He'd been given them, and he'd carry them out.

He took a deep breath and turned to Kraus. The captain's face was as bleak as the granite around him.

'Give the signal,' Bloch ordered. 'Let's do it.'

# Chapter Four

NOON HAD PASSED, and the afternoon sun began to cast long shadows from the branches of the trees. The seemingly endless pastures of long, whispering grass had given way to higher country, dotted with straggling woodland and uncultivated scrub. This was poor land. The soil was thin and the undergrowth tangled. Ever since the devastation of Ironjaw the people of the region had been slow to return to their farms, and abandoned buildings, their roofs white with age, dotted the horizon. Gorse had replaced grass on the verges, and the roads petered out into stone-clogged tracks.

Skarr pulled his horse up and the column of knights came to a halt. He rode at the front of it, accompanied by Eissen, who in the aftermath of the fighting at Averheim had assumed the position of his lieutenant by default. Leitdorf was close behind. Further down the column, protected by ranks of Reiksguard, lay Helborg. He'd been placed in a carriage taken from Leitdorf's last country residence. It was absurdly ornate, decked with florid coats of arms and a golden image of the Solland sun on its flanks. If there had been any less ostentatious choice, Skarr would have taken it. As it was, he was stuck with the late count's extravagance.

He looked over the line of troops with a commander's eye, checking for signs of weariness or indiscipline. There were none. Though they now numbered less than fifty, the company held its order impeccably. The Reiksguard, drilled from their teens to embody the perfection of the Emperor's will, had maintained the condition of their armour and steeds with stoic efficiency. They carried most of their gear and supplies with them, and the trail of baggage mules and spare horses at the rear of the column was short.

Rufus Leitdorf nudged his horse alongside Skarr's. The deposed heir had lost some of the fat around his face over the last few days. He looked better for it, less effeminate. In the face of the Reiksguard's open contempt, some of the habitual arrogance had been knocked from his manner.

'How close are we?' asked Skarr, turning his gaze back to the road ahead. The track wound through the heathland uncertainly, threatening to give out entirely. That wouldn't trouble the horses, but it would make the carriage's progress impossible. Like everywhere in the Empire, there were creatures in the dark places far from the road, ever ready to launch an assault if they sensed weakness.

'Another day,' said Leitdorf. 'No more.'

Skarr grunted. Long hours travelling in the wilds didn't bother him at all, but Helborg's condition did. The Marshal needed time to rest properly. Skarr had witnessed Helborg fighting on after taking wounds that would have laid a lesser man low, but this was different. The man's face remained bloodless. Even when awake, his eyes were glassy and listless. Something seemed broken within him, and it wasn't physical. For long periods the Marshal remained unconscious. His slumber was troubled, and on the occasions Skarr had watched over him, he'd seen Helborg mutter words in his sleep. Chief among them was always 'Schwarzhelm'.

'I'm going to check on the Marshal,' he said, dismounting. Skarr pushed his way back through the mounted knights and made his way to the carriage. The doors had been covered with a black lacquer, much of which had rubbed off during the passage south and east. Now the proud emblems were scratched and faded, and the wood was plastered with grime.

Skarr climbed up on to the footboard and pulled the door open. Helborg was slumped against the far wall of the carriage, swathed in blankets. There wasn't room to lay him flat, and he looked awkwardly twisted in the cramped interior.

Helborg was awake, staring out of the window. Days-worth of stubble covered his sunken cheeks, and his moustache was lank.

'Marshal,' acknowledged Skarr, cautiously sitting opposite him. There wasn't much that scared the preceptor, but Helborg, even in his diminished state, made everyone nervous.

Helborg didn't respond. He kept staring out of the glass.

'How do you feel?' asked Skarr.

As soon as the question left his mouth, he knew it had been a mistake. Helborg didn't want pity.

'Where are we?' Helborg's rasping voice was even worse than usual.

'Near the Drakenmoor. Leitdorf's land. Another day's riding, no more.'

'I should be on a horse. What's this damned hay-wain you've got me in?'

Skarr didn't quite know how to respond to that. The man looked like he could barely raise his arm.

'I'll see to it,' he lied.

Helborg finally looked at him. His gaze was penetrating. 'My recollection of events is... unclear,' he said. 'What has happened here?'

Skarr cleared his throat. He had no answers.

'We're being hunted. Grosslich has raised the country against us. He's been crowned elector, and there's an army on our heels.'

'Then turn and fight it. You're Reiksguard.'

'There are hundreds of them, my lord.'

Helborg grunted with disapproval, as if to say, *and when did that ever matter before?*

'Schwarzhelm was with them,' added Skarr, and it sounded like a hollow excuse. He'd never run from a fight before, but the events of the Vormeisterplatz had been horrifying. To see the two greatest sons of the Empire come to blows had been bad enough. Becoming fugitives was even worse.

'So what's your plan?' rasped Helborg. At the mention of Schwarzhelm's name, his voice had become tighter.

'Keep you and Leitdorf hidden and find out what happened. Grosslich's treachery can't stay uncovered for long, and I'll find a way of getting a message through to Altdorf.'

Helborg shot him a withering look. Skarr recoiled, recognising the imperious disdain all too well. The Marshal wasn't happy.

'Damn it, Skarr, we'll do more than that,' he growled. Something of his old cultivated savagery had returned. 'You didn't see Schwarzhelm's face. He was mad. They'd all been driven mad. It was in the air.'

He leaned forwards with difficulty. Skarr saw one of his hands slip from the cloth wrappings, and it was clenched into a tight fist.

'We'll gather our strength and strike back,' he rasped. 'Strike hard, and strike fast. Whatever treachery has taken place here will be punished.'

Like a long-cold hearth stuttering back into life, the Marshal's eyes recovered their old fire. Then, and for the first time since the fighting at Averheim, Skarr knew Helborg would live to lead him again.

'We are your men, my lord,' he said, with something like joy.

'Forget that!' Helborg snapped, his voice shaking with fervour. 'Forget your loyalties. This is about vengeance. I will recover my strength, I will return to the city, and I will find the one who did this to me.'

He looked at Skarr directly, and his expression was brutal.

'Sigmar preserves those who *fight*, Skarr. We will fight until the Aver runs dark with blood. We will fight until the last traitor drowns in his own gore. We will fight until that bastard Grosslich has been cast down and his soul flayed to the five corners of the world. They should have killed me. While a breath remains in my body I'll be too much for them. I'll raise the country against them. I'll tear down their walls and shatter their defences. I'll burn their warped dreams and rip out their traitor's hearts. All this I will do and more, for I am Kurt Helborg, master of the Emperor's endless armies, hammer of his foes, and my name itself is *vengeance*.'

BLACK FIRE KEEP was ugly. Pig ugly. The vaguely star-shaped walls jutted out unevenly, and the massive ramparts hung like brooding palls of snow over the sloping walls. Everything had been turned black by age and fire, and even the orcs hadn't found many ways to despoil further what they'd found.

'Form up!' Bloch bellowed, letting the sergeants echo his order through the ranks.

He'd pulled the army in close. The detachments of infantry were now in clear view of the battlements, arrayed in a wide semicircle to the south of the fort. All were deployed in company detachments several ranks deep, Averlanders mingled with Reiklanders. The squares formed a long, ragged line across the stony ground, and there were many gaps between the clustered companies. Pennants flew in the strong breeze, snapping and rippling over the heads of the soldiers. There was no heavy cavalry, and what artillery there was had been hauled into place on the far left flank of the army, south-west of the Keep along a narrow shelf of wind-smoothed rock. Reserves were minimal – just a couple of halberdier companies set back from the main formation.

The troops kept out of bow-range, but only just. If Bloch could tempt the defenders to waste arrows, then that was all to the good. The sun was still high in the sky, and there was plenty of time for an assault. If he had his way, the fortress would be breached by night-fall. It all came down to tactics, expectation and a generous slice of luck.

Bloch shaded his eyes and looked up at the

ramparts. There were shapes moving along them, hunched against the stone. The greenskins were agitated. He knew it wasn't fear. They were cooped up, locked behind walls. They hated that. It was that hatred he had to use.

'Artillery!' roared Bloch, and the signal was sent down the lines.

The firepower wasn't much to boast about: a handful of Helblasters, two Helstorms and a couple of light cannon. Hauling them up the mountainsides had been a miserable task; now they had to prove their worth.

On either side of the artillery, the reserve companies of halberdiers edged away. None of them trusted the gun crews, who worked fast in the cold to get the engines of war ready. Barrels were aimed and last-minute adjustments made. Buckets of water were drawn up and burning rags placed ready next to the wicks. The crew captains looked up expectantly.

'Fire,' growled Bloch.

The order went down the line. With a deafening crack that echoed around the pass, the first guns fired. Cannonballs whined into the air, smashing high up against the walls and sending the gun barrels slamming back yards. They were followed by the swish of Helstorm rockets, spiralling in their wake and exploding in balls of fire. The Helstorm batteries that followed were less effective – they'd been designed to counter infantry units, not batter down solid walls – but Bloch ordered them to open fire anyway. The task was not to reduce the walls to rubble, but to play on the nerves of the orcs. He knew they were itching to strike back. He just had to keep provoking them.

'Aim high!' he roared, reminding them of their orders. 'Dead greenskins, not cracked stone.'

Standing at Bloch's side, Kraus gestured to the commander of the archery companies. There weren't many of them – no more than two hundred – and they didn't have the range or the volume of arrows to seriously trouble the defenders. Nonetheless, they marched forwards, flanked by heavily-armed infantry carrying shields. As they came into range, the first bellows of scorn and challenge came down from the fortress. The orcs were roused.

'Remember your orders!' barked Bloch. 'No arrows wasted.'

The archers settled into position and a stream of enemy bolts began to spin down towards them. The armoured infantry formed protective ranks in front of the lightly armed archers and did their best to shelter them from the deadly hail from above. Once in position, the Imperial bows began to sing and arrows flew up at the heavily guarded battlements and windows. Even as they did so, the second round of cannon fire blazed out.

Kraus watched the flurry of bolts and shot impassively. Bloch did likewise, seeing a soldier in the front rank of the exposed archery battalion crumple to the floor, a black-barbed dart shivering in his chest. The exchange of fire was lethal in both directions, but only one army was in proper cover.

'We can't keep this up for long,' Kraus said grimly.

Bloch knew that as well as he did.

'Keep firing!' he shouted, spittle flying from his lips. The men had to know he was in charge, that this was all part of the plan.

'They'll come out,' he hissed, his voice low so only Kraus could hear.

'And if they don't?'

Bloch didn't answer. He didn't want to think about that.

THE DAY WAXED across Averheim, and all along the river barges bumped and jostled for position. Clouds had begun to drift from the east, and the sky was no longer the unbroken arch of blue it had been for so long. A light breeze whipped up the surface of the Aver, throwing flecks of foam against the bows of the vessels in the water.

Men clambered from hold to hold, carrying goods or ticking off items on requisition ledgers. Soldiers were everywhere. The number of men at arms in Averheim seemed to have trebled. Some looked like Alptraum's men, given new uniforms and new weapons. Others had an unfamiliar look about them, as if they were new to the city and out of sympathy with its residents.

Tochfel gathered his cloak around his shoulders, feeling the cool air against his skin. He had no business on the wharfs today, and since his meeting with Verstohlen he'd grown wary of any attempts to influence the traffic there. If no one but he could see the problem in suborning an entire province to the demands of a single building, then that was their problem. The time had come to make his protests at the highest level, while he still had the protection of his rank and title. He had no confidence in retaining either for long.

He hurried on down from the quayside, avoiding the glares from the roving bands of soldiers.

Grosslich's men had become officious, as if given special orders to stop and search anyone abroad without permission. Even in the middle of the afternoon, some of them were clearly the worse for wear. They were well-paid, that Tochfel knew, and there were only two things a soldier spent his money on. The taverns and bawdy-houses had never done better business.

Striding on from the Griffon Bridge and the embankment beyond, Tochfel made his way to the poor quarter. As he went, the crowds thinned out. Even the patrols lessened, and before he'd gone more than half a mile the roads and streets were eerily quiet. No taverns were open, no hearths glowed behind lead-lined windows, no brothels rang with song and laughter. Everything was buttoned-down, locked-up, shut fast.

Tochfel didn't pause, but kept his head down. He knew what kept the people away. Ahead of him, the Tower rose. It seemed to grow taller with every passing hour. Iron fronds had shot up from the base like plants, curling into the air and branching into new tendrils. The skeleton was gradually being clad, and fresh beams criss-crossed between supporting struts like the bone spurs of a lady's corset. Even at such an early stage it was clear that the final construction would be huge. When completed, the horrific needle of metal and stone would dwarf the Averburg and cast a spiked shadow over half the city. As Tochfel looked at it, he shuddered. Why could no one else see how *wrong* this was? Why was Verstohlen so relaxed about it?

Tochfel pulled his cloak tighter and pressed on. It was time to get to the bottom of things. If Grosslich wouldn't come to see him at the Averburg, Tochfel would have to come to Grosslich at the Tower.

He turned into the long, straight street which led directly to the construction site. The houses on either side of him were almost completely silent. Even in the strong sunlight he felt a strange chill settle on his bones. There were no open windows. A loose door banged in the breeze at the far end, and from somewhere else there came the sound of a rusty hinge being worked back and forth.

At the end of the street the old wooden perimeter fence had been replaced with something more permanent: iron, naturally, hammered into eight-foot poles and elaborately spiked on the top. As far as he could see, it looked like the new fence ran around the entire site, enclosing the workings of the Tower completely.

Where the street met the fence, a high gate had been raised, crowned with a stylised 'G' set amid a crown of thorns. There were other shapes sculpted there, though quite what they were was hard to make out. Despite the strong daylight, lamps burned atop twin pillars on either side of the gates. The flames within them were an odd colour, a deep orange, with the faintest blush of pink at the edges. The fires flickered within their glass caskets like grasping fingers.

Tochfel paused, suddenly uneasy. He'd heard the stories of this place, just as everyone else had. The river was less than a mile away, bustling with life, and yet it could have been left behind in another world. His resolve began to waver. Perhaps coming had been a mistake.

'Declare yourself,' came a voice from beside the gate.

A man stepped from the shadow of one of the pillars, brandishing a spear. Another approached from the opposite side. They were wearing the crimson and gold of Grosslich's army. Tochfel noticed that they were better equipped than the guards at the Averburg and wore a close-fitting breastplate, greaves and a tall helmet. Not very Averland-like. Almost... *elvish*.

'The Steward,' said Tochfel, letting his cloak fall back and trying to keep the fear out of his voice. Now that he'd been noticed, retreat was impossible. The guards recognised him and lowered their spears.

'You're here on your own, sir?'

'What does it look like? Open the gates.'

The guards looked at one another doubtfully. 'Are you expected, sir? The elector doesn't like–'

'Open the damn gates, man. Neither he nor I like being kept waiting.'

The lead guard shrugged. He went back to the pillar and pulled some kind of brass lever set into the stone. There was a hiss, and the gates swung inwards. Beyond them, a wide path had been cut, lined with some kind of thorn-bush at ground level. Dotted clumps of the strange plant were visible beside the path as it ran the several hundred yards up to the unfinished Tower.

Tochfel hurried inside, not giving the guards a second glance. Behind him, the gates sighed closed, coming together with a soft click. Like everything about the place, the motion was unsettling.

Within the fence, the ground had been cleared and flattened. Huge paving slabs of dark stone had been laid. They were interlinked, and traced out some obscure and massively complicated pattern. As Tochfel gazed at it, he thought he caught something of its outline, but the totality eluded him. It was both familiar and deeply strange. The artistry of the stones' placement looked superb, and the joins between sections were barely visible.

He went deeper in the compound. The silence

became more absolute. Only his own footfalls, soft against the polished stone, seemed to make any noise at all.

Tochfel looked up as he went. The sky had lost some of its lustre. There was a greyness to it. That was strange. As he watched, the colour seemed to run out of it. He flicked his eyes earthwards, disorientated. The mass of iron loomed ahead, a fraction more distinct than the sky behind it. It was no longer dark. Everything was going grey, as if a mist had rolled across the plain while he walked.

Tochfel could feel his heart thumping strongly. His palms grew sweaty. The air around him smelled strange. There was a metallic taste on his tongue, almost sweet. He felt light-headed and dizzy. This really had been a mistake.

His breathing quickening, he turned and started to head back. The place was cursed, and he had no place in it.

A sudden noise made him start. He felt panic rise in his throat. It sounded like the wheeze of some huge dog, close by, somewhere in the gathering mist. Tochfel hurried back the way he'd come. The scorn of the guards didn't matter now. There was something in the grey light, and it wasn't natural. Perhaps a hundred yards ahead, he could still see the dim outline of the pillars with their flame lanterns. He'd be there in moments.

Then the pillars shrank from view. Both of them. As if some order had been given from within the Tower, the colour-drenching mist swept up and across the compound. Everything but the patterned stone beneath him disappeared. Even his hands looked pale, like a cadaver's.

Tochfel found himself struggling to keep a lid on his bubbling fear. He began to run. To his left there was another dog-like sound, closer than the last, right on his shoulder. He veered away from it, losing his sense of direction. The last shreds of vision merged into the grey fog. It felt like the whole world had been torn from existence. Heart hammering, breath ragged, he stumbled blindly, mumbling prayers to Sigmar in his panic.

Then, from nowhere, a patch of curling vapour ripped from the rest and let a shaft of the world's sun into the cloud. Ahead of Tochfel was a man. No, not a man. It had an armoured snout, impossibly long, plated and dark. It crouched low, as if its joints were twisted backwards. A snarling, grating sound came from its muzzle, and it clutched a crystal-bladed halberd in a pair of clawed hands.

Tochfel screamed. He screamed like he'd never screamed in his life. Other soldiers emerged from the shifting clouds, each panting and growling like a dog, each limping towards him like a grotesque parody of both man and beast.

Then the beam of sunlight passed, obscured by the grey miasma once more. Tochfel's screams lasted for a moment longer, and were then extinguished, muffled by the mist. Silence rolled back across the construction site. After a few moments the mist sank back to earth, wavering and rippling as it sighed out of existence.

Back at the gates, the guards did their best not to pay any attention. They'd learned it wasn't wise to interfere with what went on in the Tower. They hadn't seen the mist anyway. Only one man in Averheim had seen the mist, and he was gone. Just on the edge of hearing, there was a faint noise. It could have been a trick of the wind, but it sounded like a woman laughing, cool and elegant.

Then it too was gone. The compound looked as it always did, empty and echoing. Across the wide expanse of stone there was no sign of the dog-soldiers, nor of Tochfel. If the human guards had been foolish enough to venture inside the compound, perhaps curious as to his fate, they would have found no body, and no blood.

There was no blood, because he hadn't been killed. That wasn't the way of the Tower. He'd been taken, just as the others had been, alive. And that, of course, was only the beginning.

ARROWS FLEW UP at Black Fire Keep, peppering the stone and clattering back to earth. The cannon still boomed, but only the faintest of cracks had been opened up on the ramparts. It was too old, too strong. The orcs stayed clustered in safety, locked out of harm's way. Frustration began to spread across the besieging army.

Bloch sensed it before he saw it. He was barely out of the ranks himself, plucked from being a company captain by Schwarzhelm after the engagement at Turgitz, and knew all the moods of a halberdier detachment. They were getting close to boiling over. They could all see the exposed archers being picked off from the ramparts, all hear the jeers of the capering orcs on the battlements. This was death by attrition.

'Pull them back,' hissed Kraus through clenched teeth. Nearly two dozen archers lay dead, and another score had been wounded. They were having almost no effect.

'No,' said Bloch, watching the carnage blankly. 'It's keeping their eyes where I want them. We won't pull back.'

'Damn you, commander, pull them back!' Kraus looked livid. His fingers itched at his side, eager to draw his sword and exact retribution for the losses.

'Bring out the bait,' said Bloch, clenching his jaw to hide his anguish. His faith in his plan was being sorely tested.

Kraus shook his head, but called out the order. A company of Averlander spearmen rushed from the reserve position to the front ranks of the army. Still out of bowshot, but ahead of the main body of halberdiers, they stopped. Each of them carried a heavy bag on their back. Some were bent double under the weight, and others were carried by two men.

Their captain, a veteran of the Averheim garrison who'd ridden out with Schwarzhelm, looked up to Bloch for confirmation.

'Do it!' Bloch roared, before turning to Kraus. 'Send the word out. The army holds position. Do *not* threaten the gates, d'you hear?'

The orders were passed on. The hail of artillery and arrows was kept up, nearly obscuring the Keep beyond with its drip feed of provocation.

On the plain, in full view of the Keep's massive gatehouse, the Averlanders began their work. All slammed their bags to the ground and pulled the fabric back. Within them were the bodies of fallen greenskins. Most were goblins, scrawny and spiteful-looking even in death. Some of the cadavers were of larger breeds, and there were even a couple of heavy warriors, carried by two or more men and as thick as the bole of a fallen oak.

All of the bodies had been stripped of their armour, and the naked green flesh looked almost grey in the spare light. The limbs were bound with twine, and there were bloodstains on all the corpses. There were nearly a hundred of them, the best part of a company, all dead. As the carcasses were produced, a howl of anger rose from the Keep.

'It won't work,' insisted Kraus. 'They're obviously dead.'

'They can't see that,' said Bloch, looking at the carnage grimly. 'It'll look like an execution. And even if it doesn't, would you watch while *they* butchered your comrades' bodies?'

The Averlander captain waited until the stricken orcs were all out, then brought his sword down. One by one, working from right to left, the cadavers were dragged forwards. With the maximum ceremony, the captain sliced off their limbs. He didn't work quickly, and lingered over every stroke. If the orc had been alive, it would have been howling in agony. As it was, Bloch hoped the distance would give a similar impression to those watching on the battlements.

More orc corpses were sliced apart. The growling and cursing from the Keep grew louder. Figures could be seen scurrying back and forth against the battlements, and the rain of black-feathered arrows stepped up. They were getting angrier.

'Maintain artillery barrage!' bellowed Bloch. 'Keep those arrows coming!'

He looked at the distance between the front ranks of his army and the gate. There was plenty of space. He'd deliberately kept the ground open and his forces in a loose offensive position. The orcs had to think that he was ill-prepared for a sortie, that he'd left his men wide open to attack. Even now, he could sense the boiling anger from within the castle walls. He knew the orcish commander would be holding them back, but he also knew there'd be hotheaded warriors burning to strike back. If the roles were reversed, he'd have been one of them. Better an honest fight in the open than skulking in the stinking halls of a human hovel.

'Come on,' he breathed, watching the walls intently.

A muffled cry told them that another archer had been slain. A low tide of muttering reached his ears from the halberdiers around him. More orc corpses were cut apart, their limbs thrown towards the gates with scorn. Averlanders capered around with severed heads, throwing them back and forth like children with snowballs. The cannon roared again, making the ramparts shudder with the impact.

'Come *on*...'

The gates stayed shut. The growling from within reached a fever pitch. Bloch was running out of time. Kraus put his hand on his sword, ready to draw it. His face was black with anger. Bloch knew what he was thinking. The madness had to be put to an end. They had to withdraw. The plan wasn't working.

Bloch looked up at the ramparts. The gamble was blowing up in his face, and good men were dying. Another shield-bearer went down in the front ranks, his skull crushed by a rock hurled from the Keep. The cries of agony as he writhed on the stone rent Bloch's heart.

'By Sigmar,' he hissed, knuckles white with tension as he gripped the shaft of his halberd. 'Come *on*...'

VERSTOHLEN WAITED. HE'D already been waiting for some time. It had been hard to gauge how long, but it must surely have been two hours. He was sitting in an antechamber in the Averburg. The room was almost entirely bare. There were marks against the stone where furniture and paintings had once hung, now just bleached emptiness. The one bench that remained was old and battered. The place had been stripped, and was now not much more than a draughty hall of naked rock.

Verstohlen crossed his legs and looked out of the window opposite. Doubts ran through his mind, one after the other. It was the little things that gave cause for anxiety. Traders spoke in hushed tones of a heavy military presence all along the Aver. What little dissent had remained in Averheim after Leitdorf's departure had been ruthlessly crushed. Verstohlen recalled Tochfel's look of disbelief as he'd recounted the burnings. *Two hundred*.

And Natassja was still alive. She had to be. Despite all Grosslich's assurances that she and her husband were being hunted, there was still no result. Only a body would satisfy him.

Now Tochfel had thrown doubt on the elector himself. Part of him couldn't believe the ebullient, golden-haired warrior could have been corrupted; the other part of him dwelt on the possibility endlessly. Averland seemed to have developed a knack for turning the minds of its governors. First Marius, then Schwarzhelm, now Grosslich. There had to be something deeper going on. For all his supposed acumen, all his long experience, he couldn't see it.

Verstohlen sighed, letting his head fall back against the bare stone wall. There was no pleasure in this work any more. There never had been, really. He was just Schwarzhelm's tool, the keenest of his many instruments. With the Emperor's Champion gone, Verstohlen was bereft, like a plank of old wood washed up on the shoreline. Some men made their own destinies. Verstohlen hadn't been like that since Leonora. For all his peerless attributes, the wound of that parting had never closed. He was a follower, not a leader, and the shadows were his home. Now exposed, held out in the open as the architect of Grosslich's rebellion, he was useless, a liability, an anachronism.

'My lord?'

Verstohlen snapped back into the present. He'd been drifting. Reverie was replaced with irritation.

'What is it?' he asked, looking up sharply.

An official wearing the robes of a loremaster had entered. The man's face was curiously white and smooth, rather like a woman's. He was gazing at Verstohlen with a faint air of smugness, as if glad to have caught the famous spy napping.

'I'm sorry to inform you that His Excellency is not able to grant you an audience after all. I regret extremely that you've waited so long for no purpose.'

'*His Excellency*? What in Sigmar's name is that? And who're you?'

'I am Holymon Eschenbach,' replied the official, still as smooth and untroubled as cream. 'The new under-Steward. And His Excellency has issued a proclamation on the titles and ranks to be observed in the new dispensation. You would do well to note them, counsellor.'

Verstohlen felt his frustration begin to rise. He was being snubbed, and crudely so. Or perhaps this was another message. He rose fluidly, pulling his leather overcoat closed around him.

'Well then, under-Steward,' he said, letting a note of contempt sink into that title. 'It seems I have no more business here. Perhaps you would let His Excellency know that I need to see him as soon as is convenient.'

Eschenbach bowed. 'I'll do so.'

Verstohlen made to brush past him when a faint whiff of something familiar caught his attention. He paused.

'I assume you work for Dagobert Tochfel now?' he asked.

Eschenbach couldn't suppress the ghost of a sneer across his full lips. 'Naturally.' In that one, short word, much information was conveyed. Verstohlen caught the meaning perfectly clearly. So this Eschenbach was after the Steward position. Tochfel had better watch his back.

Then he placed it. The aroma wasn't strong, but Verstohlen had spent enough time trying to trace its origins to recognise its presence. Joyroot. The man was either a user, or he'd worked on the trade in it. Grosslich couldn't possibly have missed it. So much for all the promises.

'Are you all right, my lord?' asked Eschenbach, his tone profoundly unconcerned.

'I'm fine,' said Verstohlen. His mind was working quickly, teasing out the possibilities. Tochfel had been right. This Eschenbach was a minor player, but his presence here was no accident. Perhaps the joyroot on his collar was a slip. Or perhaps he was being given a warning, a reward for the work he'd done to drive Leitdorf out and deliver the throne to Grosslich. Verstohlen felt the first stirrings of a deep nausea. More than anyone else, more than Schwarzhelm, he'd done this. He'd brought it about, the man who hated

Chaos with a fervour unequalled even by the witch hunters. The irony nearly killed him.

'This has been an instructive conversation,' he said, and pushed the door open. Outside, the guards stood to attention. There was fear in their faces. How could he have been so blind? The fear had never gone away, it had just been hidden for a while. Long enough for the damage to have been done.

Verstohlen hurried down the corridor, anxious to get into the fresh air again. He could still smell the joyroot. A dozen thoughts crowded into his mind at once. He had to find Tochfel. He had to find Schwarzhelm. He had to find help.

And then he remembered Natassja, the masks on the walls, the dreams.

With a pang of fear, he knew then what his principal objective was. They weren't quite ready to kill him in the Averburg, not while his name was so well known and there were loyal personnel still at their stations. They'd come for him at night, when he was alone, when the last of his friends had been despatched. Nowhere was safe now, perhaps not even the forge.

As he passed through the winding passages of the ancient citadel, the message Tochfel had been trying to convey to him became painfully apparent. The corruption had never been defeated, never been banished, never been suppressed.

It had always been there, and now it was coming for him.

# Chapter Five

AT LAST, THE rain had stopped falling on Altdorf. The skies remained a low grey, heavy with sodden cloud, but the dull thud of water against stone and tile ceased for a while. That didn't make much difference to the stench hanging over the old city. Though much of the water drained down into the vast network of catacombs and sink-holes far beneath the foundations of the clustered buildings, plenty of the filth and slurry had nowhere to go but the street, and large pools of foetid water sat stinking across the thorough-fares. Folk trudged through it while going about their business, making the sign of the comet to ward off pox and plague. It didn't help much. In the aftermath of the deluge, dysentery and cholera spread with the same speed they always did, and the tight-knit terraces of wattle houses were soon racked with coughs, splut-ters and phlegmy expirations. The gravediggers and the priests of Morr were the only ones who profited, revelling as they always did in misery.

Set some distance from the sprawl and splendour of the Imperial Palace, as streaked with rain as every other building in the city, was the Cathedral of Sigmar

Risen and Transformed. It had been purposefully set away from the Imperial Chapel, whose priesthood were part of the Emperor's retinue and therefore loyal to the master of the throne. The Grand Theogonists, with their long tradition of independent thought, had always seen the danger in letting the Emperor's pet priests monopolise the worship of the warrior-god in Altdorf, so funds had been set aside to create a rival institution within the city. The first stones had been laid in the year 580, before Altdorf had even been recognised as the pre-eminent settlement in the Empire. Successive masters of the Cult of Sigmar had augmented, rebuilt, extended, demolished and refashioned the structure until it came to dominate nearly half a square mile of prime Altdorf real estate.

In a conurbation already rammed with massive, vulgar piles of stone, the Cathedral of Sigmar Risen and Transformed was a serious contender for the most massive and vulgar of them all. The Church was rich, and no expense had been spared on its decoration. Huge murals had been commissioned, some by de Buenosera himself, which adorned every inch of the plastered ceilings. They mostly depicted Sigmar slaying some beast or other, although the famously dissolute Michaelangelico had managed to insert spurious vignettes of buxom Reikland maidens being carried off in various states of undress to a fate worse than death at the hands of improbably proportioned Norscans.

Every pillar was encrusted with bands of gold, studded with semi-precious stones and ringed with ingots of silver. The floor was made up of a dizzying array of marble flags, each a different colour, some engraved with trader's marks indicating passage from furthest Cathay. The windows were a riot of brightly-stained glass, most illustrating moral tales of dragon-slaying, mutant-hunting or witch-burning. In the very centre of the colossal building, where four vaulted naves met under a domed roof nearly two hundred feet high, the Altar of the Ascended Warrior stood in gaudy magnificence, crowned by a thirty-foot-high statue of Sigmar wrestling with the dragon Gauthmir cast in ever-polished bronze and ringed with forty-two censers containing the finest spices of Ind and Araby.

Every day, whether the rain was falling or the pox raging, thousands of pilgrims made their way to the holy site. Some fell on their faces before the splendour, mumbling prayers to Sigmar before being dragged away by the small army of impatient priests. Others fell into silent contemplation, marvelling at the labour required to create such a daunting monument to the human spirit. Still others, perhaps over-educated or seduced by the thin-lipped creed of Verena, found the whole thing mildly distasteful and regretted handing over the three-schilling entrance fee to the heavily-armed zealots at the north gate entrance.

For Volkmar, who had nothing but contempt for the pitiable worship of Verena, that was about the only thing he had in common with such borderline heretics. He hated the Cathedral. He hated the gold, he hated the gilt, and he hated the pilgrims. They were simpering fools, the lot of them. None knew how to wield a warhammer, and hardly any would have been able to read the scriptures or the ordinances. They would come to the Cathedral fresh from whatever petty debauchery they'd been engaged in, thinking that a donation of brass and a few genuflections would save their souls from an eternity of damnation.

Volkmar knew different. He knew what kind of god Sigmar was. Sigmar didn't value excuses, and He certainly didn't value offerings. He needed spirits forged in white-hot steel, hands willing to take up swords, feet willing to march into the cold wastes of the north to pin back the hordes of destruction.

Volkmar also knew about damnation. He'd stared into the face of it, seen the fate awaiting mankind should it falter. On the pitiless plains of the far north, he'd been struck low by the Everchosen of Chaos, Archaon the Mighty. He'd felt his life slip away, had cried out as his soul was ripped from his mortal frame. It was Chaos that had brought him back, had pulled his essence back into his ravaged body and tortured it before the gibbering hosts of ruin. The ranks of the corrupted had stretched from horizon to horizon, filling the northlands with a simmering tide of hate.

Volkmar alone of mortal men knew what it was to die and be forcibly reborn. He alone knew of the utter horror of existence on the planes of madness, and he alone had seen, however briefly, the world through the aspect of a daemon's eyes.

Most would have been driven mad. He sometimes wondered why he hadn't. No doubt there was a reason he'd endured. There was some pattern, some divine intention behind it. He wasn't sure what it was yet. In the meantime, taking the war back to the filth that had caused him such pain seemed like a reasonable way of repaying the debt. They said that familiarity bred contempt. Volkmar, uniquely amongst his peers, was familiar with the great enemy, and Volkmar, uniquely amongst his peers, held it in utter, withering, grinding contempt.

And so it was that he despised the Cathedral. It was showy, a front for the futile rivalry between the Cult of Sigmar and the officials of the Imperial Palace. He preferred the Chapel of the Fallen, or the Cathedral of Sigmar the Avenger in Talabheim, or the Abbey of Sigmar the Destroyer of Beasts in Middenheim, hard under the shadow of the imposing Ulrican temple and carved from solid granite.

He strode down the long south transept, snarling at the shiny flummery around him. Every so often, a priest would see him coming and look for an escape. If none was available, the man would bow low, desperate to avoid the wrath of the Theogonist. Even the brute mass of the populace, as ignorant as they were malodorous, knew well enough to keep out of his way. A six-foot mountain of a man, clad in heavy furs and carrying the ancient Staff of Command, was not someone to be crossed lightly.

Eventually, Volkmar reached his destination: a small door in the outer wall of the transept, barely marked and overshadowed by a tasteless frieze depicting Magnus smiting some worm or other. With a final snarl at the milling crowds around him, Volkmar pushed the door open, ducked under the lintel and went inside.

It led into a small, unadorned chamber. Centuries ago this had been a tomb. Now Volkmar had commandeered it for his private meetings. The walls were made of solid stone and had no windows. Though he was in the very heart of Altdorf, nothing of the plague-ridden, gossip-laced town ever penetrated down there.

There were men already waiting for him. They clustered around the old sarcophagus in the centre of the chamber. All around the walls, torches guttered, throwing sooty smoke curling into the vaulted roof. It was dark, cold and austere. Just how a chapel to Sigmar ought to be.

'Greetings, Theogonist,' said one of them.

Volkmar grunted, slammed the door shut behind him and shot the bolts home. Then he rose to his full height and surveyed the scene.

There were three figures waiting for him. All wore armour, notched and scored by recent fighting. They were nearly as massive as Volkmar himself and had the confident stare of men who'd faced death, or worse, in battle. Two of them Volkmar knew almost as well as he knew himself. The third was new.

On his left was his confessor, Efraim Roll. The man looked as old as the tomb he stood behind. His beard was long and matted, and his skin lined with a latticework of wrinkles. His head was bald, and old wounds decorated the bare scalp. His dark eyebrows jutted out, as did his chin, and he bore himself with the demeanour of a man fighting against a constant stream of rage. His armour was as ancient as any in the Empire, having been forged by dwarfs for the first conclave of Sigmar's personal priesthood. It was hammered from purest gromril and engraved with runes of destruction and damnation. Roll was perfectly suited to it, being Volkmar's confessor and the only man in the Empire apart from Karl Franz who ever dared to give him an order. In the flickering light of the torches, the innate savagery of his face was amplified.

To his right stood a very different figure. Odain Maljdir was a vast bear of a man, ruddy-cheeked with a blond beard bursting over his enormous breastplate. He wore his hair long, and it streamed in a series of elaborate plaits over his studded pauldrons. His skin was tanned by the ice-glare of the far north and looked as tough as old horsehide. Once the man had been a priest in the service of Ulric and had made his name smiting the Norscans on their endless raids across the Sea of Claws. They said he'd once held back an entire company of them single-handed on the steps of a pagan temple while waiting for an army of State troopers to relieve his position. Soon after that, something had changed. He never said what it was, but he'd ended up travelling south. The first Volkmar had known of it was when the huge man had hammered on his door with his two fists, blurting in heavily accented Reikspiel that he'd come to learn of the ways of Sigmar. Since then he'd been inducted into the secrets of the Cult, and given the warhammer Bloodbringer as his weapon. If he still hankered for the bleak worship of Ulric, he never gave a sign. He'd become as devoted a Sigmarite as Volkmar himself, which was a rare thing in an Empire made up of doubters, heretics and fools.

The final figure stood apart. He looked scarcely less deadly than his counterparts, though he was clearly no Templar of Sigmar. His dark hair was long, and his visage lean. Like the others, his armour was of ancient pedigree, though dented by recent sword blows. He had a haughty, noble look about him, as confident as it was pitiless. This was a man who had been forged in the keenest fires of combat, who had ridden once against the terror-inducing foes of mankind and had the stomach to do it again. He carried a longsword at his belt, sheathed in a scabbard marked with the campaign records of Araby and Tilea. It was the first day he'd been in Altdorf since being ordered to take the fight to the enemy in the wind-scoured wastes of the north. He bore the scars of that assignment in his dour expression. No man fought against the legions of the dark gods and was unchanged by it.

In other ways, though, he was still the man he'd been when standing besides Schwarzhelm at the battle of the Turgitz Cauldron. Preceptor Leonidas Gruppen of the Knights Panther had been summoned home, though at that point he had absolutely no idea why.

'Greetings to you all,' grunted Volkmar. 'Now, to business.'

DRASSLER LAY STILL amongst the boulders, his grey cloak smothering him, barely an inch of room exposed to see out from under. His breathing was shallow and he could feel his heartbeats against the stone. Around him, he knew the rest of the mountain guard, all two hundred of those who remained, were similarly concealed. As the sunlight began to wane, throwing shadows across the broken landscape, their disguise became even more effective. For generations the bergsjaeger had known how to blend into the barren landscape. The skills had originated in the hunting of game but had been perfected over the long years for warfare. Now he waited, face down and sprawled against the ice-hard rock, waiting.

Nearly two hundred yards away, the Keep stood as solid as a peak. The barrage from Bloch's artillery was being maintained and a steady stream of arrows flew up at the battlements. Drassler and his men had crept round to the east side of the castle. The gates were in view now, and he could see the Averlanders continue to goad the orcs with feigned executions and mutilations.

He didn't like the tactic. Drassler had seen too many greenskin armies use the same strategy, driving defenders mad by torturing their comrades in sight of the walls. But he knew what Bloch was doing, and saw how it gave them their chance. The commander had deliberately left his force in disarray, making it look like the overconfident approach of a novice general. The orcs would see that. They would see how far back Bloch had deployed, how little he threatened the gate-house. The sortie beckoned. If Drassler had been in charge of the Keep, he'd have been tempted.

He wouldn't have taken the bait. Unlike the orcs, Drassler knew of the opportunities for ambush, of the techniques the mountain guard could use for creeping up unawares. All his men were clad in the same stone-grey cloaks, mottled and streaked to mimic the pattern of the terrain beneath them. It had taken hours to work their way around to the east of Bloch's position and then shuffle forwards over the rock, grazing flesh and tearing the stiff leather of their jerkins.

If a watchful orc on the battlements happened to gaze straight at them, then the game would be up. Even their camouflage, as good as it was, couldn't foil direct scrutiny. So it was that Bloch kept up the nagging barrage, doing everything he could to keep the eyes of the Keep on him.

It was a dangerous tactic. A sudden rush from the gates in numbers risked overwhelming Bloch's first lines of defence. The cost of being so ostentatiously out of position was that a determined assault would cause havoc.

It was a risk worth taking. As long as the gates remained closed, the chances of driving the orcs from the Keep were slim. As soon as they opened, those odds shortened.

Drassler moved his head fractionally, looking out at the distant lines of archers. They were being given a hard time by the defending greenskins. Perhaps a third of them had been killed or wounded, and the shield-bearing infantry around them had fared little better. Orcs didn't like using ranged weapons if there was a choice, but they were more skilled shots than many Imperial generals gave them credit for.

He felt his stomach turn in disgust. The gates remained closed. The ammunition for the guns would begin to run down soon. Bloch would have to pull back. If he did so, then all his plan would have yielded would be four-score men dead and a brace of empty gun barrels.

Drassler reached slowly for the sword at his back. At any moment he expected to hear the signal for withdrawal, closely followed by bellows of derision from the orcs locked up within. Then their own position would become precarious, and they'd have to get clear of the walls. A shambles. A bloody shambles. They were running out of time.

Then came the first sound.

A heavy clang of iron, as something was unhooked from within the gates. A fresh barrage cracked out from Bloch's artillery, harmlessly smashing against the walls. Drassler felt his heart start to pound. At last. They were going for it.

He turned to the nearest of his men. The sounds of more beams being flung to the ground came from the Keep. A thin line of daylight stretched down between the mighty iron-barred doors. From behind them, a rising tide of baying and bellowing came out. Against all hope, they were going for it.

Drassler rose to a low crouch, ready for the break-neck sprint across the rock. This would all still unravel if the mountain guard couldn't close in quickly enough. He saw the massive gates begin to swing open. The noise of the horde rose in volume, a terrifying roar of pent-up aggression and frustration. The orcs had been maddened, and the storm of their emergence would be terrible.

Drassler's hand was damp with sweat as he drew his sword, keeping it under his cloak as best he could. They'd be outnumbered badly until Bloch could get to them. Surprise was all they had.

'On my mark, lads,' he hissed, knowing his men would be as taut as he, ready for the charge, knowing the danger. 'On my mark...'

There was a boom, a scrape of tortured metal, and the gates slammed back against the stone. With a torrent of bellows and roars, the orcs surged out, eyes blazing red, blades swinging, trampling over one another in their lust for combat.

The pretence was over. Now the real fighting had begun.

VOLKMAR WALKED UP to the sarcophagus, the heel of the Staff of Command clanking on the stone floor. The other three men clustered around the tomb.

'We don't have long,' said Volkmar. 'The army is gathering, but these things take time.'

'What's the state of it?' asked Maljdir.

'Twenty thousand men promised. We need twice that.'

Gruppen let slip a low whistle.

'That's big.'

Volkmar nodded. 'That it is, Herr Gruppen. I'd like it bigger. I'd like more warrior priests, and I'd like more wizards.'

Roll shook his head, looking disgusted. 'Spell-casters? Sigmar's bones, surely we can do without them this time?'

'We can't, and we won't. Most of the magisters are on duty in the north, but there are some stationed here and in Nuln. We'll take as many as we can find.'

'And the priests?'

'We'll empty the chapels here, and there's a whole company of them in Nuln. They'll all go.'

Gruppen frowned. 'Perhaps one of you would like to tell me why all this is needed?'

Volkmar turned to the preceptor. 'You served with Schwarzhelm, right?'

'Right.'

'What was he like?'

Gruppen looked nonplussed.

'Was his behaviour unusual? Any sickness evident?'

'No. None at all. He slew the doombull.'

'I'm not asking for evidence of his heroics, preceptor. I'm asking about his judgement.'

Gruppen's face flushed. He wasn't used to being talked down to. 'As sound as ever. Why are you asking me? Where is Schwarzhelm?'

'Nobody knows,' said Roll. 'We'd hoped you might.'

'Though it's not hard to guess where he's headed,' said Volkmar. 'He was sent to Averland soon after you were ordered to the northern front. Something happened to him there, and he made a serious mistake. He's now been relieved of his office, and has disappeared.'

Gruppen gripped the side of the tomb. He looked pale. 'What kind of mistake?'

'He cut down Kurt Helborg, possibly to the death. He installed a new elector whom we now believe is in league with the great enemy. He killed the swordmaster Heinrich Lassus and stole the Sword of Vengeance from the Chapel of the Fallen. That enough of a mistake for you?'

'Sweet Myrmidia,' swore Gruppen, shaking his head. Then something seemed to occur to him. 'I remember the name Lassus.'

'He's the one who ordered you north,' said Maljdir grimly. 'We checked. He had no authority to do so, but the habit of command is strong and the orderlies followed instruction.'

'I never understood why my assignment changed.'

'To keep you away from your master,' said Volkmar. 'Lassus knew Schwarzhelm trusted you. When the Emperor's Champion left for Averland, his army was commanded by Andreas Grunwald, a man whose command ability was known to be suspect.'

'He was a good soldier.'

'No doubt. Not good enough.'

Gruppen took the information in quickly. It was a lot to digest, and Volkmar saw him struggling to absorb it. To his credit, the man stayed focussed.

'So how stands the province?'

'We don't know that either,' said Roll dryly.

'Very little has come in or out of Averland since the election of Grosslich,' said Volkmar. 'We believe the new elector is training an army, and that he has gold and weapons. For the time being, his allegiance is still for the Empire, at least in public, but we can be sure that won't last.'

'How?'

'Schwarzhelm wrote a letter before he disappeared, detailing all he'd done and what it meant. We now know the great enemy is active in the city, and Grosslich's actions have left the Emperor in no doubt that we have a rogue elector.'

Gruppen leaned heavily against the cold stone. For an elector to turn traitor was almost unheard of. Minor nobles, yes, even dukes and barons, but the holders of the runefangs were different. All the resources of the province were theirs. The consequences were too dreadful to contemplate.

'And there's been no uprising in Averland?' he asked, obviously clutching for some sign of hope. 'Why have the Estates tolerated it?'

Maljdir gave a snorting laugh. 'That's the problem, preceptor. They don't *know*. If Lassus hadn't given his role in this away to Schwarzhelm, we wouldn't either.'

'Such is the beauty of the scheme,' said Roll. 'They didn't just seize power. They were *given* it. As far as anyone in Averland knows, Grosslich is the duly appointed master of the province and all that lies within it.'

'He'll play for time,' added Volkmar, 'building up his forces, keeping the cloak of respectability for as long as he can. We know he's arming, and there are reports of men being drafted from as far afield as Tilea. We have to act now.'

Gruppen nodded. 'I can see that, but what do you want from me? I'm not Schwarzhelm's physician, and I can't tell you why he did it.'

'You're coming with us,' said Volkmar. 'Schwarzhelm will be there somewhere, and I want your counsel.' He leaned forwards, and his dark eyes glittered. 'You'll bring your company of knights too, preceptor. Their swords will be needed. This is no minor insurrection. This is a new war.'

'Then you'll have them, Theogonist,' said Gruppen without hesitation. 'And as many more as I can muster.' He paused, and his eyes slipped down to the face of the tomb.

'But why Averland?' he asked.

Volkmar's face remained as grim as his appellation.

'We don't know,' he said. 'Yet.'

THE GATES HAD opened. With a mighty torrent of screams and whoops, Black Fire Keep began to disgorge its contents. The surging mass of greenskins charged straight towards the waiting ranks of Bloch's army. With frightening speed they closed the gap, loping across the uneven ground like wolves hungry for the kill.

Bloch strode forwards, heart thumping in his breast. This was what he'd prepared for, what he'd wanted, but unleashing the fury of the greenskins was perilous.

'Bring that artillery round!' he yelled, knowing the gunnery captains would already be working. All of this had been prepared, the army knew it was coming, but the impression of disarray would take time to correct. He hoped Drassler was still in position. This all depended on him. 'Archers withdraw! Get back here, you dogs!'

Trumpets blared out, giving the signal over the rising roar of the orcs. The gap between the armies shrank. Rank after rank of orcs thundered from the Keep, swinging their straight swords with furious abandon.

Bloch had fought many orcs over the long years, and he'd always hated their feral enjoyment in bloodshed. They seemed to treat battle as a sport, like a man would enjoy drinking or bear-baiting. These ones, however, had been tipped over into a blind fury. The tactic of mutilating their kin had done the work.

'Halberdiers! Form up!' All around him, slovenly looking groups of men rushed into formation, taking up their spears and halberds and assuming their positions.

The gap closed further. The orcs were tearing towards them. Bloch found himself itching to get stuck in, to tear his blade through the flesh of the scum, but he knew he couldn't. Not yet. This army needed its commander.

The archers rushed back behind the lines of infantry like birds before the storm, leaving their gear on the ground and hurrying to take up heavier weapons. As they did so, the first round shot out from the Helblasters on the left flank. Their ammunition was much more effective against infantry than walls, and the front row of orc berserkers stumbled.

It hardly dented the force of the assault. Huge warriors, roaring with incoherent fury, leapt over their fallen kin, desperate to tear into the waiting human soldiers. Ever more of them poured from the gates. The Keep was emptying.

'Hold your ground!' roared Bloch, seeing the last few yards between the armies dwindle to nothing. 'By Sigmar, hold your ground!'

Then the horde crashed into the halberdiers.

The lines slammed together with a sickening crunch. The first line of defenders buckled, driven back by the force of the assault. Behind them, the second rank was smashed apart in turn, knocked back and hurled into disarray.

The third barely held. Orcs rampaged through the broken human lines, wading into battle and plunging their weapons with abandon. The fighting spread down the long crescent of the besieging army, and soon the entire southern face of the Keep approach was engulfed in desperate combat. There must have been over a thousand orcs in the sortie, all frantically trying to get to the action, all lusting after the blood of the humans who'd taunted them for so long. The greenskins were outnumbered, but they had the initiative and plenty of anger to fuel them.

'Reserves!' cried Bloch, seeing his plans ripping away under the sudden onslaught.

The trumpet blared out and the extra men piled in to staunch the onslaught, desperately trying to blunt the force of the orc charge.

Bloch whirled around, letting his eye sweep across the battlefield. Both armies were fully committed. Fighting was heavy at every point across his long deployment. None of his detachments had broken, but several were close to it. They had to hang on, to weather the storm until they could douse its initial fury.

He turned to Kraus, who was looking over the scene with his habitual bleak expression.

'I'm going in,' he said, buckling his helmet. 'The men have their orders.'

The honour guard captain nodded, unsheathing his own sword and preparing for the melee. 'What about Drassler?'

'Give him the signal. This is when we find out what he's made of.'

* * *

DRASSLER SPRANG TO his feet, casting his cloak aside and taking up his sword. The blade flashed silver in the sunlight. All around him his men did likewise, emerging from the rock like ghosts. Some carried handguns, most swords. They immediately formed up into two companies, one led by Drassler, the other by his lieutenant, Hochmann.

'That's the signal!' he cried, as the trumpets blared out from the rear of the main army. 'Sigmar guide your blades!'

The mountain guard sprinted hard towards the gates. A few hundred yards to their left, the column of orcs had slammed into Bloch's position, no doubt aiming to drive them back so hard they'd be unable to respond. The greenskins had left almost nothing in reserve, as was their wont. The few orcs that remained in the rearguard were clearly itching to pile into combat, and saw Drassler's men coming at them far too late.

The gap closed.

'Fire!' Drassler roared, and a ripple of blackpowder detonations ran across the front rank of his men. With a confused bellow, a dozen orcs at the gate fell, tumbling down onto the rock as they clutched their eyes and midriffs.

Fifty yards to go. Drassler picked up the pace, feeling the weight of his sword as he ran, revelling in the blood pumping round his body. For too long he'd had to creep and scuttle in his own land, prevented by his paltry numbers from striking back at the orcs who'd ripped through his comrades. Now revenge had come, and it felt good.

Twenty yards. The orcs at the gate were trying to form up into some kind of defence. Some called frantically to their kin who'd rushed out to engage Bloch's men, beckoning them back. There couldn't have been more than two dozen ready to meet Drassler's assault, and it looked like there were barely more than that emerging from the interior of the fortress.

Ten yards. Drassler stole a glance to his right, seeing the mountain guard around him surge as one towards the Keep. They cried out curses in the old tongue of the mountains as they came, ancient smiting words that had echoed down the glens since before the time of the Emperors. All of them had hatred in their faces, the kind of naked anger that made a man deadly. Drassler felt pride. They were his kindred, and this was their moment.

Then he was amongst the orcs, slashing, hacking and heaving with his blade. At his shoulder, mountain guard soldiers piled in, bearing down orcs twice their size with the force of the charge and their numbers. Drassler took apart his first victim with a vicious two-handed slash, watching with satisfaction as the mighty figure bent double across the sword-edge before it was finished off by another charging member of his company.

They made the gates. The few remaining orcs broke and fled into the courtyard beyond. Some of his men rushed to follow them, consumed by the need for vengeance.

'Hold fast!' cried Drassler, seeing the danger. The mountain guard were only two hundred strong and there were five times that many orcs on the field. He whirled around, looking back over to where the greenskin column had charged out. He expected to see a morass of entangled combat, with Bloch's men holding the sortie and turning it back on itself.

What he saw was a wall of greenskins charging right back at him, their faces contorted with fury. There was no time to organise a defence. The greenskins had realised their mistake and were coming back to correct it. From inside the Keep came the noise of fresh troops arriving to bolster them. Drassler had taken the gates, but he was caught between the returning sortie and the mustering Keep defenders.

'You take the ones inside, I'll handle the rest!' snapped Drassler to Hochmann, and braced himself for the coming impact.

Around him, his men did their best to form into some kind of defensive arrangement. Under the shadow of the open gates they clustered together, watching as the horde rushed back towards them. There was no escape, and no chance of surrender. If Bloch got his timing wrong, they were all dead men.

'We've done our part,' he muttered, watching as the nearest orc warriors thundered into range. 'Now damn well do yours.'

BLOCH CHARGED INTO the fray, his halberd held low, his throat hoarse from hurling invective at the enemy. He had his men around him, the Reiklanders who'd stood at his side since the march from Altdorf. All did the same, barrelling into the charge, levering the long halberds with expert hands.

There were few armies across the wide earth that could cope with a massed charge of close-serried infantry, and the orcs before them were no different. The steel sliced through them, tearing apart leather, ripping sinew and breaking bones.

'Onward!' Bloch cried, his blood hot with the exhilaration of battle. 'Tear them apart!'

Drassler's charge had done it. The orcs had seen the mountain guard spring up as if from the stone itself, and the force of their assault had wavered. Now Bloch had to press home the advantage, pile on the pressure before they could regroup and take back the gates.

'No mercy!' he bellowed, breaking into a run. All along the lines, his men were doing likewise, striking back at the greenskins and turning the counter-assault into a rout.

Even as he went after them Bloch could see the indecision in the orcs' inhuman faces. Some opted to stay and fight, while others had broken from the horde and were racing back to the Keep. Speed was of the essence now. If Drassler's men were left isolated for too long then all they'd achieved would fall apart.

A hulking warrior loomed up before him. It crouched down low and let fly with a spittle-laced roar of defiance.

'To me!' cried Bloch, calling to the two halberdiers on either side of him. As one, they charged the greenskin, blades aimed for ribcage, legs and face. The orc was big, clad in plate armour and swinging a mighty warhammer around its head, beckoning the charge with wild-eyed relish.

The halberdier on Bloch's right plunged his blade in high, aiming to catch the shoulder. The orc whirled around, smashing him aside with the hammer, before lurching back to counter the thrust of the other blades.

Bloch ducked low, feeling the hammer-head whistle above his ears, before stabbing the shaft of the halberd up. The blade struck true, halfway up the orc's torso, but deflected from the armour and left nothing but a long scratch on the metal. Bloch staggered back, arms jarred from the impact.

The halberdier on his left had better luck, and his blade bit deep into the orc's muscle-bound arm. The creature roared in pain, shaking off the fragile shaft and swinging the warhammer round in response. Bloch's companion sprang back, but too late. The iron head crunched into his ribcage, crushing the bone and sending him sprawling in agony across the ground.

Bloch was exposed. There were men all around him, grappling with the ranks of orcs, but none were close enough to come to his aid. He grabbed the halberd from the first soldier who'd fallen, picked it up on the run and charged straight back into range. The orc saw him coming and heaved the warhammer round for the killing blow.

He had to strike hard and true. If he missed, the hammer would do for him as it had done for the others.

'Sigmar!' Bloch bellowed, plunging forwards with all his might, keeping the tip of the halberd high and controlling it with both hands.

The steel bit deep between the orc's breastplate and collar, driving into the flesh beneath and sending up a spray of hot, black blood. The warhammer flew from the orc's flailing hands, spinning into the air and sailing high over the heads of the struggling warriors. Bloch pushed the halberd in deeper, twisting the blade, churning through the flesh and severing the head from its massive shoulders.

The roars were silenced. The orc crashed to the ground, taking the shaft of the halberd with it, hitting the stone with a dull thud.

Panting, Bloch looked around for a fresh weapon. Time was running out.

'Faster!' he roared, stooping to collect the halberd of

another fallen soldier and breaking back into a run. His men were still on the offensive, hammering at the retreating orcs, trying to hack their way through to the Keep. 'Faster, damn you!'

Ahead of him, Bloch could see the Keep looming closer, still cut off by the horde of greenskins. The fighting was frenzied and brutal – both sides knew what was at stake.

Bloch raised his halberd, the blade streaked with blood, and roared his defiance. From every direction men answered his call, hurling obscenities at the orcs and slamming into their disordered defences. The counter-assault was in full swing, the fruit of the tactics he'd spent so long devising. All their hopes were with Sigmar now.

Bloch got his head down, picked his next target and charged.

DRASSLER'S MEN WERE hemmed in, surrounded on all sides by the orcs and pinned back close against the open gates of the Keep. The two companies had formed up into ranks three deep on either side, fighting under the shadow of the mighty ramparts and repelling the assaults coming at them from both directions.

The orcs returning from the sortie were the biggest and most aggressive – they'd been the vanguard of the attack and were the most heavily armoured greenskins left. Those remaining on the inside were the weaker breeds, less nakedly belligerent than their larger kindred though nearly as deadly at close quarters. Seeing the danger of losing the gates entirely, scores of them had torn across the courtyard and thrown themselves at the rear of the mountain guard position, heedless of the steel fence waiting for them when they arrived.

Drassler heard the cries of anguish as the lines clashed, but he couldn't pay them any attention. Hochmann had taken the rear ranks, and he was busy enough with his own counter-assault. The first of the returning orcs slammed into the ranks in front of him, tearing their way back to the Keep with desperation. The orcs lived for fighting, but even they could see when their position had become exposed. As savagely as they'd fought to break out of the Keep, they now fought to recover it.

'Form up!' Drassler shouted. In the midst of the ranks of defenders, he'd assembled a detachment of his own. Twenty men, all from his home village, all experienced and tempered by a lifetime fighting the greenskin. As the battle raged around them they formed into a tight column, four men deep and five across. Drassler stood in the centre of the front rank, leading as ever from the front.

'Charge!' he roared, breaking into a run. The men swept forwards, thrusting aside their comrades as they surged to the front. All were swordsmen, carrying the blades of their fathers, handed down from each generation to the next and stained with the blood of countless orcs.

Drassler's unit crashed into the front rank of the enemy, sweeping it aside and ploughing onwards. The greenskins were disorganised, broken up by their headlong race to recover ground. Each of them alone was twice as strong and quick as a man, but by acting in concert a disciplined detachment made up the shortfall.

'That one! Break them!' Drassler pointed to the right, spotting a vast, dark-skinned monster hammering away at the mountain guard's right flank. It was surrounded by a heavily-armoured bodyguard, all wielding human weapons. There were swords, maces and warhammers. Not a curved scimitar or cleaver to be seen.

Drassler's unit swung into battle, keeping their formation as they assaulted the knot of larger orcs. Drassler himself got into position quickly, pulling his sword back to strike, knowing his back was covered by those around him.

His bladed flashed, slicing clean through an orc's extended forearm. The greenskin bellowed with pain and swung a halberd straight back at him. Drassler dodged it, and a swordsman to the left of him leapt in with another strike. The orc, bleeding heavily, turned to face the new threat. Then the man on Drassler's right struck, plunging his blade deep into the orc's back.

Working in unison, swords spinning and jabbing in a united front, Drassler's men carved their way into the heart of the fighting. The greenskins retreated further, knocked aside and bludgeoned into submission by the organised ferocity of the human assault.

But the charge only lasted so long. With nowhere to go, the orcs regrouped and struck back. Dragged into a melee, the detachment formation lost its edge and soldiers began to fall. Whenever a grey-clad swordsman went down, another rushed to take his place, maintaining the line and keeping the pressure on the greenskins. The orcs were strong, though, terribly strong. When they got close, their heavy fists and crushing blows began to tell.

Drassler worked like a blacksmith at a forge, his sword heaving in arcs of destruction. Ahead of him loomed the warlord, the heart of the orc forces. Drassler lowered his sword-point and bellowed a challenge. The language of battle was universal, and the lumbering brute turned to face him. It was nearly as broad as it was tall, covered in bunched muscle and draped in plates of ill-fitting armour. It carried a halberd in one hand and an axe in the other. Seeing Drassler come at it, the orc thundered its defiance, opening its tusked mouth wide and roaring like a bull.

Then they came together. The orc struck first, bringing the axe down hard. Drassler sprang aside, dodging the blow and sweeping his sword back for a counter-thrust. The orc punched the halberd up, and the blades met with a jarring clang. Drassler withdrew a pace, keeping his blade raised, watching for the next blow. The axe fell, followed by the halberd again. The flurry of blow and counter-blow was fast and deadly. Drassler matched it as best he could, but he was driven back.

Then there was another man at his side, jabbing a halberd into the fray, going for the patches of exposed flesh. The orc turned to face him, swinging its own blade to meet the attack.

Drassler joined in, catching the axe with a sharp upward jab and knocking it out of position. Now the orc withdrew, unable to cope with every warrior at once. The halberdier pursued, working his stave with incredible skill and precision. Drassler followed suit, knowing his men around him guarded his flanks.

Together, halberdier and swordsman battered the mighty orc to its knees, raining blow after blow onto its desperate parries. Seeing the danger, it tried to break back out, powering up to its feet with a heavy lunge. The halberdier was knocked back by the thrust, rocking back on his heels and staggering two paces.

That gave Drassler the opening. Leaping forwards, he spun the sword-tip round in his hand, gripped the hilt with his fists and rammed it down. The point sank deep into the orc's ribcage, snaking between plates of metal and lodging deep.

The greenskin bellowed like a wounded ox and whirled round, axe flailing. Then the halberdier was back, scything his blade mightily. The arc swept through the creature's defences and took its head clean off. The severed hunk of flesh and bone flew high into the air, before hitting the rock and rolling to a standstill.

The decapitated body swayed for a moment, pumping hot blood into the air like a fountain, before it too slumped to the earth. Drassler pulled his sword clear as it fell. The orcs weren't bellowing now, and a kind of sullen hush fell over the entire horde.

All around him, mountain guard pressed home the advantage, sweeping past Drassler and tearing into the demoralised orcs.

Drassler turned to thank his comrade. Markus Bloch grinned back at him, his face streaked with blood. Only then did Drassler notice the swarms of Averlanders and Reiklanders breaking through the mass of orcs and smashing them aside. The relief had arrived. The orcs were broken.

'Good timing,' Drassler said.

'Not finished yet,' said Bloch, heading back into the melee. Before long his coarse voice was raised above the general roar, uttering every obscene curse known to man.

Smiling like a wolf, Drassler plunged after him.

There was hard fighting left before the day was over, but the outcome was no longer in doubt. The orcs were in disarray, the halberdiers rampant, and soon the Keep would be theirs.

# Chapter Six

PAIN. THAT WAS all that remained. Sometimes a dull, throbbing ache, distributed evenly across his body. Other times, they made it sharp and sudden. There were long, drawn-out sessions, and mercifully short ones. It all depended on her mood. He'd stopped being able to mark the passage of time, and couldn't truly remember what had brought him here. Maybe he'd been in the Tower for a few hours, maybe a few weeks. Only one thing was certain. The pain.

There was a noise, somewhere close. With effort, Tochfel dragged his eyelids open. He was suspended. He felt the flesh of his wrists, raw and angry, chafe against the rope. The muscles under his ribs had been pulled tight. He should have been dead long ago. He had no idea why he wasn't. Down on the stone floor, beneath his gently swaying feet, he could see pools of his own blood. The sight no longer nauseated him. After a while, the horror became a long, numb dream. There was only so much screaming a man could do.

He moved his head carefully, trying not to inflame the exposed muscles of his neck. The chamber looked much as it always did. There were tables on either side of him. One had the instruments. They were astonishingly beautiful, forged from steel with the precision of a master craftsman. From time to time, when they came to have their fun, he'd tried to remember which ones they'd used. It was the little things, the repetitions and rituals, that kept a fragment of sanity lodged in his mind.

The other table had the items. Some of them had already been added to him. Others had once been part of his body. His extracted organs still sat, glistening and viscid, slopped in the metal bowls.

Ahead of him was the door, the only way in and out. When they shut it, it was dark like no darkness he'd ever known. There, suspended, far from help or salvation, he could reflect on the variety of pain they'd introduced him to during the last session. He didn't have the language to describe it all, but he suspected they did. They knew all the ways of misery. They were geniuses of their craft, masters of sensation. In comparison to what they'd shown him, his former life now seemed impossibly stale and drab. He'd had no idea that existence could be so raw, so unutterably acute, so agonising.

The door opened. Tochfel had trouble focussing. Was it her? He could no longer decide whether he should scream or not. Being in her presence was unbearable. Being away from it was unbearable. He'd been transformed in so short a time. He felt his mouth hanging open, a line of drool running down to his naked chest.

'You shouldn't have come here, Steward.'

That wasn't her voice. It was a man's voice. A hunched, slender man, bowed by a curving spine.

Tochfel's eyes weren't working. Everything was blurred. He tried to screw them into focus.

'Achendorfer?' he croaked, wincing as the tendons in his throat rubbed against one another.

The man came closer. Uriens Achendorfer had changed. His skin, always grey, was now as white as snow. The bags under his eyes hung heavier than ever, purple and pulsing. His pupils were pin-pricks of red, and lines of sutures ran across his sagging cheeks. He looked heavily altered. His purple robes were loose, but when he moved they gave away the changes that had taken place. Willingly or not, the loremaster had become something more, or perhaps less, than human.

'What were you *thinking*?' asked Achendorfer scornfully. His voice rattled when he spoke. 'You must have known what was in here.'

Tochfel ignored the questions. None of the others had asked him questions. That was the confusing thing. Why torture him, if they didn't want to know anything? It was senseless.

'Where've you been?' Tochfel croaked again.

Achendorfer let slip a thin smile, and his cheeks ran like fluid around his lips. 'Here,' he replied, self-satisfied. 'When Alptraum took the Averburg, that was my signal. I had to bring the book here.'

'Alptraum?'

'He's in number seven, and still not dead. Amazing, given what she's done to him.'

Tochfel felt a tear run down his cheek. That was unusual. He'd thought all his tears had been shed. Perhaps something still lingered within him. That was bad. If they discovered it, there would be more pain.

'Why?'

Achendorfer raised a heavily plucked eyebrow. 'Why? Do you really need to know that?' He shook his head. 'This is power, Dagobert. You've no idea what these people are capable of. What *she's* capable of. I was shown a fraction of it. The scrolls, the parchments, they mean nothing to me now. Only one of them was important – the one I could bring to her. There are rewards for those who know how to serve her. There are punishments, to be sure, but rewards also.' The white-faced man grinned, exposing black teeth. 'I am no longer a petty man, Dagobert. She will make me a god.'

Tochfel found he wasn't listening. Speech bored him. Everything bored him. Only pain piqued his interest. That was all there was left. He hated it, feared it, needed it. That was what they'd driven him to.

Another figure appeared at the door. Tochfel had no trouble recognising her outline. There was something curved in her hand, shining in the dark. As she approached him, Natassja patted Achendorfer affectionately on the head.

'That's right, my foul pet,' she said. 'I have great plans for you. Just as I have for all my creatures.'

Achendorfer shivered, whether out of pleasure or fear Tochfel couldn't tell. His vision started to cloud again. What was left of his skin broke out into sweat. His heart, shivering beneath his open ribcage, beat a little faster. Why didn't he die? What malign force kept him sustained in this living hell?

'And what do you plan for me?' he asked, eyes wide with fear, locked on the approaching instrument.

Natassja smiled and began to work. 'Something very special,' she purred. 'Something very special indeed.'

* * *

DAWN BROKE OVER Averheim. The sun peered through veils of mist rising from the river, taking an age to warm the stone of the quayside buildings. Even before the light made its way down to the wharfs men were busy unloading and loading the endless train of barges. Orders were bellowed out from overseers, and the cranes wheeled back and forth with pallets of iron bars, brick and stone.

Verstohlen watched the activity from his shabby rented room on the east side of the river. From two storeys up he had a good view of the operation. As he watched, he began to wonder how he'd missed the signs. Some of the crates were clearly full of arms. One of them spilled open on landing, revealing scores of curved swords, all wickedly fashioned with trailing spikes. They were no ordinary Imperial manufacture, and he could bet they hadn't come from Nuln.

Verstohlen let his gaze run down the long harbour-side, watching as the gathering dawn brought more activity. There were soldiers everywhere. How had he not noticed the increase in their numbers? Where did Grosslich get them from? It seemed like every street corner had a group of surly-faced guards, all wearing the absurd crimson and gold of the elector's personal army. There must have been several hundred of them, milling around, threatening and cuffing the merchants doing their best to unload cargo. The Averlanders seemed to have learned not to talk back.

He turned from the window. He needed to get some sleep. It wouldn't take them long to find out where he'd gone. Even now he guessed that his rooms in the Averburg had been ransacked. Perhaps they'd slipped deathflower into his food. That would be a real spy's death.

Verstohlen rubbed his eyes. The room around him was grim. The sheets were stained and stinking, and there were long lines of grease down the faded walls. He walked from the window and sat down heavily on the bed, ignoring the cocktail of unsavoury aromas that curled up from the linen. All night he'd been kept awake by the shouts of gamblers in the chamber below, steadily getting drunker and more violent. Not that he'd have been able to sleep much anyway. He'd kept his dagger and pistol close to hand and sat watching the door until the dawn.

There was a knock.

'Come,' said Verstohlen, cocking the pistol and placing it under the sheets.

The fat landlord, a man with as many chins as he had rooms, waddled in. He wore an apron that might once have been white, but now had been stained the colour of thin gruel. In his hands he carried a mug of small beer, long past its best and reeking of spoilage.

'You're awake, then,' he grunted, placing the mug on an unsteady table and wiping his hands on the apron. 'You'll be wanting food?'

'No, thank you,' said Verstohlen. If the food was prepared here, then he wouldn't need to worry about assassins. 'I won't be staying another night. Prepare my account, and I'll settle it this morning.'

The landlord looked at him blankly. 'Suit yourself,' he muttered. 'It'll be five schillings.'

The price was exorbitant. He'd have balked at paying it even in a refined inn. For a moment, he considered challenging it, then changed his mind. He needed to keep a low profile until he could get out of the city.

'I'll bring it to you as I leave,' said Verstohlen. The

landlord hung around, as if waiting for something. 'Was there anything else?'

The fat man coughed and looked down at his hands. 'Maybe, if you're not having food...' He trailed off.

'Yes?'

'I can get it for you. Cheap price. Best this side of the river.'

Verstohlen looked at him coldly. If joyroot was available even to scum such as this, then the last pretence at controlling the trade must have been abandoned. Grosslich was flooding Averheim with it, just as before. Was he in it with the Leitdorfs? Or had he taken it over? So much still to unravel.

'No,' said Verstohlen, his voice quiet and controlled. 'A little early for me.'

The landlord shrugged and shuffled out again, closing the door behind him clumsily. Verstohlen pulled his pistol out from under the sheets and looked over the workings. It was important that everything operated flawlessly. Unless he could get out of the city soon and find his way north undetected, he knew he'd be using it soon enough.

RUFUS LEITDORF WATCHED as the land around him became steadily more familiar. The gorse and heather stretched to the horizon in all directions, rustling gently under a ceaseless wind. The air was sharper than it had been in the lowlands, and in the distance the peaks of the Grey Mountains were just visible, lost in a haze of blue in the far south. A low tide of mist rolled across the depressions in the land, shifting and miasmic, torn into tatters as the breeze across the moors ripped it away. In the far distance there were ruins, tall towers of age-whitened stone marching across the horizon. No human hand had built those places, and no human dwelt among them now. In the vast space between mankind's scattered settlements, there were still plenty of ancient secrets lying dormant. Drakenmoor was replete with them.

Leitdorf had been sent to the secret castle twice in the past, once as a child when there was a threat of assassination against him, and once as a teenager. The second time he'd travelled on his own account, albeit surrounded by household servants, Averburg officials and a retinue of armed guards. Growing up as a prince had given him precious little solitude. He found it hard to recall any occasions where there hadn't been members of the elector's court hovering around, waiting to take orders from him or pass on new requirements from his father.

That world, the one of privilege and prestige, had slipped away so fast. Less than a month ago it had seemed like the trappings of true power were firmly in his grasp. He and Natassja had planned so much together, and Averland looked set to have another Leitdorf at its helm.

He let his gaze drop from the horizon. The memory of Natassja was painful. Like a drug, being away from her was hard. He hadn't realised, perhaps, how much he'd relied on her, how far the preparations for conquest had been hers, and how many of his considerable resources had been diverted into her policies. The joyroot had been her creation. He had no idea where she'd sourced the first samples. Perhaps he should have inquired more carefully.

For all her wisdom and perceptiveness, it hadn't helped them when the hammer-blow fell. No doubt

Grosslich had tracked her down by now, and she languished in one of the dungeons of the citadel. Somehow he doubted her spirit had been broken, but feared her body might have been.

It was unpleasant to dwell too much on that. He had failed her, and he had failed his family. The experience of the entire Empire turning against him, seemingly on the whim of Schwarzhelm and his damnable spy, had shocked him to his core. He should have paid more attention to his lessons in diplomacy. The old fool Tochfel might have been worth listening to more carefully.

The situation with the Reiksguard was even more puzzling. He could understand well enough Grosslich's desire to have him hunted down and killed, but to extend it to the Emperor's own troops? That was bravery bordering on folly, and in the long run such arrogance would surely cost him dear. He'd never have dared such a thing himself, even if matters in Averheim had gone otherwise.

Leitdorf looked over his shoulder at the carriage, shaking as it was dragged along the uneven tracks towards Drakenmoor. He knew the Marshal was recovering. The knights' morale had lifted as a result, and they now went more proudly than before, as if defying Grosslich's pursuers to find them. It was amazing what the presence of a commander could do for his men.

Leitdorf found himself reflecting on what his own vassals thought of him. The closest to him, soldiers like Klopfer, were surely dead now, caught in the ruin and confusion of Averheim. Even if they hadn't been killed, none of them would have rushed to fight by his side again. He knew his temper had driven half of his allies away. Like his father, his blood ran hot, ever ready to spill out into some petulant tirade. He'd never been forced to confront the consequences of that, to examine himself against the measure of other, better men. Now, when he looked in the mirror of introspection, he saw a petty character, a bully and a tyrant.

A shadow passed across him. Skarr had drawn up alongside, controlling his horse with an enviable ease.

'You look troubled, my lord,' he said, and his severe face twisted awkwardly into something like a smile.

Skarr had become less brooding since Helborg's partial recovery. The preceptor still held him responsible for the events of the Vormeisterplatz, but an uneasy truce had developed between them. At least he was being referred to as 'my lord' again.

'I've only been here twice,' replied Leitdorf. 'And yet it feels like home. I can't tell you why.'

Skarr shrugged. 'I like this place too,' he said. 'The air's healthier. I can see what your father was thinking.'

They rode on in silence for a while. Tangled copses of black-thorned briars passed by as the horses trod the winding path. The calls of birds, or something like birds, echoed in the distance, faint against the vastness of the open sky.

'You know, he wasn't the madman everyone says he was,' said Leitdorf at length. 'He had a temper, but he wasn't mad.'

Skarr said nothing.

'When he came up here, he was more himself.' Leitdorf found himself suddenly wishing to explain everything, to make it clear why things had turned out the way they had. 'Everyone said the same about him. It was Averheim that made him angry.'

'The city?'

'I saw it for myself. He never slept properly. There were bad dreams. It was almost as if…'

Leitdorf trailed off. It was painful to recall those sleepless nights, the screams of his father echoing down the long corridors of the Averburg. Nothing the physicians could do would ease the pain. Though his father had known the courtiers were laughing at him behind his back, Marius never once shirked his duty as a result of the night terrors. Not once, even though it drove his mind to the brink of breaking.

'They say he was a proper swordsman,' acknowledged Skarr, and his voice had a grudging approval in it. 'The Marshal wanted to offer him a duel, but the opportunity never arose.' The grizzled knight smiled again, this time less forced. 'Perhaps, when he's recovered, *you* should take up the challenge.'

Leitdorf felt his pride stung at the mockery, and went red with anger.

He pushed it down. This was his problem. He had no means of coping with the banter of ordinary conversation. That was why he was feared rather than loved, ridiculed rather than respected. Instead, he did his best to return the smile.

'I'd not give him much of a fight.'

Skarr couldn't disagree, and gave an equivocal shrug. Leitdorf winced.

'You don't think much of me, do you, preceptor?' he said.

Skarr looked surprised.

'It's not important what I think. It's about survival now.'

'Perhaps.' Leitdorf looked up ahead. The road was curving round to the right, snaking steadily up a long, shallow incline. Remnants of the mist curled around the hooves of the horses as they laboured up it, ghostly and insubstantial. The Drakenmoor castle was close, staffed by members of his father's most devoted staff and safe – for the moment – from the prying eyes of Grosslich. This had been his decision, perhaps the first he'd ever truly made without his father or his wife peering over his shoulder. That was an odd thought.

'Maybe I don't think that much of myself, either,' he said. 'A man's defined by what's around him. I'm beginning to wonder if the company I've kept has always worked to my advantage.'

'War can change a man, my lord,' said Skarr. 'I've seen it happen. It asks a question of you.'

'We're at war?'

'Assuredly. The Marshal has no thoughts of escaping. He'll take the fight back to Grosslich.'

Leitdorf pondered that. Such a course was hugely dangerous. Grosslich had the resources of the entire province at his disposal. It would be easier for Leitdorf to slip over the mountains into Tilea, to lick his wounds amongst old allies of his father and gather strength slowly. Staying in Averland was the riskiest option of all.

And yet the Marshal had not built his reputation for nothing. Now Leitdorf – chubby, tantrum-ridden Rufus Leitdorf – had the chance to ride alongside the legend.

'So the question will be asked,' he mused. 'Let us hope, when the time comes, I have the right answer.'

THE IRON TOWER kept growing. Every hour, more metal beams were lowered into place, slotting into a plan of dazzling complexity. Even semi-complete, it had the

look of a building that could survive a thousand years.
Great spars shot into the air, now reinforced by hundreds of cross-beams. A thick outer shell had begun to
creep up in their wake, hard and shiny like the carapace of an insect.

Halfway up the monstrous structure, a chamber had
been created. It was small, just a foretaste of the
mighty halls which would fill out the shaft in due
course. Giant crystal windows covered three of the
walls, and in the centre a curved throne had been
placed. There was no other decoration, just blank panels of iron. Natassja's aesthetic sense had not yet been
brought to bear, for this was Grosslich's commission.

Standing by the windows, nearly a hundred feet
above the centre of the circular plain below, the elector gazed down on the majesty of his creation.
Natassja preferred to remain below ground. That
relieved him. Though she was as addictive as the narcotics she created, her presence was wearing on his
nerves. Grosslich had seen what happened to servants
who failed her. From time to time, a nagging doubt
even entered the back of his own mind.

*Will I be next?*

No. That wouldn't happen. He was the lord of this
realm, and she was his ally. They both needed each
other for the fulfilment of the great vision. Though the
mask was gradually slipping away, just as it had to,
there was still the appearance of normality in Averheim. The ordinary people could grumble about the
imposition of rules and military tithes, but none of
them suspected the truth behind the manoeuvrings.
The knowledge would come later, once all was ready.
In the meantime, they had the joyroot again to addle
their minds.

Grosslich looked down. The elaborate pattern of stonework on the courtyard below was almost complete. It was dazzlingly beautiful. From three hundred feet up, the eventual height of the Tower, it would be even more impressive. The Mark of Slaanesh, etched in circling rows of obsidian and picked out with silver. At ground level, the shapes were unintelligible, and only here was their true purpose apparent.

He followed the progress of a pack of dog-soldiers as they crept across the open space, far below him. Once he'd have baulked at having such creatures working for him. No longer. He'd seen for himself what the Empire really was: a club for the privileged and the noble-born. It didn't matter that his bloodline had sent its sons to die on the sodden fields of war, had built up a trade in cattle-rearing from nearly nothing and donated vast sums to the Church of Sigmar and the Knights of the Blazing Sun. For the elite in Altdorf, the Grosslichs would always be commoners. The electoral battle had been about nothing more than blood proofs. The fact that Grosslich was twice the warrior Leitdorf would ever be counted, seemingly, for nothing.

All that had changed with Natassja. Until she'd proposed her alliance, he'd been a minor landowner and frustrated powerbroker, nothing more. It was she who'd taught him how to use his money, how to influence the right people, buy the right alliances, smooth over the trifling difficulties of the law, and dispose of those who couldn't be bought.

Heinz-Mark had learned the lessons well. Only later had the joyroot emerged, and then soon after that the knowledge of her corruption. She'd come to his rooms at night, draped in perfume, and the seduction into the dark had begun.

Though he'd not known it at the time, that had been his last chance to turn back. By then, though, he was entangled in a thousand deals and treaties. She showed him visions of such splendour, gave him experiences of such magnificence, that he'd been unable to say no. He denied her nothing after that, trapped in the honeypot she'd so skilfully placed before him, addicted to the pleasures she doled out to him like toys to a child.

Grosslich still liked to tell himself that she needed him, that the plan would have ground to a halt without his efforts. Perhaps that was true in part, but he wasn't deluded enough to put any faith in it. He was the lesser partner, and that made things dangerous for him. When the Tower was completed and his armies mustered, perhaps Grosslich would have to do something to reinforce his position. She was powerful, to be sure, but only a woman. He was a warrior, tempered by combat since childhood and destined for command. Surely the Dark Prince would reward him when the time came. He had, after all, done so much to please him. There would be opportunities. There were always opportunities.

There was a knock from the corridor outside. Grosslich turned, his dark cloak following him like furled wings. He gestured with his finger, and twin doors slid back into the iron walls. Eschenbach and Heidegger came in. Far from the prying eyes of the Averburg, they were free to shed their appearance of normality. Eschenbach had let his eyes resume their pink hue and had donned robes of subtly shifting colour. Heidegger looked perfectly normal, although the mania in his eyes was more pronounced. The poor dupe was working under a heavy burden of interwoven spells, and still believed he was doing Sigmar's holy work. Despite the abundance of evidence of Chaos around him, the part of his mind that could discern the world truly had been drilled out by Natassja. Now he only saw what she wanted him to see.

Grosslich had to hand it to her. Subverting a witch hunter was hard.

'Report,' he ordered, walking over to the throne and taking his seat.

'The executions you ordered have been carried out,' said Heidegger, his eyes flickering back and forth. The man's mind was cracking. 'The objections of Steward Tochfel seem to have been overcome, though I wasn't able to see him personally to confirm this. More heretics have been unearthed and justice handed out according to your instructions.' The old man shook his head. 'So much corruption here,' he mused. 'When will they ever learn?'

'When indeed?' agreed Grosslich. 'Thankfully, your services have been invaluable, Herr Heidegger. Continue the programme. We cannot stop until all faithless have been uncovered, though I assume you have not yet found the spy Verstohlen?'

'Not yet, my lord. We found evidence of him at a boarding-house on the east side of the river. He must still be in the city, since the ordinance on movements prevents any unauthorised departure. The end will come soon for him, you may be sure of it.'

'Good,' said Grosslich. 'Then I will not detain you from your work. Go now, and report to me again in two days.'

The corrupted witch hunter bowed again and shuffled out, the doors sliding open to allow his passage.

Eschenbach watched him go with ill-concealed scorn. 'Do we need his services still? His stench sickens me.'

'You should learn to value him,' warned Grosslich. 'As with everything we've done, appearance is important.'

'Really?' said Eschenbach, his teeth exposed. 'Leitdorf and his men are gone, Schwarzhelm is gone, and the spy will soon be dead. It offends my sense of propriety that we continue to maintain this charade.'

Grosslich frowned. He'd promoted Eschenbach himself, one of the few members of the cabal not to be brought in by Natassja. Could he really be so stupid?

'I don't think you fully appreciate the balance here,' he said. 'The Emperor knows of our allegiance now. Do you think he will hesitate to send an army here? One is already marching, and it will be ten times the force Schwarzhelm had. While we prepare for it, we must maintain the little game, keep the province quiet and give us the space we need.'

Eschenbach shook his head. 'It disgusts me. I have to deal with dullard thugs in the Averburg as if they were equals. I would rather tear their stomachs from their fat bodies and eat them before their own eyes.'

Grosslich listened with some weariness. Eschenbach was proving a disappointment. He didn't need sadists and madmen around him – the dog-soldiers were perfectly capable of dealing out terror. He did need advisers with a clear head and a strategic grasp. He began to suspect that Natassja had let him promote Eschenbach *because* he was a liability.

'There'll be plenty of time for that,' Grosslich said. 'In the meantime, double the supply of root to the markets, and see that the price goes down. And speed up the recruitment drive. We've not got enough men yet, and she's getting impatient.'

'Gold supplies are running low. These troops aren't cheap.'

'Keep spending it. More will come. Don't disappoint me, Steward.'

Eschenbach gave out one of his fat, thick-lipped smiles. 'Of course not,' he replied smoothly.

Something about the man's manner stung Grosslich then. He extended his hand, and a nimbus of lilac quickly formed around Eschenbach's neck. The Steward clutched at it, suddenly panicked.

'What is this, my lord?' he blurted, eyes bulging.

'I'm not sure you're taking my advice seriously enough, Steward,' snarled Grosslich, giving vent to all of his many frustrations. 'Perhaps something of a lesson is in order.'

'No, my lord!' shrieked the Steward, writhing against the nimbus. 'All is perfectly well understood!'

'Even so.'

While Eschenbach writhed in the grip of his luminescent collar, Grosslich flicked out his left hand. An iron wall panel slid open, revealing a new chamber beyond.

'Look at him, Eschenbach.'

The Steward struggled, unwilling to gaze into the chamber. 'It's not necessary, my lord! Really, you've no need to–'

'*Look at him,*' commanded Grosslich, feeding the nimbus energy and twisting the man's neck round to face the revealed chamber.

Eschenbach's eyes widened further, and his pale skin went grey with horror. A figure was suspended in the chamber, seemingly hanging in the air. An angry red glow surrounded him, as if flames licked his body. The man's eyes were even wider than Eschenbach's. If he'd wanted to close them, he would have needed his skin back. The white of bone glistened amongst the glossy red of the exposed muscle. He should have been dead, killed long ago by shock, but through some forbidden power the unfortunate soul was still alive. His face, what was left of it, was fixed in an open-mouthed howl of utter, unending agony. The pupils stared straight at Eschenbach, pleading for help. From his tortured mouth came only a silent, never-ending scream. He couldn't produce anything else. He'd never be able to produce anything else.

'Watch well, Steward,' said Grosslich, ensuring the spectacle had its full effect. 'This man once thought to replace me. His family ruled this province, and saw me as a tool for returning to power. This is what happens to those who seek to use me, Herr Eschenbach. This is what they become.'

The Steward started to whimper, unable to bear looking at the horrific scene before him but prevented from looking away. His smoothness of manner had been torn away. The lesson was having its effect.

'I can see it!' he cried, desperately trying to avert his eyes. 'I understand!'

Grosslich kept him locked in place. The memory of this would keep him loyal, and now more than ever he needed men around him he could trust.

'I hope you do,' said Grosslich, enjoying the power flowing from his fingertips. It was at times like this he didn't regret the choices he'd made. 'Forget it, and you'll end up in an agony chamber. And that's *really* not something you want to happen. Isn't that right, Ferenc?'

The man in the chamber couldn't respond. There was only misery left for him, only sensation, only terror.

In such circumstances, Grosslich could allow his doubts to subside, and to glory in his future power. Averheim was already being moulded to his will. By the time the Empire armies arrived, it would be his own domain, the home of whole legions of terror troops. He would be at the forefront of them, drenched in the gifts of the Dark Prince, ready to meet the weary response of Karl Franz. It would be *his* realm, the mightiest between the mountains and the sea.

He tightened his grip on the nimbus, enjoying Eschenbach's choked crying. The prospect made all the compromises worthwhile. By whatever means, through whatever sacrifice, he would have what he'd been put on the earth for.

*Dominion.*

## Chapter Seven

THE NET WAS closing in on Verstohlen. The harder he tried to get out of the city, the closer his pursuers got to him. Things were getting difficult.

Grosslich's army had swelled to ridiculous proportions, and there were soldiers everywhere. Lines of men waited outside dingy offices in the basement of the old Alptraum residence, desperate to sign up to Grosslich's expanding ranks in return for their pile of cheap coins and promise of glory. The amount of money changing hands was phenomenal. Every hour, another hundred or so infantrymen swaggered out of the burgeoning drafting houses, each dressed in a crimson tunic and carrying a curved scimitar. Soon there would be more soldiers in Averheim than ordinary citizens.

That wasn't the worst of it. There were witch hunters among them, though they weren't like witch hunters Verstohlen had seen anywhere else. They seized people seemingly at random, dragging them off to the Averburg over the screams of their family. Fear had gripped the city again. No one would say it out loud, but it was slowly becoming apparent what kind of a man Grosslich was. Some still welcomed the firm hand of authority, judging it preferable to have a strong elector than none at all. Others kept their mouths shut, eyes sliding from side to side, waiting for the knock at the door to come for them and watching the streets empty with the coming of the dark.

All gates to the city were now watched. Verstohlen had visited every portal, hugging the shadows and assessing the chances of slipping out. Passes were now required, issued only by captains in the elector's direct employ. Only the soldiers seemed to be let in and out at will, plus the carefully scrutinised train of merchants bringing in building materials and weaponry. Some of the traders had strange looks on their faces, and Verstohlen doubted any were Averlanders. Some looked barely human at all.

So it was that he'd been forced to lay low in Averheim for a second day, observing the degeneration around him, seeing all he'd worked to prevent coming to pass. He felt disgusted at himself. Maybe he'd become arrogant, too pleased with his own skills. Whatever the reason, he'd failed. They'd all failed.

As night fell, he made his way back to the richer parts of the city, close to the Averburg and the old cathedral. Some of the richer merchants still had a measure of independence, and the streets were slightly freer of soldiers.

Verstohlen wrapped his coat around him, keeping one hand on his concealed pistol. Ahead of him a broad street ran south, flanked by three-storied townhouses. The buildings were decorated across their gables with scenes of bucolic contentment, all etched in wood by master carpenters, a sign of the wealth of the owners. In the past the windows might have glowed with firelight; now they'd all been shut fast, the doors bolted with many locks.

Verstohlen hesitated. He didn't know what to do. The hostelries were dangerous for him now. He'd not been able to get anywhere near Tochfel. Perhaps the Steward had been taken. If so, it would be another mark of guilt to set against his complacency.

Ahead of him, one of the lanterns flickered and went out. The street slid into darkness. A few still burned further ahead, but they gave off an uncertain light. Mannslieb rode high in a tortured sky, broken by fast-moving clouds from the east.

Verstohlen leaned against the wall of one of the houses, trying to think. He couldn't stay outside all night. Perhaps he could go back to Valgrind's forge, though if Tochfel had been taken that would be as unsafe as anywhere else. His fear was clouding his judgement. Two days without sleep were taking their toll.

Once again, he remembered Schwarzhelm. *There are many ways of attacking a man, subtle ways.* Had he said that? It was hard to remember.

He crept out from under the shadow of the house, determined to keep moving. There might be a safer tavern open in the poor quarter. He needed something to eat and drink, even if it carried a risk with it.

Another lantern flickered out. That was strange. Verstohlen looked back over his shoulder. The street behind was empty and sunk into darkness. He turned back, flicking his collar up against the chill.

Then he saw the figure, hunched and cloaked, standing in the middle of the road, no more than a hundred yards away and coming closer. As it came on, the lantern above it guttered and died. They were all being put out.

'*Verstohlen,*' the shape hissed, and steam curled from its mouth.

Verstohlen felt a cold fist of terror close over his heart. His mind raced back to Natassja's pets, creeping around in their world of blind misery.

The cloaked figure limped towards him. From under its cowl, something clawed and curved emerged.

Verstohlen withdrew his pistol and fired. The crack of the report echoed down the empty streets. The creature staggered, bending low. Verstohlen fired again, and the cloaked shape crouched over, rocking on its feet.

Then, slowly, terribly, it rose again. Under the cowl, two points of lilac flared into life. Metal flashed in the night. It was smiling, and its teeth were made of steel.

'*Verstohlen,*' it hissed again, as if by way of confirmation. It had a scraping, rattling voice that was only barely human, but nonetheless horribly familiar.

Verstohlen felt his breath quicken. Terror gripped him, held him tight in place. Then the creature came for him, exposing long talons, curved and gleaming in the moonlight. It loped towards him in a broken, stumbling run.

'Holy Verena...'

Verstohlen fled. Drawing his dagger as he went, he turned on his heels and sped down the streets. Behind him, he heard the horror set off after him. It was faster than the other ones, and something told him it wouldn't need Natassja nearby to maintain its strength.

Buildings sped by in the night, blurring like dreams. He felt his foot skid on a patch of slime, and nearly went down. Behind him, close on his shoulder, he could hear the clicking, the scuttle of bone against stone.

It was getting nearer. He couldn't turn to check. He couldn't fight it. He couldn't escape. With the prescience of those about to die, Verstohlen saw everything clearly. He would be overtaken. The horror would catch him. In every patch of shadow, he saw the masks leering at him, laughing at his failure. The signs had been there. He should have known. Only his pride had let him think he'd defeated them. Now it was over.

His heart hammering, his lungs bursting, Pieter Verstohlen ran for his life.

THE CANDLE BURNED low and its light began to fail. Leitdorf reached for another, lit it and held it over the flame until the wax softened, then pressed it into the brass holder. A warm, golden light flooded back across the desk. It was late. The journey had been long and he was tired. He knew he should go to bed. Something, perhaps the sense of familiarity, kept him up.

They'd arrived at the Drakenmoor castle in the late afternoon. The old stone walls had towered over the bleak land, just as he'd remembered them doing. It wasn't a true castle, more a fortified manor house in the heart of the moors. The crumbling battlements were mostly for show, and the walls wouldn't have withstood a determined attack with any kind of artillery. The sheer-sided roofs were missing a few tiles, and broken panes of glass hadn't been repaired. Still, that was hardly the point. It was secret, and it was far from Averheim. The few resident staff had welcomed him back like the forgotten son he was to them. Gerta, the old nursemaid, nearly blind and bent double with age, had kissed him on the forehead and clamped her arms around him for so long it had become embarrassing. Even Skarr had broken into a laugh at that.

Now the old house was quiet again and the hastily lit fires were burning low in the grates. Helborg had been given the old count's master bedroom. The Marshal had been able to hobble up to it unaided, but only just. Even so, it was clear the man's strength was returning.

Skarr had organised a watch. Through the night Reiksguard would patrol the countryside around them. For the first time in days, a semblance of safety had returned. It was possibly illusory, and certainly transitory, but at least it was something.

Leitdorf had taken his father's private study to sleep in. Alongside the huge desk, still stacked with parchment that the servants had been too timid to remove, there was a narrow bed set against the wall. The old man had often slept there after working late, too exhausted to drag himself along the creaking landing to the opulent master suite. Unlike most of Marius's private rooms, the study was sparsely furnished and decorated. Icons of Sigmar and Siggurd hung on the dark green walls, flaking with age.

Unwilling to sleep, Leitdorf had started to leaf through the old papers. It was a sobering business. Most of them were routine orders and reports detailing the dreary minutiae of state. A dispute over land on the Stirland border, a revision of the tax thresholds for smaller farms, a visiting delegation from Wissenland to discuss levies on wine imports. His father's bold hand was on all of them, making notes or issuing orders to his secretary. The signature, written in a heavy, flowing script, was everywhere.

Rufus remembered seeing him work when he'd still been a child. He'd managed to evade his nannies and had stolen down the winding interior of the Averburg, darting from shadow to shadow. At that age he'd imagined his father sitting on a golden throne, dictating matters of war and alliance to a waiting army of knights and battle wizards. Instead, when the young Rufus had found him, Marius had been bent over a desk much like the one he sat at now, scribbling on parchment, hunched over a flickering candle flame.

Rufus remembered the smile creasing the man's weary face, beckoning him over.

'This isn't for you, young one,' he'd said, looking over the piles of parchment with forbearance. 'Be thankful for it. Leopold will inherit this.'

Of course, Rufus hadn't been thankful then. He'd grown resentful, spoiled and fat as the years passed. Getting his father's attention had been difficult. Rufus had tried to get noticed in other ways, throwing wild parties and balls, bedding eligible women and then casting them aside, gorging on food and wine while the peasants in the fields laboured to produce it. Even after Natassja he'd continued to indulge his rampant, clumsy lusts, riding out to isolated villages on his estates and picking a girl for his enjoyment over the protests of the serfs. The last one, a few months ago, had proved hardest to tame. She'd given him a brace of scratches to remember her by. He could still recall the look of defiant hatred in her eyes, glistening with hot, furious tears.

Pathetic. He'd become a laughing stock, a figure of casual hatred, only loved by those so steeped in the

Leitdorf blood, like Gerta, that they were blind to the extent of his follies. And in the end, of course, Marius's mind had begun to turn, and it was too late. Everything was then about plots, and war, and screaming in the night. When Ironjaw had taken the old man at last, perhaps it had been a mercy.

Leitdorf pushed the papers to one side. Such was his family's legacy, and such was his inheritance.

As his fingers ran over the surface of the desk, they caught on a small, leather-bound book, buried under the heaps of paperwork. Knowing full well he should retire and keep his strength for the following day, Leitdorf flicked it open. There were handwritten entries on nearly every page, also in Marius's script. Some were written as confidently as the signature on his orders; others looked shakier, as if scribbled down in haste.

He began to read. Some of it was illegible, and other passages didn't make sense at all. Perhaps written when his father's mind was beginning to drift.

And then, as if it had been burned on to the page for that very purpose, there came a sentence that chilled his heart. He dropped the book, hearing it thud on to the desk. It fell open where he'd been reading.

Leitdorf stayed still for a moment, lost in shock. He no longer needed to read the phrase to see it. He couldn't have been mistaken. There it was, scrawled in black ink, as plain as a hawk against the open sky.

*Her name is Natassja. And she will kill me.*

VERSTOHLEN FELT HIS strength begin to give out as he ran. His coat streamed behind him, more a hindrance than a help. The houses passed by in a haze of half-seeing. The moonlight covered everything with a faint outline of silver, but the pools of shadows were ink-black and deep as souls.

The streets were deserted. He had no idea where he was. Perhaps the terror was driving him somewhere in particular. Perhaps not. There was no time to think. He felt his legs protest, his muscles burn. This would be over soon.

He tore round a corner leading into a small square. Tall buildings on all four sides cut off the light, and it felt like running into a well of shadows. Behind him, the rattling grew even louder. The creature was almost close enough to reach out and touch him.

Verstohlen veered sharply to the left, darting to one side and trying to wrong-foot his pursuer. Something snagged at his coat, tearing the leather. Footfalls echoed around the enclosed space, making it sound like there was more than one of him trying to run. The illusion was cruel, only reinforcing his desperate isolation.

Bone-hard fingers clutched at his coat again, slicing through the expensive leather as if it were the flimsiest of gauze. One more lunge, and the creature would have him.

Verstohlen spun round, bringing the dagger up hard. He had a glimpse of the monster's face. It nearly caused him to miss his aim. A ravaged visage, stripped of skin and eyes, studded with brass spikes and needle-tipped incisors. The blank eyes glowed lilac, shining in the night like corrupted stars. An inhuman shriek echoed round the square as Verstohlen's blade scraped across what remained of the flesh.

Then he was moving again, running as before, heart labouring, sweat streaming from his brow. The creature barely paused. It scuttled after him, wheezing as it came. There was no blood on the dagger, just scraps of dry skin and sinew.

Verstohlen had seen enough. The horror had once been a man he knew. Tochfel's features, or what was left of them, still existed, distorted by pain and artificial hatred.

The talons groped for him. He felt one of them scrape down his back, cutting through his clothes and drawing blood. Verstohlen roared with pain, twisting away from the agonising touch, feeling himself stumble.

Verstohlen rolled as he fell, getting his dagger up just in time to parry a fresh plunge of the talons. The Tochfel-creature's robes fell away and Verstohlen saw the full extent of the man's transformation. He was naked underneath the flimsy draping, though not much of his old human form remained. He was as much bone and iron as flesh, animated by some dread power and kept alive by forbidden sorcery. Spikes studded his ruined flesh, curved and barbed. A chasm had been cut in his chest and the ribs were still visible across the wound. Within that exposed shell beat a heart, though it was no natural organ. It pulsed with a lurid light, strapped in place with iron bands and surrounded by the eight-pointed star. Tochfel's residual flesh curled away from it, as if burned by the terrible energy within. The stink of jasmine was pungent and close, as sweet as death.

The talons raked down, aiming at Verstohlen's eyes. Frantically, driven by nothing more than pure fear, he fended off the blows, his dagger scraping along the scythes.

The end would come quickly now. Tochfel's strength had been augmented three-fold and his sorcery-laced limbs quickly pinned Verstohlen to the ground. Talons scrabbled at his face again and he only just got the dagger up in time to ward them. The blade was knocked away by the force of the strike, sent spinning across the ground. Then he was defenceless.

Verstohlen looked up into the eyes of his killer. There was no humanity left there, just a sickening grin where Natassja had inserted rows of needle teeth. The Tochfel-creature's smile widened, and its cheeks stretched impossibly taut.

'*Verstohlen*,' it whispered a final time, as if the name somehow gave it the power to kill. It opened its jaws wide and prepared to lunge.

Light exploded, blinding him. There was a heavy blow from somewhere close by, and Verstohlen felt the creature knocked into the air. He scrabbled free, rubbing his eyes. Something huge and heavy strode across his field of vision. Moonlight flashed down the length of a mighty sword, carved with runes and with the sign of the comet etched on its surface.

'You're a hard man to find,' growled Schwarzhelm, before plunging after the wounded Tochfel-creature. His sword flashed again in the night, and battle was joined.

DEEP UNDER THE Iron Tower, the screams now never ceased. Insulated from the surface by many feet of solid stone, they resounded from the polished walls of the lower dungeon, rising through the snaking vaults and shafts before spilling out across the throne chamber, mixed together in a symphony of suffering. As the catacombs had expanded, hewn from the rock by Natassja's growing army of Stone-slaves, the scope for experiments had only grown. So many of the fine young men who'd volunteered for Grosslich's forces had ended up serving a rather different mistress. No doubt those coins didn't look like such a good deal now.

Natassja knew that Grosslich didn't like her taking a tithe of his warriors for her own purposes, but that really was too bad. She understood, as he could not, what purpose they served. The inflicting of pain was not merely done for her enjoyment – though, to be sure, she did enjoy it. There was method behind it, a necessary accumulation of souls in anguish. The time was coming when the object of her labour would become apparent. Not yet, but soon.

Natassja walked down towards the Chamber of the Stone. She was already far below ground level and the floor was still sloping down. The rock walls of the corridor had been carved recently and she hadn't had time to decorate them yet. Maintaining an appropriate aesthetic was important, and she would have to set her architects to work on the lower levels without much further delay. Grosslich thought such work was a waste of effort, which only went to show how meagre his understanding of the great plan was.

Natassja reached the archway that led to the chamber. From within, she could hear Achendorfer chanting away. He'd been busy, the little lizard. Such diligence really deserved some kind of reward. Perhaps one of the slave girls from the upper pens could be given to him before too much work was done to her.

Natassja entered the domed chamber, feeling the waves of suppressed energy surge towards her, bathing her body in the raw essence of the aethyr. The Stone recognised her.

The chamber was perhaps forty feet in diameter and perfectly circular, though it rose far higher than that and the roof was lost in shadow. At floor level the rock had been ground smooth and reflected the light like a mirror. Torches had been placed high up on the walls, covering the scene in a lurid purple glow. Achendorfer stood to one side, reciting passages from the book he'd taken from the Averburg library. As he read, the flames seemed to wave and flicker in appreciation. Something in the chamber was listening to him.

Natassja looked up at the Stone, the centrepiece and foundation of everything she'd done. Only the merest tip of it had been exposed and even that was massive, thrusting up from the floor like a miniature mountain. It was pure black, shiny and diamond-hard. She didn't know exactly how long it had lain under Averheim, locked deep within the earth, cold and forgotten by men. What she did know was that it was gigantic, a vast fragment of tainted substance, hidden away since the forgotten wars of the great powers at the dawn of the world.

The Stone. Ancient and malignant, locked out of sight for millennia, exposed to human contact again just two days ago. Even now its energies were bleeding upwards, suffusing the structure of the Tower and taking it over. With every cry of agony, the slumbering giant groped more surely to awakening.

Natassja breathed in deeply, feeling the throbbing air fill her lungs, glorying in the latent, thrumming energy around her.

'How long have you been working, Uriens?' she asked, gazing fondly at the little insect.

'Six hours,' he replied, looking exhausted.

'Get some rest,' she said, stroking his bald head

absently. 'I'll have something nice sent to your chamber.'

Achendorfer closed the book and bowed, his limbs trembling from fatigue. Dried blood had collected around his cracked lips. He shuffled back into the tunnel, leaving Natassja alone with the Stone.

She walked up to it and ran her fingers down its many-faceted surface. It was warm to the touch. The spirit had been roused. Her pupils dilated, and a smile of satisfaction spread across her elegant face.

'Not long now, then,' she breathed. 'Not long now.'

SCHWARZHELM STRODE FORWARDS, whirling his sword back into position, watching as the horror before him gathered itself to strike. It was like some massive, terrible insect. Its limbs cradled around itself, stretched and distended.

It looked up and screamed at him. The sound was unearthly, like a man's and a woman's voices mixed together and stretched almost beyond recognition. The lilac eyes flashed, the teeth snapped in the dark.

Then it sprang. The talons extended, slashing at his eyes.

Schwarzhelm brought the sword up sharp, cutting the blade into the oncoming torso and bending back out of range of the swiping talons. The creature crumpled around the sword and a flash of light shot out, just as before. The horror was sent flying back, its scrawny legs cracking as it hit the stone. Quick as hate, it was back on its claws, scuttling into the attack.

It leapt at Schwarzhelm. The Champion parried the claws away, stepped back out of the range of the snapping jaws, working his blade with phenomenal speed.

The Tochfel-creature dropped low, coiling to pounce

at Schwarzhelm's legs. Its movements were fast but clumsy, like a spider trying to manage too many limbs. It sprang, both hands outstretched.

Schwarzhelm darted back again, the Rechtstahl flickering in a defensive pattern. Next to the ruined amalgam of man, machine and sorcery, he looked even more solid and immovable than usual, a bulwark of coiled force and endurance. No emotion crossed his craggy features as he worked, no fear shone in his eyes. In combat Schwarzhelm was irresistible, as elemental as the storms of nature, as unyielding as the bones of the hills.

Verstohlen staggered to his feet, dagger poised. He had no chance of intervening – this fight had been taken from him. The Tochfel-creature struck again, screaming with frustration as it tried to find a way past Schwarzhelm's wall of steel. Every time it lashed out, a flash of light broke across the square. The Rechtstahl had been forged for monsters such as this. No ordinary blade would have withstood the clattering talons or gnashing incisors, but the Sword of Justice had been wound with spells of warding and drenched in litanies of destruction.

Schwarzhelm waited patiently, watching the horror flail at him, keeping it engaged until the opening emerged. It leapt up again, trying to rake at his eyes with its sweeping claws. He slammed the sword round, connecting solidly with the Tochfel-creature's iron-bound chest and sending it spinning through the air. It hit the stone hard, and there was the sound of something snapping. The lilac light in its eyes flickered for an instant.

Schwarzhelm went after it quickly, rotating the sword in both hands and holding it point down. The horror was almost too quick. As soon as its spine hit the ground it began to gather for another strike. Only for the briefest moment was its ruined torso exposed. Schwarzhelm plunged the Rechtstahl down cleanly, through the flesh and bone. The tip went down into it all, rending as it went, impaling the abomination like a fly on a pin.

The Tochfel-creature screamed, flailing wildly, raking its talons and trying to claw at Schwarzhelm's eyes. The Emperor's Champion held firm, keeping the blade lodged in place, letting the holy steel purge and cleanse.

Slowly, punctuated by shrieks, whines and hisses, the light in the monster's eyes dimmed. Its iron heart lost its lustre and the ravaged limbs fell still. Schwarzhelm kept the sword in place, not daring to withdraw it until the last energy had been bled from the creature of Chaos. It took a long time for the final twitches to subside. Eventually, the fire extinguished, and the talons clanged to the ground, bereft of a guiding will, as inert as an unwielded dagger.

Schwarzhelm pulled the Rechtstahl free, keeping it poised for a second strike. It wasn't needed. The terror had been extinguished.

He felt Verstohlen limp to his side before he saw him. The man looked terrible. He'd lost weight, and his face had the pallor of one who'd stared at his own death. Blood stained his shirt and coat, and he looked like he was having trouble keeping his feet.

'Where've you *been*?' he demanded.

'We'll talk later,' replied Schwarzhelm, supporting him with his free hand and keeping the Rechtstahl unsheathed. 'For now we need to get out of the city. Come with me.'

He dragged Verstohlen back into the shadows, out of the square and towards the eastern gates. There'd be more fighting before they'd be out, but at least the guards there would be human.

Once they'd gone, the square sank back into silence. No lights shone from the buildings around it. The only signs of the struggle were a couple of long blood-stains on the stone, and the crumpled shape of Dagobert Tochfel, his reign as Steward finally over, his suffering ended at last.

CLEARING THE ORCS' filth from Black Fire Keep had taken long, wearying hours. Fresh from the last of the fighting, soldiers had been forced to douse the floors and scrub them until their fingers were raw. The refuse left behind by the fortress's occupiers defied belief. They'd lived worse than animals, fouling every recess or secluded corner, destroying any furniture not made of solid stone, smearing foul slogans and symbols over every open patch of wall.

The stench remained even after the last of them had been rooted out of the castle and dispatched. In the narrow bunk rooms where the exhausted infantry tried to snatch sleep, the foul reek was indescribably bad, like a mix of all the ill-kept cattle-pens, slaughterhouses and public privies in the seamiest and most dilapidated of Altdorf's slum districts, amplified and concentrated into a heady musk of singular, unforgettable horror.

Such things did little to dent Bloch's pleasure at having achieved what he'd been commanded to do. Once the last of the bitter combat had ended he'd led the victorious human armies under the gates in triumph, casting down the leering symbol of the moon and restoring the Averland coat of arms in its proper place. Now the Solland sun flew again over Black Fire Pass beside the banners of the Empire, Reikland and the bergsjaeger.

The toil hadn't ended with the fighting. Bloch had been determined to order the defence of the Keep personally before the deep of the night fell on them. Only after many hours of labour did he retire at last, retreating to a chamber high up in the Keep as the bulk of his men slept below. Once sleep took him, it took him soundly. He knew that if any orcs remained alive in the mountains, they would be pitifully few in number and unable to do more than squat in the clefts and hollows of the hills, waiting for a warlord to unite their fractious bands again and lead them to more fruitless bloodshed.

Morning broke cold and severe, as it did every day in the high peaks. The sky was low, and dark clouds had passed overhead in the night. The wind remained strong, blasting across the bare peaks and tearing down the glens towards the lowlands to the west. It brought with it rain, which did much to wash the scrawlings from the walls of the castle.

Bloch woke with a start, reaching for his weapon and wiping his eyes. It took a moment for him to remember where he was and what had happened. He'd been dreaming of the wide grasslands again, of Grunwald's last charge in the heart of the horde.

'I avenged you, at least,' muttered Bloch, swinging his legs from the narrow cot and on to the icy stone flags. 'You stupid bastard.'

His cell was narrow. From the curve of the wall it was evident it was on the edge of the fortress's outer wall, high in one of the five towers that rose above the points of the star. There wasn't much in it: just a bunk, a rickety table and a pitcher of frigid water. The sole window was an arrow slit, unglazed. A chill breeze sighed through the gap. He'd not had much more to keep him warm than his cloak and some ragged furs he'd found somewhere or other. If the chamber had once housed the trappings of a commander, the orcs had long since taken them all.

Bloch shivered and pulled his cloak tight around him. He felt as dirty and ragged as a hound. He splashed water from the pitcher across his face and rubbed it into his eyes. His temples were sore and he had bruises all across his body, but he could still walk without a limp, so that was better than usual.

He found Kraus and Drassler already awake and sitting at a long oak table in one of the tower rooms. There were four windows, all narrow but giving a panorama of the mountains in each cardinal direction. The peaks stretched off towards the far horizons, majestic, ice-bound and massive.

'Morning, commander,' said Kraus, rising gingerly. He'd taken a heavy blow to the ribs from a warhammer during the last phases of the castle recovery and only his armour had saved him. Though tough as old bones, he'd not got back on his feet quickly and it had been the Averlanders who'd saved his hide.

'So it is,' replied Bloch, coming to the table. Drassler nodded as he and Kraus sat down, the mountain guard captain looking as rangy and implacable as ever.

'Sweet dreams?' he asked.

'Very sweet,' replied Bloch, seeing a plate of stale bread and grabbing a handful greedily. 'Me and the nice girls of Madame de Guillaume's. Shame to wake up.'

Drassler grinned. Kraus looked disapproving.

'How's the Keep looking?' asked Bloch, speaking through mouthfuls of bread.

'All is in order,' muttered Kraus. In many ways he was a lesser version of Schwarzhelm, though not quite as humorous. 'The artillery and supply wains have been recovered, though we'll need to send for more food soon. The Keep has its own water supply, but ale's running low.'

'Too bad,' said Bloch. 'The men deserve a drink.'

'Watches have been arranged and the company captains given their orders. The place stinks, but it's secure.'

Bloch nodded with satisfaction.

'You've got your castle back, Herr Drassler,' he said.

'That we have. It was a bold plan.'

Bloch shrugged. 'The only plan. Now we have to decide what to do next.'

'You might want to look at these,' said Kraus, handing him some fragments of parchment.

'Have you slept?' asked Bloch, taking them.

'I don't need much.'

Bloch grunted and started to look at the papers. The edges were black and serrated, as if someone had tried to burn them. There were instructions written across them in Reikspiel. Here and there were seals and official stamps.

'Where did you find these?' he asked.

'The garrison commander's chamber,' said Kraus. 'The orcs had been in there, and not much remained.'

Bloch leafed through the remnants. It was as Drassler had said. Orders for the garrison to disperse and move out to meet several threats. There was correspondence too, from months ago. Reinforcements delayed, supplies refused. Each item, considered alone, was routine enough. Taken together, they amounted to a serious weakening of the pass defences.

'These came by courier from Averheim?' asked Bloch, speaking to Drassler.

'Just as ever.'

Bloch kept reading. It all looked in order. He'd received similar instructions himself while serving in garrisons across the Empire. Whoever had written them knew the ways of the Imperial bureaucracy.

'They're fakes,' he said, letting them fall to the table.

Kraus raised an eyebrow. 'You're sure?'

'Schwarzhelm knew it. He told me we were being used. The orcs crossed the border just when the battle for the new elector took place. This was all part of some move to frustrate him.' He balled his fists and pressed them against his temples, trying to think. 'Have we heard any word from Averheim?'

'None.'

'Grenzstadt?'

'From nowhere, commander. We're on our own.'

It was too convenient. All those troops, drawn east, away from where the real decisions were being made.

'How many men do we have left?'

'A thousand men able to bear arms, plus the mountain guard,' said Kraus. 'Many of the wounded will recover, given time.'

'Not as much as I'd like.'

'So what do you intend?'

Bloch pushed his chair back and sighed heavily.

'Here's how I see it. We know the orcs had gear and money from Altdorf. Plenty of people in the capital have a stake in the new Elector of Averland. Someone in the army could have issued those orders, and you'd never have known. They had to know the codes, sure, but nothing's impossible at the right price. Maybe they wanted to keep us fighting for months, bogged down against the horde. If they did, then Schwarzhelm put paid to that when he broke them open on the plain. So they may not have banked on us recovering the Keep so soon, and that might be a good thing.'

Drassler said nothing. These affairs were beyond his experience, and there was little for him to contribute.

Kraus listened intently, his narrow eyes glittering. 'I was in Averheim with Schwarzhelm,' he said. 'Verstohlen said there'd been letters being sent back and forth from Altdorf, though he didn't know what was in them. He was more worried about the joyroot.'

'The what?'

'Smuggling. He thought it might lead to something bigger.'

'Maybe it has.'

Bloch felt indecision creep across him. Battlefield tactics were one thing, but making the larger choices was still unfamiliar. He'd been told to recover the Keep and wait for orders. After so much labour, so much hardship, that would have been the safest option. It was the one he'd be expected to take. Not so long ago, he'd been a halberdier captain, hardly more senior than Drassler was now. Every once in a while, he still felt like one.

'I'm going back,' he said.

'To Averheim?' asked Kraus.

'Yes, and you're coming with me.' He turned to Drassler. 'We'll take two companies of infantry, the Reiklanders. The rest will stay here. You'll have supplies and artillery, and almost as many men at your command as before.'

Drassler looked unsure. 'There's much to do here.'

Bloch nodded. 'We'll stay to secure the Keep and pass. The way-stations need re-manning, and the damage done here repairing. A few days, but no more.'

'Why Averheim?' asked Kraus, just as warily. 'We could send messengers down to Grenzstadt. If Schwarzhelm needs you, he'll summon you.'

Bloch shook his head. 'Don't you get it, Kraus? Whoever arranged this was arranging things there as well. I want to see what's been happening with my own eyes.'

He looked at the honour guard captain, and his expression was dark.

'There's work to do here, and I won't leave until it's done, but I won't stay on the edges forever. Schwarzhelm knew something was happening in Averheim and he was worried about it. Now that we're finished here, I'm worried too.'

Kraus looked unconvinced, but didn't voice any objection.

'Call it instinct,' said Bloch, feeling only half as confident as he sounded. 'Something's not right down there. It's about time we found out what.'

# Chapter Eight

THE SKY WAS chopped up and stormy. Far to the east, heavy clouds had built up on the horizon. A chill wind whipped the grass, tousling it like hair. Stirred by the breeze, the crowns of the trees swayed to and fro, an endless rustling that preyed on the nerves.

Verstohlen woke late. As he moved, he felt a dull pain in his back. Slowly, the memory of the previous night returned to him. He shivered, trying to blot it out.

He pulled himself upright, moving slowly to avoid opening the wounds on either side of his spine. The air smelled of charred meat. Something was cooking.

A few yards away, crouching over a fire, was Schwarzhelm. Two rabbits were roasting, their discarded skins glistening on the grass close by. There were trees all around, and between their slender trunks Verstohlen could see the open, rolling plains of Averland. Not much in the way of cover, but better than nothing.

The big man looked over his shoulder. He didn't smile, and went back to cooking breakfast.

'You slept late,' he grunted. He was right; the sun was high in the sky.

Verstohlen tried to stretch, but the movement sent pangs of pain down his back. He shuffled closer to the fire, limbs stiff and unresponsive.

'How did we get here?' he asked. The events of the previous night were confused. He remembered Tochfel and he remembered a chase through the streets of Averheim. Schwarzhelm had killed men, many of them. Then the gates had slammed open, and there was more running. After that, everything was hazy.

'I brought you here,' he replied. 'When you passed out, I carried you. We're twenty miles east of Averheim. Not far enough. We'll have to move again soon.'

*Twenty miles.* Schwarzhelm must have walked all night and into the morning. Had he slept at all?

Verstohlen crawled closer to the fire. The rabbit smelled good. He couldn't remember the last time he'd eaten properly.

'I had no idea what happened to you,' he said, staring at the flames, remembering the long days with no communication.

Schwarzhelm didn't reply, and turned the rabbits over on their twig spits.

'I was wrong,' said Verstohlen again. He thought of Natassja, of Grosslich, of Leitdorf. 'I was wrong about everything.'

'We were both wrong,' said Schwarzhelm. 'Blame won't change that.'

He pulled the rabbit meat from the fire and tore it into chunks. He gave Verstohlen half and started munching on the rest. Verstohlen ate quickly, ramming the hot meat down his throat, feeling a bloom of warmth and energy return. Schwarzhelm kicked earth over the fire, killing the smoke. Then he sat back to chew.

'I sent you messages from Altdorf,' he said, his great jaw working steadily. 'You didn't get them?'

Verstohlen shook his head. 'Not much has come and gone out of Averland.'

'So how much do you know about what's happened?'

'Not as much, I guess, as you.'

'You guess right.'

Schwarzhelm sucked at his fingers, leaving flecks of fat in his beard. He looked somehow older than when Verstohlen had last seen him. A cold grief marked his features that hadn't been there before.

'Helborg was no traitor,' said Schwarzhelm. There was no emotion in his voice, no condemnation, just the bald facts. 'But there was corruption. Heinrich Lassus, my old tutor. He was the one who arranged for me to come here. He knew me better than any man alive. He knew what would prey on my mind, and what would cloud my judgement.'

As he spoke, the trees hissed in the wind. Verstohlen kept eating, saying nothing.

'Above all, he knew I'd make the wrong decision. You were allowed to see Natassja Leitdorf, and you were allowed to escape to pass on the tidings. Certain things are now clear to me. She and Grosslich were in league with one another. I don't know whether Rufus, the husband, knew of their plans or not. Is he dead?'

'No one knows.'

'In any case, he's irrelevant. Grosslich has what he wants. The province is his, and there are men streaming to join him every day. Natassja, you may be sure, is by his side. We have delivered Averland to Chaos, you and I. No mean feat.'

Verstohlen let the tidings sink in. With every revelation, his part in things seemed more sordid, more damaging.

'Does the Emperor know?'

'An army is being gathered. I left him in no doubt of the threat.'

'But what's Grosslich's purpose? He must know he can't fight the whole Empire, not once the deception is unravelled. There's something more to this.' He looked up at Schwarzhelm, doubt etched on his face. 'Why was Lassus involved?'

Schwarzhelm swallowed the last of a gristly chunk of meat, wiped his fingers and reached into his jerkin. He withdrew a bundle of letters.

'These are from his private chambers. The answer will be in them.'

'So what do they say?'

'I've no idea.' Schwarzhelm tossed them to Verstohlen. 'They're written in cipher. Not one I recognise.'

Verstohlen unwrapped the bundle and started to look through the leaves. The script was unintelligible. As he scanned the characters, nothing meaningful formed.

'Me neither.'

'Then you should get to work. You're the spy. There'll be plenty of time to look at them as we travel.'

Schwarzhelm hauled himself to his feet and went over to his sword, hung from a nearby branch. Leaning against a tree trunk was another blade. It was naked, and a notch had been taken from it halfway along its length.

'Where are we going?' asked Verstohlen. He knew they needed to move, but his body still ached. He could have slept for another whole day under the shade of the trees.

'East,' replied Schwarzhelm, buckling the Rechtstahl to his swordbelt. He took up the other sword and gazed at the steel blade for a moment. 'This is Helborg's weapon. It needs to be returned.'

'But we don't know if he's still alive,' protested Verstohlen, getting to his feet with effort. 'There's been no news since–'

'He's alive,' snarled Schwarzhelm. For a moment, his eyes flashed with a savage light. 'The spirit of the blade is eager to be made whole. It will lead us to the shard.'

Verstohlen looked doubtful. Averland was a big place, and the mystical power of ancient swords seemed like a poor guide.

Unconcerned, Schwarzhelm hoisted his bag over his shoulder and began to walk. He had the grim, almost cavalier air of a man who had nothing more to lose. It made Verstohlen uneasy. He looked down at the letters, still clenched in his hand. Nothing made sense. Nothing had made sense for a long time.

'If you say so,' he muttered to himself, limping after Schwarzhelm and trying to ignore the pain in his back.

THE PARADE GROUND of the Imperial College of Arms was full of men. Regiment after regiment entered the open space, wheeled around, paraded across the gravel and wheeled back again. Sergeants shouted orders and cuffed those who failed to keep up. The pace was relentless. The white and grey of Reikland was predominant, but there were many other State colours on display.

Over eight thousand men, all marching in step. The earth shook under their boots, and this was less than a quarter of the army Volkmar was assembling. When the final host departed for Averheim, it would clog the roads for miles. The baggage train alone was nearly as well-manned as the entire force Schwarzhelm had taken with him to Averland. Chasing greenskins was one thing. Taking back a renegade province was another.

'They look sloppy,' said Gruppen, standing with Volkmar on an observation platform on the south side of the parade ground. The two of them were alone behind the railing. Above them, the sky was a lighter grey than it had been. The rain was clearing, driven west by powerful winds piling in from the far distant mountains.

'What do you expect?' said Volkmar. 'They'll learn discipline on the road.'

'Where do these men come from? I thought the regiments were all in the north.'

'Some were called back. Some are from the reserves. Some are fresh-drafted.'

As Volkmar spoke, one unfortunate infantryman stumbled, bringing three of his comrades down with him. The detachment halted in confusion, earning them a tirade of abuse from the sergeants clustered around them. Gruppen shook his head.

'Little better than murder, sending *them* into battle.'

Volkmar scowled. 'If I had more time, things would be different.' He turned away from the pacing ranks. 'The Emperor wants more speed. The Celestial College has seen portents of a terror growing. We can't afford to linger until they know how to hold a halberd.'

Gruppen narrowed his eyes disapprovingly. 'A shame they didn't report such portents before,' he said. 'Have they released any magisters?'

'Two. And we have three Bright wizards, and a trio of Light magisters. Not the best, of course – they're in Middenheim still – but powerful, all the same.'

Volkmar had once marched at the head of a host that filled the valleys of Ostland from peak to peak. He'd commanded whole batteries of heavy artillery, capable of razing companies in a single barrage. At the city of the White Wolf he'd stood alongside the defenders while the numberless hordes of Archaon had besieged the walls and the skies had been torn apart by the shadows of madness. Those campaigns had taken weeks to muster. For the retaking of Averheim, Karl Franz had given him days.

And there was still the doubt gnawing at him. He had yet to discover if Archaon had destroyed more than his body in that duel. He suppressed the doubts, pushing them down beneath an external shell of calm.

'I won't lie to you, Gruppen,' he said, his expression like flint. 'We could have a hundred thousand such men, and it wouldn't matter. This battle will be fought by others. The priests. The magisters. The knights. You've faced the great enemy before, so you know what to expect.'

Gruppen nodded bleakly. 'How many of those poor scum do, I wonder?' he said, gesturing to the parading regiments.

'They'll do their duty,' said Volkmar. 'A man should expect nothing more from life.'

More men filed into the parade ground. These were

Middenheimers, greatswords by the look of them, and they marched with the confidence of seasoned campaigners. Gruppen broke into a grim smile.

'That's better,' he said. 'They look like they won't run at the first sight of killing.'

Volkmar said nothing. War was always a dirty, terrifying business, but he wasn't worried about that. Even the meanest peasant in the Empire had seen killing, and they could all be taught to hold their ground.

But Chaos was different. He'd seen the reports from the Celestial College, and the looks of fear on the faces of the seers. Something terrifying was growing in Averheim, and if it wasn't staunched at the source, that terror would just keep spreading. The Emperor was right. They had to meet it head-on, and there was no time to waste.

'There's no running from this, Gruppen,' said Volkmar, his voice low. 'Not for any of them. It's stand fast, or die.'

KURT HELBORG LIMPED along the landing of the Drakenmoor castle, his shoulder aflame with pain, sweat beading on his forehead. He leaned on a staff like an old man, wincing with every step. The infirmity made him furious. Every passing hour wasted in the cause of recovery fuelled the smouldering sense of injustice and frustration. He needed to escape, to take up his sword again, to find the ones who'd done this to him.

The wound Schwarzhelm had given him was still weeping blood. He'd seen off the fever, but his sinews needed time to knit together. All he could do was rest and wait. The enforced inaction was far more of a torment than the stabs of pain that still ran across his upper body.

He barely noticed the finery around him. Though the bronze busts of ancient warriors were coated in dust and the woodwork was showing signs of worm, Drakenmoor was still a place of shadowy majesty. The stairways were broad and sweeping, the floor laid with slate tiles, the ceiling plastered and richly decorated. Marius Leitdorf had been wealthy even by the standards of his office, and as Helborg shuffled along he passed priceless urns, irreplaceable statues and portraits by the finest painters in the Empire.

None of it made the slightest impression. He might as well have been limping through a desolate wasteland. As he went, his breath came in ragged gasps and his teeth clenched hard. His waxed moustache, once his pride and joy, had become straggling and wild, and his dark hair hung down to his collar in matted clumps. Only his eyes, the clear blue eyes that had won the hearts of so many women across so many provinces, still flashed with their old icy intensity.

Helborg reached the door to Marius's old study. The old count's feckless son had spent most of his time locked away in there since they'd arrived. That was no longer good enough. If they were going to survive the storm to come, he'd have to make himself more useful.

Without knocking, Helborg kicked the door open. It swung back heavily, banging against the wooden panels of the wall.

Leitdorf was sitting with his back to the door, hunched over his father's old desk, surrounded by papers. The deposed elector spun round, snapping closed the book he'd been reading. His face was pale, as if he'd been reading horror stories. By the redness of his eyes, Helborg guessed he'd been at it for some time.

Helborg shook his head. The boy was no warrior. Never would be.

'Found anything interesting?' the Marshal growled, hobbling over to the single bed against the wall.

Leitdorf pushed the book under a pile of parchment.

'My lord,' he replied, ignoring the question. 'How are you feeling?'

'Like a newborn lamb on a warm spring morning,' Helborg rasped, hoping the sweat on his brow wasn't too obvious. 'Any more stupid questions?'

Leitdorf looked instantly chastened.

'Then I'm glad you're recovering,' he said.

The last time Helborg had spoken to Leitdorf had been in the Vormeisterplatz. After that, there hadn't been the chance. It felt strange to be looking at his face again. Leitdorf had lost some weight. Something of the old arrogance had been knocked out of him too, maybe. If so, that was all to the good. Helborg settled on the bed, feeling his muscles protest as he moved.

'And what are you doing with yourself, Herr Leitdorf?' he said. 'How will you aid our fight for survival?'

'I'm no warrior, Marshal. But if you order me to fight for you, I'll do what I can.'

So meek, so defeated. The old Leitdorf would at least have shown some spirit. Helborg didn't know which incarnation was worse.

'Damn right you'll fight,' he snarled, letting his disdain come to the surface. 'If you hadn't brought this province to the edge of ruin, none of this would have happened. Sigmar's bones, I *still* don't know why we're being chased down by this provincial rabble, nor why that madman Schwarzhelm did what he did.'

'I do,' said Leitdorf quietly. 'I didn't up until now. Truly, I was as deceived as you. But now some things are becoming apparent to me that should have been clear a long time ago.'

Helborg paused.

'Maybe you'd better tell me what you know.'

Leitdorf turned back to the desk and retrieved the book.

'I don't know why I tried to hide it from you,' he said, looking at the cover mournfully. He opened it and began flicking through the pages. 'This is my father's journal. It's nearly full. The last months of his reign are chronicled here, when the madness was at its height. The final entry describes his preparations to face Ironjaw. A few weeks later, he was dead.'

Leitdorf had a crushed expression on his fleshy face. As he spoke, there was little sign of the shrill self-importance that had coloured his speech in Averheim.

'Much of it will be of interest only to me, I suspect. But there's something else. He mentions dreams, terrible dreams in which the great enemy comes to him, tempting him to turn to darkness. He sees war over Averland, vast armies clashing under a tower of iron. Again and again, he mentions a woman, tempting him to join her, offering herself to him if only he will turn. Each time he resists, the madness gets worse. He knows it's killing him. That's why the coming of Ironjaw was, in its own way, a relief. Better to die fighting than lose his mind.'

Helborg listened carefully, resisting the temptation to interrupt.

'She had a name,' said Leitdorf. 'Natassja. Not a common name in the Empire, as you know. The kind of name you'd remember. He mentions it over and over again. Sometimes he descends into gibberish, but always returns to Natassja. He knows she's trying to turn him to the darkness, and can't do anything about it. He couldn't find her in the real world, just in the dreams, but he knew as surely as anything that she was going to drive him mad.'

'Your wife,' said Helborg, finally remembering the name from the briefing Skarr had given him in Nuln.

Leitdorf nodded bitterly. 'The same.' He looked up at the Marshal, horror in his eyes. 'Even now, even after being driven out of Averheim, I thought she was the one ally I had left. The worst of my many errors. She destroyed my father, and now she's destroyed me.'

Helborg let the information sink in, weighing up the implications. A sorceress, then, working to subvert the ruling line of Averland. If she could turn minds to insanity, then that explained Schwarzhelm's rages. Helborg had always assumed Marius's madness was due to a weakness in the man's blood, just as had the rest of the Empire. Perhaps that explanation had been too simple.

'Your *wife*,' he mused. 'So what are you telling me, that you didn't know she was corrupted?'

Leitdorf shook his head. 'I thought the accusations were lies, spread by Grosslich. By all that's holy, Marshal, by the blood of Sigmar and all the saints, I swear I never knew.' His eyes seemed to lose focus. 'I never knew…'

Helborg pushed himself up from the bed with difficulty and got to his feet.

'Don't you *dare* start whimpering, man,' he growled. 'She was your responsibility, and you let her play you for a cuckold. A sorceress and an elector. Morr's teeth, Leitdorf, can you see what you've done?'

Rufus looked up at him, a flash of the old anger in his eyes.

'Remember who you're talking to!' he snarled. 'I may have lost the city, but I *am* the rightful Elector of Averland.'

Helborg smiled inwardly. This was better.

'So you say. You've nothing to back up that claim but old heirlooms and a crumbling castle. I'm not impressed.'

Leitdorf sprang to his feet. He looked more comical than threatening, clad in his sagging, travel-worn clothes and carrying the vestiges of his pot-belly. The fury on his face was real enough, though, and he drew his ancestral sword, the Wolfsklinge, with a deadly flourish.

'I have this,' he hissed. 'Where is your blade, mighty hero of the Empire?'

They locked eyes. Helborg met his gaze. For a moment, Leitdorf managed to hold it, driven by his anger. Then his face fell. Next to Helborg he was little more than a soft, aristocratic fop, and he knew it.

'I have no sword,' said Helborg. 'You know why that is. But you have an armoury here – I'll take one of yours. And we'll use it to arm the others who will come.'

He leaned forwards and grasped Leitdorf's shoulder. The grip was tight, and his fingers dug into the pudgy flesh unmercifully.

'We've all been betrayed,' he said. His voice was as hard as pack-ice. 'You can sit here and cry about it, or look for a way to strike back. You have natural allies here, men whose allegiance was to your father. We can use that loyalty. Today, we have fifty men under arms. Tomorrow, we'll add another fifty from the villages around. By the time Grosslich gets here, the country-side will be alive with his enemies.'

Leitdorf raised his head again. There was a kind of strangled hope in his face, but also doubt. He'd never been forced to command before. For all his bluster, the man was afraid, deeply afraid.

'They'll follow you,' he said. 'Why would they follow me?'

Helborg maintained the vice-like grip on his shoulder. It burned his wound to hold the position, but he ignored the pain.

'Because you're the *elector*, Herr Leitdorf. It's what you said you wanted. Now it's here, what will you do? Will you keep running? Will you bury yourself in old books, hunting for answers? Or will you turn and fight? This is the test, my friend. Your father faced it. Now you must choose.'

Leitdorf stood still for a moment, his body tense, his face wrought with indecision. He wavered. For a moment, Helborg thought he'd turn away again. Then the torment passed. Leitdorf withdrew from Helborg's grip and sheathed his sword, sliding the steel back into the scabbard clumsily.

'There's more in the notebooks,' he said, his voice calmer than before. 'I'll study them. But when the time comes, I will ride beside you, Marshal. I'll find the one who wounded me, even as you will find the one who wounded you. Averland will be restored, and I will lead it.'

Helborg smiled again, this time with no rancour. There were challenges ahead, but first test had been passed.

'So be it,' he said. 'We'll ride together.'

* * *

GERHARD MULLEREN LOCKED the doors carefully and headed back to the kitchen. The geese were still hissing in the yard as if the End Times were upon them, but he couldn't see anything out there. A fox, perhaps, prowling round the edge of the farm, sniffing for loose chickens. Wolfen, his old hound, slunk along beside him, eager to get himself in front of the range and warm up. The air had a chill in it which didn't bode well for winter. A cold mist had rolled down from the highlands, out of season and unwelcome.

Gerhard sat down in front of the range, opened the iron door and threw another log on the fire. The still-warm embers flared up. It was late, nearly two hours after dark. The old farmer sat forwards, warming his hands as the timber crackled and spat. He had to get some rest. He'd be up before dawn with the animals. The summer had been a good one, but there were always shortages, always things to buy. The long plough had finally given out, and there was only so long he could rely on the ancient shire horse to keep going.

He was getting too old for this himself. It was about time one of his sons took the business over. They were too fond of ale, and too fond of the women that came with it. The time had long passed for them to take a step forwards and assume a man's proper role.

Wolfen gave a weary snort and lay down in front of the range. The old hound had stopped shivering, which was a relief. Gerhard had never seen him so agitated. The mist had done it to him, probably. Spooked him. Anything out of season would spook a farmer's dog.

There was a noise behind him, and he spun round, heart beating. Rosamunde stood at the foot of the stairs, carrying a candle and looking full of slumber.

'What in Morr're you doing, woman?' he snapped irritably.

'Can't sleep,' she mumbled, coming over to the fire.

She was a big-boned woman, and always had been. When she sat next to him on the bench, the wood flexed under her weight. Gerhard couldn't complain about that. He liked a bit of meat to hold on to in the cold winters, and she'd given him five sons, two daughters and a handsome dowry. At least one of them was bound to turn out for the good. For all her carping, Rosamunde was a fine woman.

'I'll draw you a cup of milk,' said Gerhard, getting up and heading to the corner of the kitchen where a collection of earthenware jugs stood, covered in fabric. Outside, the wind was getting up. The geese kept hissing, and in the far distance he heard a dog barking wildly. Wolfen pricked his ears up.

'That Dieter's hound?' asked Rosamunde, waking up a little.

'Guess so. There's a wind up tonight.'

Rosamunde shook her head to clear it. 'I had bad dreams.'

Gerhard brought a mug of milk over, frothy and pungent from the udder. 'Forget about it. It's a wild night.'

She took the mug and cradled it in her palms. Her normally rosy cheeks were pale.

There was a rattling sound from outside the window. Rosamunde stiffened.

'What's that?' she asked, eyes suddenly wide open.

Gerhard felt his heart start to thump again. He'd heard it in the yard, and it had sent the geese wild. They were still hissing and honking like a crowd of flagellants on a holy day. He was beginning to get unnerved himself. Something was out there.

'Ignore it,' he said, failing to keep the fear from his voice. 'Go to bed. I'll take Wolfen out for a look.'

More rattling. The hound started to whine, and crept under a bench, tail shivering between his legs. Much use he was.

Rosamunde stood up. The mug of milk fell to the ground, and the liquid streaked across the rushes on the floor.

'There's someone in the yard, Gerhard,' she insisted, looking more scared by the moment. What had her dream been about? 'Get the axe.'

'It's in the shed.'

'What's it doing in the shed?'

'I left it there.'

'Morr's bones! Go and get it!'

Panic was rising. Gerhard knew he wasn't going outside, not for all the jewels of Ind. He threw another log on the fire, sending more light across the kitchen. As the wood left his hands, he saw how much they were shaking. He was scared. He hadn't been this scared since his service in the regiment, and that was now years ago.

'What're you going to do?' demanded Rosamunde. Her voice was climbing up the register, getting higher pitched with fear. The clicking got louder.

'Go to bed, woman,' growled Gerhard, picking up a poker from next to the range. Wolfen whimpered and crept further out of harm's way. 'I'll handle this. It'll be lads from the village, playing a prank.'

She stayed where she was, rooted to the spot. She spun round, looking at the window on the far side of the room. It was beginning to open.

'Gerhard!' she screamed, pointing at it and shaking.

Gerhard found that he couldn't move. His limbs seemed welded together, as stiff as beams of iron.

'Do something!' she shrieked, equally unable to move. Something was climbing inside. Bone fingers crept over the sill, scraping against the plaster. A vase was knocked over, sending the cut flowers skittering across the floor.

'Wolfen!' ordered Gerhard, pointing at the window with trembling fingers. 'Get 'im!'

The dog bolted, not for the window but for the stairway leading up to the bedrooms above. He'd never been allowed up there. The terror had overridden any commands Gerhard could have given him.

*'Who are you?'* Gerhard cried out, feeling himself lose control of his voice. He backed towards Rosamunde, clutching at her instinctively. She clutched back, and the two of them huddled in the middle of the room.

The bone fingers reached down to the floor, followed by a thin arm. A cowled head emerged, pushing the lace curtains aside.

More rattling sounded from the other side of the room. Something was scrabbling at the door. There were more of them.

'Get out!' screamed Rosamunde, tearing at her hair. 'Get out of my house!'

The figure at the window dropped inside, sprawled on the floor like a crushed spider. Its hair hung lank around its slim face, and iron studs gleamed from its limbs. It looked like a girl, near-naked. She must have been perishing cold, and her skin was as white as the moon.

Gerhard wanted to say something, do something

heroic, get them out of his farmhouse. The door was now rattling on his hinges. They were going to knock it down.

'What do you *want*?' he pleaded, nearly sobbing with terror. They kept rattling, just like mechanical dolls.

The first one lifted her head. She had no eyes, just blank plates of metal. She grinned wide, exposing drilled-sharp teeth. Her fingers clacked together, dagger-quick blades rubbing against each other like a butcher's sharpening knives.

'*Helborg!*' she hissed, her voice echoing from the walls. '*Helborg!*'

'What?' screamed Gerhard. 'This is Mofligen, by Ruppelstadt! Not Helborg! Leave us!'

The door slammed open, ripped from its hangings. Another horror came in, clad in rags like the first, hissing and wheezing. Its knife-like fingers trailed on the ground, leaving grooves in the hard stone.

'*Helborg!*' it cried.

There was another one behind it, just like the rest. Three of them. They limped towards Gerhard and Rosamunde, their grins impossibly wide, skin stretched tight, teeth snapping as they came.

'*Helborg!*'

Gerhard felt his heart hammer so hard he thought it would explode. Rosamunde snatched at him frantically, pushing him in front of her, anything to get away from the creeping terrors.

He knew he should run. Do something. Try and get away. But there was nothing he could do. His body was drenched with sweat. The terrible maidens closed in on him, raising their fingers high.

'*Helborg!*'

'I can't help you!' cried Gerhard, falling to his knees and bursting into horrified tears. 'Sigmar's *mercy*, I can't help you! Leave us alone!'

Then the first talon fell, slicing down with speed and skill. The others joined in, carving up the huddled pair like raptors on the carcass of a stricken deer. For a few moments, the screams of the victims rose into the windy night, mingling with the cries of the geese and the howling from upstairs. Then all was silent. The kitchen was still, apart from the crackle of the fire-wood, the distant whimper of the dog and the expanding pools of blood on the floor.

The three handmaidens stepped back, admiring their work. Flesh was strewn all across the rushes, diced into neat segments. For a moment, they paused, each breathing gently, lost in appreciation of their art.

Then one of them looked at the others, and the grin left her face. A signal was given, and they limped back to the door. This quarry hadn't been what they sought, but killing was good. It reminded them of a life before the one they had now, when there was more than simply pain and orders. For some reason, the pleading for mercy, the desperate entreaties to be left alone, appealed to them. Maybe they had done the same thing, a long time ago before their minds had been taken away and all had descended into the long grind of horror. There was no clear memory of it, just a vague sense.

They passed through the door, rattling as they went. Outside, the wind howled around the farmhouse, and a loose shutter banged wildly. A gale was coming, a storm wind from the Grey Mountains to the south.

The maidens departed. They knew they were getting close. They never tired, they never gave in, they never lost hope. All they had was the single word, the reason for their existence.

'*Helborg*,' whispered the last of them, before they stalked off into the night, heading south and east, away from the pastureland and up into the gorse of the high moors. Their prey was drawing closer.

# Chapter Nine

VERSTOHLEN LOOKED ACROSS the scattered fragments of parchment again. The light was beginning to fail. His limbs throbbed from the long march across country, and that affected his mind. Nothing came easily, and the cipher remained firmly locked in place.

Over the past two days Schwarzhelm had driven them hard, striding across the countryside with the iron resolve he'd used in the past to lead armies. He spoke even less than normal. Apart from the Recht-stahl at his side, he'd eschewed his armour, and seemed diminished both physically and mentally. Something had broken within him.

Though Schwarzhelm never explained how, he seemed to know where he was going. Every so often, he'd stop walking for no reason at all. Once he'd drawn Helborg's sword and held it up to the sun, turning the metal and watching the reflection in it. Then he'd set off again, silent and brooding, striding purposefully as if nothing had happened.

They kept clear of the roads, lying low whenever they sighted Grosslich's men on the horizon. Even so far into the wilds there were patrols. They'd seen one column of men, at least five hundred strong, heading east. The new elector's reach was extending.

As the hours of furtive trekking had passed, Verstohlen had watched his master carefully. There was none of the mania that had affected him in Averheim. He now had a cold, calculated fury, directed inwards. The cure to this sickness was obvious. If Helborg were alive, Schwarzhelm would return the sword. Verstohlen didn't like to speculate too much on what Helborg would do when he got it – the Marshal wasn't renowned for his compassion. Still, one way or another it would bring some kind of resolution.

On the rare breaks between the marches, Verstohlen had plenty of time to contemplate the coded messages taken from Lassus's chambers. At first glance, he'd assumed the code would be relatively easy to break. Ciphers used for routine messages were rarely complex – if they were, uncovering the meaning for the recipient would be too arduous and time consuming to be useful. In the normal run of things, in a world where so few men could read, Imperial codes were generally only used to keep messages secret from opportunistic thieves.

Lassus's code, on the other hand, looked like total gibberish. Verstohlen had started on the assumption that some kind of substitution code was being used, and had drawn out a table of alphabets using a stick of charcoal on parchment Schwarzhelm had brought from Altdorf. After that, he'd worked on a single phrase, the opening words of the final letter. Every variation produced a fresh line of nonsense. If he'd had more leisure to work, Verstohlen might have been able to do things more thoroughly. Even so, after hammering away at the problem, he knew he was missing something.

Schwarzhelm didn't appreciate the difficulties. As they travelled, he'd demanded answers. The man was a near indestructible master of swordcraft, but he had little appreciation of the literary and philosophical arts. He could read, it was true, but his penchant for language games didn't extend far. Verstohlen found it hard even to explain the nature of the problem. Whenever he had to confess his lack of progress, Schwarzhelm didn't fail to show his frustration.

'This is important, Pieter,' he'd say.

'I know it is.'

'We don't have time to speculate.'

'I know we don't.'

'Then crack it.'

On the second day out from Averheim, they'd come across an abandoned farmhouse on the edge of what looked like fallow fields. There were no settlements within eyesight. The light was beginning to fail, and even Schwarzhelm looked ready to halt the march.

Verstohlen looked at the roofless building before him, watching the way the evening sun struck the stone. Around them, beyond the margins of the ploughed and empty fields, the endless seas of grass whispered. Schwarzhelm looked as if he was remembering something. Whatever it was, the memory wasn't a happy one.

'How close are you?' he asked again.

'Are we stopping here?' replied Verstohlen. 'If so, I might be able to concentrate.'

'I'll gather wood for a fire,' Schwarzhelm said, stalking off. 'Do what you can.'

So it was that Verstohlen found himself huddled in

the corner of the ruined farmhouse, surrounded by scraps of yellowing paper. The characters, all written in a small, discursive hand, began to stream in front of his eyes. He ran the substitution tests again, this time isolating a different phrase in the letter, near the end. He worked on the sentences in his head, trying to spot patterns emerging for each shift. Whatever he tried, nonsense emerged. By the time Schwarzhelm came back, Verstohlen was tired and frustrated. Lassus was no fool. Verstohlen needed time, space, the use of a desk, quill and mathematical tables. It was hopeless.

Schwarzhelm crouched down some distance from him and began to pile the wood. A few moments later he'd struck his flint and the kindling at its base began to burn. It wasn't until Verstohlen saw the fire flare into life that he realised how cold he'd been getting. The nights were drawing in across Averland, turned chill by the gathering storms in the east.

'Progress?' asked Schwarzhelm curtly, sitting down with his back against the wall. Verstohlen shook his head, knowing the reaction it would provoke.

To his surprise, Schwarzhelm didn't admonish him. The big man stared into the growing flames moodily, watching the dry wood catch. All around them, the shadows began to lengthen. Another day had passed and they were no closer to their goal.

'We'll have to work without the letters, then,' he said. 'Maybe things will become clearer when we're back in Averheim.'

Verstohlen raised an eyebrow. Schwarzhelm clearly had the future all mapped out. Verstohlen almost asked him to explain what he had in mind, but then decided against it. He was too tired. As far as he could see, the quest to find Helborg was doomed to failure, and the march across the countryside was merely a way for Schwarzhelm to exorcise his inner demons. He sighed, and began to collect the scraps of paper together. He could start work on them again in the morning.

'I need to get my bearings,' said Schwarzhelm, looking like he was speaking half to himself. 'This whole place seems foreign to me.'

'So it should,' muttered Verstohlen. 'It's changed since you were a child.'

Schwarzhelm grunted in agreement. Verstohlen returned to the fire and held his hands against it.

'You never told me much about your time here,' he said.

'What do you want, my life story?'

'Not all of it.' Verstohlen was inured to Schwarzhelm's prickliness. 'But you're a hard man to understand, my lord. Is there a man alive who knows anything about you?'

Schwarzhelm remained stony-faced.

'Not alive,' he said.

Verstohlen took the hint and fell quiet. For a while, the only sound was the crackle of the fire and the sounds of the land. In the distance, a triangle of geese flew low across the setting sun, crying as they went. Below them ran the sound of the grasses, rushing endlessly in the wind. Verstohlen resigned himself to a long, sullen evening, but then Schwarzhelm, against all expectation, spoke.

'I was born a few days' ride from here,' he said. He continued to look into the flames, and they lit his eyes with a dancing light. 'In a village like any across the Empire. Less than a hundred souls, all of them poor. Getting into the army was my dream then, just like any other lad's. I didn't expect much from it, just a schilling in my pocket and the chance to escape the grind. Turned out I was good at killing. My one true talent. I got noticed, then got sent to Altdorf. After I started to train with Lassus, I never came back. Even now, I've never been back. The Empire became my home, and my roots seemed unimportant. Maybe that was a mistake.'

By Schwarzhelm's standards, it was an unprecedented confession. For a man who rarely strung more than a few words together, and those usually curt commands, his answers to Verstohlen's questions were a revelation. Perhaps it was necessary. Maybe the wounds opened up by his failure in Averheim needed some kind of purgation before they were closed. Even the Emperor's Champion could be damaged.

'Close to here, eh?' said Verstohlen. 'So this is your country.'

Schwarzhelm nodded. 'That it is. Wenenlich, the village was called. I don't even know if it still exists.'

At the mention of the village's name, Verstohlen froze.

'What was it called?'

'Wenenlich.'

Verstohlen felt his mind start to race. That wasn't the first time he'd heard that word. Someone had uttered it recently, somewhere important. He sat back, leaning his head against the wall and looking into the darkening sky, trying to think.

'Holy Verena,' he swore, feeling the memory return. 'They used that word.'

'Who?'

'It was the password. To get into Natassja's sanctum. The soldier at the gates required it.'

Verstohlen got to his feet, brushing his clothes down as he rose. Something had occurred to him. Schwarzhelm followed him more slowly, clambering to his feet stiffly.

'What is it?'

'An idea,' said Verstohlen, taking out the letter again.

He scrabbled for the crude table of characters he'd drawn up, talking rapidly as he did so.

'Suppose you create a table of characters, each axis being the alphabet in sequence, and each row starting with the letter in the leftmost column – like this one. This is what Menningen uses, based on a system devised by Vignius. Now suppose you read an "a". Take the first letter of the key, say "w". Find the row starting with the key, and move along to the cell containing the cipher character. The character of the column header will be the one you write.'

As he spoke, Verstohlen turned one of the parchment scraps over and scribbled on it with the blunt charcoal. Schwarzhelm looked completely blank, watching Verstohlen work with little comprehension.

'If you say so.'

Verstohlen kept writing, referring back to the original letter. The stream of letters looked as impenetrable as ever.

*jlyvrataakpnwgxmuzwkrpfdmpaoshxusqutwrtvhaxguerb-wgwipkkryctccpdwpqvrxikuossgbxuuawjsavwtdlsmgllzcuvkr peaywvoapcjrpttlcvrxszzrhnxvrgsqudwwgmzpejljpbzropk-twwfsapdgujsjhbywvadmaojttnininorlaksutesppmfzfslvbzbf poxeipomrvomgiqdmebniycnwtgsoivrulvfzpmypplcvp-krnkntvuadiyfbcodbpcbyzlsgvsrzmaocrhbxrvzfkjdkvxkepmp zgmawepiffpscpnjxcyphrjrykgzsinorymfhjhsyaoatlyfsoflng-suly*

'The important thing is the key. Using the word unlocks the meaning.'

'Why Wenenlich?'

Verstohlen shot Schwarzhelm a wry look. 'Perhaps their idea of a joke. Lassus knew you like no one else.'

His fingers ran across the table, cross-referencing each character in the letter with the one the key pointed to. Letters emerged. As he wrote, Verstohlen could feel his hands begin to shake. It didn't exactly make sense, but it wasn't gibberish. The letters followed one another without a break as Verstohlen decoded them.

*ndfundsrecbfksafehl*

Verstohlen stopped transcribing and ran the charcoal stub back along the letters.

'It'll still be truncated, and may start mid-word.' He began to draw a line between the likely words, watching for abbreviation and filling out the expansion. 'Some of this is guesswork, but maybe this will make more sense.'

*and funds received black fire keep safely hl*

Verstohlen stared at his handiwork, his heart thumping. He'd cracked it.

'About time,' said Schwarzhelm gruffly. 'I'll get us some food. You can make a start in the morning.'

Verstohlen smiled to himself. Effusive praise wasn't the big man's style. More importantly, though, the tone of his voice had changed. The cold note of self-judgement was diminished. In its place, and for the first time since he'd returned to Averland, there was hope for some answers.

THE MUSTER WAS complete. Across the plains south of Pohlbad in the lower Reikland, Volkmar's host was ready to march at last. Companies had been moving down the short distance from Altdorf in an incessant stream for days and gathering in the sprawling country estate of Duke Raffenburg Olsehn. With every new arrival, the numbers of men stationed in the huge marshalling yards swelled by another few hundred. Caravans of food and supplies had already set off, heading south under heavy armed guard. Messengers had been sent on fast horses, handing out warrants from the Imperial Palace for more materiel and men. Requisitions had been made of the Gunnery School in Nuln, already working at breakneck pace to supply the war in the north and now expected to arm another whole army with only days' notice. The fabric of the Empire, its finances and its resolve, were being stretched to their very limit.

Volkmar stood on a high stepped platform overlooking the duke's grand parade ground, watching the fruit of his labours stand in row after row, detachment after detachment. The standards of the various companies hung limply from their poles. The morning had dawned overcast and still, turning the stone of the mansion house behind them a dark, dull grey.

'Good enough?' mused Maljdir, watching the final units take their places in the muster. He was standing beside Volkmar, as was Roll. Volkmar was arrayed in the ceremonial robes of his office, and the eagle of Sigmar, cast in steel, adorned his breast. The collar of his cloak, a deep ceremonial red, rose high above his head, making his already massive frame even more imposing. Roll wore the robes of a warrior priest and carried a double-headed axe in his clenched fists. Maljdir wore the plate armour and chainmail of his Middenheim heritage. His cloak was white, trimmed with the dark blue of the northern province.

'We'll see,' said Volkmar, his eyes trained on the host below. 'Give the signal.'

The message was passed down from the platform, and a trumpet blared out from rear of the parade ground, soon repeated across the open space. Men stood to attention, and the sound of their boots snapping together echoed through the air.

'Men of the Empire!' roared Volkmar. His huge voice boomed out, spreading to all corners of the parade ground. Few men would have been able to make themselves heard across such a wide area, but Volkmar's oratory, honed by a lifetime's service to the Cult of Sigmar, was fuelled by his inexhaustible faith. 'You know why you've been summoned here. I'll not weary your ears by talking of Averland and its troubles. You need know only one thing. The great enemy has made Averheim its home, and we march to expunge it from the face of the Empire.'

As he spoke, Volkmar swept his eyes across the ranks. Every man present, nearly thirty thousand infantrymen, remained silent, listening intently to his words. None dared raise so much as a smile in his presence. The Grand Theogonist, master of the arcane mysteries of the Church of Sigmar, was a figure of awe and majesty.

'There will be no deception between us. The task will be arduous. Before the victory, there will be death. Even as we assemble here, they are recruiting men of their own, arming them and readying for the battle to come. By such means do they hope to destroy our resolve, to crush our spirit when the time of testing comes.'

He took a step forwards, gripping the brass railing and leaning out over the masses.

'Do *not* be afraid!' he roared. 'Do *not* give in! We know, as they will never do, of the secret power of mankind, the source of his greatness! Only in purity and steadfastness is there salvation. The mind of the loyal soldier is more terrible to the false gods than anything our weapons of steel and blackpowder can devise. While we profess our faith, they are powerless against us!'

The host remained rapt, hanging on every word. Volkmar knew how important the speech was. There would be few chances to address the entire army again. He had to inspire them while the sun shone and the world seemed hopeful, for he knew how dark the road would be.

'Look around you, my sons,' he said, sweeping his arms in a wide gesture. 'See what the hand of man has built here. Look at the powers ranged in our defence. We have gunnery from Nuln capable of tearing down the walls of any castle standing. We will have magisters of the colleges in our ranks, each of them masters of the winds of magic. I myself will command a full regiment of warrior priests, all sworn enemies of the heretic and the daemon. Alongside them will ride the Knights Panther, deadliest swords of the Empire.'

He pointed out each elite company as he spoke, noting Gruppen's nod of acknowledgement as his finger isolated the proud regiment of knights, standing not more than thirty yards from him.

'And so you do not march alone. For every sword they possess, we possess a sharper. For every fallen sorcerer, we have an exalted master of magic. For every twisted warrior, cursed with the warping gifts of their dark masters, we have armoured knights wearing sanctified armour and carrying the blades of their forebears. So when the moment comes, stride forth with confidence! Let anger be your guide, not fear. Let fury drive you, the fury of the just man at the insolence of those who have taken our lands and despoiled them!'

Volkmar's voice rose, channelling the anger he felt himself. It was always there, just beneath the surface. As he spoke, he remembered Be'lakor's twisted face, the savage leer of the daemon as it turned to horror in the face of his implacable wrath. He had triumphed then, and the taste of victory had never left his lips. He was strong enough for this.

'We will give them no mercy!' he bellowed, and a ripple of agreement passed across the army. 'We will drive them into the ground! We will rip their false idols down, burn their blasphemous temples and tear their souls from their gibbering carcasses! We will sweep through Averland like an avenging storm, with the fire of Holy Sigmar in our hearts and the steel of His Empire in our hands!'

The army pressed forwards. Men raised their fists, stirred by the emotion shaking in Volkmar's words. They were almost ready to be unleashed.

'Remember who you are!' he shouted, his knuckles white as they gripped the railing. 'You are *men*, the rightful masters of the world! None shall stand before us, not the beast of the forest, the orc of the mountain, nor the corruption from within! We shall cleanse Averland just as Middenheim was cleansed, as Praag was cleansed, and as every city will be cleansed that is defiled by those without faith, without honour, and without hope!'

The murmur turned into a swell of acclamation.

'So we ride, men of the Empire! We ride to glory, not

for ourselves, but for the one who leads us. For Karl Franz! For Sigmar! For the Empire!'

The army raised its fist as one, hurling cries of 'For the Empire!' into the air. The noise was deafening, a wall of sound that rose up from the gravel of the parade ground and swelled up to the highest pinnacle of the mansion house beyond. The earth drummed as the stamp of thirty thousand feet hit home. As if a gale had been sent by Sigmar Himself, the standards of the massed regiments suddenly burst into life, streaking out and displaying the proud devices of the myriad companies.

Volkmar felt his heart beat powerfully. On either side of him, Roll and Maljdir had raised their weapons high, and were stirring the host into new heights of fervour. The sea of men, filling the ground before him, had been roused. They would remember this moment on the long march ahead, and when the clash finally came, it would fill their hearts with the courage they would need to weather the storm.

Volkmar raised his arms high in a gesture of defiance, then stepped back from the edge of the platform. The host continued to roar with undiminished enthusiasm. He turned to Maljdir, and his grim face was set.

'Bring my charger,' he growled. 'Now we march.'

HIGH IN THE Iron Tower, work continued apace. Metal was twisted around metal, ever rising, ever growing. The pinnacle now dominated the city, casting its shadow over the poor quarter and stretching to the river. Nowhere in the city was now free of its gaze, and the skeleton framework of the topmost chambers was already snaking into the sky. A thousand Stone-slaves now toiled on its construction, their spirits crushed by the malevolence of the shard buried beneath them, their eyes glazed and wills destroyed.

Night was falling. Outside the perimeter fence the ceremony was starting up again. Hundreds of soldiers moved through the streets of Averheim, isolating those not performing their duties with sufficient zeal and dragging them to the holding pens. Iron lamps had been lit at every street corner, throwing an angry red glow across the stone. Numbly, the citizens of the city emerged to do obeisance to their new lords and masters. Most had the tell-tale signs of joyroot addiction around their eyes.

The populace had been told the ceremony was a ritual of praise to Sigmar, held to erase the sins of the citizens during the time without an elector. Many of them believed that, and sang the words with devout fervour. Others, knowing that they weren't Reikspiel and had the ring of some unholy foreign tongue, did so reluctantly. They had little choice but to comply.

Many of the people still supported Grosslich, despite the steel fist that had descended on the city. Money continued to flow, and the food and root were both plentiful. Relaxations on long-standing edicts against drunkenness and fornication were popular in the slums, and the nobles who would normally have opposed such measures were Grosslich's allies, or had been cowed into submission, or were dead.

From his crystal chamber in the Tower, the elector looked out across the city, watching with satisfaction as the points of light spread out from the centre like a spider's web of flame. Far below, he could see shuffling masses in the streets, whipped into a frenzy of chanting by the soldiers around them. Some of them had looks of religious transport on their faces.

Though they were doing his work, he despised them more than he could express. At least those who opposed him had some backbone. Until Natassja got her hands on them, that was.

'Enjoying the view?'

He hadn't heard her enter. No doubt she enjoyed these demonstrations of her superiority, but they were beginning to become trying. He turned slowly, attempting to look as if he'd known she'd been behind him all along.

'The mask has almost slipped now,' he said. 'Few will be fooled for much longer. Is any of this pretence worth keeping up?'

Natassja came over to stand beside him and looked out across the twinkling mass of lights.

'It most certainly is,' she said. The blue tinge in her skin had become more pronounced and the pure black of her eyes glistened. 'Why reveal ourselves before deception becomes impossible?'

Grosslich shook his head. 'I can't understand how they don't see it.'

Natassja shrugged. 'Because they don't want to see it. You were chosen to end the anarchy. Right up until the end, there will be those who fail to see what you've done with your power.'

She turned away from the window. As ever, her manner was cool and controlled. Despite the outlandish nature of her appearance, it was hard to reconcile the grace of her bearing with the terror she was capable of inflicting.

'Maintain the ceremony,' she said. 'The hymns aid the awakening of the Stone, and it gives the rabble something to do.'

Grosslich didn't like the tone of command in her voice. For so long, he'd been willing to let her dominate him, aware he had much to learn, but now his own powers were increasing. The issue of respect was something he'd have to address.

'Is the chamber below complete?' he asked.

Natassja nodded. 'Achendorfer has been busy. The process will quicken soon, and then you'll have tools at your disposal no mortal elector has ever possessed.'

'I'll look forward to it.'

'Enjoy them while you can. The Stone is useful in other ways. I've seen a great army heading south, commanded by the master of the boy-god's church. They're travelling fast.'

'Do they pose a danger?'

'Everything is dangerous.'

'And do you ever give a straight answer?'

Something like a smile played across Natassja's purple lips. With a sudden pang, Grosslich realised how well she was playing him.

'You can handle them, my love,' she said, coming up to him and placing a slender hand on his chest. Despite everything, Grosslich felt a shudder of desire at her touch. 'With the powers I will give you, no mortal army will be able to stand against us.'

She came closer, her lips parted, her dark eyes shining. Grosslich could feel her breath, laced with lilac perfume. This was her most potent weapon. Herself. He had no means of combating it.

'Have no fear,' she whispered, pressing her body against his. 'The outcome has already been determined. By the time they arrive, this place will be a fragment of the Realm of Pain on earth. We will crush them, my love, just as we have crushed Averland.'

From down in the city, the noise of frenzied revels was growing. Grosslich felt his will sapped, his resolve weaken. Natassja was more beautiful then than she'd ever been. Thoughts of trying to resist her divine mastery seemed not so much foolish as pointless.

'We *have* crushed Averland, have we not?' he murmured, running his fingers up to her hair.

'Oh, we've only just started,' breathed Natassja, and her pupils seemed like chasms to a whole new realm of terrible wonder. 'Believe me, my love, this is only the beginning.'

# Chapter Ten

BLOCH PAUSED FOR a moment from the march, shading his eyes against the setting sun. The sinking orb was huge and red, and the sky above was angry and inflamed like a giant wound. He stood with Kraus at the head of his small force, less than two hundred men, poised at the mouth of the passes. The Keep was several miles behind, garrisoned and provisioned after two days of hard work. Ahead of him, the land fell sharply, falling in a cascade of cliffs and sharp defiles. The road threaded through the broken land before snaking eventually down through the highlands and towards distant Grenzstadt. On either side, the shoulders of the mountains reared into the evening sky, their snow-streaked flanks rosy from the dying sun.

'You all right?' asked Kraus, looking at him keenly.

'Fine,' said Bloch, starting to walk again. He'd be pleased enough to get down out of the high passes and back into warmer climes. There was still another hour before they'd make the next way-fort, and he'd kept the pace hard.

In truth, though, something about the sunset troubled him. He remembered Schwarzhelm's face before he'd left. Whatever he was returning to face in Averheim had scared him. And that was where he was headed too.

'We need to pick up the pace,' he muttered, striding down the road with purpose. 'Marching down here in the dark will be dangerous.'

Behind him, the column wearily picked up their weapons, and the trek resumed.

SKARR CROUCHED DOWN low under the cover of the trees. The sky was a light grey, overcast with high cloud and full of the chill of a failing summer. Around him his men did likewise, keeping their blades sheathed and armour covered. There were thirty of the Reiksguard with him, the majority of those who'd escaped Averheim and joined Helborg in the wilderness. He felt his body tense for action, his muscles responding instantly despite the long days in the wilds. His fingers remained tight around the hilt of his sword, still in its scabbard but ready to be drawn.

His eyes narrowed. After a couple of yards the trees gave out, revealing a slope of grassland and gorse. Thirty yards away, down at the base of a shallow depression, was the road, one of the main trade routes running east towards Heideck. On the far side of it the land rose again, enclosing the route on either flank.

The position was far north of Drakenmoor. Word had come to Leitdorf's men that Grosslich was using the road for the transport of arms and supplies. No doubt thinking the province entirely subdued, the guard was light. Such complacence would have to be punished.

Skarr studied the descent carefully, noting the quickest routes down.

'I see them,' hissed Eissen, crouching to Skarr's left.

From the west, to the left of the hidden Reiksguard, a caravan of wagons and carts made its way steadily towards the cleft in the hills. There were about a dozen of them, heavily built and drawn by a team of four horses each. All were covered, and the scarlet boar's head of Grosslich had been painted on their wooden flanks. In front of the wagons was an escort of twelve mounted troops armed with spears and round shields. At the rear were perhaps two dozen more, marching on foot and arranged in a loose column formation.

Skarr watched carefully, judging the character of the guards and their likely responses from the way they moved. Their captain, mounted on a sable charger at the head of the escort, was a burly man with a shaven head and a heavy coat of mail over his broad shoulders. He didn't look like an Averlander. A mercenary, perhaps, brought into the province by Grosslich's famed bottomless coffers.

The trail of wagons crawled closer. As it neared the depression an order was barked out from the head of the escort and the guards drew closer together. There was no real urgency about their movements, just a calm, professional caution. They had no reason to suspect resistance; as far as they knew, Averland was entirely at peace.

The first horsemen came into range. Skarr gestured to Eissen in Reiksguard battle-signals, flickering his fingers to indicate deployment and tactics. He was to take ten men to deal with the rearguard, while Skarr and ten more dealt with the armoured column at the front. The remainder would hang back, mopping up stragglers and ensuring none got back to Averheim to report the ambush.

*Wait for my signal*, he gestured, then turned back to the road.

The head of the escort passed them and the carriages came into the centre of the view, swaying on their heavy axles under the weight of the cargo.

*Now*, signalled Skarr, balling his fist and plunging it down.

Silent as ghouls, moving as one, the Reiksguard burst from cover. Skarr tore down the slope, drawing his sword and aiming for the leader.

It took a few moments for them to be noticed. By the time the alarm was raised, the Reiksguard were almost on them.

'Ambush!' came a cry from one of the horsemen, and the carriages ground to a halt. From the rear of the column the infantry guards reached for their weapons, hurriedly pulling on helmets and buckling up loose breastplates. A second later and Eissen's men tore into them, felling three before the rest began to mount any kind of defence.

Skarr felt his blood pumping fiercely. After so long skulking around like thieves, it was a savage joy to get back to proper fighting.

The escort leader kicked his horse towards him, shouting invective in some foreign tongue and pulling a curve-bladed halberd from his back. Skarr ran straight at him, keeping his sword loose in his hand. On either side his comrades fanned out, running at full tilt into the heart of the cavalry formation. They all knew the effectiveness of cavalry on the charge, but also how vulnerable the animals were once men got among them.

The black charger went for him, hooves kicking up turf as it laboured up the slope. Skarr waited until the last possible moment before swerving sharply to his right, dropping low and ducking under the swing of the rider's halberd.

The horse thundered past him. Skarr spun sharply, stabbing his sword-edge deep into the beast's hamstrings, severing them cleanly. With a scream, the horse tried to rear, buckled, and collapsed onto its side, pinning its rider beneath half a ton of muscle, tack and armour.

Skarr whirled round, hearing a second horse go down as his men carved their way into the panicking squadron. Another halberd blade plunged at him, stabbed down by a rider kicking a chestnut mount straight towards him.

Skarr spun his sword round, switching to a two-handed grip just in time to meet the strike. He parried it away and leapt clear of the charge. As the rider careered past, Skarr pulled a knife from his belt and hurled it at the man's back. He turned away to his next target, hearing with satisfaction his blade thump into its target and unseat the rider.

The Reiksguard were everywhere by then, hacking at the horses to bring them down or pulling the riders from their saddles. Two of the convoy guards, seeing the destruction of their unit, tried to ride off down the road and away from danger. Both were soon toppled from their steeds, clutching at the daggers flung with expert precision at their backs.

As the defence collapsed, a third rider attempted to engage Skarr, spurring his terrified horse at him and working to bring his halberd to bear. Skarr danced away from the challenge, watching with contempt as the panicked swipe missed him by half a yard. The rider's horse stumbled on the uneven terrain, caught up in the confusion of rearing steeds and flashing steel. Skarr powered forwards, leaping up and grabbing the jerkin of the struggling rider with his free hand. He pulled the man from the saddle and the two of them hit the ground hard. In an instant the Reiksguard was on top of the stricken soldier, sword edge at his throat, pressing deep into the skin.

'Mercy!' the man screamed, scrabbling for his own weapon.

'Not for you,' Skarr rasped, and yanked the blade down, severing the man's head cleanly. Then he was up on his feet again, poised for a fresh attack, sword swinging into position.

The skirmish was over. Eissen's men had wiped out the rearguard and were hastening to the head of the column to join him. The convoy's riders lay amongst their dead mounts, slaughtered to a man by the sudden assault. The Reiksguard were the deadliest troops in the Imperial army, and the fighting had been almost embarrassingly one-sided.

'Secure those carts,' spat Skarr to Eissen, wiping the gore from his face and looking round to check for casualties.

On the ground, whimpering from pain, the leader of the escort still lived. Half of him was trapped under the flank of his steed, and his attempts to crawl free were pitiful. Skarr walked up to him and crouched down close, keeping his blade unsheathed. The man's face was pale, and lines of blood ran down from the corners of his mouth. It looked like his ribcage had been driven in, and his breathing was thin and halting.

Skarr grabbed him by his hair and yanked his head back sharply.

'Who sent you?' he hissed. 'You're no Averlander.'

The man's eyes narrowed in pain, but he somehow managed to spit a gobbet of phlegm into the Reiksguard captain's eyes.

Skarr laughed harshly.

'Good man,' he said, wiping his face and letting the man's head fall back against the turf. 'Do it again, though, and I'll cut your balls off.'

He pressed his blade against the man's neck, watching as the honed edge parted the flesh. The rider grimaced, and his defiance ebbed.

'So I say again, who sent you?'

'You no Averlander neither,' the captain panted, his teeth red with blood, his speech slurred and heavy with a north Tilean accent. 'All this for she. You stand no chance of it. Not against she.'

He tried a crooked smile, but the effort was too much. Blood and phlegm rose up his throat, and he began to retch.

Skarr withdrew, watching the man die impassively. Eissen came up to him, wiping his blade down with a handful of grass.

'Get anything from him?'

Skarr shook his head. 'Dogs of war,' he said. 'They know nothing. Let's get the carts open.'

As the Reiksguard dragged the bodies into a pile at the front of the caravan and retrieved the surviving horses, Skarr and Eissen mounted the first of the wagons. The driver shrank back from them as they climbed up, face white with fear. Unlike his escort, he looked like a proper Averland merchant, full-cheeked and running to a comfortable layer of fat. Skarr ignored him. Behind the driver's position there was a locked door. He kicked it heavily and the wood around the lock splintered and broke. Inside the wagon were crates, all of them bound with iron and locked tight. He pulled one out with difficulty. It was heavy, and the clink of metal came from within.

'Money,' said Skarr.

'Lots of it,' agreed Eissen. He turned to the cart's driver. 'Are all the wagons full of this stuff?'

The man nodded emphatically, eager to please. 'And arms. The elector's been recruiting hard.'

Further down the convoy there came the sound of Reiksguard breaking into more caches. Skarr clapped his hand on the shoulder of the driver, and the man winced under the impact.

'You're a good Averlander,' the preceptor said. 'You don't need to spend your time working for these people.'

The driver looked back at him, still terrified, his fingers clutching the reins of his horses tightly.

'What'll I do? What do you want me to do?'

Skarr smiled, and the lattice of pale lines on his face creased.

'My men'll take these carts south. Take heart, my friend. An army is growing, and you're going to be a part of it.'

The driver didn't seem to know whether to look pleased by that or not.

'Play that part well, and this could be good for you,' continued Skarr. 'Lord Helborg knows how to reward those who serve him.'

'Helborg!' gasped the driver, eyes widening further.

'That's right. Get used it. You're working for the Reiksmarshal now.'

* * *

VOLKMAR PUSHED HIS warhorse up the ridge above the road, feeling the cleansing wind ruffle his cloak. Efraim Roll was with him, as was a guard of twenty mounted warrior priests, all clad in heavy plate armour and carrying warhammers inscribed with the livery of the Cult of Sigmar. The Theogonist himself had donned bronze-lined armour of an ancient lineage, covered in runes of destruction and adorned across the breastplate with a priceless jade griffon, pinions outstretched.

He carried the massive Staff of Command in his hands at all times. A lesser commander would have had it taken up by an underling, but such luxuries were not for Volkmar. Though his palms were already raw from the weight of the iron and ash he kept his grip on the sacred weapon tight.

Below them, his army crawled along the road. In the vanguard came the companies of knights, Gruppen riding at their head. Their squires, spare horses, armour and lances came in a long caravan behind them, such that they almost constituted a small army in their own right. Behind them came the long train of halberdier and spearman regiments, marching in close-knit squares and decked out in their State colours. Drummers kept the pace tight. There was little of the casual joking and bawdiness of a regular campaign. Volkmar drove them hard, and the sergeants had kept the men on a short leash.

It took some time for the long lines of infantry to pass Volkmar's position. He watched them as a hawk watches its prey, scouring the ranks for weakness and insubordination. Some of his own warrior priests were among them, clustered in tight groups of half a dozen. Those fanatics asked for neither rest nor privilege.

Behind them came the artillery train. Huge assault cannons were hauled by teams of horses up to six strong, followed by the infantry-killing pieces, the Helblasters and Helstorms. Handgunners, artillery crew and engineers sat on their carts in their wake, keeping a close eye on the wagons of blackpowder, matchcords, ammunition and spare parts. Volkmar's brow creased with disapproval as he surveyed them. He trusted blackpowder less than he trusted faith and steel. Still, they would be called on, just as every other part of the massive force would be called on.

Behind the artillery caravan came the auxiliary companies, archers and irregular troops who'd been drafted in since the march had begun. There was never a shortage of men willing to fight for a schilling, and much as Volkmar loathed mercenaries too, he had the resources to employ them and turned no man away.

The main baggage train followed, wagon after wagon loaded with stores. Barrels of ale were piled high on open carts, mixed up with cloth-covered food wains. Armour, cloaks, bundles of arrows, heaps of firewood and fodder for the horses were all stacked closely and guarded watchfully by Roll's own men, as incorruptible as zealots. Dozens of his soldiers, clad in the scarlet colours of Altdorf's Church of Sigmar Risen and Transformed, swarmed around the pay wains, the all-important guardians of the cases of coin that kept the soldiers loyal.

Finally, bringing up the rear, were three companies of greatswords and a unit of pistolier outriders, their steeds stepping impatiently. Every so often a squadron of six of them would kick into action and ride up the flanks of the huge army, peeling off into the terrain on either side of the road to scout ahead before returning to the long slog, their need for adventure satisfied for the moment.

Over thirty thousand regular troops, with maybe five thousand more dogs of war who'd joined on the march from Pohlbad. More would come at the rendezvous south of Nuln. A whole regiment of warrior priests to augment those he already had, plus more artillery and heavy cavalry. It was a formidable force, scarcely less powerful than the massive armies that marched across the north of the Empire against the scattered warbands of Archaon's invasion. If the predictions of the Celestial magisters proved reliable, it would need to be.

'You look displeased,' said Roll, his bald head gleaming in the cold light. The tone was one of mild remonstration. No other man in the Empire would have dared to speak thus to the Theogonist.

'What use are mortal men here?' Volkmar muttered. 'When have they ever been able to stand firm against the great enemy? We're leading them to their deaths.'

Roll spat on the ground.

'It's as you said. They'll do their duty. The enemy will have mortals too.'

Volkmar said nothing. He remembered the ranks of men marching into ruin in the Troll Country with him at their head. As the daemons had screamed across the sky and the rivers run with blood, mortal faith had done little to stem the tide of insanity and pain. Above all, he remembered Be'lakor, grinning from ear to ear, the daemon's eyes little more than windows on to a world of utter, terrifying horror.

'This will all come down to us, Roll,' he said.

'Don't forget Helborg.'

'Helborg? Even if he lives, what can he do?'

'And Schwarzhelm.'

He looked south. The dark leagues of endless forests were behind them, and the country was now beginning to open up. Far in the distance lay the wide ribbon of the Aver, winding through the grassland ahead.

'Schwarzhelm has done enough. If he attempts to interfere again before this thing is ended, I have the authority to prevent him.'

He turned to Roll, and his gaze was bleak.

'I have *all* authority in this. The Emperor's Champion has served faithfully for a generation of men, but weakness is weakness. I will judge the matter when he's found.'

Roll raised an eyebrow, but said nothing. Volkmar paused for a few more moments on the ridge, before kicking his horse onwards, back down to join the vanguard of the immense host. His guard did likewise, and soon the high place was bare once more, home to nothing more than the sigh of the wind and the rustle of grass.

THE TOWER WAS nearly complete, and the last veils over the charade were close to being lifted. Smaller versions of the Tower were being built at six points on the city walls, each also made of iron and given the same spiked profile as the master construction. The vista across Averheim had been marred irrevocably. Ancient halls had been demolished, the stone carted off to bolster the new fortifications springing up across the old walls. Merchants' townhouses had been commandeered for garrisons, while the Averburg was now nothing more than a vast store of arms. Soldiers were everywhere, thronging the streets, clustering in the squares, camped out to the north of the city on the flat plains running towards Stirland.

Above it all, the Grosslich banner hung proud. The six-pronged crown of the Tower had been completed at last, and long pennants with the crimson boar's head draped down towards the massive courtyard, three hundred feet below. Red and gold were ubiquitous, drowning out the memory of any other allegiance the city may once have had. Alptraums and Leitdorfs were forgotten. Now only the new dispensation had any meaning.

As night fell, the new aspect of the city showed itself to most effect. The Tower was lit along its entire height by a series of lilac beads, each glowing like stars. At the summit a pale flame burned incessantly. Lanterns in the streets below shone with a range of intense shades, banishing shadows from the night and bathing the city in a mingled fog of colour. Those citizens not steeped in joyroot found their sleep interrupted and fractious. A certain faded elegance had been replaced by rampant excess.

Those few clear-sighted citizens who remained now knew beyond all doubt that Grosslich was a tyrant, and one whose perversion of the Imperial Law had only just started. Insurrections were ruthlessly put down, and the hated witch hunters of Odo Heidegger kept the furnaces burning. Any faint flicker of revolt was overwhelmed by the vast numbers of troops arriving every day from every corner of the wastelands south of the Grey Mountains, drawn by the promise of money and glory. Some were paid in joyroot, and that seemed to satisfy them. Just as it had been in the spring, the roads were lined with drooling, vacant-eyed figures, slumped against the stone and lost in dreaming.

All of them, deep in their reverie, whispered the same thing.

*She is coming. She is coming. Blessed be her path, everlasting be her reign. Queen of pleasure, mistress of the world. She is coming. She is coming.*

Endlessly they mumbled the mantra until their lips were calloused and cracked, and they crawled off to find more root to numb the pain. Whatever debaucheries Averheim had known before, it suffered a hundredfold more then, stepping down a path of ruin as surely as if guided by the Lord of Pain himself.

Elector Grosslich now rarely ventured from the pinnacle of his precious Tower. The topmost chamber had been fitted out in silks and upholstered with fine soft leather. The floor was polished marble, veined like a flayed muscle, shining in the light of a dozen suspended orbs. There were six windows in the iron walls, each overlooking one of the massive suspended spikes.

The view was commanding. Grosslich's armies, so long in the mustering, were now mobilising. The numbers astounded even him. Where there was corruption and power, humans seemed to drawn to it like insects around a candle flame.

Grosslich himself was swathed in crimson robes, beautifully lined with fur and monogrammed with the flowing 'G' motif. A tall crown had been forged for him in the hidden pits of the Tower below, a swirling sculpture in steel which tapered to a point above his forehead and sent tendrils of slender metal curling down across his cheeks. Natassja had designed it herself, but he'd made it his own.

The city was his too, locked in an iron grip of control. More dog-soldiers were being spawned in the basements, all answering to his command. There were other creatures down there too, terrible products of Natassja's imagination, taking shape under her pitiless tutelage. Soon the whole host would be ready, a legion of terror ready to sweep across the river and destroy the army he knew had been sent from Altdorf to rein him in.

A chime sounded from outside the chamber. Grosslich turned from the windows and sat down on his throne, an obsidian block composed of tortured limbs, just like the one Natassja had used to dupe Verstohlen.

'Come,' he said, and marvelled at how his voice had changed. Gone were the gruff, plain tones that had drawn peasants flocking to his banner in the early days. Now his speech was clipped and refined, almost as smooth as Natassja's own. The Dark Prince had changed him in many ways, not all of them to Grosslich's liking. Still, it was too late for regrets.

A glass door at the far end of the chamber swung open silently and Holymon Eschenbach entered. The man had continued to change. His eyes were now entirely white-less and glowed a subtle pink. His flesh was bleached and his lips stained the colour of old wine. Like Achendorfer, he walked with a pronounced limp, as if some terrible rearrangement had taken place beneath his robes of swirling colour. The old smugness had gone, wiped from his features by Grosslich's merciless drive to bring the city under his control. Eschenbach had assumed all the duties of Stewardship in the wake of Tochfel's unfortunate demise, and the burden had proved heavy.

'You asked to see me, your Excellency?' he whispered. He could barely speak above a sibilant hiss these days, another result of the improvements made to his otherwise unremarkable body.

'Steward, perhaps you could tell me the names of the fugitives we have been so assiduously pursuing since our ascension to the electorship.'

Eschenbach looked nervous. He knew what was coming.

'The traitors Leitdorf and Helborg, as well as the spy Verstohlen.'

'Well done. And can you inform me how close we are to tracking them down?'

'Your armies are spreading further east with every day. Courts of enquiry have opened in Heideck, and Grenzstadt will not be far behind. It cannot be–'

Grosslich extended a hand lazily and clenched his fist. Eschenbach gasped and fell to his knees. As he did so, his neck seemed to constrict, veins bulging on his temples. He choked, falling forwards, scrabbling to release the pressure.

'You think I don't *know* this?' Grosslich hissed, watching with only mild pleasure as the fat Steward writhed in agony. 'You have the entire resources of a province at your disposal. Your orders are simple. Find them and kill them.'

Grosslich released the vice around Eschenbach's neck, and the man fell forwards, panting like a dog.

'All Leitdorf's houses have been stormed,' the Steward gasped. 'His estates have been plundered. I have men scouring the countryside. What more could I do?'

'Listen carefully,' snarled Grosslich, leaning forwards in his throne. 'Things are approaching a delicate stage. The mistress's plans are nearing fruition, and the Empire is beginning to wake up. An army will be here within days. It is imperative that this matter is concluded before then.'

Eschenbach nodded miserably.

'There's another aspect to this,' continued Grosslich, choosing his words carefully. 'The mistress has dispatched creatures of her own to dispose of Helborg. It would be... *preferable* for my own troops to find the Marshal first. As for the Leitdorf pup, I want to bring him in myself. This is very important to me. I'm not convinced you're giving your work the attention it deserves.'

Eschenbach began to panic. He'd been on the end of too many punishments from Grosslich already.

'I am, your Excellency! A thousand men have been sent east this very day. They have orders to bring in Helborg and the pretender. There have been reports of supply columns being raided in the far south, towards the moors. If he's there, he'll be uncovered.'

'Double the numbers,' he ordered. 'They have licence to burn the countryside to a husk if they have to. Spare no expense, and give them no respite. Helborg must be found.'

Eschenbach nodded. His eyes gave away his misery. Raising that many troops would be difficult, especially given the numbers he'd been instructed to make ready for the defence of Averheim.

'And the ceremony?'

'No delays. It goes ahead as planned. There's no point in further secrecy, whatever the mistress says.'

He narrowed his eyes, thinking of the power on the cusp of grasping. His army was nearly ready, the one that would deliver the dominion he craved.

'Ensure the root supply remains high, and give your

orders to the priests,' he said. 'The mask will be removed. It is time to show the people what they've taken on by serving me.'

## Chapter Eleven

DAWN HAD BROKEN. The moors were still shrouded in a
fine mist. Scraps of cloud hurried westwards above the
drifting pall, driven by the relentless winds from the
mountains. The weather was converging on Averheim,
as if the world's winds were being sucked into a vortex
above the distant city. Out on the high fells, though,
the air was crisp and damp, as cold and clear as a crystal goblet in the Imperial Palace.

Eissen came to a halt. He'd been riding through the
night to return to the Drakenmoor, carrying with him
welcome tidings for the Marshal. Before Eissen had
left, Skarr had captured three supply trains and roused
half a dozen villages to the cause. His men under arms
now numbered more than a hundred, and more
joined them daily. Part of this was due to the plentiful
supply of gold and weapons they'd obtained since the
capture of the caravans, but there was also no love for
Grosslich in this part of the world and recruits were
ready converts.

Most of the Reiksguard had remained with Skarr to
press home the assault and spread dissent in the lands
running towards Heideck. A couple of others had

been assigned to the caravans to guard their passage to
Drakenmoor. Eissen had gone on ahead to deliver his
report to Helborg. He'd covered many leagues in the
night, riding his steed hard.

Now he gave it some respite, dismounting and letting it walk through the gorse and heather. The animal
went warily, treading in between the glistening clumps
of dew-bedecked grass, clouds of steam snorting from
its nostrils. Eissen led it through the meandering
moorland paths carefully, keeping one hand on the
reins and the other on his sword. In every direction,
the mist curled up about him, grey and thin like gruel.
Lone trees, blasted and curled over by the wind, came
and went before the gauze-like clouds swallowed
them up again. Only the ground beneath his feet was
solid, and everything else was as shifting and fickle as
a woman's promise.

'Easy, girl,' Eissen whispered, noticing his steed's
shivering flanks. She needed to be rubbed down and
given a bucket of hot oats. Still, Drakenmoor wasn't
far. He'd wait for the mist to lift, get his bearings, and
be there before the end of the day.

Then the horse stiffened, tugging back on the reins
and stamping. Its eyes began to roll.

'Mist got you spooked?' asked Eissen, looking
around. There was no sound except for the faint rustle
of the gorse. 'Better get over it.'

The Reiksguard shook his head and smiled to himself.

'Talking to my horse? Time to get–'

He froze. There was something out there. Eissen felt
the hairs on the back of his neck stand up stiff. The
chill was still acute and he shivered under his leather
jerkin.

Ahead of him, the curtain of grey sighed past, driven by the breeze, as cloudy and opaque as milk. Still no sound.

Eissen drew his sword. The steel was dull in the diffuse light. After a night's riding his muscles felt sluggish and stiff.

'Declare yourself!' he cried. His voice was sucked into the fog like water draining from a sink. There was no reply.

Eissen's horse was beginning to panic. It tried to rear away, only held firm by Eissen's tight grip. A line of foam appeared at its mouth.

Eissen pulled it savagely back into line, keeping his blade raised defensively. Despite all his training and experience, his heart was hammering like a maiden's on her wedding night. He felt a line of sweat run down his chest, cold against his flesh. He backed towards his horse, head craning to see anything among the shifting sea of occlusion.

'Helborg.'

The voice was unearthly, a bizarre mix of a young woman's and a boy's, scraped over metal and given the sibilant whisper of a snake. As soon as he heard it, Eissen's resolve was shaken. He gripped his sword, keeping hold of his tugging steed with difficulty.

'Show yourself, ghoul,' he commanded, but his voice sounded reedy and foolish.

Ahead of him, three figures slowly emerged from the clouds. They were hunched like old women, draped in rags, limping uncertainly across the uneven ground. At twenty paces away they were wreathed in a shifting cloak of translucence, as muffled and indistinct as shades. Only their eyes were solid, six points of lilac brilliance, emerging from the obscurity like stars.

Eissen felt the dread grow stronger. His steed reared, snatching the reins from his fingers. He turned quickly, grabbing at the leather straps, but he was too late. It turned and broke into a gallop, bounding back into the gloom and disappearing from view. He was alone. Heart thudding, he turned to face the newcomers.

'*Helborg,*' they hissed again in perfect unison. The words were taut with malice.

Eissen grabbed the hilt of his sword with both hands. He'd faced the undead before – where was his courage?

'He's not here,' he replied, trying to keep his voice level. 'Who sent you?'

The creatures seemed not to hear, and advanced slowly. One of them extended a hand from under its rags. Eissen stared in horror as the long talons extended. Another reached out, exposing ravaged flesh, white as ice, studded with metal and knots of protruding bone.

'Sigmar preserves!' he roared, trying to summon up some kind of resolve. As the nearest horror drew close, he charged at it, swinging his sword round to decapitate.

Something like laughter burst out. The creature snapped up its talon to block the strike and steel clanged against bone. The horror's movements were staggeringly fast, more like those of an insect than a human. Eissen sprang back, moving his blade warily, watching for the attack.

'*Helborg!*' they hissed, driven into some kind of ecstasy. The lilac glow became piercing, and they lost their stooped hunches. The one in the centre pounced, leaping into the air and spreading its claws wide.

Eissen withdrew, swinging his sword up to block the swipe. Again the metal clanged, and he felt the force of the blow shiver down his arm.

Another sprang at him, screaming with glee. Eissen spun round to deflect, only to feel the burn of a raking claw plunge into his back. He cried aloud, ripping the talons from the wound as he turned, seeing his own blood fly into the faces of the horrors. Another pounced, and something stabbed into his stomach, slicing into the flesh as smoothly as a stick into water.

Eissen lurched back, trying to shake them off him, slashing at their brass-bound hides with his sword. They ignored his blows and dragged him down, tearing at his flesh, pulling the muscles from the bones, cackling with a childish delight.

Eissen lost his sword when he lost his fingers, cleaved from his forearm with a single jab from a barbed set of claws. He heard screaming, lost in the fog, before realising it was his own. Then he was on his knees, and the creatures really got to work. They didn't go for the kill, but for the dissection, taking off chunk after chunk of flesh until what was left of Eissen finally collapsed in a gore-bedraggled mess, bereft of eyes, hoarse from screaming, lost in a world of pain, beyond wishing for death and sucked into a slough of horror.

The final blow was reluctant, a grudging stab to silence his jaw-less mewls of agony, regretfully delivered by the lead ghoul. As before, they stood in silence for a while, admiring what they'd done. One of them raised a taloned hand to its ruined face and licked at the blood-soaked bone with a black tongue. Its eyes glowed brightest then, perhaps blazing in remembrance of what it was like to be hot-blooded and encased in mortal flesh.

When they'd finished they hunched over once more and the light in their eyes faded. In the far distance, a frenzied whinnying could still be heard, growing fainter with every second.

Then, one by one, they turned south, trudging after their real prey again, insatiable until the one whose name they carried was found. If they were capable of feeling any emotion other than malice, they didn't show it. Perhaps, though, there was a faintest trace of excitement in their movements. The journey had been long, but they knew they were getting close. They shuffled into the fog, rags trailing behind them, whispering the name, the one name they still knew how to say.

When they were gone, the moor returned to silence. The mist curled around the long grasses, pale and ephemeral. Down in the mud, the sweet smell of death, mingled with the faint aroma of jasmine, stained the chill air, and the blood sank slowly into the soil.

SCHWARZHELM LOOKED UP. The moors were high on the southern horizon, still laced with scraps of mist. In the far distance he thought he could hear some strange bird's cry, repeated over and over until it faded away. He listened for a repeat, but none came.

The sky remained grey and the light of the sun was weak. The cold didn't bother him much, but he pulled his cloak tighter across his huge shoulders in any case. As surely as he knew his own name, he knew the Sword of Vengeance had guided him well. Somewhere up on those bleak, wind-tousled moors lay Helborg.

The spirit of the blade longed to return to its master.

As the day of their meeting drew ever closer, Schwarzhelm found his iron will begin to waver. His dreams were still haunted by the old warrior's face.

*Why are you doing this, Ludwig?*

He looked away from the brooding highlands. He'd made up his mind. Justice demanded the return of the sword. Schwarzhelm's entire existence depended on honour, on keeping his word, on being the very embodiment of the law. Without that, he was nothing, just a killer in the service of the Emperor. He didn't know whether he'd ever raise the Imperial standard again on the field of battle, but he was certain that if he didn't carry through this duty then he'd never regain the right to. Redemption was never handed over; it was always earned.

He stamped back up to the tree line he'd come down from, slinging the brace of hares over his shoulder. The forest had sheltered them for the night and had yielded a rich bounty. It was a good thing he knew how to hunt and trap. If he'd been relying on Verstohlen, all they'd have eaten would have been air and fine words.

Once back under the cover of the trees, he found the spy trying to light a fire with trembling fingers. He looked cold, and crouched low over the pile of damp wood, his coat flapping over his slim form as he moved. Verstohlen was as clumsy out in the wilds as he was accomplished in the city. Schwarzhelm almost felt like smiling.

'So you've decoded the letters,' he said, flinging the carcasses on the ground and reaching for his flint.

Verstohlen sat back from his abortive fire, giving up in disgust.

'Indeed. They made for interesting reading.'

Schwarzhelm ignored Verstohlen's tumbled pile of branches and began building a fresh fire from the dry scrub he'd collected at the edge of the forest.

'Tell me.'

Verstohlen pulled a sheaf of notes from his coat pocket, covered in messy scribblings from the charcoal. He'd been busy in the rare moments Schwarzhelm had halted the march and allowed him to decipher.

'They were mostly replies to messages sent by Lassus,' Verstohlen said. 'I don't know who wrote them. The final one is from Lassus himself. It's unfinished, no doubt because you interrupted him before he could send it.'

Schwarzhelm watched as his kindling took. Gradually, shakily, washed-out flames began to flicker. He fed the nascent blaze with more twigs, trying not to let his feelings about Lassus impair his attention to Verstohlen's findings.

'The conspiracy didn't start with him,' said Verstohlen. 'The power behind it was a woman. There's no name here, but I'd stake my life it's Natassja.'

'So you've always maintained.'

'Whether or not she intended me to see her engaged in those rites, I could not have been mistaken about the fact of her sorcery. From this, it's clear she approached Lassus three years ago, soon after the death of Marius Leitdorf. At that point she wasn't Rufus's wife – they married eighteen months later. The two of them, Lassus and she, evidently found much of mutual interest to discuss.'

The fire grew. Schwarzhelm began to prepare the carcasses, ripping at the skin with expert fingers.

'Lassus had been passed over for promotion,' said Verstohlen. 'He felt wounded by the Imperial establishment. He was also old. He hid it from you, I suspect, but he was a bitter man, bereft of an honourable position in the hierarchy and banished to a retirement in a part of Altdorf he hated.'

Schwarzhelm remembered the old man's words at their first meeting in Altdorf. *There are more ways than one to make a success of one's life. Maybe when you're as old as I am, you'll see that. My battles are over. I've been granted the grace to retire from the field and see out the rest of my days in peace.* At the time, the words had seemed like such calm, resigned wisdom. All of it had been lies, then, just another layer of deception.

'Natassja's powers were strong. She's a beautiful woman, and he was a frustrated failure. I've no idea how she corrupted him, but I'm certain she did so. From then on, he was her tool, using his money and influence in support of her and Grosslich's ends. The letters make it clear that Lassus arranged the weakening of the defences at Black Fire Keep. Gold was found to induce the orcs to invade, and weapons too. It was all timed with impressive precision. By the time he'd seen to it that you would be sent to handle the succession, the passes were already under attack.'

'The greenskins had Imperial weapons.'

'A novelty for them, no doubt. Though I can't imagine what they did with the gold.'

Schwarzhelm tore the skin from the hare carcasses roughly. As he remembered the fighting on the plains of Averland, the memory of Grunwald came unbidden to his mind.

'What did he hope to achieve?'

'He would have joined Natassja and Grosslich in

Averheim. The Ruinous Powers offer the foolish an extension of their natural span, and he expected to live for another hundred years. You should reflect on that, my lord. Had you not killed him, the powers in Altdorf would only now be learning of their danger, and Lassus would be safely hidden and growing in strength again.'

Schwarzhelm grunted. Such attempts to placate his sense of guilt were unwelcome.

'And after that?'

'I can't tell what their plans were beyond the coronation of Grosslich, but they weren't stupid. They knew the deception would only last for so long. They needed time to do something else, something involving Averheim. By deflecting accusations of treachery towards Rufus they let the world believe that corruption in Averland had been defeated, and that has given them the space they needed.'

Schwarzhelm let the tidings sink in, dissecting each morsel of information, weighing it up against what he already knew. The process was painful. He himself had been the tool by which Natassja and Grosslich had corrupted the province, and the knowledge weighed heavily on him.

'So Rufus Leitdorf was an innocent in this.'

'He was. A dupe. I was to blame, my lord. When I witnessed his wife, I assumed he was implicated. Grosslich and she played their parts well.'

'That they did.'

Schwarzhelm finished skinning and dressing the hares, and skewered them roughly. The fire was now burning fiercely, and at last the warmth began to cut through the chill of the early morning.

'Anything else?' he asked.

'Not that I can decipher. There's some link with the Leitdorfs that I don't yet understand, and I have no idea why Averheim is so important to them. If you truly want to fight this, then we should go back there.'

'We will,' muttered Schwarzhelm. 'I've thought of little else, besides finding Kurt.'

Verstohlen paused. 'And you're still sure you want to do that? You don't have to. He may be dead, or he may be–'

'He's alive, and he's close,' snapped Schwarzhelm, shoving the skinned hare into the fire. 'Don't try to dissuade me. I know some things about this that you cannot. I had the dreams, sent to me by that witch. They didn't expect Helborg. He's the element in this they couldn't control. That's why Grosslich was so keen to kill him, and that's why we have to find him first. Kurt Helborg with the Sword of Vengeance will be a foe they cannot ignore.'

Verstohlen looked at Schwarzhelm for a long time then, pondering his words.

'He's not a forgiving man.'

Schwarzhelm nodded, watching the flesh of the hares crisp and char in the flames.

'Of course,' he said, and his voice was low and steady. 'So it's always been with him.'

He turned the meat in the fire, roasting it gently.

'Not long now, Pieter,' he said. 'He's nearby. The sword and its master cannot be kept apart.'

LEITDORF TOOK A deep breath before emerging on to the balcony. He could hear the expectant mutter of the crowd outside, and they were getting impatient.

'How many are there?' he whispered to Helmut

Gram, the seasoned Reiksguard who'd been assigned to him as bodyguard.

'Five hundred,' replied the knight, showing no trace of emotion. 'Not many. Better than nothing.'

Leitdorf swallowed. Addressing armed men had always been something he'd dreaded. Not much of a soldier himself, he'd never been able to look them in the eye. He'd made up for his natural reticence with a kind of studied arrogance, but he knew it had fooled few of them. When he remembered his churlish behaviour with Schwarzhelm back in Averheim, he shuddered.

'Should I take the sword?'

Gram's eyebrow rose in surprise. 'The Wolfsklinge? Of course. It is a holy blade.'

All this fuss about swords. That was the one thing that seemed to unite the fighting men of the Empire, a universal reverence for their antique blades. His father's weapon was hardly as prestigious as the rune-fangs or the Sword of Justice, but it had a long and proud history nonetheless. Like all such blades, there were runes hammered into the steel, augmenting the belligerence of the wielder and guiding the edge to its target. He'd never felt comfortable in its presence, and it hung heavily from his sword-belt.

'Yes, of course,' he mumbled, and stepped closer to the balcony. Outside, clustered in the courtyard of the Drakenmoor castle, were the recruits the Reiksguard had worked so hard to draw together. There were hundreds more, he'd been told, flocking south to be armed and trained to fight for him. As a result of all that activity, Grosslich must surely have discovered where they were by now. The only option left was to take the battle to him.

'They're waiting, my lord.'

Leitdorf swallowed, then pushed aside the doors leading to the balcony and stepped outside.

Below him, rammed tight into the enclosed space, the core of his new army stared up expectantly. Most were well armed, the product of his own armouries as well as Skarr's raids on the supply caravans. Here and there he could see men wearing the blue and burgundy of the Leitdorf house, as well as the black and yellow livery of Averland. Such men were to be the captains and sergeants of the greater host to come, the leaders of the peasants and farm-hands who'd flesh out the ranks. Many of them looked experienced and capable. Others looked worryingly callow.

'Men of Averland!' Leitdorf cried. His voice sounded thin, snatched away by the breeze, and he worked to lower it. 'You all know why you've been summoned here. The traitor Grosslich has seized this province and plans to deliver it to the great enemy. This muster marks the very beginning of our struggle. We will fight our way north of here, gathering men as we go, raising the countryside against those who dare to take it from us. I will lead you, Rufus Leitdorf, son of electors and master of this realm!'

There was a sporadic burst of applause, and a few men broke into a cheer. It wasn't convincing. With a sick feeling in his stomach, Leitdorf realised he was losing them. They all knew his reputation. He tried to remember what he'd planned to say, but the words slipped from his grasp.

'So I say, do not fear! The five hundred of you here today will be a thousand by dawn tomorrow. As we march, more will flock to our standard. By the time we reach Averheim, the hills will tremble at our coming.'

The murmurs of approval began to die out.

'I have fought Grosslich before!' shouted Leitdorf, trying to work up some enthusiasm. 'He is nothing but a peasant, a low-born master of horse manure! I, on the other hand, am a noble-born leader of men and hence blessed by Sigmar. March with me, and I will return Averland to the rule of those fitted for it!'

That didn't go down well. Most of the troops were low-born, even those given command roles. Grosslich's popularity had always stemmed from his mastery of the common touch. Leitdorf realised his error too late, and began to lose his thread. The crowd had fallen silent.

Then the doors behind him slammed open. Leitdorf turned to see Helborg striding to stand beside him, though for a moment he hardly recognised the man.

The Marshal was wearing the heavy plate of the Reiksguard once more, cleaned and restored by his knights and shining like polished ithilmar. He'd donned his hawk-winged helmet, and the sun glinted from the steel pins holding the feathers in place. A heavy cloak hung from his shoulders, draped across massive pauldrons. Helborg's visor was lifted, his craggy face exposed. The moustache had been trimmed, waxed and moulded back to its former glory, the envy of men and fascination of women. His skin was no longer grey, but full of a tight, uncompromising vigour. His blue eyes, two points of sapphire set deep in that lean, handsome face, fixed the crowd below with an unwavering gaze. Beside his imposing frame, Leitdorf suddenly felt meagre and superfluous.

Helborg placed his gauntlets on the balcony railing with a heavy clang. The murmuring of the crowd picked up again. All of them knew who he was, though most had only dreamt of seeing him in the flesh. Men shuffled closer, eager to catch a glimpse of the legend.

'Men of the Empire!' roared Helborg, his voice echoing in the narrow courtyard and resounding from the high walls of the Drakenmoor castle. Leitdorf's entreaties were instantly forgotten. Helborg's voice was grinding, rumbling, stone-hard, tempered by years of command on the battlefield and infused with the expectation of obeisance. When the Reiksmarshal spoke, all other voices were stilled.

'You have heard the words of your elector. Listen to them! He is the rightful heir of the realm of Siggurd and the true bearer of the runefang. Averheim is in the hands of a traitor, one who has sold his soul to the great enemy and even now plots to deliver this proud province into ruin.'

His voice softened, but his glare remained fierce. As his eyes swept the crowd, each man felt his soul being examined, tested on the anvil of Helborg's unyielding conviction.

'Perhaps some of you supported Grosslich in the early days. Maybe you thought a man of the people would right the wrongs of the past and give you a life of comfort and justice.'

Helborg's gauntlet balled into a fist and slammed the railing. Fragments of stone showered on to the crowd below.

'Lies!' he bellowed, spittle flying from his mouth. 'The man is a creeping worm, the most contemptible of animals, the progeny of traitors and the scion of whores. The least of you is worth a hundred such crawling beasts, for they have forgotten themselves and become less than the insects of the dung heap. For as long as he remembers the law and the word of Sigmar, the lowliest serf towers over such degenerate scum.'

His eyes narrowed, and he pulled himself to his full height. Sunlight glinted from his helm, and his cloak lifted in the wind.

'Maybe you joined this army for gold, or for glory, or out of some long-earned pledge of allegiance. If so, then you may as well return to your homes now and live the rest of your life cowering in fear. Gold you will have, and glory there will be, but it is for *honour* that we are mustered here today. Your realm has been stolen from you, your heritage debased and your future ransomed to the fickle will of the Dark Gods. Have you no shame for that, men of Averland? Have you no *anger*?'

The crowd started to murmur again. Helborg's words held them rapt.

'*This* is why we march!' he roared, sweeping out his sword and holding it aloft. 'To take back our birthright. To hold our heads high and resist the usurper, the heretic and the traitor. I will lead you in this, men of Siggurd. I, who have commanded armies that made the very earth tremble, whose holy blade has run dark with the blood of the Emperor's enemies. I, Grand Marshal of the Reiksguard, Hammer of Chaos, Kreigsmeister, the hand of vengeance!'

His voice rose in fervour. Men below were shouting in acclamation now, fists clenched, roused to a pitch of emotion. They would do anything for him. Leitdorf watched in awe as Helborg moulded them to his will. So *this* was why he inspired such devotion.

'Go back to your villages!' he roared, sweeping his

sword down and pointing the tip at each man in turn. 'Bring your men to me and I will make them killers. With me at your head, no army shall dare oppose our will. We will not relent until we have cleansed the city of the filth that squats in it. They sowed the seeds of this war through treachery, but we will repay them twenty times over in their own blood. March with me, men of Averland, and I will deliver you! For the Empire! For your elector! For the holy blood of Sigmar!'

As one, the men below rose up, shaking their fists and repeating the cry. They were seething, ready to sell their lives for the cause. The army had been born.

As *For the Empire!* rang out across the courtyard, Helborg swept his imperious gaze back to Leitdorf.

'How do you *do* that?' asked Rufus, still watching the frenzied crowd below.

'Learn from it,' snapped Helborg. 'And learn it fast.'

As he pulled back from the balcony, Helborg winced. His wounds had not entirely healed.

'I'll not wait here any longer,' he rasped. 'The time has come to lead these men. War calls, Herr Leitdorf, and I will answer.'

THE MAYOR OF Grenzstadt was no fool. Unlike in Heideck, the proximity of the eastern town to the Worlds Edge Mountains had bred a certain toughness in the place. Klaus Meuningen was a lean, angular man, grey-haired and clean-shaven with a warrior's bearing. In his youth he'd commanded a regiment of mountain guard, and knew the ways of a soldier. When Schwarzhelm's commander had passed through the town on the route to Black Fire Pass, he'd spared every man from his garrison that he could. The news that none of them would be coming back was an unwelcome reward for his generosity.

'And what I am supposed to do about the defence of Grenzstadt?' he asked, placing his pitcher of beer heavily on the table in front of him.

He sat behind the desk in his chambers facing Bloch once again. The commander looked like he'd taken a few more knocks in the mountains. He'd lost weight, and his stocky frame was beginning to look ravaged. The man's aide, Kraus, was at his side, still in his plate armour and looking as grim-faced as he had before.

Bloch shrugged.

'Why do you need a garrison here, mayor?' He seemed impatient, as if some pressing need was nagging away at him. 'The passes are secure. We've done what we came to do.'

Meuningen sighed. Many things had been preying on his mind recently, and this was unwelcome in the extreme.

'Matters have moved on since you left for the passes,' he said. 'News has come of the new elector in Averheim, Count Heinz-Mark Grosslich. The issue has been decided.'

'You must welcome that,' Bloch said. 'Schwarzhelm has given his verdict. That's what he came for.'

Meuningen shrugged.

'Schwarzhelm? I'm told he's left the province. We're alone again here, ignored by the rest of the Empire, just as before.'

Bloch frowned. Despite his blunt manners and street-brawler appearance, the man was as astute as his master.

'There's something you're not telling me.'

'Of course.'

Meuningen reached for the roll of parchment lying on the desk and took it up. His eyes scanned the message for the fourth time.

'This arrived yesterday by courier from the Averburg. It's signed by Grosslich himself. By revealing the contents to you I'm breaking the first order my new liege-lord has given me. Perhaps now you understand why I'm feeling rather exposed without my garrison here.'

'Just tell me what's in it.'

'The elector knows of your presence at Black Fire Pass, and knew you'd come back here. He's ordered me to detain you in Grenzstadt until his men arrive in force. He says he wishes to convey you back to Averheim with a guard of honour. As it happens, I'm forbidden to reveal these instructions to you. Make of that what you will.'

Bloch was unmoved. He looked as if some suspicion he'd been cradling had been confirmed.

'Detained, eh?' he said, and a wry smile creased his weather-worn features. 'Some reward for what we've done. I don't take orders from him, mayor. Until I receive notice from Schwarzhelm, I'll go where I please and when I please. We've earned that right in blood.'

Bloch spat the last few words out forcefully. Meuningen could appreciate the sentiment. He'd lost men under command too.

'I agree entirely, commander,' he said. 'If I didn't, do you think I'd be telling you this?'

He took another swig of beer. As he did so, he noticed the trembling in his hands. He was getting too old for these kind of risks.

'I've seen many years of service in Averland,' he

continued, wiping his mouth. 'A man learns a few things about the arts of state as he ages. Grosslich will want to install his own man here sooner or later. He's sending a battalion of troops already, and I'm not stupid enough to think they'll take orders from me.

He leaned forwards, hoping Bloch would be wise enough to see the danger.

'We owe you a debt of thanks in Grenzstadt. Take this advice as repayment. Grosslich has no love for you, and nor does he wish to have an army in his province that he doesn't control. You should leave. Now. Find your Schwarzhelm if you can, or get out. There's only room for one victor in Averland.'

Bloch sat back in his chair, pondering the tidings. He didn't look massively surprised by them, though the news that Schwarzhelm was missing clearly bothered him.

'What'll you do when we're gone?' he asked, rubbing his stubbled chin. 'Grosslich won't be slow to send more men.'

Meuningen smiled coldly. 'Make the best of it. What else can we do?'

Bloch turned to Kraus. 'How soon can we leave?'

'We could be on the road at dawn. You'll have trouble pulling the men from the taverns until then. They haven't seen a tankard or a woman for a long time.'

Bloch didn't smile. 'Me neither,' he said ruefully.

'Where will you go?' asked Meuningen.

Bloch sighed, and ran his hands through his cropped hair.

'I said to the men we'd go back to Averheim. We'll have to head west for a while, maybe as far as Heideck. We're small enough to keep out of trouble until then, and I'll have a look at things when we get closer. I'll not run across the fields again like a fugitive. There are two hundred of us, all battle-scarred. If Grosslich wants to bring us in, he'll have to work for it.'

Meuningen nodded.

'Very well. The grace of Sigmar be with you. You deserve it.'

'As do you, mayor,' replied Bloch, looking sincere enough. 'So I hope he has grace enough for the both of us.'

THE VILLAGERS CROWDED round, suspicion heavy in their dull, stupid faces. The settlement of Urblinken was as unremittingly grim as most of the hamlets on the slopes, untouched by the prosperity of the lower Aver valley and left to scratch a living on the unproductive highlands. In that respect, it resembled many of the grimy places of the northern Empire, beds of poverty, incest, disease and superstition.

Perfect recruiting grounds, mused Skarr, sweeping his gaze across the murmuring throng, gathered in what passed for a marketplace. All around him, low, mean buildings crowded. Their wattle and daub walls were streaked with filth and stained from cooking fires. Chickens pecked through the refuse and children splashed through grimy puddles. An ill-repaired wall ran around the perimeter of the houses, crumbling at the summit and with a flimsy iron gate at the opening.

The Reiksguard, all twenty-seven of them, looked like messengers from some mighty deity compared with the mean folk who'd clustered to hear him speak. Their armour flashed in the afternoon sun and the iron cross of their regiment fluttered proudly from their banner. The villagers had no real idea what *Reiksguard* were, but they knew the power and reputation of knights. If Skarr had told them the Emperor himself had sent them, they would have believed him readily enough.

'How many men can you muster?' he asked the headman, a slack-jawed, unshaven brute with a lazy eye and unspeakably foul breath.

'How much're you paying?' asked the man again, fixated on the idea of gold.

'You needn't worry about that,' said Skarr coldly. 'Have you no idea of honour? Your lands have been usurped. You can be part of the campaign to take them back.'

The man looked blank.

'All recruits will be paid,' Skarr added grudgingly. 'They'll be fed too. If they fight well, the Lord Helborg will find ways to reward them.'

At the mention of the Marshal, a ripple of excitement passed through the crowd.

'Helborg!' gasped several of the men.

Skarr never ceased to be amazed by that. Even in the darkest corner of the Empire, the name was spoken with reverence.

'Is it true he can summon fire from the heavens?' blurted a hulking blacksmith. He wore a fearsome beard and his head was shaven. Piercings glinted from his muscled arms. He looked as belligerent as an orc, but at the mention of Helborg's name his expression had taken on a childlike curiosity.

'Is he really twelve foot tall?'

'Can he level the hills?'

Skarr looked at the throng contemptuously. Just by talking to them he felt sullied, dragged down to their bone-headed level.

'Yes, and more,' he said. 'If you march with him,

you'll be able to tell your children's children of it.'

Some of the younger men gained an eager light in their eyes. Getting out of the village always appealed to the young bucks who hadn't yet been crushed by the tedium of rural life. They had aspirations, girls to impress, dreams of riches and adventure to nurture.

Even the headman looked fleetingly interested.

'We've fifty men who can bear arms here. There are more in the valleys to the north.'

Skarr nodded. The forces were coming together. Grosslich hadn't penetrated this far east yet. Until he did, these men were Helborg's.

'Then muster all you can,' he said. 'Every man will need his own boots and must be ready to march at an hour's notice. We'll provide the weapons.'

He let a sliver of threat enter his voice.

'You're under orders now, headman,' he said, holding the fat man's gaze. 'Don't let me down. I'll come through here again in two days. If your men aren't waiting, the vengeance of Helborg will be on your heads.'

The man's eyes widened and a murmur of fear passed through the crowd.

'Don't worry,' said the headman, looking over his shoulder for encouragement. 'We'll be ready.'

Skarr turned away from them, indicating to his men to pass through the crowd and get a closer estimate of numbers. If even half of the villages provided what they said they would then he'd have added over a thousand men to the Marshal's tally. This whole region was ready to march, for gold if for nothing else.

Adro Vorster, his deputy in Eissen's absence, strode up to him.

'Word from Drakenmoor,' he said, clutching a roll of

orders in his hand. 'The Marshal's back on his feet. We're to press on south of Heideck and continue the muster, but the march won't be long now.'

'That order can't come soon enough,' grumbled Skarr, brushing some accumulated grime from the edge of his cloak. 'These people sicken me.'

Vorster smiled in sympathy.

'They're scum, sir,' he agreed. 'But they're our scum.'

'And Sigmar be praised for that,' muttered Skarr, shaking his head.

# Chapter Twelve

NIGHT IN AVERHEIM. Fires burned in the braziers placed across the city. The dull sound of massed chanting resounded along the narrow streets. Broken clouds circled the pinnacle of the Iron Tower, ripping away from it as the arcane energies thrumming along its massive flanks flared and whipped around the six-pronged crown.

The citadel was complete, glinting darkly, a vast spike of curling metal erupting from the very heart of the corrupted city. It dominated the entire valley, thrusting into the tormented air from the great circular courtyard below.

No sane man could possibly have doubted its baleful intent now. Lilac tongues of flame licked at it from pits sunk deep into the heart of the earth. Vast engines had been chanted into life by gangs of shackled supplicants, constructed in secret by scores of mutated workers and branded with smouldering icons of ruin. The machines churned with a deep, pounding murmur, gouts of coal-black smoke rising around them like pillars, billowing up through deep-sunk vents and fouling the air above the ground. Deep vibrations cracked the older buildings of Averheim, shattering walls that had stood since the very foundation of the Empire and jarring the rich merchant townhouses into piles of rubble.

From deep within the dungeons of the Tower, ranks of dog-soldiers emerged. They marched in close formation, wheezing and growling, their humanity now long forgotten behind masks of beaten metal, riveted to their tortured bones and daubed with the blood of their live human prey. They swung crystal-bladed halberds fresh from the underground forges where packs of Stone-slaves toiled without hope of release. The dog-soldiers fanned out from the Tower and into the streets, thousands of them, all once men, now turned into voiceless, inexorable bringers of death.

The populace of Averheim had been addled by joy-root, now billowing in vast columns of lilac smoke from furnaces all across the city. The six lesser towers burned night and day with the narcotic fumes, dousing the houses, garrisons and taverns with the mind-altering cocktail prepared in hulking underground vats. As the twisted warriors marched to their allotted stations, mortal men cheered them wildly, lost in a haze of visions. None slept. None had slept for days. The houses were empty, and the squares were full. Madness had come to Averheim, and the debased populace revelled in it.

At the summit of the Tower, out on the open platform at the very pinnacle of the huge citadel, Grosslich and Natassja stood alone.

Natassja was revealed in all her dark majesty. The wind, whipped up by the latent forces surging beneath Averheim, screamed past her, rippling her black robes and tousling her long raven hair. Her body now glowed a deep, luminous blue, and tattoos as black as night writhed across her exposed skin. Her white-less eyes glittered in the night air and her lips were parted. She gazed on the maelstrom, and the maelstrom gazed back.

'It begins,' she murmured.

Grosslich wore a new suit of armour, blood-red and forged from some unnatural alloy created in Natassja's forges. It shone like an insect's shell, jointed with astonishing precision, encasing his entire body below the neck. In place of a sword he carried a slender wand of bone, carved from skulls and fused into a single channel for his forbidden magicks. He was a sorcerer in his own right now, gifted by the Dark Prince for the damage he'd wrought to the Empire he'd once called his homeland. His expression was eager, though there was a note of uncertainty.

'The lesser towers are lighting,' he said.

One by one, the six smaller spikes of iron protruding from the old city walls burst into sudden flame. Each was a different colour, vivid and searing. As the torches kindled, the florescent hues mingled in the air above the rooftops, turning the deep of the night into a bizarre and perverted copy of the day. Shadows swayed wildly across the city as the illumination switched from one shade to another. All of Averheim was ablaze, drenched in a riot of sorcerous, sickening colour. Only the central Tower, massive and nightshade-black, remained untouched by the luminous blooms. It was waiting, biding its time, holding for the moment.

More mutant soldiers, some bearing bronze studs in their flesh as the handmaidens did, began to file from the gates at the base of the Tower, marching behind the dog-soldiers to take up their places within the city. The ranks of troops emerging from the surgeries and dungeons seemed endless, hundreds upon hundreds of twisted creatures who'd once been men. The mortal inhabitants of Averheim cheered them on, their own senses distorted and insensible to anything but a vague impression of excitement. The madness was now universal, soaked into the walls and stained deep at the roots.

Below it all, the Stone waited. Its spirit was alive, sentient and searching. In its hidden chamber, Achendorfer read the rites endlessly, the blood flowing over his chin and dripping to the polished floor. It remained as black as a corrupted soul. As the chanting continued, it became *more* black, sinking into an utter absence of light impossible to create in the world of untainted matter. As Achendorfer stumbled over his spells, the glossy sheen disappeared, replaced by a purity of darkness he'd never seen before. It deepened, falling away to a shade he could only describe as *oblivion*.

Out on the pinnacle, Natassja sensed it. She sighed, flexing her long, taloned fingers. The aethyric energies surging up the Tower resonated with her body, fuelling the transformations within. She felt subtle harmonics, so long cultivated, shift into alignment.

'Here it comes...' she whispered.

Far above, the clouds broke. High in the sky, the Deathmoon rode, as yellow as a goblin's tooth, full-faced and leering. Morrslieb, bleeding corruption, was abroad. As the final shreds moved away from it, baleful light flooded across blighted Averheim, blending with the fires on the walls and drenching the Aver valley in more layers of diseased virulence.

'*Ah...*' Natassja breathed, feeling the tainted essence of the moon sink over her. The tattoos on her flesh whirled into new shapes, spinning and extending like a nest of snakes.

Below, in the fevered city, the chanting broke out with fresh ardour. The fires on the towers sent plumes high into the sky, tearing up towards the glowing disc, wreathing it in fingers of outstretched witch-lightning.

'Will you say the word?' asked Grosslich, fingering the wand. He looked half-enraptured, half-terrified.

Natassja hardly heard him. She was lost on a higher plane of sensation. Below her, the Stone sang. Above her, the vast ball of warpstone sailed through the heavens. Between them was the Tower, the fulcrum on which everything rested. She could feel massive waves of power run up the spell-infused iron, resonating like the peals of great bronze bells. The earth cried out, though only she could hear its tortured wails. The barriers separating her from the raw essence of Chaos were finger-thin.

Then the moment came, the conjunction of all she'd worked for. After so much suffering, so many years of toil, her vision was realised. The failure with Marius now meant nothing. Lassus's failure meant nothing. She had the tools she needed to complete the great work. The servants now answering her call would be of a different order to any who had come before.

She raised her arms high, and coruscating energy blazed from her palms. The Tower beneath her shuddered, trembling as a vast, uncontainable force suddenly surged along its frame.

'*Now*,' she hissed.

And Averheim exploded.

* * *

VERSTOHLEN AWOKE, COVERED in sweat. It was still the deep of the night. He rolled over, tangled in his cloak. The wind was rippling across the moors, racing through the tussocks of grass. A storm was brewing.

That wasn't what had woken him.

Schwarzhelm was already standing, arms folded, gazing into the north-west. Overhead, the clouds were racing. Morrslieb had risen, just as it had over the Vormeisterplatz. The heavens were in motion.

'I dreamt of...' Verstohlen started, but his words trailed away. The nightmares had come back. Visions of daemons leaping from roof to roof. An endless cycle of screams, flesh pulled from the bones of living men, soldiers with the faces of dogs. Above it all, a tall, slender tower of dark metal, looming across the carnage, covering the world in a shadow of insanity.

'You weren't dreaming.'

Verstohlen clambered to his feet, shivering against the cold. Far in the west, a tongue of flame burned bright on the horizon. It was like a column of blood, impossibly distant, impossibly tall. It stood sentinel over the land, neither flickering nor weakening, a pillar of fire.

'Holy Verena,' Verstohlen breathed, making the sign of the scales on his chest. 'What *is* that?'

'It is Averheim, Pieter,' said Schwarzhelm, voice grim. 'It is what we've done.'

'That's impossible. Averheim must be over a hundred...'

Verstohlen broke off again. As he watched, he knew the truth of it. The city was burning.

The two men remained silent, watching, unable to move or look away. The column remained still, staining the boiling clouds above it crimson. If there had been any doubt in his mind, it was banished now.

The city was damned. With a terrible insight, Verstohlen knew that no force within the province could hope to counter such terrible sorcery. Whether Helborg received the Sword of Vengeance or not made no difference now.

This was a power no mortal could hope to contest, and it had entered the world of the living.

THE WIZARD SCREAMED. Drool flew from his lips, splattering against the dirt of the camp floor. His fine sky-blue robes ripped as he rolled across the ground in his agony, eyes staring, nostrils flared. Blood ran down from his ears in thin trails and his fingers clutched at the air impotently.

'What is this?' roared Volkmar, lurching to his feet. He'd sensed something too, but Magister Alonysius von Hettram, Celestial Wizard and the Master of the Seers, evidently felt it more keenly.

'*She is coming!*' he shrieked, scrabbling at his eyes feverishly. '*She is coming!*'

Efraim Roll strode forwards, lifting the man from the ground and shaking him like a doll. The other members of Volkmar's command retinue, clustered in his tent overlooking the encampment, hung back in horror. Hettram was now vomiting, his limbs shaking uncontrollably.

'*She... is... coming!*' he blurted between heaves.

'Enough of this,' snapped Volkmar, moving to the tent entrance. He pushed the canvas to one side and strode out into the night.

Below him, the lights of the camp glowed in the darkness. Men slept in their rank order, curled in cloaks and watched over by teams of sentries. Far to the south, a storm had been brewing for days. Now it had broken.

'Sigmar's blood,' murmured Roll, coming to stand beside him.

Many miles away, a column of fire, slim as a plumbline, disfigured the southern horizon. The swirling clouds above it were as red and angry as an open wound.

'How far is-?'

'Averheim,' said Volkmar. He felt a cold fist clench around his heart. It was the Troll Country all over again. Chaos ascendant.

'Are you sure?'

'What else could it be?'

Above the vision of flame, the malignant orb of Morrslieb peered through the tattered streams of cloud. The line of fire rushed to meet it, streaming into the high airs and tainting the very arch of the sky. The pillar was far away, very far away, but even so the stench of Dark magic clogged his nostrils. Something of awesome magnitude had been discharged, and the natural world recoiled from it in horror.

Back in the tent, the Celestial wizard was busy raving. All across the camp, men were woken from their slumber, knowing even in their mean, base way that some terrible event had taken place. When they saw the distant column, voices were raised in alarm.

Volkmar felt his resolve waver. Anything capable of rending the heavens in such a way would be untroubled by blackpowder or halberds. What had Schwarzhelm unleashed here? How deep did the corruption run?

'Theogonist?' asked Roll, his voice as flat and savage as ever. 'What are your orders?'

Volkmar said nothing. He could think of nothing to say. The commotion across the camp grew. More of his commanders stumbled from the tent, gaping at the distant glow. Maljdir was among them, for once speechless. Gruppen too. They all looked to him.

He clasped his staff. It gave him no comfort. Placed beside the abomination ahead, all the weapons they had seemed like so many trinkets and charms. He felt despair creep up, just as it had when Archaon had come for him in the north. The great enemy were too strong. They were *too strong*.

'Theogonist?' asked Roll again.

Volkmar looked away from it. That helped. Just gazing on the searing line of flame seemed to bleed the hope from him. He looked down. His palm was raw from clutching the ash shaft of the Staff of Command. He remembered Karl Franz's final words to him in Altdorf. *Can I trust you, Volkmar? Can you succeed where both my generals have failed?*

'Yes, my liege,' he muttered through clenched teeth. 'You can.'

Roll looked confused. 'My lord?'

Volkmar whirled on him.

'Light fires of our own. Banish the dark, and the men will no longer be plagued by it. Get an apothecary for the wizard, and minister to him yourself too. He cannot be allowed to die – we'll need him.'

Then he turned on the rest of his men, his face lit with a dark certainty.

'What did you *expect*?' he snarled, feeling both faith and fury return to him. 'That they'd welcome us with open arms? Know your danger, but do not fear it. That is our destination. That is the crucible upon which your devotion will be tested.'

He turned back to the face the pillar of flame. This time his resolve was solid.

'Search your souls, men. Purge all weakness. The storm is coming. If we fail here, then all the world will know the horror that Averheim knows now.'

BALLS OF BLOOD-RED fire soared high into the sky, racing upwards, coiling round the Tower in a vortex of dizzying speed. Screams from below fractured the very air, ripping it open and exposing the shimmering lattice of emotion beneath, the naked stuff of Chaos.

All along the length of the Tower, iron panels withdrew. The citadel's innards glowed an angry crimson, like hot coals. From the newly-revealed recesses, *things* emerged.

To Natassja, they were objects of transcendent beauty, diaphanous intelligences, winged and noble, possessed of an ineffable wisdom derived from the realm of the infinite. They soared into the fire-flecked air like angels, swimming in the void, drinking in the unleashed power crackling through the air.

To mortal eyes, they were women, lilac-skinned, claw-handed, clad in scraps of leather and iron, lissom and fleshy, screaming from mouths lined with fangs, trailing cloven hooves as they swooped. They were visions of lust and death, fusions of sudden pain and lingering pleasure, the incarnation of the debauchery of their Dark Prince and the fragments of his divine will.

They flew down like harpies, crashing into the roofs of the houses and shattering the tiles, drinking in the sheets of flame lurching up around them, growing larger and more substantial as the aethyr bled into the world of matter, sustaining them and firming up insubstantial sinews.

In Averheim, the sky no longer existed. The air was as red as blood, thundering upwards in a vast column of roaring aethyric essence. In the midst of it all was the Tower, focussing the torrent, keeping it together, directing the inexhaustible will of the Stone.

Natassja laughed out loud, glorying in the rush of the fire as it surged past her, rippling her skirts and tearing at her hair.

'Behold the Stone!' she cried, and from hundreds of feet below a rolling boom echoed across the city.

Grosslich staggered away from her, his face drained. Torrents of aethyr latched on to him, clutching at his armour and then ripping away in shreds. The daemons came soon after, tugging at his hair and laughing.

'Unhand me!' he commanded, brandishing the wand. They laughed all the harder, but none dared harm him. Instead they limited themselves to lascivious gestures, wheeling around the pinnacle like birds flocking to a storm-tossed ship. As they screeched, their voices echoed across registers, at once as flighty as a girl's and as deep as the pits of the abyss.

'What is this, Natassja?' he demanded, turning on her, eyes blazing with fear and anger.

The queen of Averheim gave him a scornful look.

'The allies we seek,' she said. 'What mortal army would dare to venture here now? The Stone sustains a portal, one which can last for centuries if I will it. This is the stuff of Chaos, Heinz-Mark, the raw material of dreams. Daemons will come. While the column of fire lasts they will endure, terrible and deadly. We have created what we wished for, my love! A foothold of the Infinite Realm in the heart of Sigmar's kingdom!'

Grosslich looked as angry as before. His armour

made him nearly invulnerable and he'd developed powers of his own – he would be a formidable enemy if she chose to pick a fight with him. Formidable, but not insuperable.

'This is not what I wanted!' he roared over the torrent. 'I wanted dominion over men, not a realm of magic! What good is this to me?'

Natassja's eyes narrowed dangerously. She was flush with power, suffused with all the roaring energy of the Stone. Grosslich had served a useful purpose and at one time she'd been fond of him, but he was playing a perilous game.

'This mortal realm is yours for the taking, my love,' she said, keeping her voice low. 'Only the daemons cannot venture from the column of fire. All my other creations will serve you in the realm of the five senses.'

'But you have destroyed them!'

'Look around you, fool!' she snapped, tested almost beyond endurance by his stupidity. 'Do you see the buildings burning? Do you see your troops withering? This is no earth-bound fire. These flames burn souls, not flesh.'

Grosslich hesitated, then stalked to the edge of the platform. Bracing against a huge buttress of iron and stone, he leaned far out over the void. Natassja came to his side, fearing nothing of the precipitous drop. She was fast becoming impervious to physical harm.

'Watch them, my love,' she purred. She couldn't stay angry for long, not when so much had been accomplished. 'See how they relish what we have done for them.'

Far down on the streets of Averheim, the dog-soldiers still marched, filing from the gates and assuming defensive positions outside the walls. The citizens of the city had been transformed in their turn, moulded by the power of the Stone and warped into something greater. Where their eyes had been there were now smouldering points of light, blazing in the smog of the furnaces like stars. All their previous cares and infirmities had been shaken off, and they stood tall, glorying in the rush of aethyr around them. Grosslich's army, already huge, had been bolstered by thousands more, their wills bound to the Stone, their bodies hale and ready to bear arms.

'Don't you see it?' murmured Natassja, caressing Grosslich's cheek and speaking softly into his ear. 'The daemons are for me, here in the Tower. Your realm will stretch for many leagues to the north, to the south, to wherever you wish it. Only here will the raw essence of the world of nightmares be permitted to endure.'

Grosslich looked sullen but impressed. Far below, the hordes of Stone-bound slaves had begun to form into crowds and head towards the courtyard below them. Even as they did so, dog-soldiers prepared to hand them weapons. The Everchosen himself could hardly have wished for a more devastating host to command. The joyroot had prepared them, and the Stone had completed the great work.

'I believed we would rule Averland together, you and I,' he muttered, torn between rival lusts. 'I thought that's what you wanted too.'

'I do, my love,' said Natassja, pulling his head round from the scenes below. The furnaces, the screams, the capering daemons, the palls of smoke, all of these were forgotten for a moment.

'This is what we have done, you and I,' she said, pulling him close to her. 'Why can't you be happy with it?'

'I am, my queen,' Grosslich replied, his anger dissipating as her eyes bored deep into his. Resisting her was never easy, even after he'd been taught so much. 'It's just that... my vision was different.'

'Then revel in *this*. See what glories will be achieved here. Our names will pass into the annals of legend, not in this fading world, but in the libraries of the gods, etched on tablets of marble and placed in halls of perpetual wonder. You have taken a step towards a new world, Heinz-Mark. Do not falter now, for there is no way back.'

He nodded weakly, all resistance crumbling. His will was always so easy to break. Not like Schwarzhelm, and not like Marius – they had been made of more enduring material. As she spoke, she sensed the doubt in his mind. Had it always been there? Perhaps she should have paid more attention.

'Remember my words,' she warned, making sure he'd taken her meaning. 'This is the future for us, the future for mankind. I will say it again, in case you failed to hear me: there is *no* way back.'

KURT HELBORG TURNED uneasily in his sleep. In the past, his slumber had been that of a warrior, complete and unbroken. Ever since the fires of the Vormeisterplatz, though, the pattern had been broken. He saw visions before waking, faces leering at him in the dark. There was Rufus Leitdorf, fat and pallid, gloating over his failure to secure the city. Skarr was there too, mocking him for the loss of the runefang. And there was Schwarzhelm, his face unlocked by madness, brandishing the Sword of Justice and inviting the duel once again. It was all mockery and scorn, the things he'd never encountered in the world of waking.

At the vision of the Emperor's Champion, Helborg awoke suddenly. The sheets around him were clammy and blood had leaked from his wound again. The pain was ever-present, a dull ache in his side. He could ignore it in battle, just as he'd ignored a thousand lesser wounds before, but the architect of it would not leave him in peace.

Helborg lay still, letting his breathing return to normal. The room around him was dark and cold. Dawn was some hours away and the shutters had been bolted closed. At the foot of his massive four-poster bed hung the sword he'd been lent by Leitdorf. It was a good blade, well-balanced and forged by master smiths of Nuln. It was nothing compared to the Klingerach.

Helborg swung his legs from the bed and walked over to the window. He unlocked the shutters, letting the moonlight flood into his chamber. Mannslieb was low in the eastern sky, almost invisible. It was Morrslieb, the Cursed Moon, that rode high. Helborg made the sign of the comet across his chest, more out of reflex than anything else. He feared the Chaos moon as little as he feared anything else. Far out in the north-west, he noticed a faint smudge of red against the horizon. Perhaps a fire, lost out on the bleak moorland.

He limped back to the bed and sat heavily on it. Being isolated, cut off from the Imperial chain of command, was an experience he'd not had for over twenty years. Even in the fiercest fighting he'd always had access to some indication of how things stood in Altdorf. Now things were different. For all he knew, Schwarzhelm still hunted him. If so, then the man's soul was surely damned.

Leitdorf had told him of the corruption recorded in Marius's diaries, the sickness at the heart of Averheim. He'd seen it for himself at the Vormeisterplatz. Whatever force had the power to turn Schwarzhelm's mighty hands to the cause of darkness was potent indeed. The old curmudgeon had always been infuriating, stubborn, grim, taciturn, inflexible, proud and prickly, but he'd never shown the slightest lack of faith in the Empire and its masters. Not until now.

Prompted by some random inclination, Helborg took up his borrowed sword and withdrew the blade from the scabbard. He turned it slowly, watching the metal reflect the tainted moonlight. A weak instrument, but it would have to do. Nothing about his current situation was ideal. Leitdorf was a simpering, self-pitying fool, the men at his command were half-trained and liable to bolt at the first sign of trouble, and Helborg had almost no idea what Grosslich's intentions or tactics were.

So be it. He'd never asked for anything other than a life of testing. Being Grand Marshal of the Empire brought with it certain privileges – the loyalty of powerful men and the favours of beautiful women – but these were not the things that drove him onwards. It had always been about faith, an ideal, something to aspire to. He'd come closer than ever to death in Averheim, and no man remained unchanged in the face of his own mortality. Maybe he'd been too flamboyant in the past, too ready to orchestrate the defence of the Empire around his own ambition. Maybe Schwarzhelm had been right to resent his success. Maybe some of this had been his fault, despite the long, painful hours he'd spent blaming his great rival for all that had befallen.

Things would have to change. Whatever the result of the war, he could not go back to Altdorf as if nothing had happened.

He began to re-sheathe the sword when a faint rattling sound caught his attention. He paused, listening carefully. It was coming from outside the window. Helborg's room was on the first storey of the mansion, more than twenty feet up from ground level. Leitdorf's chambers were down the corridor, and the other rooms were empty.

The rattling sounded again. Helborg placed the scabbard on the bed and took the naked sword up in his right hand. For some reason his heart began to beat faster. His armour had been hung in the room below, and he wore nothing more protective than a threadbare nightshirt. There should have been Reiksguard patrolling the grounds. The noise outside was like nothing he'd heard in his life, at once artificial and full of a strange, scuttling kind of life.

He stood up from the bed and edged towards the window. He listened carefully. Nothing, save the faint creak of the floorboards beneath him and the rush of the wind from outside. Helborg stayed perfectly still, blade poised for the strike, watching.

Still nothing. Heartbeats passed, gradually slowing. Perhaps he'd imagined it.

The window shattered with a smash that resounded across the chamber. A bone claw thrust through the jagged panes, scrabbling at the stone sill, hauling something up behind it.

Helborg sprang forwards, bringing the sword down on the talons with a massive, two-handed hammer-blow. The stone fractured, sending shards spinning into the air, but the blade rebounded from the claw, jarring his arms and sending him staggering back. There was a thin scream and something crashed back down to earth. Helborg regained his feet. The talons had gone. Whatever had tried to get in had been sent plummeting back to the courtyard.

It had not been alone. With a spider-like pounce, another creature leapt through the shattered glass, crouched on the floor and coiled for another spring.

'*Helborg!*' it hissed, and there was something like ecstasy in its warped voice.

Helborg stared at it in horror. The stink of Chaos rose from it, pungent and sweet. The body of a young woman, naked and covered in scars, squatted on the floor, draped in the remnants of rags. The flesh was as pale as the Deathmoon and caked with mud and filth from the moors. Old blood had dried on its needle teeth and ribbons of dry skin clung to the talons. Its eyes glinted with the dull sheen of tarnished iron, then blazed into a pale lilac fire.

It pounced. Helborg swung the sword to parry, using all his strength to ward the scything claws. The horror's strength and speed were incredible. It lashed out, striking at his eyes and fingers, following him across the chamber as he withdrew, step by step.

Helborg's sword moved in a blur, countering the strikes and thrusting back. He was the foremost swordsman of the Empire, but this blade was no rune-fang. The curved talons of the handmaiden scored the edge of it, scraping down its length in a shower of sparks and shivering the metal.

More clambered in, two of them, their eyes lit up with the same lilac blaze. They rushed into the attack, limbs flailing, trying to break through Helborg's guard.

He pulled back to the door, whirling his blade in tighter and faster arcs. The edge seemed to have no effect on them. Every time his sword connected with flesh, a hidden layer of bone or iron bounced the shaft back. The creatures were like the automata of a crazed surgeon's imagination, pitiless and unstoppable.

One dropped down low and went for his legs. He kicked the creature hard in the face, knocking it on its back, before leaping away to dodge the attack from the others. As he withdrew again he felt hot blood running down his shin. Morr's teeth, the thing had *bitten* him.

The first creature pressed the attack, trying to impale him against the wooden doorframe, jabbing its talons in hard and straight. Its face came close, locked in a contortion of pain. Helborg veered his head out of the way and blocked a sideswipe from the second with the flat of his sword. The third got back on its feet and coiled to leap again. They were all over him.

Feeling the door at his back, Helborg kicked it open and retreated out to the landing beyond. It was darker there, and the pursuing horrors' eyes glowed with malice in the gloom. Step by step they pushed him back, slicing at his exposed flesh, pushing for the opening. It was only a matter of time. He couldn't hurt them, and they never tired. Even as he knocked away a lunge, Helborg felt a sharp stab of pain as one of the talons got past his guard.

He broke away, fresh blood dripping from the wound, twisting and blocking to evade the merciless attack. They were going to break through. They'd blooded him, and the taste of it in the air drove them into a fresh mania.

'*Helborg!*' they cried together, gathering themselves

for the strike like coiling snakes. Helborg held the sword steady, waiting for them in the dark. His teeth clenched, breath coming in ragged gasps. He tensed, ready for the impact.

'Sigmar!'

He heard the cry, but the voice wasn't his. A dark shape plunged past him, wielding a blade and swinging it with clumsy abandon.

The new sword swung down, connecting with the lead creature as it made to leap. A flash of blinding light broke out across the landing, briefly showing up the scene in stark, dazzling relief.

Leitdorf was there. *Leitdorf*. The fat, slovenly man laid into the horrors with his broadsword, as naked as the day he'd been born, roaring with a kind of blind, panicked fury. Helborg lurched after him, desperate to stop the man being cut to pieces. The elector was no swordsman – he was a fool, a buffoon, a spoiled brat.

The horrors fell back. Incredibly, they shrank away from the heavy swipes of the Wolfsklinge, eyes dull with horror, talons curled up into impotent fists. Leitdorf ploughed into them, jabbing left and right with slow, inexpert strokes. Every step he took, they scrabbled back, screaming at him with an unmistakable expression of terror.

They were *afraid* of him.

There was no time to be astounded. In a heartbeat, Helborg was at his side, matching the elector's clumsy blows with precision strikes. Under the twin assault, the creatures seemed to shrivel into a tortured impotence, holding their tortured hands up in front of their ravaged faces, scuttling to escape, desperate not to face the heavy bite of the Wolfsklinge.

'Follow my lead!' roared Helborg, dazzling one of

the creatures with a glittering backhand swipe before bringing the edge back sharply. The horror, so eerily efficient before, clattered backwards. Its guard destroyed, Leitdorf landed the killer blow, his sword cleaving the creature from neck to stomach in a single movement. Old flesh, iron bindings, clockwork bearings and rune-stamped plates scattered across the landing floor, skittering and bouncing as the creature was ripped apart. A cloud of jasmine perfume billowed out, sighing across the darkness of the landing before rippling into nothingness.

The two remaining handmaidens turned to flee, wailing like lost children in the night. With every blow from Leitdorf's blade a fresh blaze of light seemed to cow them further. Leitdorf and Helborg pushed them back into the bedchamber, steel ringing against bone and exploding in flashes of light and sparks.

One of them coiled for a counter-attack, jaws wide in a scream of fear and hatred, talons extended for a desperate, gouging assault. Helborg was on it in an instant, his blade hurtling round to sever the horror's wrists. As ever, his weapon bounced from the creature without biting, but the impact was enough to knock it off balance.

'Now!' he roared, and Leitdorf was quick enough to obey. The elector jabbed down, his grip two-handed, and the creature was smashed apart by the power of the Wolfsklinge.

One remained. It scrabbled backwards, face contorted in terror. It stared at Leitdorf with anguish, all thoughts of its mission forgotten.

Helborg shot Leitdorf a quick look. The man's face was white with terror and his temples were drenched in sweat. He was panting heavily, mouth open and jaw loose. He looked like he'd stumbled into a nightmare.

'Finish it,' Helborg growled, edging forwards. He had to provide the opening. He let the tip of his sword sway back and forth, distracting the creature as it crouched miserably.

Then he struck, darting forwards, slipping the blade under the horror's outstretched talons, going for the midriff.

It slapped the sword away contemptuously, ignoring his attack, eyes still on Leitdorf. But the distraction had been enough. The elector was on it, hammering down with the Wolfsklinge, shattering iron bonds and ripping dry skin.

The handmaiden, Natassja's killing machine, the perfect assassin, shattered under the flurry of blows, its tortured hide carved open, its spell-locked innards dented and smashed. Helborg staggered out of the way, ducking under a wild swipe from Leitdorf. The man hacked and hammered in a frenzy of rage and fear, obliterating the cowering horror with blow after crushing blow. Even when it was nothing more than a heap of dented iron and twitching sinews he kept going, pounding away until the floorboards beneath were hacked up and in danger of collapsing.

'Leitdorf!' cried Helborg.

The man kept going, eyes wild, hair swinging around his head like flails.

'*Leitdorf!*' roared Helborg, grabbing him by the shoulder and swinging him round. For a moment, he thought Leitdorf was going to attack him. The elector stared at him wide-eyed, his face lost in a mask of terror.

'It's *me*, Rufus,' said Helborg, eyes locked with his, hand clamped on his shoulder.

Leitdorf froze, sword ready to strike. His limbs were shivering. His fat belly was streaked with sweat. Slowly, haltingly, he let the Wolfsklinge fall from his fingers. It clanged amongst the shattered carcasses of the handmaidens, now lost in the darkness of the chamber.

'What... I...' he mumbled, frenzy giving way to shock. The blood had drained from his face. He looked ready to pass out.

'Get some clothes on,' said Helborg, keeping the grip on his shoulder tight. Already there were sounds of commotion from below. 'I'll get some guards up here. Then we need to talk.'

# Chapter Thirteen

LEITDORF SAT IN his father's study. His hands still shook each time he raised the glass of wine to his lips. From the landing outside he could hear the guards clearing away the last of the wreckage of the assassin creatures.

Dawn had broken, and a meagre light had slowly crept over the moorland outside. The clouds that had been building up for days continued to mount, blocking the light of the sun and turning the sky as dark and sullen as a musket-barrel.

Leitdorf placed his goblet back on the desk. In front of him, as always, was his father's diary. He'd read it all, some parts several times over. Even the most obscure passages had begun to make some sense. Over the final few weeks' entries, though, Marius's handwriting was near-illegible, and there were still long sections where Rufus could make nothing out. In the centre of the page he was looking it, the old elector seemed to have drifted off into random scrawlings.

*...bedarruzibarr'zagarratumnan'akz'akz'berau...*

There was more of the same. One page was entirely covered in such nonsense. As he reflected on a proud mind laid low, his spirits sank further. He'd not been close to his father in life, but no son wanted to witness such degeneration. If he'd known at the time, maybe he'd have done something. Or maybe he'd have stayed mired in the excess and privilege he'd always known.

There was a knock at the door.

'Come.'

Helborg pushed the door open. It had been courteous of him to knock. Over the past few days, the Marshal had got into the habit of bursting in uninvited. Helborg walked over to the desk and leaned against the wall beside Leitdorf. He looked untroubled by the events of a few hours ago. No doubt he'd seen worse.

'Feeling better?' asked the Marshal.

'Yes, thank you.' The wine had helped calm his nerves. Leitdorf noticed Helborg had had his wound freshly bound again. He looked a lot more formidable out of his nightshirt and back in his standard military uniform. Not many men would have seen the Master of the Reiksguard fighting in his nightwear. Then again, at least the man had been wearing *some* clothes.

'Interesting reading?'

Leitdorf glanced back down at the page. 'Like looking inside the mind of a dead man.'

He pushed his chair back from the desk and turned to face the Marshal.

'You know what's been bothering me?' Leitdorf said. 'For over a year we lived as a couple in Altdorf. She had access to all of my resources, all of my men. Why didn't she ever try to corrupt me? Why did she use Grosslich?'

Helborg shrugged. 'You're sure she never tried? The ways of the enemy are–'

'Subtle, yes, I know,' muttered Leitdorf. 'And yes, I'm

sure. She tried to subvert my father – and failed. How could that be *possible*? She had the power to walk in men's dreams. Just look what she did to Schwarzhelm. Somehow, Marius resisted her for all those years where the Emperor's Champion couldn't. He was untouchable.'

As he spoke, Leitdorf felt a fugitive pride in that.

'Not all men give in to temptation,' said Helborg.

'Of course. But something else is at work here. You saw what happened with those... creatures. It's only confirmed a suspicion I've had for some time, ever since I first read this book.'

Helborg looked doubtful, but said nothing.

'You know as well as I that the bloodlines of the electors are ancient. There have been many ruling families in Averland over the centuries, but the Leitdorfs have always been among them. Ever since the time of Siggurd my people have taken up swords in the defence of this realm. We're bound to Averheim like none of the others. This has always been the root of our hold over the runefang, even during the dark times when it was wielded by others. We were the first ones.'

As he spoke, Leitdorf thought of all the fine words he'd rehearsed for this speech. It sounded ludicrous, contemptible even, in his head. Still, he had to say it.

'My father believed there was a hidden presence in the city. *Under* the city. His dreams were full of it – a source of power, or evil, or knowledge. That's why he hated Averheim, even as he fought to retain it. Men have long joked that the place was cursed, destined forever to be ruled by the insane. My father thought he knew why. There were always clandestine forces at work there, nagging away in the shadows, whispering in the silences.'

Helborg narrowed his eyes, still listening intently.

'And then there was this woman, this Natassja, making all those fears explicit, coming to him in his sleep. Despite everything, she failed to turn him to the enemy. Why? He was too strong, too indomitable. In the end, tiring of her seduction, she let him ride out to face Ironjaw and turned her ambitions away from the Leitdorfs. She had to.'

As he spoke, Rufus held Helborg's gaze, his brown eyes steadier than they'd ever been.

'It's in our blood, Marshal,' he said. 'We can't be turned. I'd always been told it by nursemaids and tutors, but I never really knew what they meant until now. We have our failings, to be sure, but one kind of corruption we are free of. The whispers of the great enemy are useless against us. It's not just a matter of will. It's in the *blood*.'

Helborg looked sceptical. 'You think that explains what happened here?'

Leitdorf smiled. 'You know my reputation as a fighter, my lord. And yet, against her creations, I had the mastery. I will always have the mastery. She must have known that. So she needed to find another champion.'

Helborg remained incredulous. Leitdorf couldn't blame him. The idea sounded preposterous to him too in the cold light of day. And yet only he – fat, stupid Rufus – had been able to defeat the creatures. The hero of the Empire, the Hammer of Chaos, would have been carved apart by them. There was some link between the Leitdorfs and Natassja, something that made him powerful.

'I've heard of such things,' said the Marshal at last, evidently unconvinced. 'There are weapons, the

Wolfsklinge maybe, which have power over individuals and their works. Maybe some long-forgotten father of your line performed a distant feat of faith which explains your victory. Beyond that, I would not safely go.'

Leitdorf smiled again, this time with resignation. He couldn't expect anyone else to understand. This was between him, his father and Natassja.

'No doubt you're right, my lord,' he said. 'Only consider this. There is a force for corruption in the city that my family has resisted for generations, even to the extent of being driven into madness. Is it not possible that we have developed some counterpart power of our own? And if this were so, would it not be a matter of great hope for the Empire? For mankind, even?'

Helborg thought for a moment, then gave a non-committal gesture. 'There are many strange things in the world. Be careful where your pride takes you, elector. Many have thought themselves immune to the call of corruption. They have always been the first to fall.'

Leitdorf bowed his head. 'Of course. These are just speculations.'

Helborg looked at Leitdorf carefully then, like a farmer sizing up an unpromising foal with a view to producing a future prize stallion. Some of the unconscious scorn had left the Marshal's manner, even if his habitual pride still remained sunk deep in his battle-ravaged features.

'In any case,' he said, 'you have my thanks. Whatever the reason, your sword bit into those creatures where mine did not. When the grace of Sigmar descends, it is foolish to ask too closely the reason why.'

The unaccustomed praise made Leitdorf feel

awkward. He'd never been complimented on his swordplay before by anyone, let alone by a legend such as Helborg.

'Then maybe you should take the Wolfsklinge, my lord,' he said, although, deep down, he was loath to lose it. 'Your hands will wield it more skilfully than mine.'

Helborg laughed and shook his head. 'A generous offer! Maybe this war will make a man of you yet, Rufus.' He pushed himself away from the wall and made to leave the room. 'I'll not take it up. There's only one sword for me, and I still plan on recovering it. Until then, I'll make do with what weapons I can find.'

He started to walk towards the door.

'We'll both have the opportunity to use our blades again soon. Our army, such as it is, is ready, and I've given Skarr his deadline to make the rendezvous. We march within the hour. Collect yourself, elector. Averheim beckons.'

THE TOWN OF Streissen lay between Nuln and Averheim, the first of the large market towns that straddled the main trading route into the heart of the Empire. It was the only settlement of any note before the capital and commanded a key crossing point over the river. Like most Imperial towns it was walled and garrisoned. Tiled roofs rose up within the ramparts, close-packed and divided only by narrow, winding streets. In its own way it was an attractive place, a bustling, hard-nosed town made rich through trade and commerce.

In the days between the electors its defences had fallen into disrepair. Grosslich had put that right soon after his coronation. The walls had been strengthened and an extra two thousand men drafted into the garrison. The old icons of the province had been removed and the crimson boar's head now hung from the gatehouse. Streissen had always been home to many Grosslich supporters, and it was far in both distance and sympathy from the lands once controlled by the Leitdorfs. The merchants had welcomed the changes brought in by the new elector, and for a brief time the trade had picked up again.

Now it was paying for its choices. Volkmar had given the burgomeisters almost no time to consider his demands for surrender. Before any reply had come back the walls had been surrounded by his army, nearly forty thousand strong since taking on reinforcements from Nuln and itching for a fight.

The Theogonist stood to the north of the city on a conical hill, his commanders, musicians and messengers around him. The storm in the south had grown fiercer, and black clouds raged on the horizon, flecked with lightning. The column of fire was still visible, though far paler in the daylight. It was ever-present, a reminder to all of the destination that awaited them.

On the plain below, his army was deployed in a wide circle, out of bow-shot and musket-range of the walls but close enough to advance at a moment's notice. Placed in readiness for combat, the volume of men looked fearsome. They covered the undulating land in front of the gates like a vast chequered carpet, over a mile wide from flank to flank. The auxiliaries were desperate to mount an assault; the regular troops less so. Morale had been strangely affected by the apparition in the night sky. Some men had responded with aggression, others with fear, others with fatalism.

'We still haven't heard from the burgomeisters,' said Maljdir, frowning at the beleaguered town as if it had personally offended him. 'Give them more time?'

Volkmar shook his head.

'They've damned themselves by waiting. Launch the assault.'

Maljdir hesitated, then bowed and gestured to the trumpeter standing to his left. The man blew a series of long notes into the air, which were then taken up by other musicians. The signal passed to the west flank, where the big guns had been placed along the edge of a low ridge.

As soon as the notes reached them the crews sprang into action. Shot was rammed home and fuses lit. With a deafening boom, the great cannons roared out, hurling their shot straight and true. As the smoke rolled across the battlefield, the walls of Streissen cracked and buckled. To the right of the cannons, arranged high on the north flank of the battlefield, men began to shuffle forwards. Cavalry units mounted and adjusted their armour, taking up lances and handguns. The vast bulk of the infantry, the halberdiers, spearmen and swordsmen, held their positions, watching the destruction begin with a mix of relish and anxiety.

The cannons roared out again, a thunderous barrage of stone-cracking power, shaking the earth beneath them and rocking the town to its foundations. A jagged line appeared in the north-west corner of the walls, showering dust and mortar as the blocks were knocked loose.

'There's the breach,' said Volkmar, watching the action unfold through his spyglass. 'Order the Third and Ninth into position. Knights Panther on their left flank, Horstman's cavalry on their right.'

The orders were conveyed and a mass of men crept forwards, still in company order, nearly three thousand halberdiers marching cautiously in offensive formation. Squadrons of armoured horsemen drew alongside them, guarding their flanks from counter-assault. As the infantry pulled itself into position, the first arrows whined down from the walls. Ranged against the might of Volkmar's forces, the defences looked pitiably weak.

The cannons roared a third time, then a fourth. The breach opened further, exposing the masonry within. The halberdiers moved closer, kept in tight ranks by their sergeants, shadowed by the cavalry, waiting for the order to charge.

'Move the auxiliaries to close the leaguer,' said Volkmar, watching the movement of men below him intently. 'Maintain the barrage. Assault on my word.'

'My lord, there are flags on the ramparts,' said Maljdir, pointing at Streissen's turrets, only half-visible through the rolling clouds of blackpowder smoke from the cannon barrels. 'They wish to submit.'

'How is that relevant, Odain?' Volkmar said, observing the fifth barrage as it blasted the breach wider. The gap was now wide enough to drive a carriage through. There were defenders swarming over it like flies round a wound. 'They've had their chance, and we'll show them the price of defiance. Order the advance.'

Maljdir looked hesitant. The huge Nordlander was not a man given to pity, but still he paused.

'They're asking for quarter, my lord. They're men of the Empire.'

Volkmar let the spyglass drop and rounded on the priest, eyes blazing.

'They're *traitors*,' he growled. 'Order the advance.'

Maljdir resisted for a moment longer, eyes locked with Volkmar's. Then they dropped. He turned to the musician and gave him the instruction. Fresh trumpet calls blared out, and a roar of recognition rippled across the army. They knew what was coming.

The final cannon barrage boomed out, shattering the broken section of wall further. The cries of those crushed under the stone rang out, audible even over the roar of the charging halberdiers. Volkmar's vanguard was unleashed and surged forwards en masse, loping over the broken ground, blades kept low in the front rank, raised high in the following. They swarmed across the shattered walls and the sound of killing rose above all others.

'Fourth and Eighth in behind them!' ordered Volkmar, his pulse beginning to race. This was the first action of the campaign, and the men needed a crushing success to bolster their morale. 'Greatswords into reserve!'

His orders were conveyed and the massed companies of men moved to follow them. The halberdiers were still pouring through the walls, storming across the overwhelmed breach and piling into the town, blades flashing in the grey light. There were plumes of smoke as enemy handgunners returned fire, but they were soon extinguished under the weight of the assault. Like a single, massive animal, the invading army began to wheel around the centre of tactical gravity and close in on its prey.

As the last of the cannon smoke lazily drifted across the plain, it was already evident the defence was doomed. Volkmar stowed his spyglass with satisfaction and turned to Maljdir.

'Come with me,' he ordered, his eyes alight with savagery. 'We've cut our way in. Time to follow the halberds.'

With that, the Grand Theogonist strode down the slope of the hill, flanked by plate-armoured warrior priests, to take his prize.

Maljdir watched him go, arms crossed over his massive chest, unmoving, unwilling to be a part of a slaughter with no glory in it. He'd come to hunt Chaos troops, not misguided merchants and farmhands.

The power of command was too strong, though. In the end Maljdir shook his head, took up the vast, gold-studded warhammer Bloodbringer and stalked down after his general. For the first time since leaving Altdorf, the big man found himself eager to get to the real fighting in Averheim. At least there was an enemy there which deserved to be put to the sword.

And they'd be in range soon enough.

BLOCH SCREWED HIS eyes tight, peering into the distance. The sun had started to lower in the west, obscuring the land ahead in a lowering haze.

'It's a blockade,' he said.

Kraus shook his head. 'More than that. There must be hundreds of them. It's a camp. They're on the march.'

Bloch looked back at the horizon. The road west ran over the grassland before them. They were in the cattle-country south of Heideck, having made good progress on the long journey from Grenzstadt. As they'd neared Averland's second city, Bloch had decided to take a detour to the south. He had no desire to run into Grosslich's men before they drew nearer to Averheim. With only two hundred troops still under his command, he was vulnerable.

For a few days, his strategy seemed to be working. They'd seen merchant convoys on the roads, all heavily guarded by private militia. Apart from them, there had been almost no movement on the highways. Bloch's company had been able to travel quickly and in the open, lodging in or around villages where the people had heard nothing from Averheim in days. The province of Averland seemed to have shut down. That would have been cause for more concern if it hadn't aided their passage so much, and of Grosslich's vaunted armies in particular there had been no sign.

Until now.

Thankfully, Bloch had stumbled across the encampment while his men were still under cover, overshadowed by the crumbling walls of a ruined farmhouse high on the hill. He, Kraus and a handful of men had scouted ahead of the main column of soldiers, planning the remainder of the day's trek and looking for a site to make camp.

It seemed Grosslich's men had had a similar idea. They straddled the road ahead, dozens of soldiers wearing the crimson and gold tunics of the new elector, starting the laborious process of erecting tents and raising an embankment for the night. They clearly expected trouble from someone. Perhaps Meuningen had been wrong about the succession issue being completely resolved.

'Nice colours,' said Bloch.

'Helpfully visible,' agreed Kraus.

'So what are we going to do about them?'

Kraus pursed his cracked lips. The weeks in the wilderness had given him a ragged, almost canine look. Like all of them, he'd lost weight and gained muscle.

'We can't evade Grosslich's forces forever. Perhaps now we'll see what his intentions are.'

Bloch pondered that.

'Too many to fight,' he said.

'What d'you mean? It can't be more than two to one. We'll tear them apart.'

Bloch grinned. 'Don't get cocky. I want to get back to Altdorf in one piece.'

'You're in the wrong trade, then.'

Bloch motioned to one of his men, a sandy-haired halberdier. Like all the troops marching with him still, this one had fought under his command since the death of Grunwald. They were good men, these, the kind you'd trust with your life.

'Bring the lads up here,' he told him. 'We'll form up and march towards them with our heads held high. No reason for us to suspect they'll be hostile.'

But there was. Meuningen's warning still echoed in his thoughts. Everything about Averland since his return had felt deeply, terribly wrong. The further west they went, the stranger it felt.

The halberdier slipped off to muster the rest of the men.

Kraus was satisfied. He'd never been happy with avoiding conflict, and looked eager for another fight. He drew his sword and looked carefully along the edge, searching for defects.

'Keep that sheathed when we get up there,' warned Bloch.

'You really think they'll let us pass?'

Bloch shrugged.

'Your guess is as good as mine. Since Schwarzhelm

left, I've got no idea what's been going on here.'

'And if they don't?'

'Same as always,' he said. His voice was flat. 'We'll kill 'em all.'

VERSTOHLEN SHADED HIS eyes against the grey sky and shivered. Either autumn was approaching very fast or there was something decidedly strange about the weather. Each day dawned colder than the last and the rush of clouds from the mountains continued unabated. The scudding masses seemed to be drawn north-west like water rushing down a whirlpool. In the distance, where the column of fire was still just visible on the edge of sight, a vast maelstrom of circling storm-bringers had accumulated. Tongues of forked lightning flickered against the dark shadow of the rolling grassland.

He flipped the collar of his Kartor-Bruessol coat up around his neck and stuffed his hands in his pockets. The attire he was so proud of was suffering badly out in the wilds. He knew that he was worse than useless in such an environment. The skills he prided himself on were suited to cities and stately houses, places where information was more deadly than swords. Since decoding Lassus's missives, he'd not been able to contribute much more to Schwarzhelm's quest than the occasional grumble. He was tired, dog-tired, and the pain of his wounds still throbbed in his back.

Schwarzhelm himself strode on as powerfully as ever, thrusting aside bushes and clumps of overgrown gorse with unconscious ease. The trials of the past month had done little to dent his sheer physical presence. Even out of his customary plate armour he still exuded a raw, almost bestial menace. He'd been described as a force of nature, and such a description served him well. Verstohlen had known him for years, but only on this journey had he displayed more than the most fleeting of weaknesses. This journey had been remarkable in many ways, though, none of which Verstohlen wanted to see repeated.

'Keep up, man,' Schwarzhelm growled irritably, pushing through a briar patch and hauling himself on to a shallow ridge of crumbling clay soil.

Verstohlen sighed, hoisted his bag over his shoulder once more and followed wearily. They'd been on the highlands for two days now and there was little enough sign of any habitation at all, let alone the hiding place of Kurt Helborg. The country had gone from open moor to a twisting landscape of defiles and narrow coombs, all thickly forested or choked with undergrowth. The going had got harder, and tempers had frayed.

'I'm coming, damn you,' muttered Verstohlen, crawling up the ridge with difficulty. When he crested it, Schwarzhelm was waiting for him with a face like thunder. Behind him, a wall of low, wind-blasted trees clustered darkly, cutting off the grey light of the sun.

'Can you go no faster?' he snapped, eyes glittering with impatience.

'*Faster?*' gasped Verstohlen, breathing heavily. His head felt light from the exertions he'd already made. 'Verena's scales, we'd need wings to get across here in less than a week. This is a fool's errand, my lord. We should turn back.'

Schwarzhelm glowered at him. Though the man would never admit it, the fatigue was playing on him too.

'Remember who you're talking to,' he rasped, moving a hand instinctively to the hilt of the Rechtstahl. 'You have your orders.'

Verstohlen's eyes widened. 'What're you going to do? *Draw* that on me?'

Schwarzhelm took a step towards him, his expression one of gathering fury.

'Don't tempt me. I've marched with Tileans with stronger stomachs than–'

He broke off, suddenly tensing. From the tree line, a twig snapped.

Schwarzhelm whirled around, both swords drawn. Verstohlen was at his shoulder in an instant, dagger in hand. They were being watched.

Men broke from the cover of the branches, clad in leather jerkins and open-faced helmets. Their swords were naked and they were ready for a fight. There were six of them, all with the grizzled faces of professional soldiers. With a sudden lurch of remembrance, Verstohlen realised what they were.

Reiksguard.

'Lower your blades!' cried their captain, pointing his sword-tip at Schwarzhelm and advancing menacingly.

Schwarzhelm stood still, slowly letting the Swords of Vengeance and Justice down until the points grazed the ground. He knew what they were as well as Verstohlen did, but for the moment at least the knights didn't recognise him. They'd probably never seen him out of armour before.

'Perhaps you don't remember me,' he said.

As soon as he spoke, a ripple of amazement passed across the faces of the knights.

'Schwarzhelm!' one of them gasped aloud. Another advanced with purpose, looking like he wanted to run his blade through the big man's chest. Schwarzhelm remained motionless, keeping both his swords out of position. Verstohlen clutched his dagger tight, ready to act. This was dangerous.

'Wait!' snapped the leader, holding his fist up. His stubble-lined face was grimy and studded with scabs. He'd been in the wilderness for a long time. He kept his blade raised, watching both of them intently. Schwarzhelm's reputation preceded him, and the knight seemed lost in a mix of awe and hatred.

'Are you alone?' he asked.

Schwarzhelm nodded.

'Why are you here?'

'I seek the Lord Helborg, if he still lives.'

One of the Reiksguard snorted with derision. 'If he lives!'

'Silence!' ordered the captain. 'He's alive, though no thanks to you. Tell me why I shouldn't kill you now myself, traitor?'

Schwarzhelm looked directly at the knight. His gaze was blunt, hard to read. There was defiance there, belligerence too, but also shame.

'Do you really think you could harm me, Reiksguard, if I chose to prevent you?' His voice came in a deep growl. 'I have two swords in my hands, both as ancient as the bones of the earth. You're walking a dangerous path.'

Verstohlen thought he was going to strike then, and sweat broke out across his forehead. He clutched his dagger more tightly. The Reiksguard held their ground. The merest spark would light this fire.

Then Schwarzhelm's massive shoulders slumped.

'I did not come here to spill fresh blood,' he muttered. Sorrow weighed heavily on each word, and the threat drained from his speech. 'Take me to the Lord Helborg, and he shall be the judge of things. There are tidings he must hear.'

The Reiksguard captain made no move.

'Surrender your swords, then,' he said.

'Not to you.'

'How can I take you to him when you will not disarm?'

Schwarzhelm grunted with disdain.

'You forget yourself, Reiksguard. I am the Emperor's Champion. I will come as I am.'

Still the tension remained. The knights looked to their captain. If he ordered it, they would charge. The man frowned, wrestling with the decision. Verstohlen could see the frustration in his eyes, but the Reiksguard's respect for the sanctity of rank was near-absolute.

'I will take you to him,' he said at last, nearly spitting the words out. 'There is an army on these moors, Schwarzhelm, an army raised to right the wrongs you have caused. Think on that, should you choose to wield your swords in anger. Your reputation goes before you, but if you raise them again, you will die before the blade leaves the scabbard. This I swear, as do all the Reiksguard that remain in Averland.'

Schwarzhelm said nothing, but nodded wearily. He sheathed the Rechtstahl and the Klingerach in a single movement. The captain gave a signal to his men and they fanned around the two of them, blades in hand.

Then they started walking. There was no conversation, and the atmosphere was frigid. As they went, the wind howled across the gorse like mocking laughter.

'Merciful Verena,' muttered Verstohlen to himself as

he stumbled along behind the implacable form of his master. 'This just gets better.'

BLOCH STRODE CASUALLY at the head of his column, Kraus by his side. Behind him, his men marched in formation, six abreast, a compact column of fighting men. After so long on campaign they looked more than a little shabby, but their manner of quiet, efficient confidence was unfeigned. They were the remnants of an army that had driven the greenskins over the mountains, and they had every reason to walk tall.

As they drew closer to the camp, shouts went up from the sentries and the guards took up their places. By the time Bloch approached the perimeter the detachment commander was waiting at the camp entrance. He was flanked by several dozen men, all heavily armed. More clustered within, protected by the spiked embankment. They were wearing crimson tunics over plate breastplates. Their swords were strangely curved, and some had barbs forged into them. Not very Imperial. Half the troops looked like Averlanders, but the rest had the darker colouring of Tileans, Estalians or even soldiers of Araby. Grosslich must have paid out handsomely to get mercenaries from so far.

Behind the camp commander the earthworks rose up several feet, surmounted by a row of stakes. The deployment looked well organised. Kraus was right; this was a part of an army at war.

'Halt,' ordered the camp commander. 'State your name and business.'

Bloch took a good look at his opposite number. The man had the air of a seasoned warrior. His armour was more elaborate than that of his men, and a golden boar's head had been sewn into the breast of his tunic. He wore a crimson cloak that fell to the ground behind him. Like the rest of his men he wore a close-fitting, open-faced helm. As with all else, it didn't look Imperial. Everything was too bright, too clean. Too beautiful.

'I answer to the Lord Schwarzhelm,' Bloch responded, keeping his voice carefully neutral. 'Who are you?'

'Captain Erasmus Euler of the First Averheim Reavers, and Schwarzhelm has no authority here. You've overstayed your welcome in Averland, Commander Bloch.'

Bloch was instantly irritated by the man's manner. If he'd known who he was, why ask for a name?

'I was warned there was a shortage of gratitude in Averheim,' he replied coolly. 'I can live with that. Let us pass, and we'll be on our way.'

'Your men may pass. You're wanted by the elector.'

'Is that right?' Bloch let his free hand creep an inch closer towards his halberd stave. 'Sadly, that won't be possible. Your elector has no jurisdiction over me. Like I said, I answer to Schwarzhelm.'

Euler withdrew a step and grasped his sword-hilt. His men did likewise.

'Don't push your luck, commander. You're outnumbered two to one.'

Kraus let slip a low, growling laugh. 'I knew it,' he muttered. 'We'll tear 'em apart.'

That settled it.

'As far as I'm concerned, you can bring it on, captain,' said Bloch, sweeping up his halberd in both hands and swinging the blade into position. 'We've been fighting greenskins for weeks. If you reckon you're a match for them, be my guest to prove it.'

Behind him, Bloch's men instantly snapped into position, halberds gripped for the charge, faces set like flint.

For a moment, a ghost of doubt crossed Euler's face. The two forces stood facing one another, both bristling for combat.

Then, from behind the camp, there came sudden cries of alarm. There were horses galloping and metal clashing against metal. A trumpet blared out in warning. A long, strangled scream was followed by a massed roar of aggression. Something was attacking the camp's defences from the far side, and whatever it was had hit it hard.

Euler stared round in confusion, backing away from Bloch's column, clearly unsure how to react.

'Reiksguard!' came a cry from within the encampment. At that, some of Euler's guards started to run back through the entrance, swords drawn. Others stayed with their captain, confusion and apprehension marked on their faces.

'Reiksguard?' asked Kraus, incredulous. 'What in the nine hells are they doing here?'

'Morr knows,' said Bloch, picking out Euler with his blade and preparing to charge. 'And I don't care. We've had the luck of Ranald here, so let's use it.'

At that, with the tight-knit, lung-bursting roar they'd perfected out on the grasslands, Bloch's halberdiers surged forwards, blades lowered and murder in their eyes.

GROSSLICH SAT ON his throne of obsidian in the pinnacle, watching the clouds churn above him. Lightning streaked down, licking against the Iron Tower and screaming down to the courtyard far below. The aethyric fire still coursed through the air, staining everything a deep, throbbing red. Even the daylight failed to penetrate it. The maelstrom gathering above the Tower made the waking hours almost as dark as night.

The daemons still swam in the shifting winds, end-lessly circling the Tower, forever screeching their delight at being embodied in the world of mortals. Every so often they would swoop down to ground level and bring up some unfortunate to be torn to pieces for their pleasure. Not that the denizens of Averheim seemed capable of horror any longer. They'd been transformed into shambling automata, driven by the will of the Stone and blind to all else.

The Stone controlled the slaves, and Natassja con-trolled the Stone. Now that there was no longer any attempt to hide what they were doing from the Empire, Grosslich's position had become more per-ilous than ever. He was no fool. He'd known it when Alptraum had tried to manipulate him, and he recog-nised the signs again. He'd never be as powerful as Natassja in terms of sorcery, and there were few other cards left to play.

As Grosslich brooded on the throne, chin resting on his fist, a daemon slipped through the iron walls of the pinnacle chamber and pirouetted in front of him. He'd tried to place wards to prevent them from doing that, but the whole city was so drenched in Dark magic that it had proved impossible. They were deeply irritating, these capricious horrors, and they enjoyed provoking him.

The daemon stopped spinning and blew a kiss

towards him. She was impossibly lithe, as they all were, shimmering like a mirage, her flesh taut and rich and tantalisingly exposed. For some reason the fact that her hands were crab-like claws and her feet ended in talons failed to detract from the powerful allure. Even as steeped as he'd become in the arts of magic, it was hard not to rush towards her, arms extended, ready to be lost in the delicious pain of oblivion.

'What d'you want?' Grosslich drawled, at once aroused and put out by her presence.

'To watch you, mortal,' she replied. The voice was like a choir of children, all slightly out of sync with one another. 'It amuses me. Your desire is palpable. Why not give in to me? I might not even kill you afterwards.'

Grosslich sneered. 'And I might not kill you.'

'Kill *me*? Impossible.'

'Maybe. I'm learning new things every day.'

The daemon laughed, revealing her pointed incisors and a long, flickering tongue like a lizard's.

'What a good boy,' she said. 'That'll keep her happy.'

Grosslich scowled. The inane chatter was supremely annoying. Eschenbach would be here soon, and there were important matters to discuss. The Steward was one of the few humans left in the city with a mind of his own. Whatever she'd said about it, Natassja had destroyed his ambitions in that damned rite of hers. He had no wish to rule over a city of psychotic imbeciles.

'I could help you, you know,' said the daemon, sliding up to the throne and draping herself across one of the arms. Her fragrance was powerful, as intoxicating as the root.

'I doubt that,' said Grosslich, ignoring her and hoping she'd go away.

'Don't be so sure. You have no idea what she's going to do.'

'And you do.'

'Of course. I know everything.'

The daemon came close. Her eyes were as yellow as a cat's, blank and pupil-less. Grosslich looked away too late. The orbs were mirrored. He caught himself in them, faint and rippling as if seen from underwater. There were other things in there too, fragments of other men's dreams and nightmares. Terrible things. The stuff of which daemons were made.

'Just what do you think her ambition is in all this?' the daemon murmured. Her choir of voices became ever more seductive, curling around the syllables like the caress of a lover. 'Do you think she'll rest content turning this city into a playground for the likes of us?'

'She has what she wanted,' said Grosslich, trying to avoid the eyes. The daemon's sweet musk was beginning to affect his judgement. 'This is what we planned.'

The daemon laughed again.

'I know you don't really think that. She's given you a fortress of puppets. Of course, *we* love it here. At the end of time the whole world will be like this. In the meantime, I feel sorry for you. We don't like to see a handsome man disappointed.'

'There's no pity in your body,' Grosslich growled. 'You're an *absence* of pity, so don't try to tell me you feel sorry for anything.' He turned to face her. 'Your words don't impress me, for all they impress you. You're *nothing* next to a man, daemon. You're just echoes of our dreams. You talk of the realm of the senses. You cannot know it, not like we can. You exist only in a world of reflections.'

He lashed out and clasped his gauntlet around her neck, squeezing the aethyr-born muscle tight. The daemon's eyes widened in surprise.

'*Feel* it,' he hissed. '*This* is the flesh you can never know. You may mock us, but you envy this.'

The daemon blinked and was suddenly several feet away, eyes shining with delight. Grosslich's armoured fingers snapped closed on thin air.

'Masterful!' she laughed, rubbing her neck lasciviously. 'I knew a man like you once. He said much the same thing. I kept his eyes as baubles.'

'Just say what you came to say or go,' muttered Grosslich. The daemon sickened him. Much of what he'd done had begun to sicken him.

She sidled back close.

'Natassja cares nothing for the realms of men,' she whispered. 'The Stone is just the beginning. This is all about her. You'd better act fast, or you'll be the one with no eyes.'

'And what do you advise?'

The daemon looked suddenly serious. Her pouting lips calmed down.

'You have an army,' she breathed. 'Only a mortal can command it. That's the one thing you still own. Remember that.'

Then she shot up into the air, spinning with the supernatural grace of her sisters, diving and swooping with astonishing suppleness.

'I've enjoyed this chat,' she laughed, winking at him as she circled around the chamber. 'Come outside and see me some time. I'm sure we could have fun.'

Then she was gone, slipping through the window as if the glass wasn't there. Grosslich slumped back on the throne, his mood darkening. He knew better than to trust the words of daemons.

Still, they rankled.

A chime sounded from outside the chamber. Grosslich flicked a finger and the doors slid open. Eschenbach shuffled in. He looked emaciated, his skin drawn tight over his bones and his eyes staring from their sockets. The Dark Prince only knew why – there was plenty of food in the Tower storerooms. Perhaps he'd lost his appetite.

'You asked to see me, your Excellency.'

'I did, but I've changed my mind,' said Grosslich. 'I have another task for you. A simple one.'

Eschenbach swallowed.

'Go down to the dungeons,' said Grosslich. 'Enter the chamber of the Stone. Discover what the mistress intends for it. Then report back.'

Eschenbach's eyes widened, exposing red threads of veins. 'You cannot mean...' he began. His fingers started to tremble. 'Why do you not–'

He seemed to see the futility of the question, and stopped talking. Resignation shuddered through his tortured body. He, like so many others, had found service in the Tower less fulfilling than he might have hoped.

'I will do it,' he said, and bowed as low as his rearranged spine would let him. Then he was gone, limping back down into the central shaft of the Tower, broken in spirit as well as in body.

Grosslich remained silent. He gestured with another finger, and the braziers in the chamber guttered and went out. Alone in the dark, surrounded by the whoops of the daemons in the sky outside, the Elector of Averland pondered his next move.

As things stood, they didn't look good. He was alone, lord of a realm of nightmares, master of nothing. Something would have to be done.

Something *would* be done.

# Chapter Fourteen

SKARR KICKED HIS steed forwards, hacking on either side
with his broadsword. Grosslich's men scattered before
him, running for cover. The rest of the Reiksguard
swept along in his wake, cutting down any of the
guards too slow or too stupid to get out of the way.
Behind the horsemen came the footsoldiers he'd
equipped over the past few days. They were a ragged
tide of soldiery, wielding their weapons clumsily and
clad in a whole range of drab peasant garb, but at least
they were enthusiastic. They ransacked the rows of
tents, stabbing at any men they found inside or dragging them out to be butchered.

The raid seemed to have taken Grosslich's camp
entirely by surprise. Storming the embankment at the
west end of the enclosure had taken mere moments,
and the defence was cleared out by the first cavalry
charge. Once the perimeter had been seized, the interior was theirs and the knights ran amok, slaughtering
any who got in their way.

A knot of the elector's men, two dozen strong, some
still with helmets or breastplates missing, mustered
near the centre of the encampment, swords clutched

with both hands, desperate to form some kind of resistance.

Skarr laughed harshly.

'Reiksguard, to me!' he cried, spurring his horse on. The stand was brave but foolish. Few detachments in the Empire could withstand a massed charge from nearly thirty of the Emperor's finest knights, and these startled mercenaries would barely make him miss a stride.

The spearhead of Reiksguard thundered onwards, hooves drumming on the beaten earth. Even before the crash of the impact half the defenders had broken, turning and running wildly towards the east end of the encampment.

Skarr kicked his horse on and the knights crunched into the wavering band of men. Hooves lashed out, cracking ribs, breaking necks and knocking men cold. Behind them came the flickering blades, swooping down to kill like raptors. The few survivors turned tail, fleeing in almost comical terror, their spirits broken by the speed and power of the charge.

Skarr pursued them with cold efficiency, cutting down any he caught up with, maintaining the gallop. The momentum took him to the other end of the camp.

As the far embankment neared he slowed his pace, struck by the sight before him. There was fresh fighting ahead. The captain of Grosslich's troops was surrounded, pushed back into the compound in a concerted assault by a column of halberdiers in Reikland colours. Caught between twin attacks, the elector's troops were being hammered into submission.

The rest of the Reiksguard squadron drew alongside

Skarr. Behind them, the camp had been overrun. The preceptor's newly recruited troops were going after the few defenders that remained, killing with a zeal that promised good things for the future.

'Relieve those halberdiers,' Skarr ordered his men, kicking his horse back into a canter. 'Let's finish this.'

The Reiksguard plunged into action again, tearing through the dispirited resistance with disdainful ease. The halberdiers were equally savage. They fought expertly in close formation, supporting one another at the shoulder and wheeling to avoid the flank attack. Their captain, a thick-set man with the look of a brawler about him, was devastating at close range, wielding his heavy halberd as a lesser man might swing a longsword. Even as Skarr watched, he felled Grosslich's commander.

'Here's my name *and* business!' the man cried as he plunged his blade straight through the stricken captain's neck. His comrades laughed coarsely, finishing off the remainder of the defenders with a savage, feral energy.

They were serious fighters, thought Skarr, almost unconsciously hacking down a fleeing soldier as he careered from their assault and into his path. Possibly useful fighters.

The slaughter came to an end. In truth, it had been rank butchery. Several hundred of Grosslich's troops lay dead, strewn across the camp, their broken bodies trampled into the dirt by the rampaging peasant mob.

Skarr dismounted heavily, thumping to the ground in his plate armour. He'd have to impose some discipline on the worst of his troops in time, but for now they could enjoy their victory. Sterner trials lay ahead for them.

He strode over the heaps of crimson-clad corpses towards the halberdier captain. The man was being congratulated by his peers, all of whom were still whooping with the brutal enjoyment of the kill.

'Master halberdier!' cried Skarr, extending his gauntlet in friendship. 'I'd thought there were no foes of Grosslich left in Averland.'

The halberdier turned to face him and returned the handshake. He was grinning from ear to ear, his face splattered with blood and with a purple swelling disfiguring his left eye. He could have stumbled out of a fight in any disreputable tavern of the Empire.

'Nor I,' he said. 'That was good riding.'

The remainder of the Reiksguard dismounted. Most walked over to Skarr, swords in hand; others began to fan back through the camp, hunting for survivors.

'We could use men like yours,' said Skarr, looking over the body of halberdiers with approval. 'You're wearing Reikland colours. Who's your commander?'

'The Lord Schwarzhelm,' replied the halberdier, still smiling.

Skarr moved instantly. His dagger was out of his scabbard before the man could move. He whirled the halberdier round, got his left arm in a lock and hooked the blade up against his neck, pressing hard against the muscle. By the time the man knew what was happening, he was pinned.

'Schwarzhelm?' Skarr hissed, his good mood immediately shifting to a cold, heartfelt hatred. 'Well, this *is* my lucky day. Now tell me how to get to him, or you die where you stand.'

STREISSEN LAY IN ruins. The walls to the north of the town were little more than piles of rubble, smoking

gently from the cannon barrage. The boar's head of
Grosslich had been torn down and replaced with the
Imperial griffon and the old colours of Averland. The
dead lay in their hundreds on the streets, mostly
defenders, too numerous for the priests of Morr to
handle. Women wept openly as carts were loaded with
cadavers, some of them showing signs of mistreat-
ment after the combat had ended. All had been
stripped of their weapons and valuable items. The
dogs of war in Volkmar's army had paid scant regard
to the conventions of combat and only the strenuous
efforts of the warrior priests had prevented a whole-
sale massacre of innocents.

Resistance had been sporadic during the assault,
and most of it had concentrated around the large central square, once enclosed by richly decorated houses
and an elegant, tree-lined fountain. Now the foun-
tainhead was smashed and the cobbled space covered
in a stinking brown lake. The trees had been felled for
firewood and the grandest townhouse taken over by
Volkmar's retinue.

As the long, slow task of securing the city began, the
Grand Theogonist sat in the uppermost chamber,
flanked by his captains of war. He had taken the high
seat, a tall-backed chair carved from a single block of
oak. The others sat in two long rows on either side,
facing inwards. The subject of their interrogation
stood alone, dwarfed by the armoured figures bearing
down on him.

'That's *all* you know?' Volkmar snarled, leaning forwards, his hands gripping the chair arms tightly. His
hard face was twisted with disbelief.

The man standing before him didn't look like he
was lying. He hardly looked like he could stammer his

name out. Hans von Bohm, mayor of Streissen, had had plenty of time to regret his delay in coming to terms. The stench of smoke and burned flesh was a potent reminder of his failure.

'It is, my lord,' the mayor insisted. 'The elector–'

'The traitor.'

'The *traitor* sent us men from Averheim to bolster the garrison. They were all normal men, good stock from the land around these parts. None of them were tainted. If they had been, we wouldn't have taken them.'

Volkmar grunted with dissatisfaction, turning to Roll.

'Is he telling the truth?' he asked his confessor.

Roll shrugged. 'There's no aura of a lie.'

Volkmar turned back to the mayor.

'If you weren't in league with Grosslich, why did you not submit earlier? There are many deaths on your head.'

The mayor looked dumbfounded. 'We had barely time to read your demands! No war has been declared. What was I supposed to think, when an army suddenly appeared from the north and began to deploy? I was charged with the defence of this place.'

'And the column of fire did not alert you? The lack of contact from the Empire? At no stage did you doubt the loyalty of your new masters?'

'There had been no time!' cried the mayor, his exasperation getting the better of his fear. 'We are loyal subjects of the Empire, and you're asking us to know the impossible!'

Volkmar rose from his seat, glowering like thunder. The mayor shrank back, looking around him for some kind of support. None came.

'There are no excuses for ignorance,' the Theogonist said, looking like he wanted to leap across the floor and tear the man apart. 'You were placed in authority here. You should have acted sooner.'

The mayor said nothing, and hope left his eyes. Like a bewildered child asked to learn some lesson beyond his capability, he froze.

'Go now,' ordered Volkmar, bristling with suppressed anger. 'Gather what remains of your men and see that they're re-ordered into marching companies. They're under my command now. Fail me in this and I'll have you hanged.'

The mayor bowed and scuttled from the chamber, face flushed and sweaty. As he left, Volkmar slowly took his seat again. He sat, brooding, for a few moments. The sound of men working to clear the streets rose up from outside the townhouse, mixed with the sound of weeping and bells tolling.

'How quickly can we move again?' Volkmar asked at last.

'Whenever you order it, my lord,' said Gruppen.

'Then we leave within the hour,' said Volkmar.

'The men need rest,' objected Maljdir.

'They will get none.'

The big Nordlander raised his bearded chin, looking defiant. 'If you expect them to fight when they reach Averheim, they cannot march again.'

Volkmar looked at his priest darkly. It was one thing to have dissension from others of the command council, but to have it from one of his own retinue was intolerable.

'Are you telling me how to conduct this war, priest?' Volkmar asked, and there was a low note of threat in his gravelly voice.

Maljdir held the Theogonist's gaze. 'It is my counsel,' he replied. 'Why have a council of war, if you will not listen to its views?'

There was an intake of breath from one of the more junior captains. Roll, used to the fearless ways of his comrade, made no sign.

Volkmar's face went pale with anger. When he spoke, the muscles in his broad neck tensed.

'In the years we have fought together, you and I, you have never dared to speak thus. Perhaps you have more to say.'

'I do,' replied Maljdir. 'There were deaths here that should never have taken place. You know me well, Theogonist. Never have I hesitated to kill in the name of the law, but we could have taken Streissen without this bloodshed.'

'They were *heretics*,' hissed Volkmar, eyes blazing. 'They deserved nothing better. This will warn the others.'

'Heretics? They were instruments, as blind as moles.'

'So you *are* telling me how to conduct the war.' Volkmar's voice lowered, and the threat remained in it.

'And if I am? You've not commanded an army since your return from the wastes, my lord. What happened to you would change any man. You never relished slaughter before.'

Volkmar leapt to his feet and grabbed the Staff of Command. The shaft burst into a blazing golden light, cracking and spitting as it channelled his rage.

'You *dare* to accuse me!'

Gruppen and Roll rose from their seats, consternation etched on their faces.

'We don't have time for this,' warned Roll.

'That is right, confessor,' spat Volkmar, staring belligerently at Maljdir. 'Retract your words, priest, or this matter will be taken further.'

For a moment, Maljdir's fingers crept towards the handle of Bloodbringer, still by his side. He remained seated, his vast bulk crammed into a scholar's chair. His broad face was sullen and defiant.

Then, slowly, he withdrew.

'I do not intend disloyalty,' he said, his jaw tight. 'But the men need more time.'

Volkmar remained on his feet. The Staff continued to shimmer with angry golden energy. No one spoke. Eventually, grudgingly, Volkmar let the aura fade and flicker out.

'I will consider it. For now, this council is over. We have real work to do.'

He shot a final look of warning at Maljdir, then swept from the chamber, cloak streaming out from behind him, staff thudding on the floor as he went.

Once he'd gone, Gruppen moved his hand discreetly away from the pommel of his sword and relaxed.

'What're you *doing*?' said Roll to Maljdir.

'He's losing it. Surely you can see it.'

'I see nothing but your thick neck.'

'This is personal for him. He wants to make up for Archaon. Tell me truly, does this fury seem *normal* to you?'

Roll shook his head. 'You should have spoken out earlier. Averheim beckons. He will lead us there, whatever qualms you've suddenly developed.'

Maljdir clambered to his feet. 'If he directs it at Grosslich, I'll be right beside him. If he takes it out on our own kind, I'll not stand aside again.'

He hefted Bloodbringer lightly, and his expression was grim.

'You may count on it.'

BLOCH FROZE. THE dagger parted his skin, worming through the flesh. The pain was sharp. His day had just gone from surprising to downright insane.

'Get back!' he yelled at his men, some of whom had started to edge forwards. He knew something of Reiksguard from his time in the ranks. They were terrifying bastards and he had no doubt the preceptor would twist home his knife in an instant if he felt the slightest justification for it.

'Time's running out,' the preceptor warned, keeping the metal close.

Bloch felt a line of sweat run down his temple. After all he'd done, this continual ingratitude was getting ridiculous.

'I've no idea where he is,' he said, trying to keep his voice as steady as possible. 'On Sigmar's honour I don't. Now why don't you tell me why you're so happy to kill me to find out?'

The Reiksguard kept his scarred, ugly face close. Bloch could feel the man's breath on his cheek.

'Not good enough,' he snarled. Something had made him very angry indeed. 'One more chance.'

Bloch swallowed. The knife dug a little deeper. A hot trickle of blood slipped down his collar. It would be important to get the next few words right.

'I can't tell you, because I don't know,' he said, speaking slowly and carefully. 'The last time I saw him was weeks ago. He ordered me to retake Black Fire Keep from the orcs. I did that. Now I come back here, and everybody wants to kill me. Perhaps I wouldn't be so angry about that if I had any idea why.'

The Reiksguard paused. Bloch dared to start hoping again. From the corner of his eye he could see Kraus, itching to pile in.

'You weren't in Averheim with him?'

'No, though I was hoping to find him there.'

Another pause.

'You really have no idea why I might want to spill blood to find him?'

'No idea at all. Less than none. Though if you do find a lead, perhaps you'd let me come along with you. There's a lot I'd like to ask him too.'

As suddenly as he'd struck, the preceptor withdrew the knife. Bloch spun out of the armlock and staggered away, feeling his neck gingerly. His men took a menacing pace forwards again.

'Enough!' he rasped, waving them back. Something very strange was going on, and this was his best chance to find out what. 'Morr's balls, that *hurt*.'

The preceptor didn't look obviously sorry. He and his men radiated aggression.

'Be thankful I didn't finish the job. If I hadn't seen you fighting against Grosslich's men, you'd have died a lot sooner.'

Bloch winced. That didn't make him feel a lot better.

'Look, we could put all this behind us if you'd just tell me what in the nine hells is happening here. When I headed east, there was a battle for succession going on. Now it seems like this Grosslich is in charge and he's killing anyone left who isn't him. I'm pretty sure that's not what Schwarzhelm intended.'

The preceptor regarded him suspiciously. His knights stayed poised to attack. It didn't seem to matter to them that it was thirty knights and a rabble of ill-trained peasant filth against two hundred battle-hardened infantry. Reiksguard were crazy like that. They'd take on anyone.

'You haven't heard about Lord Helborg, then?' asked the Reiksguard darkly.

Bloch shook his head. The last he'd heard, Helborg had been in Nuln.

'Then we have much to discuss, you and I,' said the preceptor. 'I will tell you what I know. Perhaps you can explain the rest. Then, once things are a little clearer between us, I'll decide what to do with you.'

ANOTHER DREAR, COLD day was drawing to a close. Blankets of cloud obscured the sunset, but the darkness stealing from the east came on quickly enough. Helborg stood on a ridge, his gaze drawn north. He was alone. The rest of the army was busy erecting camp half a mile away. While the light remained, the Marshal surveyed the country ahead, planning the next day's march, weighing up the dangers ahead, choosing where to recover more supplies, horses and fodder to fuel their onward progress.

The army had reached the edge of the highlands. To the north the land fell away sharply, turning from barren scrub into the rich grassland for which Averland was famous. From Helborg's position, right on the summit of a scarp on the borders of the moor-country, he could see for miles. The heart of the province beckoned, its grasses ruffled by the ceaseless wind, its open skies marred by storms.

The column of fire weighed on his mind. Now, just as the army was poised on the cusp of descending into the interior, it was ever-present, visible even during the middle of the day. The broken clouds swirled above it, drawn inwards as if summoned by a Celestial magister of awesome power.

The Marshal gazed at the angry glow for a while, reflecting on the paucity of men he had under arms. Nearly two thousand now marched with him, the gleanings of Leitdorf's ancestral lands. As a result of Skarr's plunder he had money to pay them, supplies to give them and weapons to arm them with. That might well not be enough. The more Leitdorf told him what was in Marius's notebooks, the more he dreaded the encounter to come. Not for his own sake – he was a fighting man, and battle had never held any terrors for him – but for the sake of the Empire. If the corruption was not staunched at its source then it would spread as surely as the pox in a whorehouse. The Empire was already overstretched with the endless war in the north. A drawn-out campaign in Averland would be disastrous. Maybe even fatal.

Two thousand men. On such meagre forces did so much depend.

'My lord.'

Helborg turned to see a group of Reiksguard standing to attention. They were led by Rainer Hausman, the one he'd sent ahead to scout the flanks of the rearguard.

'I gave instructions to be left alone,' he said.

Hausman bowed in apology.

'I know. We have a prisoner.'

As the man spoke, his captive stepped forwards.

It was perfectly clear the man was no prisoner. He stood nearly a head taller than the knights around him and was more powerfully built than them even out of his armour. His beard looked a little greyer, his skin a little tighter, his stance a little less upright, but there could be no mistake about it.

It was him. After so many nights of dreaming of that mighty face, contorted with rage and madness, he was back.

Helborg felt his blood begin to pump. The wound in his shoulder suddenly flared, as if recognising the man that had dealt it. His hand flew for his sword quicker than thought and his fingers curled around the grip. His jaw locked. For once, his fluent speech deserted him. His knuckles went white.

Schwarzhelm stood motionless. His face was as grim as it had ever been. He said nothing. The Reiksguard withdrew, leaving the two peerless warriors alone, exposed on the escarpment, facing one another as the wind whipped about them. From the northwest, a rumble of distant thunder rolled across the plains.

Helborg took a step forwards, face taut with rage. The anger burned him; the deep, smouldering sense of injustice that had burned since the duel in Averheim. For so many nights, drifting on the borders of death, that rage had sustained him. For so long he'd lived for nothing more than the thought of vengeance. Now his fury flared into the real world, animating his sinews, firing his lungs, screaming at him to wield the blade.

It felt unreal, like the lingering memory of a dream. The grip on his sword grew tighter. He couldn't lift his arm.

On the far horizon, the column of fire flared, angry and raw.

Schwarzhelm moved first. Keeping his gestures obvious, unthreatening, he unfastened a naked sword from his belt. The blade was notched halfway along its length. In the low light, the metal looked black with age. There were runes on the steel, obscured in the darkness.

Helborg remained frozen, driven by fury, imprisoned by indecision. This was *wrong*. Schwarzhelm was his brother.

He was a traitor.

The big man edged forwards, carrying the Sword of Vengeance on his upturned palms. As he drew closer, Helborg saw the grief on his face. The man was wracked with it. The last time he'd seen those features, they'd been lit with a fire of madness. Now what was left was grey and empty, like embers that had long since burned into husks.

Schwarzhelm halted less than a yard away. He extended his arms, offering Helborg the Klingerach. With stiff fingers, Helborg loosed his grip on his borrowed blade, raised his right hand and took it at the hilt.

The weight was familiar, the balance almost the same as before. Helborg bore it up. The spirit of the weapon was coiled within, as ancient and powerful as the lost forges on which it had been made. As Helborg took the grip, he felt death locked into the instrument. It had killed for millennia, this thing, drinking deep of the blood of men and their enemies alike. It thirsted still. It would thirst until the end of time, never satisfied, never at peace.

Only one taint remained on its glinting surface, the shard Schwarzhelm had taken from it. That had still to be healed.

Schwarzhelm sank to one knee then, his limbs moving awkwardly. Only then, kneeling before Helborg, did he speak. When they came, his words were shaky and thick with emotion.

'This is yours, Kurt. Wield it as your heart dictates.'

The tide of rage broke. Schwarzhelm's voice unlocked it.

'Damn you!' Helborg roared, snatching up the blade in two hands and raising it high. 'Damn your arrogance! You should *not* have come.'

Helborg held the Klingerach high over his head, grip tight, poised to strike. He locked it in place, shivering with anger, waiting for the resolve to bring it down. Schwarzhelm bared his neck, looking Helborg in the eye, refusing to flinch. He said nothing more.

*I will find the one who did this to me.*

Still Helborg hesitated. He felt as if his fury had become so great that it would destroy them both if he moved. The fire within him raged beyond all control, greedy and consuming. His shoulder flared again, sending jets of pain coursing through his body. The wound goaded him, his anger goaded him, the sword goaded him.

*My name itself is vengeance.*

Still they remained, locked in a grotesque masque of execution. Heartbeats drummed, heavy and lingering. The runefang wavered, eager to plunge.

When it fell at last, toppling from his fingers to land in the grass, he hardly heard it. It rolled away, discarded in the mud like a child's toy.

'Not this way.'

Helborg reached down. Extending a hand, he raised Schwarzhelm to his feet. The big man hauled himself up slowly, unready to face him again.

The anger was still there. The grief was stronger now. Even during the darkest times, it had always been stronger. They were the titans of the Empire, the two of them, the foundations upon which all else was built. That could never be forgotten, not while any shred of forgiveness existed within the world.

Helborg looked into the man's face. There were the familiar features he had fought alongside for so many years, the cracked cheeks, the deep-set eyes, the unsmiling mouth. The madness had gone from them. Schwarzhelm was diminished in some respects, unchanged in others.

Emperor's Champion.

'*Brother,*' said Helborg, gripping him by the shoulders.

Schwarzhelm met his gaze. The old warrior had seen it all. Loss and victory, faith and treachery. He'd witnessed the fires of war tear across the Empire. He'd watched, defiant, as the tides of ruin had swept down from the wastes of the north and the hopes of mankind had dimmed. In all of this he had been unmoving, implacable, emotionless.

Only now did he falter. Only now, as Helborg embraced him at last, did his eyes glisten with tears. Clumsily, he returned the gesture, his mighty arms locked round the shoulders of his rival. There they stood, together once more as brothers in arms, the bitterness purged, the anger drained away.

The Reiksguard watched, silent as tombs, none daring to move. At their side was Verstohlen, lost in contemplation. After so long in the wilderness, the circle had been completed. About this, as with so much else, he had been wrong.

Forgiveness had been sought. Honour had been satisfied. Restitution had been made.

* * *

ACHENDORFER HURRIED THROUGH the corridors of the under-Tower, clutching the book to his breast as he always did. He had no choice. The leather-bound tome had merged with the fingers of his left hand. The book was one with him now, and he was one with the book. Little by little, the pages of spells and arcane recipes of death within had melted away from the parchment, all except the one he needed, the one he recited every day. The one that coaxed the Stone into life.

All around him, muffled moans and sighs ran down the twisting passages. Every so often a pale hand would reach out from the ornately carved walls, clutching at him desperately. So many slaves had been trapped within the filigree of iron that he'd lost count of them. They couldn't die in there, but neither was their agonised existence truly life. Some brave souls retained enough of a sense of self to implore him to release them, their fingers scrabbling against the cage walls to gain his attention.

Achendorfer ignored them. Where could they go, even if they were set free? All of Averheim was a furnace now, a shrine to the singular lust of one individual. They didn't matter to her, no more than they had in their former miserable lives.

He turned a corner sharply and followed a winding path between high, arching walls of obsidian. He went as surely as a rat in a cellar. He knew all the routes, all the myriad ways of the under-Tower. Another gift from the queen. Even when the walls shifted, as they often did, he could still follow them.

Achendorfer scurried quickly, knowing the penalties for missing an appointment. On his right, the wall suddenly fell away, exposing a huge shaft. Hot air blossomed up from it, flaked with ash. Deep down below, massive engines toiled and churned. Natassja's thousands of minions had been busy. Such infernal devices magnified her power many times over, storing the energies of the Stone in vast crystal cylinders. The machines growled angrily as they turned, fed incessantly by a host of Stone-slaves.

Achendorfer pressed on, feeling the book crackle expectantly under his touch. How long had it lain, forgotten, in the library of the Averburg? It had been a spoil of war, probably, recovered by an elector count and dumped, unread, in his stash of trophies and trinkets. Now, after so many thousands of years, the words were being heard again in the lands of the living. Perhaps the author, if some shred of him still existed, was pleased about that.

Achendorfer left the shaft behind and drew closer to the heart of the under-Tower. The walls began to throb with a suffused pink light, bleeding from behind the black iron like the organs of a dissected corpse. Natassja liked those little touches.

He paused for a second, reflecting on how far he'd come. It was five years ago that the dreams had started, leading him to the library under the Averburg and its terrible secret. Back then Natassja had kept her face covered, whispering secrets to him and promising the wealth of Araby if he would interpret the scripts for her. And so he had done so, working night and day in the gloomy recesses of the archives, his skin turning grey and his hair falling free in clumps.

It had been worth it. All the pain, all the humiliation. He was now her *true* lieutenant in the Tower, whatever Grosslich thought about such things. Achendorfer had been given gifts beyond measure and had seen things no mortal could dream of. He had a personal guard of fifty augmented dog-soldiers, exclusive chambers near the centre of the under-Tower and a playroom lined with shackled, quiescent pets.

All of that was immaterial, of course, besides the *power*. That was what convinced him he'd been right to turn. For the first time in his life he held the lives of men in his hands. The knowledge of that thrilled him. By the time this was over, she would make him a god. That's what she said. The prospect made him moisten his purple lips with anticipation. She'd promised so much, and always kept her word.

A scream broke out from up ahead, resounding down the curved walls. Achendorfer smiled. So it had started.

He came to a set of double doors, each inscribed with a glowing lilac sigil of Slaanesh. He gestured with his free hand and they slid open.

The room beyond was circular and lined with marble. There was no furniture or adornment, just perfectly smooth, faintly reflective walls. There was no ceiling either. The polished walls went up, on and on, hundreds of feet, until they emerged near the summit of the Tower, far above the roofs of Averheim. The laughter of daemons could be heard from the distant opening, and fire flickered around the rim.

A single figure crouched on the floor, hands clasped over his ears. Odo Heidegger, Templar of Sigmar.

'So you know the truth,' said Achendorfer, closing the doors behind him.

Heidegger looked at him imploringly. His skin was white with fear and horror. He'd torn his scarlet robes apart. Beneath them Achendorfer could see protruding ribs, stark across the man's wasted torso.

'What is this... *madness*?' he cried, spittle flying from his dribbling mouth, eyes staring.

Achendorfer smiled.

'What you've helped to create. All of this has been built by you, witch hunter.'

Heidegger's horror grew. His mind, for so long on the brink of insanity, was breaking. Natassja had lifted the veil from him, and the pleasure of the moment was exquisite.

'You killed every enemy who could have worked against us,' said Achendorfer. 'You delivered Alptraum to us. You killed Morven and let Tochfel be taken. You burned the rebellious and tortured the questioning. The queen is pleased with your work. She asked me to thank you in person.'

Heidegger looked like he might be sick, but there was nothing to retch up in his ravaged frame. He fell to his knees and wracking sobs shook his body.

'No,' he gasped. 'This is an illusion. I have been working for the Lord Sigmar, who protects and guides. Long may He–'

Achendorfer laughed, and his distended stomach wobbled beneath his white robes.

'Oh, you are subject to an illusion,' he admitted, coming to crouch down beside the distraught Templar. 'All that you did *before* was an illusion. This is real. This is more real than anything you've ever known.'

Heidegger's eyes began to flicker rapidly back and forth. Lines of foamy drool ran down his chin, glistening in the light of the fires above.

'I do not...' he started, then seemed to lose the power of speech. A low howl broke from his bloodstained lips.

'You were a *sadist*, master witch hunter,' whispered

Achendorfer, loading his words with malice. 'You broke men for pleasure, whatever stories you told yourself about righteousness and duty. You were no different from us, except perhaps in honesty.'

From far above, the howling was reciprocated. Something was coming down the shaft, travelling fast.

'How many of our kind did you hunt down in your career? Dozens? Not a bad total. Now you have killed *hundreds*. All of them innocent. You are a murderer and a traitor, Herr Heidegger. The blood of Grosslich's treachery is on your hands. When your soul is dragged before the throne of your boy-god, he will not deign to look at it. It's *ours* now.'

The howling grew in volume. It was nearly upon them. Achendorfer got up and withdrew, looking down with satisfaction at the weeping, broken man before him. He backed towards the door, wishing he could stay to see the final act.

'Do not fool yourself that this death will be the last one,' he sneered. 'The Lord of Pain has plans for you. Eternity, in your case, will seem like a very long time.'

Then the daemons landed, slamming down from their screaming descent, eyes lit with infinite joy and malignance. They opened their fanged mouths, and the tongues flickered.

Achendorfer slipped through the doors and closed them just in time. As the barriers fell into place something heavy slammed against them and was taken up the shaft. There was no more screaming from the witch hunter. Heidegger's mortal body had been broken and the daemons had taken it. Unfortunately for him, physical death meant little to a daemon. Their sport was only just beginning.

\* \* \*

THE CAMP HAD settled for the night. Watch fires burned on the edge of it, throwing dancing shadows across the gorse. The guards patrolled the perimeter in detachments of six men, all fully armoured. The rotation was strict. Rumours still ran through the army about creatures made of bone and iron that stalked the moors at night, unstoppable and eager to drink the blood of men. Some said they had talons of wire and eyes that glowed with a pale flame, though the more level-headed troops were quick to disregard such exaggeration. Since leaving Drakenmoor, the columns had encountered nothing more threatening than foxes and kites, though they were all perfectly aware things would change as they neared the city. The watch fires were burned partly for security, but also to blot out the terrible fire on the western horizon, the one that never went out.

Verstohlen sat on the edge of one such camp fire, cradling a cup of beer in his hands and watching the men nearby as they noisily prepared for the night. They slept in their cloaks, huddled around their own small fires, laughing and telling obscene stories. Soldiers were the same across the whole Empire. Verstohlen remembered how they'd been at Turgitz. Then, as now, he was on the outside. Now, as then, men looked at him askance, questioning his presence, unsure of his role.

A dark shape loomed up from the shadows and stood before him. Unlike the rest of the troops, he didn't hurry on by. Verstohlen looked up, and his heart sank.

Rufus Leitdorf stood there, dressed in a breastplate and greaves, a sword at his belt. He'd lost weight, and looked less bloated than he'd done in Averheim. He still had the long hair and ruddy cheeks of old, but there was a residual hollow expression that marred his fleshy face.

'Verstohlen,' he said, and the tone was cold.

Verstohlen sighed. The meeting had to happen sooner or later. Perhaps best to get it over with now.

'My lord elector,' he said, inclining his head but remaining seated. 'Will you join me?'

Leitdorf shook his head.

'No,' he said. 'That might indicate to the world that we were friends. That is not the way of it, nor will it ever be.'

'I see.'

Leitdorf moved to stand in the light of the fire. His features, lit from below, looked distorted.

'I have spoken to the Lord Schwarzhelm,' he said. Verstohlen thought his voice was less haughty than before, and there was a gravity to it that he'd never noticed in Averheim. 'After reconciling with the Marshal, he apologised to me. Profusely. I have accepted it. Do you have anything you wish to add?'

'I'm glad you two made up,' said Verstohlen flatly. 'You don't want to prolong a feud with Schwarzhelm.'

'Is that all you have to say? Gods, your arrogance knows no bounds. Truly, I don't know why you came back. You offer us nothing now.'

Verstohlen swept to his feet in a single, fluid movement. He was taller than Leitdorf and considerably more deadly. Leitdorf, startled, held his ground, and the two of them faced off.

'There were errors,' Verstohlen said coolly. 'For these, I am sorry. But you *lived* with her, Leitdorf. If she could deceive you so completely, then perhaps you will understand why we made the decisions we did.'

'You should have contacted me. The war you started was unnecessary.'

'Don't fool yourself. If it hadn't been me, she'd have found another way to implicate you.' Verstohlen's face edged closer to the elector's, lit with threat. 'It might make you feel better to blame me for what took place, but you'd do well to reflect on your own conduct. If you'd not taken Natassja to your bed, there'd be no joyroot, and no corruption. We have erred, my lord, but you set this thing in motion.'

Leitdorf's hand slipped to his sword-belt.

'Even now, you dare–'

'I dare nothing. I state the facts.' Verstohlen shook his head in disgust. He was too tired for this. 'What do you want from me? Guilt? Oh, I've got plenty of that. We both have. Every night when I close my eyes I see Tochfel's face. He tried to warn me. Do you know what they did to him? They cut out his heart and replaced it with a ball of iron. *Your wife.*'

Verstohlen looked away, filled with revulsion by the memory.

'So don't try to pretend this is something you don't share responsibility for,' he muttered. 'We're all guilty, and we all had choices.'

Leitdorf removed his hand from his sword-belt. Verstohlen expected him to fly off into some tirade. To his surprise, the man remained calm.

'And you don't think much of mine, do you?' he said.

'It hardly matters now.'

'I disagree.' Leitdorf raised his chin defiantly. 'Whether you can stomach it or not, Herr Verstohlen, I am the elector now. Kurt Helborg leads my army, and Ludwig Schwarzhelm stands beside him. Soon my claim will be put to the test, and this time there can be no doubt about its legitimacy. Either we will die in battle, or I will rule Averland. Those are the only outcomes possible. Which one would you prefer?'

Verstohlen smiled grimly.

'I have no wish to see you dead, Leitdorf. Nor, for that matter, myself. But unless you've grown much wiser in a short space of time, I have no wish to see a dissolute count ruling in Averheim either. I do not say this to wound you, but your reputation does you no credit.'

Leitdorf returned the thin smile. 'So others have said.' He looked back over his shoulder. Near the centre of the encampment, Helborg was conversing with Schwarzhelm and the other captains. 'I see the warmth between us has not grown. If you'd spoken to me thus in Averheim, I'd have had you driven from the province in disgrace. Even now, a part of me would not regret to see you leave.'

He took a deep breath. As his chest rose and fell, Verstohlen noticed a book, wrapped in fabric and strapped to his belt. An unusual ornament for the battlefield.

'I've changed, Verstohlen,' he said, 'even if you haven't. Perhaps, when this is over, you'll see the proof of it.'

Verstohlen paused before replying. There *was* something different about the man. Not enough to be sure about, but hardly insignificant either.

'Perhaps I will,' was all he said, and he returned to the fire.

# Chapter Fifteen

HOLYMON ESCHENBACH MADE his way down the spiral stairway in the central shaft of the Tower. As he limped from one step to the next, the dull rumble from below grew louder. The iron around him reverberated with the drumming sound of machines turning in the depths. The lower he climbed, the hotter it became. In every sense, he was coming to the source of things.

The stairs finally came to an end, and he stood at the base of the Tower. A long gallery led away in front of him, shrouded in shadow. There were doorways along either side, each with a different rune inscribed over the lintel. At the far end was an octagonal chamber containing an obsidian throne. There were no dog-soldiers around. The only noise was the muffled growl of the machines and the endless rush of the fire as it swirled in the air outside.

Eschenbach swallowed painfully, feeling his neck muscles constrict around the pitiful trickle of saliva he was capable of generating. His transformations had built up over the past few days. What he'd initially thought of as improvements had turned out to be serious handicaps. For some reason, the Dark Prince seemed displeased with him. Eschenbach knew of no cause for that – he'd faithfully served the elector since his coronation – but that didn't make the pain go away.

He knew his death was close. He could feel it stealing up behind him, padding in the dark like a cat. The only question was when, at whose hand, and how painful they'd make it. Some reward for the service he'd rendered.

Eschenbach shuffled forwards awkwardly, feeling his altered bones grind against one another. The rooms on either side of him were deserted. In the earliest days Natassja had conducted her experiments here, creating the first of the Stone-slaves. Now she had whole levels of the under-Tower devoted to her invasive surgeries, and the screams of the tormented and augmented echoed into the vaults like massed choruses in a cathedral. Dog-soldiers had been born in their thousands there, filled with bestial savagery and strength, utterly loyal and without fear.

Other horrors had been made. He'd seen trios of handmaidens, eyes glowing, scuttling through the lower reaches like a gaggle of bronze-tipped spiders. There were men's heads grafted on to women's bodies, eyeless and earless horrors stumbling around in the dark, lost beyond hope of rescue. They had no conceivable use in the war, just amusement value for the queen.

The earliest augmentation chambers now lay abandoned, the instruments lying where she'd left them, the tables stained with old blood and the stone walls as cold and silent as ice.

'I see you, Steward,' came her voice.

It was as familiar as a recurrent nightmare. Eschenbach shivered to his core. It came from the chamber at the end of the gallery.

There was no choice but to follow it. He limped forwards, trying to ignore the residue of agony in the open doorways as he passed them by.

Natassja was waiting for him. She sat on the throne, painfully elegant, searingly beautiful, radiating an aura of such terrifying power and malice that he nearly broke down in front of her before managing his first bow. Elector Grosslich had his powers, to be sure, but Natassja was something else.

'Why are you here?' she asked. There was little emotion in her voice. No anger, no spite, just a faint trace of boredom. She looked at him with the same casual disinterest a man might use on a particularly nondescript worm.

Eschenbach did his best to look her in the face.

'I was sent by the Lord Grosslich,' he rasped, feeling his jaw nearly seize up with the effort.

'For what purpose?'

'He wished me to check on the progress of the Stone.'

'He is welcome to come himself.'

'Shall I ask him to, my lady?'

Natassja shook her head. The movement was so slight, so perfectly poised. The queen seemed incapable of making a clumsy or ill-considered gesture. She was flawless, the living embodiment of a dark and perfect symmetry.

'No need. You may see for yourself.'

She raised a slender hand. Behind her throne the stone walls shifted. Soundlessly, gliding on rails of polished bronze, two panels slid backwards and out, revealing a roaring, blood-red space beyond. Some-thing astonishing had been exposed out there – even Eschenbach's paltry skills could detect the volume of power being directed from below. He held back, reluc-tant to venture any closer.

'Take a look,' said Natassja. Her voice sang as softly as it ever did, but the tone of command was absolute. If she'd ordered him to pluck his own eyes out, he would have done it then without question. As he shuf-fled into place, Natassja rose from the throne, her dress falling about her like wine slipping down a grateful throat, and followed him.

The rear walls of the chamber opened out into the side of a massive shaft. The scale of it took Eschen-bach's breath away. Sheer walls were clad in dark iron, moulded into a thousand pillars, arches and but-tresses. Sigils of Slaanesh and Chaos had been beaten into the metal and shone an angry crimson. A hun-dred feet below, the base of the shaft was lost in a ball of slowly rotating fire. Above him, the columns soared into the far distance, lined along their whole length with elaborate sculptures and gothic ornamentation, before being lost in a fog of flame and shadow. Beau-tiful, terrible figures carved from iron and steel peered out from lofty perches on the high walls, their blank eyes bathed in flames.

Eschenbach knew without having to ask that the shaft went all the way to the summit of the Tower. Whenever he'd had his audiences with Grosslich, he'd been standing on top of it. The elector's chamber was nothing more than the fragile cap on this mighty well of fire. He wondered if Grosslich knew that.

The air inside was a mass of roaring, rushing and booming energy. Aethyric matter surged up the narrow space, pressing against its iron shackles, throbbing and fighting to be released. Now, at last, Eschenbach knew the purpose of the citadel. The whole thing was a device with a single purpose: to conduct the will of the Stone, to magnify and condense it into a point, far above the level of the city. As he watched the titanic levels of arcane puissance balloon along the spine of the Tower, as he heard the roar from below, he began to gain some appreciation of the scale of what had been achieved here.

'What do you think?' asked Natassja, standing by his side on the edge of the precipice. The rush of flames licked against her ankles, curling around her body like whips. The red light lit up her face, and her dark eyes glowed.

'Magnificent,' murmured Eschenbach, for a moment forgetting the pains in his mortal body. Beside this, nothing else seemed significant. 'It's magnificent.'

Natassja looked like she barely heard him. She was gazing into the shaft herself, eyes lost in rapture.

'This is what the suffering has achieved,' she murmured. 'The merest savage can inflict misery. We never act but for a higher purpose. The Stone is roused by agony. It *is* agony.'

Eschenbach listened, rapt. Natassja ignored him, speaking to herself.

'Every spar of this Tower, every stone of it, is in place for a reason. There lies the true beauty of this place. The *necessity* of it. Only that which is necessary is beautiful, and the beautiful is all that is necessary. That shall be my creed, when all is done here.'

She smiled, exposing her impossibly delicate incisors, tapered to a vanishing point of sharpness.

'My *creed*. Ah, the blasphemy of it.'

Natassja turned to Eschenbach.

'Enough of this. Have you seen what you came for?'

'I have, my queen.'

The pain in Eschenbach's body had lessened. His senses were operating at a heightened pitch of awareness. Visions rushed towards him like waking dreams. He saw the numberless host of Grosslich's men, legions of darkness, marching in endless ranks, unstoppable and remorseless. He saw the daemons circling the Tower like crows, ancient and malevolent, glorious and perfect. He saw the full extent of the Stone buried in the earth below, as black as the infinite void, a mere fragment of the future.

Some things began to make sense then. He no longer regretted his choices.

'Will you report back to your master?'

Eschenbach shook his head.

'No, my queen.'

'Good. So you know what will please me.'

'I do.'

'Then please me.'

Eschenbach grinned. The movement ripped his mouth at the edges, the muscles having long wasted into nothingness. He didn't care. Pain was nothing. There would be more pain, but that was nothing too. Only the Stone mattered.

He stepped from the ledge and was swept upwards by the vast power of the shaft. The flames seared him, crackling his flesh and curling it from the bone. He laughed as he was borne aloft, feeling his tortured face fracture. He was rising fast, buoyed up by the column of fire, speeding past the sigils of Slaanesh. They glowed back at him with pleasure. He had finally done well.

His eyes were burned away. He breathed in, and fire tore through his body and into his lungs. At the end, before his charred figure slammed into the roof of the shaft, he felt his soul pulled from his mortal form, immolated by the will of the Stone, sucked into its dark heart and consumed. In a final sliver of awareness, he knew just how much closer his sacrifice had brought forward the great awakening. Before he could be pleased by that, he was gone, the candle-flame of his life extinguished within the inferno of something far, far greater.

On her ledge below, Natassja remained still, watching the flames as they screamed past.

'Now then, Heinz-Mark,' she breathed, stretching out her hand and watching the torrents caress her flesh. 'Your servants are all gone. The time has come, I think, for you to face me.'

HELBORG'S ARMY HAD descended from the highlands and made good progress across the rolling fields of Averland. The men had been organised into standard Imperial formations and strode down the wide merchants' roads in squares of halberdier and spearman companies. Their livery was patchy and irregular, but they were well-armed and highly motivated. Helborg had made sure they were fed and paid, and they rewarded him by maintaining good discipline. With every mile they travelled, more came to join them. All the villagers in the region had seen the column of fire in the west, and even their simple minds had felt the corruption bleeding from it. Carts and supplies were commandeered and added to the straggling baggage caravan. At the end of the first full day of marching into the interior, his forces had swelled to near three thousand. The few remaining Reiksguard were the only truly deadly troops among them, but the rest at least had blades and some idea of how to use them.

At the end of each day, the army established camp in the Imperial manner, raising earthworks around a close-packed formation of tents and ramming stakes into the defences. As the army had grown, this task had become more arduous and time-consuming, but it was necessary work. Grosslich's forces had yet to engage them, but the closer they came to the capital the more inevitable an attack became. They were now little more than a day's march away, almost close enough to see the tips of the city's spires on the north-west horizon.

With the raising of the encampment, the men retired to their positions for the night, sitting around fires and speculating about the booty they'd receive for aiding the Reiksmarshal on campaign. They avoided discussion of the forces ranged against them, or the growing presence of the pillar of fire, or the reports from the forward scouts of a strange dark tower thrusting up from the heart of the city.

In the centre of the camp the command group held council, screened from the rank and file by canvas hoardings and sitting around a huge fire. Helborg stood in the place of honour, his breastplate glowing red from the flames. The Sword of Vengeance hung again from his belt, and it had made him complete. His habitual flamboyance seemed to have been replaced with a kind of grim majesty, and in the fire-light he resembled nothing so much as the statue of Magnus the Pious in the Chapel of Fallen.

On his left stood Hausman, in Skarr's absence the most senior Reiksguard. On his right was Leitdorf, looking uncomfortable in his armour. There were four other captains drawn from the ranks, all veteran soldiers and Leitdorf loyalists wearing the blue and burgundy.

Opposite Helborg, completing the circle, was Schwarzhelm. The Emperor's Champion looked almost as imposing as Helborg. He was back in armour, and it seemed to have had a restorative effect on his demeanour. Verstohlen stood, as ever, by his side. He remained in the margins, observing the deliberations rather than contributing, just as his long service in the clandestine arts had equipped him to do.

'You have all seen the pillar of fire,' said Helborg. 'You know the story of treachery we march to avenge. But there are greater forces at work here. Lord Schwarzhelm has more knowledge of the foe we face than any of us, so I have asked him to speak.'

All turned to the big man. The bad blood between him and Helborg seemed purged after the drama of their first meeting, but the atmosphere remained brittle. None of the captains seemed to know how to act around him. Schwarzhelm, as was his manner, gave away nothing.

'We do not march alone,' he said, and his growling voice seemed to reverberate from his newly-donned battle-plate. 'The Emperor has been warned, and we can be sure there will be Imperial forces hastening to counter the threat. How close they are, I do not know. We may encounter them at Averheim, or they may still be weeks away.'

His eyes swept the captains. There was a light kindled in them, one Verstohlen hadn't seen for many days. Not since Schwarzhelm had ridden east from the succession debate to crush the orcs. He lived for this kind of test.

'In either case, we cannot wait. I have been in Averheim. It has been turned into a den of Chaos, and our duty is to purge it. We must do all in our power to weaken the defences, whether or not other Imperial forces are committed. Our survival is unimportant.'

The Averlander captains looked concerned by that. Helborg had promised them victory, not sacrifice.

'How many men does Grosslich have under command?' asked one of them.

'We don't know,' said Helborg. 'Nor does it matter. Schwarzhelm's verdict is the only one – as soon as we're within range, we'll commit to an assault. I've sent messages to my lieutenant to gather all the men he commands. We'll join forces south of the city and make directly for it. The bulk of the troops will engage the enemy while a strike force composed of myself, the Lord Schwarzhelm and the Reiksguard will penetrate the Tower. Grosslich is the heart of this – if we kill him, the edifice around him will crumble.'

Leitdorf shook his head.

'Madness,' he muttered.

All eyes turned to him. The elector looked up guiltily, as if he'd been talking to himself.

'Well, it is,' he said defiantly. 'Even Ironjaw couldn't storm the heart of the city. It's built to withstand a siege from armies five times as big as this.'

Helborg glowered at him. 'You forget who marches with you. The Swords of Vengeance and Justice are not to be taken lightly.'

'No doubt. Neither is Natassja. And perhaps you've noticed the bonfire she's created over there – it'll take more than two pointy sticks to put it out.'

Verstohlen smiled in the dark. Against his better judgement, he was beginning to like the elector.

Helborg showed no such tolerance. 'Then I take it you have a better plan,' he said, and his voice was icy.

Leitdorf shrugged. 'The only hope is to rendezvous with this Empire army. Your swords may be of help against the sorcery within the Tower, but you'll have to get close enough first.'

There was an uncomfortable silence. Helborg was unused to being challenged, but Leitdorf had grown in stature over the past few weeks. He'd also saved the Marshal's life, which gave him something of an edge in the discussion.

'They'll come from the north,' said Leitdorf. 'Invading armies have always taken the high ground above the city before attempting an assault. That's where we should join them. You say that Preceptor Skarr has more men? Good. We can sweep up the eastern side of Averheim, rendezvous with his troops and then march to occupy the Averpeak. From there we'll be able to hold our ground until the Imperial forces arrive. If they're already there, we'll be well placed to reinforce them ourselves. It's the only course of action.'

Leitdorf's voice had grown more confident the more he'd spoken. Unlike at Drakenmoor, his captains actually listened.

Helborg said nothing, pondering the counsel. He still looked undecided. Leitdorf's manoeuvre would take longer, and they all knew time was running short. Despite that, there was sense to it – this was his country, and the elector knew the way the land was laid.

'We cannot be sure the Empire has responded yet,' said Schwarzhelm.

'Indeed,' said Verstohlen, giving Leitdorf a wry nod

of support. The elector had the self-command not to look surprised. 'But they are our best chance of success in this. We should plan our advance around them. If we arrive and they're not there, then we can consider the other options.'

'We'll lose the element of surprise,' muttered Helborg. 'They'll see us come up from the east flank.'

'There *is* no element of surprise,' said Leitdorf grimly. 'They know where we are as surely as they know the positions of the stars. Trust me, I was married to the woman.'

There was another long silence. Helborg shot an enquiring glance at Schwarzhelm, but the big man said nothing. Eventually, the Marshal let slip a scraping laugh.

'So be it!' he said. 'The elector has made his judgement. Skarr will rendezvous with us to the east of Averheim, from where we'll take position in the north. Messengers will ride out tonight, and we break camp at dawn.'

He looked over at Leitdorf, and his expression was a mix of amusement and approval.

'Not many men overrule my judgement in matters of war, Herr Leitdorf. Let us hope your confidence repays us with a victory.'

Leitdorf bowed in return. There was neither diffidence nor arrogance in the gesture.

'This is my realm, Reiksmarshal,' he said. 'It is time I took control of it.'


THE PLAINS NORTH of Averheim had once been lush, covered in the thick grass that had made the wealth of the province. The wide river Aver had fed a dozen smaller tributaries, all of which had watered the fertile black soil and nurtured the thick vegetation. Herds of cattle had been driven across the rolling country for centuries, growing fat and sleek on the goodness of the land.

Now all had changed. The city was still consumed by the column of fire. Its streets were havens of horror and madness, its residual inhabitants in hopeless thrall to the Dark Gods. Though the daemons did not venture outside the cordon set by their mistress, others of Natassja's creatures had not been slow to venture beyond the city walls. They marched in file, rank after rank, trampling the grass beneath their iron-shod feet. Great engines of war were hauled up from the depths of the forges, swaying on iron chains the width of a man's waist. Channels of witch-fire were kindled in the six lesser towers. These ran swiftly from their source, burning what little remained of the once healthy country and turning it into a bare, stark waste-land of choking ash. For miles in every direction, the canker spread. Averheim stood alone, a city of twisted iron spires amid a desolate plain of ruin.

Upon that charred and fouled wilderness, the Army of the Stone made its camp. Lines of tents were raised, each surmounted with the skulls of those slain resisting the elector. Braziers were set up, sending clouds of smog rolling over the land and coating it in a cloying pall of soot. Massive spikes were hauled from the forges under the Tower and placed around the edges of the vast encampment. Trenches were dug by a horde of mute slave labour, then filled with quick-kindling oils, roaring with green-tinged flames.

Above it all, the Tower loomed, vast and brooding, isolate and defiant, a shard of night-black metal thrusting up from the tortured land like a blade. The storm circled around it, its clouds drawn to the pinnacle by the rupture in the world's fabric, furious and yet impotent. Lightning danced under the eaves of the piled mass of darkness, flickering along the flanks of the Tower, throwing rare glimpses of light into the perpetual gloom of the lost city. It might have been night, it might have been day – beneath the wings of the storm it was impossible to tell. The aegis of fire remained, boiling and churning as it tore into the heavens, drowning out all other sounds, the terrible mark of the corruption of Averland.

Two miles distant, a high ridge ran around the northern approaches to the city. No trees had grown there even in the days of health and plenty, and from its vantage one could see across the entire Aver floodplain. South of the ridge, the land fell smoothly down to the level of the river, the road looping and circling towards the flat ground before the mighty gates of the city. Men had long called the ridge the Averpeak, and they said it was Siggurd's barrow that caused the earth to rise. At its summit it was broad and smooth, running east–west for several miles before the rolling hills broke its curving outline. In the semi-remembered past, armies had camped on the mighty bulwark, poised like eagles to swoop down on the city below them. Only Ironjaw, the last great besieger of the city, had rejected its advantages, so drunk had he been on the wine of conquest.

Grosslich knew his history, as did the silent commanders who now stalked among his legions. So it was that the camp was set in opposition to the Averpeak, and the trenches cut off the lines of assault from the high places. The old road was dug up and embankments raised across it. As if the embellished walls of Averheim with their six subordinate towers were not deterrent enough, the plains before the gates had been turned into killing fields, laced with instruments of murder and marked with rivers of unholy fire.

All this Volkmar saw as he crested the summit of the Averpeak. He rode at the head of the army, the first to come to the edge of the ridge and gaze down on the plain below. As the view unfolded, he halted, staff in hand, and was silent.

Behind him the rest of the army took up their positions. Maljdir, Roll and the warrior priests lined up in the centre, standing grim and resolute with the light of the fires reflecting from their breastplates. The battle wizards came behind them. There were two Celestial wizards, including the recovered Hettram, their sky-blue robes reflecting the fires like mirrors. Alongside them were three Bright wizards, their staffs already kindling with flame, and a triad of Light magisters clad in bone-white robes and already making preparations for their communal spellcasting.

Once the command retinue was in place, the massed ranks of halberdiers, spearmen and swordsmen spread out across the Averpeak, arranged in assault formation. They too were silent. There were no songs of defiance as they edged towards their positions. They stood in their companies, mutely staring at the horror below, only half-listening to the hymns of hate and defiance droned out by the priests. On the far left flank, to the east of the battlefield, came the light cavalry, pistoliers and handgunners. The horses, even those used to the ways of war, stamped nervously.

Only when the artillery was hauled into position

did something of a cheer run through the ranks of men. Mighty iron-belchers were dragged into place by their teams of sweating horses. Piles of cannonballs were unloaded from the heavy carts and made ready. Helblasters, Helstorms and mortars were brought up from the engineers' caravan. There were dozens of them, alongside over thirty cannons of various sizes. The broadside from such a collection would be monstrous indeed.

Volkmar had chosen to place his heavy guns on the right flank of his army, to the west of the city. Here the Averpeak came closest to the city walls, and the cannon had a devastating view over the plains. As soon as they were in position, earthworks were raised around them. Six auxiliary companies fell into place to guard the guns from assault, bolstered by a detachment of greatswords decked in the colours of Altdorf.

Behind the front lines, Volkmar placed nearly five thousand men in reserve. For the time being they were deployed among the baggage train, though no one doubted they would be called into action before long. There were also archer companies, fast-moving and lightly armed, held back behind the front ranks for rapid deployment. These took their allotted places as nervously as the rest of their peers, double-checking their strings and anxiously making sure fresh arrows were close to hand.

Aside from Volkmar and the warrior priests, only one detachment of the entire army truly marched without fear. Gruppen was last into position, his four hundred Knights Panther having held back to allow the rest of the army to spread along the ridge. As he took his station with the artillery on the extreme right flank, the cheers from the men around him took on some real enthusiasm. His men were decked in their full plate armour and exotic pelts, mounted on chargers with broadswords at their sides. Their pennants were raised defiantly against the swirling winds of the storm, a forest of leaping panthers and slender figures of Myrmidia.

Leonidas Gruppen was foremost among the knights, his visor up and his harsh face exposed to the horrors below. He went proudly, his armour draped in the hide of a black panther from furthest Ind, his standard-bearer at his side. The preceptor gave the word and the banner was unfurled, a glorious tapestry to Myrmidia picked out in gold and ivory.

Gruppen turned to Volkmar's position and raised his fist in salute. As he did so, the remaining banners of the army were swung into position. Standards of Reikland, Nuln, Middenheim, Talabecland, city-states of Tilea, Averland and the mercenary companies all flew out, caught by the buffets of the storm and exposed in all their varied splendour.

In the centre of the ridge, Volkmar gave Maljdir a curt nod. The burly Nordlander strode forwards, Bloodbringer swinging from his belt. He carried the Imperial Standard in both mighty hands. Planting the shaft firmly in the soil, he let the Theogonist's own banner stream out. The golden fabric rushed into view, exposing the Emperor's own coat of arms: two crimson griffons rampant flanking a sable shield with the initials *KF* emblazoned in dazzling argent. At the sight of the famous colours, the most revered in all the lands of men, the infantry regiments cried out with genuine fervour. If the Emperor had gifted Volkmar his own devices, men reasoned, then all hope had not gone.

With that gesture, the army was in place. Forty

thousand troops deployed along the ridge, all facing south, all armed and ready for combat.

Volkmar looked back over the plain. The enemy army waited silently a mile distant, sprawled before the walls of the city in their sullen magnificence, spread like a vast black contagion over the once pristine plains. No banners flew. No brazen trumpets called them to arms. Instead, the braziers continued to belch smoke, the fires continued to blaze, the engines continued to churn.

Then the sign was given. High up in the Iron Tower, a lilac star blazed out briefly, cutting through the columns of fire for an instant. A sigh seemed to pass through the distant ranks of waiting troops. Drums started to beat across the walls. All over the waiting host, men – or things like men – took up their crystal halberds and locked them into readiness.

Volkmar looked across the enemy formation impassively. The traitor host was larger than the Imperial army, though the smog made it hard to gauge by how much. This Grosslich had been busy. Now his designs would be put to the test.

'So we come to it at last,' he growled to Roll, taking up the Staff of Command. The gold reflected the distant lightning, glowing proudly against the gathering dark.

'Sigmar preserve us,' said Roll grimly, drawing his sword. 'Sigmar preserve us all.'

NATASSJA WAITED IN the throne room. The doors to the shaft beyond had been closed and the roar of the fires was subdued. She could feel the power beneath her feet growing, though. The time was fast approaching. Both her body and mind were changing. Her awareness, already more acute than the limited senses of mortal women, had magnified a thousandfold. She could feel the heartbeat of every soul within the city, could feel the slow burn of their stunted emotions as they readied themselves for the coming assault. From the augmentation chambers in the pits of the Tower to the daemons circling above, they were all transparent to her.

The transformation had some drawbacks. Her grasp on the material world was becoming ever more tenuous, and she had to concentrate to ensure that she retained her proper place within it. This was a dangerous time for her. If she lost her grip too soon, before the Stone had reached the appropriate pitch of awareness, the process would never complete and she'd be left torn and rootless.

That would *not* happen. Not after so many decades in the preparation.

Ever since her youth, almost forgotten on the plains of Kislev, she had known she was destined for greater things. The life of a serf had never been enough for her. Even before she'd known of any existence other than the casual brutality of the ice-bound villages, some voice had reassured her that the future held improvements. That voice had never left her, her constant companion as the years had worn on.

It had all changed with the coming of the dark ones. Out of the wastes they'd ridden, tall and slender and bearing the curved scimitars of raiders. She'd loved them at once, relishing their cruelty and skill. The villagers hadn't stood a chance. The headman had been the last to go, roaring with pointless resistance right up until the lead horseman put a spike through his temple.

Then they'd taken her. She'd been pretty and young enough to be worth corrupting. Ah, that had been a hard time. Even during the worst of her misery, manacled in the hut of the bandit chieftain, subject to the crude tastes of a savage and ignorant man, the voice hadn't gone away. The raiders were His people, and He promised to deliver her from them. If she was just patient for a while and accepted the trials He sent her, then the path would open up to worlds of discovery.

And so it had proved. In the far north, there were wonders fit for a mind of her subtlety. Her knowledge grew, fed by the snatched tutelage of shamans and their slaves. Beauty was an asset amongst such people, and in time she learned to use it. Each night she abased herself before the Dark Prince, and He gifted her luck. When she finally escaped the chieftain and was free to explore the fringes of the realm of madness, He gave her the Vision. She could remember it as clearly as ever. It had been *so beautiful*. By comparison, the bleak steppes became dreary and tedious to her. So she worked harder as she traversed the hidden realms, studied forbidden books, learned secret rites, delved into the wellspring of Dark magic which gushed so fulsomely on the edge of the mortal world of matter.

The years passed. Others aged, and she did not. When after so long in the far north she finally discovered the old bandit chieftain again he was in failing health, ready to put aside the cares of mortal life and join the symphony of souls in the hereafter. Natassja kept him alive for another fifty years, every day of which was a fresh and unique agony. By the time she was ready to let his shrivelled soul slink into oblivion, her powers had become swollen and overripe. The hunt for a greater challenge was on. She needed to find a way to fulfil the Vision.

She never regretted leaving the steppes. The warmer lands were so much more interesting, bursting with opportunity and places to practise the art. Over the long, wearing years she'd lived in many places – Marienburg, Altdorf of course, Talabheim, the heart of the Drakwald, a Lahmian citadel in the Middle Mountains, a hundred other places great and small. The world aged and grew colder while her blood and flesh remained hot and vital. The Vision never left her. She was just waiting for the right moment.

She thought it had come with Marius, but he'd proved impossible to subvert. Then she'd found Lassus, and the possibilities began to coalesce. Four hundred years of searching, and the Vision had been vindicated in Averheim, that most provincial of Imperial cities. Turning the dull, prosperous, strait-laced pile of dung into a cacophonous oratory to the Lord of Pain had been the most pleasurable thing she'd ever done. The men of Averland were no better than the cattle they reared, and their fate was well and truly deserved. It was an appropriate place to begin her new life, and her gratitude to the Dark Prince was profound and sincere. To those that pleased Him, He asked for so little, and gave so much.

Now she'd passed beyond the power of any in the province to hinder her. Helborg, for so long the one she'd feared, could do nothing in the time that remained to him. Schwarzhelm even less so. Volkmar and his little band of sword-wavers might be an irritation, but her vast legions stood between her and the Theogonist. All she needed now was a breathing space, just enough for the harmonies to reach their optimum pitch. It wouldn't be long.

'Natassja!'

Grosslich's voice was thick with anger. She turned to see him framed in the doorway to her throne room. He was still dressed in his ridiculous red armour. The Dark Prince only knew what had made him design such a thing. He carried his bone wand in one hand and a black-bladed sword in the other.

He looked hugely annoyed. She didn't blame him for that. If she'd been him, she'd have been hugely annoyed too.

'My love,' she murmured, walking over to the throne and taking her place on it. The little gestures were important, even now. 'What brings you–'

'You know damn well what brings me here,' Grosslich said, advancing towards her. There was a powerful aura about him. He'd grown strong. In another place and another time, he'd have been a mighty warlord. The waste of it saddened her.

'You seek Eschenbach.'

'Seek? No. I know full well what you did to him. Sacrificed to your power, just as you intend to sacrifice me.'

'And why would I want that?'

'To rule this place alone,' spat Grosslich, eyes blazing. 'That's why you made it a home of capering devils. None of this is what I wanted.'

Natassja raised an eyebrow. 'Then stay here with me. I'll show you how to enjoy it. I never lied to you, Heinz-Mark. Believe me. If you stay in the Tower, there are still many things we could accomplish together.'

Grosslich laughed harshly. A fey light had kindled across his features. The power he'd accumulated was already leaking, spilling out from his fingertips like water. He couldn't handle what he'd been given. Ach, the *waste*.

'Perhaps you'd like that,' he said. 'Perhaps that would give you all you wanted from this arrangement.'

He laughed again, a bitter, choking sound. 'I won't do it, Natassja. There's one role left I know how to play. Your army needs a commander. I'm leaving to take them. I'll destroy the challengers, and then I'll make my next move. Perhaps I'll bring them back here. Perhaps I won't. You've given me the tools to carve out a realm of my own – it doesn't need to be here.'

'I could prevent you,' Natassja said, and the sadness in her voice was unfeigned.

Grosslich shook his head. 'I don't think so. My skills are greater than you think.'

Natassja knew that wasn't so. She could kill him with a word, but to do so would solve nothing. Out of affection, she would give him a final chance, after which he would have to make his own decisions.

'If you leave the Tower, I cannot protect you. If you stay, you will remain safe. You have my word. You will never be the master, but you will be provided for. You may yet become truly mighty, a regent worthy of long service.'

Grosslich smiled to himself, as if a joke he'd heard a lifetime ago had suddenly made sense.

'A *regent*. Tempting. I'll bear it in mind.'

He bowed low.

'Farewell, Natassja. When I return, master of the armies you've created, perhaps our negotiations will go differently.'

He turned on his heel flamboyantly and marched out of the chamber. Natassja watched him go. Despite everything, despite the centuries of malice and intrigue, she was not unmoved. There had been a path for the two of them she'd foreseen, one of discovery, knowledge and enlightenment. The fact that he'd chosen to reject it was regrettable.

'So you let him go,' came a sibilant voice from behind the throne.

A daemon curled up from the floor, her naked flesh snaking lewdly across the obsidian. Natassja ignored the gratuitous attempt at provocation. For beings of infinite intelligence and power, daemons could be tediously infantile.

'Of course,' she replied. 'Maybe it was wrong of me to expect more of him.'

The daemon laughed. 'Or maybe he decided his position was no longer secure. That *is* a mighty army out there. It will make him feel safer.'

Natassja turned to look at the daemon and frowned with disapproval.

'Did you plant that idea in his head? If so, I'll rend you apart.'

The daemon giggled, though the laughter was suffused with a note of fear. She darted away, hovering near the outlet to the shaft.

'That's not in your gift, my queen,' she reminded her.

'Not yet,' said Natassja, rising from the throne. 'But watch yourself.'

She began to walk from the chamber.

'Are you *starting* it, then?' asked the daemon excitedly, following at a safe distance.

'Why not? I have the city to myself now.'

The daemon whooped with pleasure. 'Then you're not worried about their armies? Helborg draws close, and he carries the sword.'

'What can he do now? His time has passed.' Natassja turned to the floating daemon and gave her an affectionate, tolerant smile. 'Return to your sisters, dark one. There'll be more play for you before the day is out.'

Then she turned back, heading down the long gallery and towards the spiral staircase.

'The Chamber of the Stone will be warded until all is complete,' she warned. 'Wait for me outside the Tower. It is, at last, time for my birth.'

# Chapter Sixteen

OUT ON THE plain, something had changed. The legions continued to take up their positions, but a new presence had come among them. Volkmar strode forwards, peering down into the smog-clad gloom of the battlefield.

'My spyglass,' he snapped, and a priest hurried to bring it.

He swept across the ranks of enemy troops. Some were men, clad in Grosslich's colours, their eyes glowing strangely. Others were obscene corruptions of men, their legs twisted backwards and crouching like dogs.

Then he found his quarry. The gates of the city had opened, and a man had emerged, mounted on a coal-black charger. The horse was as corrupt and twisted as everything else in that host. It had clawed pads in place of hooves and a scaled hide in place of skin. Its mane and tail shone like polished onyx and had been plaited and decorated with jewels. Tabards decorated with forbidden sigils hung from its flanks, and its eyes smouldered like hot embers. It was massive, at least a foot taller and broader than a mortal beast, and when it trod on the broken earth the claws sunk deep.

The figure mounted on it was no less impressive. Enclosed from head to foot in crimson armour, glistening from the fires around him, the master of Averheim had emerged. He wore a tall helm crested with a plume of gold, the only opening of which was a narrow slit for his eyes. In his right hand he carried a black-bladed broadsword with a serrated edge. It looked as if molten pitch were continually dripping from the dagger-sharp points, pooling like blood on the earth as he passed into the heart of his men. In his left hand he bore a wand of bone.

As he made his way through the ranks of soldiers they withdrew silently. Perhaps once they had fought under him as mortal men, hopeful of the new dawn he would bring to Averland. Now such memories were lost, subsumed beneath the crushing will of the Stone and its mistress.

With their commander among them, the legions began to advance.

'So it begins,' said Volkmar, handing the spyglass back. 'The master has left his lair. Give the signal.'

Trumpets blared out from the command position and passed down the line. The gunnery crews sprang into action. Just as they had done at Streissen, they worked quickly and well. These were crews from Nuln, the best in the Empire, and they were masters of their deadly trade.

Orders roared out, cannonballs were rammed home and rags doused in flame. Crews and escorts scrambled to get out of the way as the iron-belchers were primed and loaded. Seconds later the thundering boom of ignition shook the earth and a wall of death screamed out from the Averpeak on to the plain below. Huge clouds of blackpowder smoke billowed from the gun-line, swept up into the air by the swirling storm and dragged across the battlefield.

The enemy vanguard continued to advance into range, heedless of the power of the artillery. They were cut down in clumps, blasted apart by the sudden wrath of the heavy guns. Heedless and undaunted, they came onwards, clambering over their fallen without pause. Like a massive pall of black fog, the enemy rolled across the plain, marching slowly, claiming more ruined ground with every step.

'Maintain fire!' ordered Volkmar, looking down at the enemy ranks. All along the ridge, men were poised to counter-attack. Soldiers fingered their weapons, sweat on their brows and ice in their heart. Minutes passed while the iron-belchers reloaded. The waiting was the worst part.

The cannons bellowed out again and a fresh cloud of blackpowder discharge tumbled down the slope. This time the barrage was laced with the scything fire of the Helblasters, slamming into the front ranks of the Army of the Stone and tearing open whole companies of marching troops. In their wake the fizzing trails of Helstorm rockets screamed, spinning into the sea of men and detonating with devastating effect. Limbs were torn free and armour shattered by the volleys as they thudded home, round after round of murderous power.

But Grosslich was no savage or raving maniac. In his der of men, and he didn't send his vanguard idly into harm's way. After the advance had gone so far, they halted, halberds raised, and began to dig in. Spikes the length of a man were brought up from the heart of the host and rammed into the ground. Earthworks were raised and the ground behind them cleared. Under withering fire from the Imperial guns, the forces of Grosslich toiled with neither fear nor hurry. Whenever an exposed company was torn apart by a well-aimed salvo, another would take its place. The artillery barrage was costing them dear, but it couldn't dislodge them.

Horns blared from the walls of the city, and the reason for their death-clogged advance became apparent. Huge engines of war, each forged in the hells of fire beneath the Tower, were dragged from the open gates by straining teams of mutated horses. Their wide mouths gaped twice as wide as the largest Imperial cannon. Each device was decorated with writhing bands of bronze and encased in a spiked cage of iron. Smoke poured from beneath them where furnaces had been stoked and fuelled to a flesh-blistering heat. Stone-slaves crawled all over them, polishing the bronze and adjusting the spider webs of pistons and valves even as the towering constructs were hauled towards the forward positions. As the line of guns ground on, each monstrous engine was flanked by whole companies of heavily armoured infantry, all covered in thick iron plate, their faces hidden behind masks in the form of leering beasts.

From the angle of those mighty barrels, it looked as if their range was less than the Imperial guns. What they lacked in distance, however, it was clear they made up for in power. As Volkmar gazed at the rumbling tide of death his eyes narrowed, calculating the distances and gauging the outcome of a volley.

'Target those embankments!' he roared, and the order went down through the ranks.

'We have to *advance*,' hissed Maljdir, his hands eager to clasp Bloodbringer. 'Once those things–'

A fresh boom of cannon fire echoed across the battlefield, backed up with a hail of rockets. The gunnery crews weren't fools, and had adjusted their aim to meet the new threat. One of the rumbling war machines was hit by a whole flurry of artillery fire. It cracked open, leaking green-tinged flames. The horrific structure listed for a moment, wracked by internal explosions, then blasted apart, showering the troops around it with white-hot metal shards.

A cheer went up from the watching Imperial forces, but it was short-lived. Other war machines were hit and suffered little, protected by their thick iron plating. More than a dozen still remained, all crawling into position, all aimed up at the ridge. The nearest drew up to the allotted positions, their bronze-lined maws grinning like hungry wolves.

Still Volkmar held back the charge.

'Magisters,' growled Volkmar, determined to delay the engagement until the last possible moment. 'Destroy them.'

The Celestial wizards strode forwards, staffs crackling with sapphire lightning and their robes rippling from winds seen and unseen. Alonysius von Hettram, the senior battle wizard of the entire army, gave the Theogonist a proud look.

'It will be done,' he said, and the winds of magic began to race.

BLOCH WATCHED THE column of fire grow as he rode west. The sight was enough to render him mute. He'd seen nothing like it in his life, and he'd done a lot of campaigning. The spectacle at Turgitz had been something, but the destruction of Averheim was on a whole different register of impressive.

Kraus was beside him as ever, riding a grey steed and keeping his mouth shut. The honour guard captain hadn't liked what he'd heard about Schwarzhelm any more than Bloch had. The big man inspired near-fanatical loyalty from the fighting men close to him, and hearing of his actions at the Vormeisterplatz had made sobering listening.

Behind the two of them, Skarr's army of infantry streamed out, marching in a semi-organised rabble. A rabble, that was, except for Bloch's own halberdiers, who stuck to the well-drilled squares he'd insisted on. They'd keep their discipline even in the fires of hell.

Ahead of them rode the Reiksguard. Skarr hadn't spoken much to Bloch since they'd exchanged their stories. He was still angry. Bloch couldn't help but think the preceptor would have liked to punish him for Schwarzhelm's alleged crimes just to make himself feel better. Typical high-born.

Despite it all though, he couldn't entirely blame the preceptor. Bloch remembered the strain on Schwarzhelm's face east of Heideck. His words had remained with him. *Since arriving in Averland I've not felt myself. It's been as if some force has turned against me, weighing down on my mind. The city is at the heart of it. It may be that Averheim is perilous for me.*

Perhaps he'd been right about that. There was little else that could explain Skarr's testimony. The few details Bloch had been able to add – Leitdorf's treachery, the long process of legal divination, the Imperial armour on the greenskins – hadn't really helped matters.

Even after the preceptor had allowed Bloch to accompany him to the rendezvous with Helborg, much still remained to be settled. The Reiksguard were suspicious, and their blood-oath against Schwarzhelm remained intact. Bloch found himself confronted with the terrible scenario of marching against his old master. For all he knew, Schwarzhelm *had* turned to darkness. He couldn't quite bring himself to believe that, but the thought wouldn't leave him alone.

'So is this what we drove the orcs out of Averland for?' muttered Kraus, staring sullenly at the distant red clouds.

Skarr's column was little more than a day's march from Averheim, summoned by Helborg's orders of a muster. At the appointed location, Skarr's two thousand troops would join up with Helborg's three thousand. Not much of an army to take on the forces of the great enemy, especially as over three-quarters of them could barely point their sword in the right direction without being shown how.

'I'd rather have one enemy than two.'

Kraus shook his head irritably.

'I don't believe it,' he said. 'He hasn't turned. And I won't believe he made a mistake either.'

'You said yourself he was acting strangely.'

'The man's commanded armies for thirty years. He's no weakling.'

'Skarr never said he was. This is the great enemy.'

Kraus said nothing, and turned his eyes away from the angry sky. On the far horizon there came a low, grinding rumble, as if the earth were as troubled as the heavens above it.

'We should be glad we made it back here, Kraus,' said Bloch. 'We've been part of this from the beginning. It'll all be decided in Averheim, one way or the other. Couldn't miss that.'

Kraus remained stubbornly quiet. Bloch looked up, watching the way the clouds were sucked across the sky into such a massive, slowly rotating spiral. He knew as well as anyone that their army couldn't fight power of that magnitude, whether or not Helborg rode with them. Just more crazy Reiksguard heroism, a final fling of bravado before they all died.

That suited him. Fighting was what he'd been born for. It had to end some time or other, and it might as well be against a decent enemy. All he'd need was a sign that the sacrifices had been worth something and he'd happily march into that storm of fire, halberd in his hand as always, searching for the next victim, doing what he'd been put on the earth to do.

HETTRAM WAS FIRST to cast. Raising his hands high, he cried aloud, summoning the storm to his aid. His companion, barely out of his twenties and with a lean face, joined him, adding his raw power to that of his master.

Above the battlefield, the clouds swirled fast. The storm, already raging, accelerated into a frenzy of anger. Lightning slammed down from the boiling tumult above, immolating all it struck and sending fresh fires blazing up from the heart of the belea-guered city.

'Storm, unleash thy wrath!' roared Hettram, sum-moning fresh power from the elements.

Rain began to hammer down, whipped into flurries by the wind. It bounced from the streaming barrels of the war engines, fizzing and hissing. Bolts of silver fire scored the heavens, streaking and tearing into the lumbering hosts below.

Another of the war engines tilted over, hit by a

thunderous blast from the skies and cracked down the length of its gaping muzzle. Still it was dragged on, listing in the mud, gouging a huge furrow as the horses strained against their chains. The beasts had been driven mad by whatever foul experiments had been performed on them, and they foamed against their halters, churning up the mire until it became a blood-coloured soup.

'We're not stopping them,' muttered Maljdir, watching darkly as the rest of the guns were hauled into their firing positions.

The Imperial cannons roared out again, sending blackpowder plumes rolling into the heart of the maelstrom. More lightning slammed down on to the field, burning brightly as it plunged into the heart of Grosslich's legions.

Still the engines came on, rolling as the chains pulled tight, islands of iron amidst a morass of men.

'More power!' snarled Volkmar, seeing the engines settle into place and chains being run across their armoured backs.

The Bright wizards joined their Celestial counterparts. Their art was better suited to close-pitched combat, but they raised their staffs and summoned up the Wind of Aqshy. Chanting in unison, they called the words of their pyromantic craft aloud and shook their blazing shafts, eyes wide and riddled with sparks.

Now the lightning was laced with a consuming fire. The bolts summoned from the skies smashed into the advancing horde and burst into waves of hungry flame. The immolation spread quickly, taking the shapes of ravening wolves, sweeping across the ranks of glow-eyed figures and wrapping them in an agonising, rolling death. Every artillery impact exploded in a ball of orange, surging across the blasted land and leaping up into the braziers and trenches.

Hundreds perished in that onslaught, burned alive by the sheets of fire-laced lightning, caught up in the heaven-summoned inferno. Two more engines were consumed, wreathed in leaping tongues of flame before exploding in a halo of spinning iron and bronze. Horses screamed and reared against their bonds, tugging the vast engines out of position. Another toppled over, lost in a welter of chains, hooves and struggling limbs. Cannons bellowed again, and the shell was cracked.

Still the rest came on.

Volkmar watched as the first engine was made secure, protected by earthworks, crowned with a bristling cordon of spikes and surrounded by the massed ranks of Grosslich's elite guard. Fresh fire was kindled at its base and huge piles of shot were unloaded behind it, ready to be hoisted into the unholy mechanism and hurled into the waiting ranks of Empire troops.

Volkmar looked round at the Light wizards. They were still preparing their magic, locked as it was in complex rites and rituals. The Celestial wizards were beginning to tire, and their powers would be needed later. He had no more to give. The advance of the guns had been slowed but not halted. Their deadly power would soon be unleashed.

He turned to Maljdir.

'We've done what we can,' he said. 'Give the order to charge.'

OUT ON THE far west flank, Leonidas Gruppen heard the trumpet blare out and his heart leapt. The moment had come.

'Lances!' he roared, and his squires rushed forwards with the steel-tipped shafts, staggering as they tried to keep their footing on the slippery ground.

All around him his knights formed up into squadrons of twenty, each man with a lance and all prepared for the first, vital charge. Behind them, the second wave waited impatiently. In two sweeping assaults, all four hundred Knights Panther would slam into the enemy lines, clearing a path for the infantry and carving their way towards the war engines. They were the tip of the spear, the sharpest instrument in the armoury of Sigmar's heirs.

More trumpets resounded from the centre of the ridge and the massed host of halberdiers began to run down the shallow slope of the Averpeak, hollering cries to Sigmar and Ranald as they went.

Gruppen looked down at the battlefield below. Less than half a mile distant, the first ranks of the enemy waited. They'd had time to dig in, but not enough. Empire artillery had blasted huge gouges in their lines of trenches and swathes of the vanguard were in disarray from the bombardment.

He picked his target and took up his lance.

'For Myrmidia!' he cried. All around him his brother knights did likewise, and for a brief moment the shout of the Knights Panther drowned out the rest of the Imperial army.

Then he snapped his visor down and kicked his horse down the slope. The squires sprinted clear and the squadrons tore towards the enemy line, picking up speed as they hurtled towards the front ranks.

Gruppen felt his heart thumping within his armoured chest as his steed accelerated into a pounding gallop. The gap between the armies shrank rapidly.

As at the Turgitz Cauldron, the knights formed into a wall of steel, their lances swinging down into position as each man picked his enemy.

Gruppen narrowed his eyes. The battlefield was a riot of fire and smoke. Flashes of lightning still arced down, exposing the vast extent of the enemy formations in vivid detail. He saw men lumbering into his path, hauling pikes into place to frustrate the charge.

Too slow. The ride of the Knights Panther was like a sudden deluge from the high peaks. Travelling at speed, their hooves a thudding blur, the squadrons smashed into the lines of defenders.

Gruppen was at the forefront. He aimed for a knot of men trying to erect fresh spikes. They tried to pull back when they saw him bearing down, but they had no chance. He spurred his charger on, sweeping through them and impaling the leader clean through with his lance. On either side of him his knights did likewise, slicing open the defences and scattering the loose formations.

Then they were amongst the press of men and the charge ground into its first resistance. Gruppen dropped his lance and drew his broadsword, whirling it round in the air as it left the scabbard. His men ploughed deep into the enemy ranks, crunching aside any obstacle. At this range, Gruppen's horse was as deadly as he was. His charger's hooves lashed out as it slowed from the gallop, crushing skulls and cracking ribs. His blade followed up, sweeping in mighty wheels to slash out at any infantry foolish enough to get close.

Gruppen spurred his horse on further, maintaining the momentum, carving his way towards his objective. It loomed up in the dark, far larger than he'd guessed from atop the ridge. The war engine towered thirty feet into the air, a heavy muzzle of iron and bronze, studded with rivets and underpinned with its growling furnace. Iron-masked men milled around it like ants, readying it to fire.

As the knights swept closer the defence became more stubborn. Grosslich's heavy infantry, rendered impervious to glancing blows by their plate armour, formed a defensive line between the knights and the war engine.

'Onwards!' roared Gruppen, kicking his steed back into speed, knowing they had to break them on the charge. The knights swept into range, still in formation, their line intact and deadly. They crashed together, a solid bastion of iron against a thundering curtain of steel.

The assault instantly descended into confusion. Knights were knocked from their steeds, hurled back in the saddle by halberd jabs. Defending infantry were tossed aside, trampled into the mud, their armour cracked.

Gruppen felled his target, riding him down and swinging heavily with his sword on the follow-through. His right-hand man was not so lucky, steering his horse into a thicket of blades and being dragged from the saddle by a dozen armoured hands.

Gruppen whirled his steed round. He needed to keep moving. A soldier lumbered towards him, halberd stabbing at the flanks of his horse. The charger kicked out at him, shattering the staff before Gruppen could bring his sword round in a decapitating arc, aimed precisely for the gap between helm and breast-plate.

Gruppen looked up. The knights had carved a trail of death, just as they'd been commanded. Now the melee would undo them. Already four of his men were down, and the rest were struggling.

'Withdraw!' he roared, kicking his steed back into motion.

As one, displaying their peerless horsemanship, the knights pulled their mounts round and fought their way free. Another rider was dragged to earth as they turned, unable to escape the grasping fingers of the defenders, but the rest broke clear.

'To the ridge!' cried Gruppen, urging his horse onwards. The knights swept back, pulling away from the avenue of death they'd created. As they galloped back for fresh lances and fresh steeds, they swept past Imperial infantry heading the other way, swarming along the cleared territory, desperate to engage at last.

Gruppen smiled. His blood was up. Another pass and the engine would be destroyed. The enemy seemed to have no answer to the sudden cavalry charge. Just as the beasts had found at Turgitz, there was little in the Empire that could withstand their driving wedge of steel.

Then the engines fired.

The massed boom of their report made the earth itself reel. All along the enemy lines, the infernal devices detonated their charges and sent their cargo of death sailing into the sky. Vast streaks of blazing red fire scored the storm-wracked heavens, tearing through the bolts of the Celestial magisters. Whips of flame wrapped themselves like serpents around the discharges, flicking and snapping angrily. The massive engines slammed back hard from the recoil, crushing the men behind them before the binding chains went taut with a shower of sparks.

The Averpeak ridge disappeared. As the shot impacted it bloomed into a screaming inferno, hurtling across the exploding earth as if kindled on a lake of oil. Lilac and crimson blasts ripped the skyline apart, flaring up with sudden, eye-watering brilliance. Echoes of the impact resounded across the battlefield, swiftly followed by the anguished cries of men caught in a sudden and terrible wall of fire. It felt as if the world had been shattered, cracked open by the devastating power of the Chaos engines.

As the backwash from the explosions rippled out, the vast plumes of lilac-edged smoke rolled clear. Huge sections of the ridge had been demolished, crushing men beneath the earth, burying them under the bodies of their comrades. Fires kindled on nothing, sweeping through what was left of the defences. Some standards still flew, but whole companies had been destroyed. Gruppen couldn't see Volkmar's position for the smog.

One of his knights rode up alongside him, pulling his steed to a halt. Gruppen did likewise, shaken to the core by what he'd seen. Nothing could resist that degree of firepower. Nothing.

'Orders, sir?' the knight asked. The man's voice was tight.

Gruppen took a deep breath, looking about him for some evidence that his senses had deceived him, that what he'd just seen hadn't been quite as devastating as it looked. None came.

'Send the second wave in,' he growled. 'Then get a fresh horse. We've got to get those engines down, or this'll be over in an hour.'

* * *

VOLKMAR PICKED HIMSELF up from the ground, his robes covered in mud and blood. He tried to stand, and staggered, falling to one knee. His vision was black, picked out with spinning points of light. The roar of the battle rushed back to him slowly, as if coming from far away.

'My lord!' Maljdir was at his elbow, helping him up. The priest was similarly covered with debris. All around them men were regaining their feet. Others didn't get up.

'Unhand me!' growled Volkmar, shaking himself loose. Signs of weakness were the last thing he needed to convey. 'Do we have the musicians?'

'Some.'

'Order the second wave in. We can't survive another barrage – we have to get amongst them.'

Maljdir nodded sharply and rushed off to find a surviving trumpeter. Volkmar looked around him. The dying and wounded stretched along the ridge in both directions. Some companies had been entirely destroyed, others only maimed. Those who'd been quickest on the charge had escaped the volley, though they now grappled with the front ranks of the enemy alone. Those who'd been held back for the second wave had been decimated.

Volkmar retrieved his staff. His men were outnumbered and outgunned. He needed to act fast.

'Where are the wizards?' he demanded. The younger Celestial magister limped forwards, blood running down his face. Two of the Bright wizards had survived the blast, and the Light magisters were untouched, set back as they were further down the far side of the ridge, still working. Hettram was gone, lying face down in the filth and debris, his robes stained dark red.

'Come with me,' Volkmar rasped to the Bright wizards. 'We're going down there. As for the rest of you, I need something big, and I need it soon.'

The Celestial wizard nodded numbly, still in shock. His Light counterparts, lost in their preparations, made no response.

All along the ridge, the army was beginning to recover. Maljdir's orders blared out, and the infantry companies still held in reserve started to stream down the slope. The warrior priests, grim-faced and bearing their warhammers, formed up around Volkmar, ready to take the battle to the enemy. Maljdir was among them, carrying the torn and charred standard in his massive hands. Roll was at his side hefting his broadsword eagerly.

Lightning still lanced down, the residue of the Celestial wizards' casting. The Army of the Stone was advancing again, rank after rank of steadily marching troops, eyes glowing in the dark. All across the battlefield, loyalist and traitor clashed with desperate ferocity. As company after company committed to action, the battlefront unfurled to over a mile long, a seething mass of straining bodies broken only by the avenues carved by the cavalry charges and artillery fire.

Volkmar looked across the plain and cursed under his breath. The bulk of his forces were engaged and the rest were racing to do so. There was no pulling back, and no room to manoeuvre. Those damned engines had turned the pattern of the battle and he was now dancing to the traitor's tune.

The Theogonist felt the rage well up within him, the desperate mania that had afflicted him since Middenheim. Like a tide pushing against a dam, cracking it and poised to overflow, the currents of his fervour rose to breaking point. Streissen had unlocked it, and Averheim had pushed wide the door.

There was no point in suppressing it now. Frenzy had a purpose, and he had to use it.

'Follow me,' Volkmar growled, planting the Staff of Command firmly in the soil. As he did so it roared into life, blazing with a swirling golden aura. 'We'll find the bastard who caused this. I want his *eyes*.'

SEEN FROM FIVE miles to the east, the column of fire was shrouded in a thick grey pall of smoke. It rose from the base of the city like a rolling sea mist, dousing the angry blood-red of the pillar until the shaft of it pierced the obscurity again a hundred feet up in the air. The very earth vibrated with its muffled roar, thrumming under the hooves of the horses.

Helborg had driven his forces hard. Leitdorf's decision had been vindicated by the obvious signs of battle around Averheim. Judging by the drifting shreds of blackpowder smoke in the air, the Empire had arrived to the north of the city. Despite the presence of the looming Tower, hope had spread across his own men like a fire through dry scrub. Eager to join up with the besieging forces from the north, the infantry columns had speeded up and left the lumbering baggage train far behind.

Helborg rode with his Reiksguard escort at the vanguard, willing the miles to pass quicker, itching to draw the runefang in anger. If they went as quickly as they were able, his men would arrive at Averheim before the day's end and in time to make a difference. All depended on Skarr being at the designated muster, now imminent. Helborg had no doubt he would be.

As the vanguard rounded a long, shallow bend in

the road, his expectations of the preceptor were vindicated. Under the lee of a sweeping curve of grassland
the reinforcements waited, Skarr at their head, the
banners of Leitdorf and the Reiksguard fluttering in
the swirling, unnatural winds.

The Marshal kicked his horse on ahead, casting a
critical eye over the ranks of soldiers as he approached
them. Some looked very useful, standing in ordered
ranks and with the proper air of belligerence. Others
looked little better than flagellants. Still, that was to
be expected. The numbers were impressive, given the
time in which they'd had to work. Helborg estimated
the combined total under arms at five thousand on
foot, plus a hundred or so horse.

'Preceptor,' he said gruffly.

Skarr saluted, fist on breastplate.

'My lord,' he replied. 'The men are ready to be led.'

'Very good. Take up the rearguard and ensure they
keep the pace tight. I'll be at the spearhead. We leave
at once – I don't want to arrive when this is over.'

Skarr bowed and made ready to take up his place
when he suddenly pulled up.

'My lord,' he started hesitantly. 'Is that... but forgive
me.'

'Is it what?' snapped Helborg.

'Your sword. It's the...'

As the words left his mouth, Ludwig Schwarzhelm
loomed up from amongst the column of men at Helborg's rear. The Emperor's Champion was
unmistakable, a massive and brooding presence even
among the escorting Reiksguard. Skarr's jaw fell open.
For a moment he looked like he might draw his blade
and charge. Then he whirled back to the Marshal, confusion etched on his face.

'The runefang, yes,' said Helborg, his expression as hard as ever. 'Much has changed since you rode north. You'll have to learn the rest on the ride.'

As Schwarzhelm drew closer, some of the halberdiers under Skarr's command recognised him and rushed forwards in greeting. In the forefront was a thick-set man with a bruised face and the look of a tavern brawler.

Skarr shook his head in disbelief, hand still on the pommel of his sword.

'I thought...'

'Did you not hear me, Skarr?' asked Helborg. 'Your vengeance can wait.'

The preceptor snapped back into focus.

'Forgive me,' he said again. Then he reached around his neck and unhooked the trophy he'd been wearing ever since the last battle of Averheim. The shard of the runefang, salvaged from the Marshal's own wounded cheek, kept safe even while the blade itself had been taken hundreds of miles away.

'At least let me give you this.'

Helborg extended his gauntlet and took the fragment of steel. He held it up to the glowing red of the sky. It twisted on its cord of leather, winking in the dull light.

'The final piece,' he mused, watching the metal turn.

Then, reverently, he hung the shard around his own neck, threading it under his breastplate for protection. The metal was cold against his skin, a reminder of what had been warded for so long, preserved against the day when the Sword of Vengeance would be united with its wielder.

'You did well, Skarr,' Helborg said, taking up the reins. This time his voice was a little less harsh. 'When this is over, I *will* explain. Until then, trust my judgement. We ride together, Schwarzhelm and I. That very fact should give you hope.'

He looked up then, gazing west across the heads of his men towards the Iron Tower, visible in the distance as a spear of darkness at the foot of the shaft of fire. Clouds of smoke billowed around it, driven into great eddies by the unnatural storm. There were blackpowder plumes among them.

'Enough talk,' he said, and his expression was dark. 'The threads gather on the loom. We've done what we can to prepare. To the city.'

GRUPPEN WHEELED HIS steed around under the shadow of the Averpeak and prepared for the charge. It would be his third foray into the enemy ranks. Of his original squadron, only six remained. He quickly commandeered more troops from two of the other depleted detachments, making up a restored line of twenty-two knights.

'One more time!' he yelled, his voice cracking. The resistance around the big guns was tough, far tougher than he'd expected. Two more of the bronze-bound monsters had been destroyed by cannon fire but the rest still thundered out, reducing any exposed Imperial positions to scorched earth and scraps of bone.

In order to survive, the bulk of the Empire troops had piled forwards, locked in close melee combat with the enemy infantry. They fought bravely, but they were outmatched by Grosslich's troops. Things had been *done* to the defenders. The Averheim troops fought without fear and their formations never broke, no matter how savagely they were mauled.

That was just the human soldiers. There were others

among them, more like beasts than men. Gruppen had nearly been felled by one such creature on the last withdrawal, a vast armoured brute with a face like that of a dog. Rumours ran wild along the ranks that there were worse horrors along the east flanks: scuttling fiends with talons for hands, unstoppable killing machines tearing a swathe through horrified Imperial companies.

Gruppen shook his head. No point in worrying about that. The battle was on a knife edge. The enemy had been hurt by the initial barrage of cannon fire, but now the field was swinging back their way. Above it all, the Tower glowered, dark and forbidding.

'Stay close!' he bellowed at the knights mustering around him. The men were gathered at the base of the ridge where the squires had hurried to avoid the worst of the artillery punishment higher up. 'Tight formation, keep on my shoulder. We strike fast, we strike hard. Remember who you are! For Myrmidia!'

The knights shouted back the name of their goddess, fists clenched, their martial spirits undaunted. The Knights Panther were the finest soldiers in the Imperial ranks and they knew it.

'Come about!' bellowed Gruppen, kicking his charger into position. 'Charge!'

Just as before, the line of riders tore across the battlefield, lances lowering, accelerating towards the enemy lines with a thunderous chorus of hooves.

Those lines were closer than they had been. Gruppen had barely made full gallop before the first defenders came into view. A company of the hideous dog-soldiers was loping up towards a beleaguered regiment of Empire swordsmen, halberds held two-handed and faces hidden behind iron masks.

'Take them!' Gruppen roared, spurring his horse even faster, feeling the beast's muscles strain as it propelled the burden of man, armour and weapon. His men remained at his shoulder, lances down, visors closed, all moving as a single body. As he ever did, Gruppen whispered a prayer to his patron goddess before bracing for impact, teeth clenched, heart pounding.

Impact came. The line of knights slammed into the dog-soldiers, knocking the foremost aside and riding them down. Six of the mutants took lances full in the chest. The wooden shafts shattered as their victims crumpled to the earth. One knight was unhorsed as his lance shattered against a breastplate, spinning through the air before crashing headlong into the ranks of fresh terror troops. The rest tore onwards.

Gruppen speared his victim, feeling the sharp recoil as the lance bit deep. He dropped the shaft and reached for his sword. A dog-soldier, eerily silent as it moved into position, swung at his horse as it charged on. Gruppen leaned out, switched grip on his sword and plunged it into the creature's neck before wheeling away, kicking at his mount's flanks to maintain momentum.

'Onwards!' he roared, pointing his bloodstained blade ahead. 'To the engines!'

His horse bounded forwards, leaping over the grasping hands of another dog-soldier and riding down a second. The surviving knights thundered along beside him. Three more had been felled, but the dog-soldier column had been utterly torn apart. The charge remained strong, sweeping resistance before it as the Knights Panther bore deep into the heart of the defenders.

Gruppen knew the danger. If they plunged in too far, they'd not be able to cut their way back out. Despite all that, he was unwilling to withdraw just yet. The enemy continued to fall back before him, dropping under the advance of the knights' hooves and blades, opening up a road to the towering war engine ahead.

Gruppen surged onwards, slashing left and right, heedless of his personal danger. The engine had to be taken down. He held his speed and the horrific machinery drew nearer. The enemy melted away before him.

They were drawing him in.

The realisation hit him too late. Gruppen pulled his horse up sharply, twisting around in the saddle, trying to gauge his position. Only ten of his squadron had followed him so deep. They formed up around him, facing outwards, swords held ready. On every side, dog-soldiers and mortal troops recovered their structure and began to turn back in. The space around the knights shrank. They'd come too far. The nearest Imperial ranks were distant, kept busy with desperate combat of their own.

'Easy, men,' growled Gruppen, keeping his nervous, bucking steed under control. 'We'll cut our way back. Take the–'

'*Leave him.*'

The new voice came from up ahead. It dominated the sounds of battle, slicing through the bedlam like a knife through cooked flesh. It was thick with a world-weary scorn, echoing into the night and resounding from the iron belly of the war engines close to hand. It was no human tongue that spoke the words, though it belonged to a speaker who had once been a man.

Gruppen wheeled round, feeling a sudden chill strike his breast. The ranks of dog-soldiers parted. In their midst was a figure on a dark horse, clad in crimson armour and carrying a black sword. The rider came forwards slowly, deliberately, singling out Gruppen and lowering his blade towards him.

'You can take the others,' Grosslich snarled to his men. 'This one's mine.'

VOLKMAR STRODE DOWN the slope and into the thick of the fighting, his staff burning with a corona of golden flame, his face locked into a mask of mania. The Bright wizards flanked him, pouring bolts of screaming orange brilliance into the ranks before them. Warrior priests came in their wake, deadly and unbreakable, swinging their warhammers to crack the skulls of any who survived the magisters' barrage. Maljdir was among them, holding the standard aloft, bellowing hymns to Sigmar and rousing the troops in earshot. Behind came the columns of regular infantry, pulled along by Volkmar's spearhead, sheltering behind the white-hot path he carved through the sea of enemy blades.

None could stand before the Grand Theogonist. Working from afar, the Light wizards had cast at last, and their protection was on him. He shimmered beneath an aegis of swirling luminescence. Those closest to him in the Imperial ranks could see that he'd lost all semblance of control. His whole being was suffused with the searing drive of faith. His armour blazed like the morning sun, throwing spring-yellow beams of dazzling brilliance into the heart of the horde. Grosslich's troops, immune to fear, blundered into his path only to be blasted apart limb from limb, ripped into flapping shreds of flesh by the power of the Staff.

Stride by stride, the golden vanguard ploughed deep into the massed ranks, an isolated pool of streaming light amid the spreading cloud of ash-streaked darkness.

'There!' roared Volkmar, pointing ahead.

A war engine loomed out of the fiery gloom, surrounded by ordered ranks of iron-clad infantry. It was preparing to fire again. Coils of steam rose from the furnace at its base and a dozen Stone-slaves crawled across its surface, adjusting levers and mumbling prayers to the Lord of Pain. The daemon-bound machine soared into the night, vast and terrible, as large as a siege tower and glowing with the angry sigils of the Dark Prince.

Undeterred, the Theogonist raised his bare arms into the air and swung the tip of his staff at the mighty construction.

'Shatter!'

His staff exploded in a nimbus of blinding light. A ball of golden fire kindled in the heart of the cannon barrel, shining in the well of darkness like the full face of Mannslieb. The florescent sphere grew, rushing outwards, bulging at the iron flanks of the massive machine and cracking its metal hide.

The infantry around it surged forwards, crystal-bladed halberds lowered, lumbering towards the bellowing Theogonist. From within their narrow visors a lilac glow bled out, and a low canine growl rumbled in their iron-cased chests.

'Forward!' roared Maljdir, rushing into the fray to protect his master, swinging the standard aloft as he went. Warrior priests swept around Volkmar and crashed into the advancing ranks of masked dog-soldiers, their warhammers coming into play with devastating, neck-breaking force.

The Bright wizards stood back and sent a hail of crackling bolts spinning into the flanks of the war engine. The bolts caught and kindled on Volkmar's holy fire and exploded in their turn. The cannon barrel expanded further, stretched almost to breaking point by the vast forces unfurling within it. A filigree of cracks, each leaking golden light, rushed across the beaten iron. The furnace began to stutter, sending rolls of soot-clogged smoke coughing into the night.

'Shatter!' Volkmar roared again, eliciting a fresh inferno from the Staff of Command.

Still the war engine resisted, somehow maintaining its structure in the face of the onslaught. The swirling maelstrom within it bulged further, bleeding golden incandescence from the growing web of cracks. Metal, hot as coals, showered down from the hulking barrel as the iron fractured. Bronze bindings broke and spun free. The furnace choked out and flared back up again, knocked out of rhythm by the ceaseless, grinding power of the Theogonist.

Then there was a great crack, a rolling boom. The air shuddered, and the earth rocked. With titanic force, the vast war engine blasted itself apart.

The huge shell of iron flew high into the air, pursued by a deafening explosion of shimmering gold. The carcass of the monster was cloven into pieces, reeling in all directions as the heart of the cannon was torn asunder. Men and beasts alike were blasted from their feet, lost in the whirling storm of consuming power.

Volkmar's fire flared up against the daemonic

energies locked in the core of the device, flattening the troops beyond and tearing up the earth on which it rested. Priests were bowled over alongside the creatures they grappled with. The wizards were hurled back and the Imperial standard ripped from Maljdir's desperate grip. A backdraft of green-tinged flame rushed out in a corona of destruction, spiralling into the night and blasting aside all in its path. Men were thrown up like leaves in a gale, their armour shattered, and hurled into the cowering forms of their comrades further back.

Only Volkmar stood firm, his robes rippling against the howling aftershock of the cannon's demise. He kept his arms raised, defiantly screaming his wrath amid the shards of spinning iron. The halo of unleashed power expanded further, ripping through the ranks of soldiers, shaking the ground and echoing out across the plain.

As the worst of the backwash passed, Maljdir clambered to his feet and staggered back to Volkmar's position. All was confusion. Bodies, twisted and broken, were heaped up against the steaming hide of the ruined war machine. Dog-soldiers lay amongst warrior priests, steeped in a cocktail of their own blood. The Empire spearhead was in ruins. The device had been destroyed, but at a massive cost.

'What are you *doing*?' Maljdir roared. This was no strategy, no tactical advance, just a headlong charge into the heart of darkness. Already the vast hosts of enemy soldiers were coalescing around Volkmar's position, drawn by the destruction of one of their totems. Elsewhere across the plain the Imperial forces were being driven back. Only Volkmar pressed forwards, carving his way deeper into peril. The unity of the army was fracturing.

The Theogonist looked back at Maljdir, hardly seeming to recognise him. His eyes were wild and staring. His knuckles were white from grasping the Staff of Command and a sheen of glistening sweat covered his exposed flesh. His torso shivered with hatred.

'I will find him, Odain,' Volkmar hissed. 'Do you not see it? *He* is here.'

Maljdir recoiled in horror.

'You do not–' he started.

It was too late. Volkmar brushed past him, striding through the wreckage of the war engine, his staff a golden halo amid the fire-wracked gloom.

'*Everchosen,*' he whispered as he went, and his staff kindled again with snapping, crackling fire.

In his wake came the surviving priests, the limping wizards, the remnants of the halberdier vanguard. Inspired by his rampage, the Empire troops just kept on coming.

'Tears of Sigmar,' cursed Maljdir, ignoring them and stooping to retrieve the charred standard from the blood-soaked earth. Efraim Roll came to his side, emerging from the press of men, his sword running with blood. The confessor had a long weal across his neck and his armour was dented. The man had been busy.

'We've lost him,' reported Maljdir grimly. 'He's gone mad. You should've let me restrain him at Streissen.'

'*Restrain* him?' Roll shook his head in disbelief. All around them the Imperial troops piled forwards, filling in the wounds in the defence rent open by the Theogonist's inexorable advance. 'You're the madman. He's the only hope we have left.'

'But his soul...'

'Damn his soul!' Roll's voice shook with fervour as

he barged past Maljdir in pursuit of Volkmar. 'This is about survival now. Keep waving that damn flag, priest. If we falter now, *all* our souls will be forfeit.'

# Chapter Seventeen

GROSSLICH FLICKED AN armoured finger and his dog-soldiers surged forwards. They crashed into the circling Knights Panther, studiously avoiding the one he'd picked out. The preceptor was soon isolated, cut off from the battle raging around and left for Grosslich to deal with. Gruppen remained on his horse, raging pointlessly as his comrades were driven further from him, hacking at the dog-soldiers swarming around them in ever greater numbers.

'You have doomed them, knight,' said Grosslich, waiting patiently.

The preceptor whirled to face him. His visor was still down and his expression hidden, but Grosslich could sense the anger boiling within him. He knew he'd pushed too deep.

'Do not *speak* to me, traitor!' spat Gruppen. 'You *disgust* me. You're filth. Worse than filth. The lowliest serf on my estate–'

Grosslich snapped his fingers again, and the tirade stopped. The preceptor would never speak again. If he'd wanted, Grosslich could have killed him then with a single casting, but he had no intention of doing so. Sorcery was a useful tool, but it was no substitute for proper combat, fighting the way a man should. Despite all Natassja had done to him, Grosslich had still not forgotten his roots.

'Save it,' he said, wearily. 'You're a dead man, so at least try to make this worthy of a song.'

He kicked his steed, and the hell-beast lurched forwards. Gruppen did likewise, sword whirling, and the two men crashed together. The preceptor was quick. He got his blade round sharply against Grosslich's flank before he could respond. The metal bounced from the spell-wound armour and the knight was nearly knocked from his saddle by the recoil.

Then Grosslich brought his own blade to bear, lashing heavily with his broadsword. The edge of it bit hard, carving through the knight's plate and digging into the leather beneath. The preceptor pulled back, somehow managing to haul his steed round in the tight space and drag himself away from the assault. Grosslich pressed the attack, bringing his blade back for a decapitating lunge.

Instead of pulling away, Gruppen darted back towards him, displaying incredible mastery of his steed. He ducked low to evade Grosslich's blow and slashed at his mutant steed instead. The knight aimed truly, slicing into the warped creature's scaly face and pulling the flesh from the bone.

The monster reared, almost throwing Grosslich from the saddle. Its clawed legs kicked out in agony. Grosslich cursed, trying to bring it under control, reeling around and out of position. The knight pursued the advantage, landing a heavy strike on Grosslich's back. Again, the armour was his saviour, though the force of the blow knocked him forwards, further maddening his pain-deranged mount.

Grosslich snaked back round in his saddle just in time to see the knight's blade coming back at him again, aimed for the head and moving with bone-breaking force. Grosslich snatched his gauntlet up. He grabbed the sword-edge and held it tight. Gruppen frantically tried to pull it back, seizing it with both hands and yanking at the hilt.

Smiling beneath his helmet, Grosslich crushed his fingers together, squeezing the metal and bending it out of shape. With a final twist, the sword shattered. Still the knight didn't give up. He continued to attack, jabbing with the broken stump of his weapon, trying to find some way to penetrate the spell-soaked armour.

Grosslich kicked his steed forwards and the pain-maddened beast lurched straight into the knight's skittish mount, knocking it sideways and causing it to stumble. Whip-fast, Grosslich grabbed Gruppen's cloak and hauled him from the saddle, hurling him to the ground with a sickening crack.

Gruppen tried to rise again, dragging himself to one knee and bringing his broken blade up for a new lunge at the mutant's shanks. The beast was now in range, though, and the animal knew the author of its pain. With a throaty scream it reared again, scything its clawed feet before bringing them down on the still-rising preceptor. One taloned hoof slammed against his breastplate, crushing the plate and cracking the man's chest. The other crunched hard against his helmet, breaking the metal open and shattering his skull.

Gruppen fell back, choked on his own blood and bone. Grosslich rode over his body, trampling it into the slick of mud beneath, letting his wounded creature take its revenge. Only when there was nothing left to stamp on did he pull the raging beast away, tugging at the reins hard. The scourge of the Drakwald was gone, his proud career ended at last on the corrupted plains of Averland, alone and surrounded by the enemy.

'Enough,' said Grosslich, calming his snorting mount. 'There'll be more.'

The dog-soldiers had finished off the others. They stood around stupidly, waiting for fresh orders. Beyond them the battle raged, intensifying in scope as more and more troops were committed by their desperate commanders. The Imperials were showing commendable spirit, but there weren't enough of them and they weren't of the same calibre as Natassja's creatures.

Grosslich wished he could take some pleasure in that. Slaughtering such men was nothing to be proud of. Even as victory edged towards his grasp, he felt a deep and stubborn sickness lodge deep within him.

He'd dreamed of *glory*. Of a realm that men would admire and envy. Whatever the result of this battle, he'd never be granted that now.

'Oh, go and find something to kill,' he muttered to his guards, and watched bitterly as they loped back towards the fiercest fighting. They never questioned a thing. They'd never question anything.

With a heavy heart, his armour streaked with blood, the elector withdrew from the frontline, back to the position of command, leaving his slaves to continue the struggle. Above him, the Tower loomed, a roost of daemons and sorcery, the mark of his failure.

* * *

MALJDIR LOOKED AROUND him, blood and sweat clouding his vision. Volkmar's vanguard had penetrated far across the plains, fighting their way through the maze of trenches and across the ridges of spikes. Even though the Light magisters' spell had waned, Volkmar still blazed a trail. Though the casualties around him grew ever heavier, the Imperial army still clustered to his call. As the day waned and the meagre scraps of shrouded sunlight bled away, his was the only pure fire left on the battlefield. Like moths around a candle-flame they huddled close to its warmth, given heart in the face of the endless hordes raging towards them. The Theogonist was heading to the centre of the defences, and a light of madness was in his eyes.

Maljdir took up the standard in his left hand, hefting the heavy stave against his shoulder. In his right hand he carried Bloodbringer, swinging it with as much vigour as the other warrior priests. The dog-soldiers were everywhere now, snarling and tearing at the Imperial troops, bringing them down through sheer savagery. The armour-plated priests were the only infantry in Volkmar's retinue capable of taking them on one-to-one. The mutants were taller, faster and stronger than the average halberdier and killed two of them for every one of their warped kin that was taken down. Against such losses, Volkmar's surge was doomed. Soon they'd be cut off entirely, their defences whittled away and the spearhead isolated.

A dog-soldier leapt across Maljdir's path, growling as it swept up its halberd, aiming for his chest. Its iron mask had been torn from its head, exposing the distended muzzle and canine teeth. The flesh was human-like, ripped and moulded into its new shape by surgery and sorcery. Maljdir dodged the blow, dropping back with surprising speed before spinning back with a counter-strike. Bloodbringer swung heavily, slamming into the soldier's flank, smashing the breastplate in and cracking the ribs beneath it. The mutant was knocked sideways, stumbling across the ground before recovering and coiling for a second attack.

It never came. Bloodbringer swept back on the reverse angle, catching the horror square in the face. With a rip and a snap the dog-soldier's head came off, dragging the body up after it on a string of sinews before the whole corpse thumped down into the mud, feet away.

Maljdir hardly broke stride, crushing the severed skull under his boots as he ploughed after Volkmar and looked for the next victim. The momentum was relentless, exhausting. The Theogonist seemed to have no tactics other than rampage. The vanguard was moving ever closer to the walls of Averheim, still barred by a sea of foes and clothed in a thundering wall of flame. Dark shapes swam within that blood-red curtain, curling like fish around the column of madness. Maljdir could sense the corruption there, spilling out from the inferno.

Volkmar must have sensed it too. That was where the Theogonist was heading. He cared nothing for the battlefield now, nothing for the lives of the thousands of men who still fought in the trenches and under the shadow of the war machines. He was after Archaon, and the rest of the army was expendable to that delusion.

'He'll damn us all,' growled Maljdir, dispatching another dog-soldier with a crunching blow, hardly pausing in his onward march.

Bloodbringer felt light in his hands. Volkmar was only a few paces ahead, raving and spilling golden light from his fingers. His back was unprotected.

'Sigmar's blood,' he said, judging the path his hammer would have to take to end it. 'He'll damn us all.'

'REIKSGUARD, TO ME!'

Helborg crested the final rise before the city, and its damnation was laid out before him. They'd arrived to the east of the battlefield. The fighting was less than a mile away, spread out across the plain below.

All thought of gaining the Averpeak was instantly abandoned. The ridge smouldered away in the north, its flanks broken by the power of Grosslich's war engines. Six infernal devices still survived, their jaws gaping red and angry. Around each of them were thousands of troops, staining the land black with their numbers. At the very foot of the Averpeak, a mile distant from the walls of the city, the line of battle ran in a vast, snaking curve.

Helborg squinted through the drifting smog. There were banners flying. Many infantry companies fought, but they were heavily outnumbered by Grosslich's defenders. There was no *shape* to the Imperial assault, just a straggling melee towards the walls. Only at one point did the Empire army seem to be making headway. A column of soldiers had pierced deep into the enemy lines, moving fast towards the city gates. There was a brilliant golden light at the tip of the column, blazing in the heart of the darkness.

'Volkmar,' said Helborg as his knights clustered around him. Forty-six Reiksguard remained. The swirling clouds reflected from their armour, glowing red from the fires on the plain below. 'I've seen that power wielded before.'

'He's out of position,' said Skarr, frowning. 'His army's coming apart.'

Schwarzhelm came alongside them. The Rechtstahl was naked in his hands, ready for action. There was no time for deliberation. The Empire army was in disarray, outnumbered, out-fought and leaderless.

'Lord Schwarzhelm, lead the infantry to bolster the Imperial lines. Rally the men, and give them some purpose.'

'And the Reiksguard?' asked Schwarzhelm.

Helborg drew the Klingerach. The dark metal glinted, still marred by the notch on the blade.

'We can cut through those troops,' he said, snapping his visor down. All thought of the long days of sickness had left him. His heart pumped powerfully in his chest again, fuelling the arms that carried the runefang. 'We'll fight to Volkmar's position. This field isn't lost yet.'

Last of all, Leitdorf drew up to the height of the rise, his ruddy face aghast at the devastation below.

'My inheritance,' he announced grimly, gazing across the carnage.

'Indeed so, my lord,' said Helborg, readying for the charge down into the inferno. 'You will ride with me. My blade is keener than it was the last time we fought together and my body is restored.'

Unholy winds, laced with ash and throbbing with heat, rushed up from the battlefield. Helborg's cloak billowed out, revealing the splendour of his ancient armour. The hawk-pinions of his helmet seemed to catch an echo of the golden rays streaming from Volkmar's staff, etching the metal with a faint sheen against the shadows.

'If Sigmar wills it,' he said, raising the Sword of Vengeance and pointing it towards the heart of the horde below, 'we will yet bring destruction to those who have turned away from His light. Ride now, and may His protection be with all of you.'

ACHENDORFER LET THE last pages of the book crackle and fade away. His long fingers, warped and melded with the leather, curled back round, free from the weight at last. The grimoire had been burned away like so much else.

No matter. Its work had been done.

He gazed up lovingly at the Stone. No light reflected from its sides even though the lamps in the walls of the chamber still burned strongly. It was as black as a pupil, a void at the base of the city. By contrast, everything around it was flickering and ephemeral. The shaft above it soared into the far distance, hundreds of feet of thundering fire. He stood alone at the base. This was the origin, the source of all that was to come. The thought pleased him.

Achendorfer took a deep breath and closed his eyes, feeling the heat of the flames enter his lungs. Down here, the bloodfire was at its thickest. It didn't consume or damage mortal flesh, but it *hurt*. He felt the searing heat of it against his throat, scraping at the flesh, testing him and probing for weakness.

'Is all ready, lizard?'

Achendorfer hadn't heard the queen enter. He snapped back to attention, whipping round to face her.

'Of course. The Stone is waiting.'

Natassja didn't smile. Such mortal gestures were losing their grip on her. Her humanity was now little more than a skein, a fragile barrier between the world of laws and the raging Chaos within her. Achendorfer could see it in her eyes. Those white-less orbs, for so long two cool, tolerant points within that sleek face, had now sunk into darkness, mirroring the Stone. He doubted that she even saw the world of matter truly any more. For such as her, a realm of pure sensation awaited, a flux of emotion and desire. Perhaps the same would come for him one day.

'Then begin again,' she said.

Achendorfer bowed. He no longer needed the book for such work. The words had been burned on to his mind across the many hours of labour. His lips formed around the words unbidden, his muscles fully attuned to the shapes of the forbidden speech.

'*Bedarruzibarr,*' he intoned. The bloodfire in the chamber flared up at the sound. '*Bedarruzibarr'zagarra-tumnan'akz'akz'berau.*'

On and on the syllables droned, just as they had for weeks, soaked into the walls of iron and etched in the blazing sigils far up the shaft.

Natassja walked slowly towards the stone, her steps mannered and ceremonial. From far above, beyond the wards, there came the sounds of daemons singing.

'*Akz'akz'berau,*' they chorused, and a feral joy was locked into their fractured, cherubic voices. '*Malaman-uar'neramumo'klza'jhehennum.*'

Natassja raised her slender arms in supplication. Her skin darkened to nightshade, glowing darkly like embers. With a faint hiss, her sheer gown slipped from her shoulders and coiled around her feet.

Achendorfer knew he should look away then. He remained rapt, and a thin line of drool ran down his chin.

He kept chanting. The daemons kept chanting. The bloodfire seared the air, pregnant with the coming storm. Natassja's hair began to lift, rippling like wind-lashed silk, exposing the sweeping curves of her flawless outline. Across her flesh, signs of Slaanesh glowed into life, swimming over the skin and moulding into new and wonderful shapes.

She began to grow.

Blood replaced the drool on Achendorfer's skin. A kind of ecstasy gripped him.

'*Abbadonnodo'neherata'gradarruminam!*' he raved, swaying with the movement of the bloodfire.

This was it. This was what the root had been for, the deception, the armies, the torture, the construction, the book, what all of it had been for.

For so long She had been coming. Now, finally, She was here.


BLOCH MARCHED AT the head of his detachment. His halberdiers went steadily. There was no running or hollering, only a disciplined, well-ordered advance. He'd arranged the men into four companies of forty men, ten across and four deep. A few extra men had been tacked on to his lead group. Not much of a return from the thousands who'd marched under Grunwald.

As he went, he muttered a prayer to Sigmar, to Ranald, to Shallya, and a general benediction to any-one he'd left off the list. The enemy ranks were within sight and the charge would not be long coming. The clash of arms was huge and heavy, echoing across the plains and rebounding from the ruined Averpeak. The nearer they came to it, the darker the skies became.

The rest of Helborg's irregular infantry marched in

semi-ordered detachments on either flank of Bloch's troops. They looked scared and uncertain. The prospect of liberating Averland, so attractive under the warm sun, now seemed like a fool's errand. They were heading into the depths of Chaos, and even the simple-minded knew the great enemy when they saw it. Bloch placed little faith in them. At the first sign of serious trouble, they'd break. The only hope was to join up with the larger Imperial forces before that happened.

Ahead of them all rode Schwarzhelm, Kraus and the few cavalry Helborg had given them. The Emperor's Champion looked as stern and unyielding as a mountain. He, and he alone, inspired some faith that this wasn't merely a vainglorious march to death.

'Herr Bloch.'

A forgotten voice rose over the growing clamour. Bloch felt his heart sink.

'Herr Verstohlen,' he replied, looking up to see the familiar figure of the spy riding alongside. Something of the habitual smug expression had been erased from the man's lean face. His eyes were ringed and heavy with fatigue, and his tailored clothes were ripped and stained. 'You're still here, then.'

'Just about.' Schwarzhelm's agent had his pistol in his free hand, loaded and ready to fire. 'I've not seen you for some time.'

'Strange, that.'

'And you've lost your lieutenant.'

'Captain Kraus is back where he belongs.'

Verstohlen smiled. There was little mirth in it, just a wry grin at the foolishness of the world.

'As we all are,' he said. 'Look, I'm not much at home on the battlefield, commander. It disagrees with me.

The last time I fought under Schwarzhelm, you were good enough to let me tag along.'

Bloch squinted up at him, wondering, as ever, whether Verstohlen was mocking him.

'We're infantry,' he said. 'Your horse won't fit in.'

Verstohlen swung down from the saddle, landing lightly beside Bloch. He gave his steed a thump on the flanks, and it lurched away from the approaching battlefront, no doubt pleased to be heading away from the horrors ahead.

'Any better?'

Bloch scowled. He'd not known what to make of Verstohlen at Turgitz, and he had little enough idea now. The man was an enigma, and enigmas were no use to him.

'If you want to use that gun, then be my guest. But get in the way, and I'll skewer you myself.'

Verstohlen nodded seriously.

'Quite right, commander,' he said. 'I wouldn't expect anything less.'

Ahead of them, the rearguard of the enemy finally spotted the advancing ranks of Schwarzhelm's troops. Soldiers began to turn to face them, still several hundred yards off.

'To arms!' came the cry from Kraus.

All along the line, steel glittered as it was swung into position. Men made the sign of the comet, adjusted their helmets, pulled breastplates down, mumbled prayers.

Steadily, silently, Grosslich's men broke into a run towards them. The soldiers looked strange, as if their eyes had been replaced with pools of witch-fire.

'On my mark!' roared Kraus.

Schwarzhelm clutched the Rechtstahl with his right

hand and bowed his head in a silent dedication. He'd be the first one in.

'I feel that we never had the chance to get to know one another properly,' said Verstohlen as the pace of the march picked up. Though he tried to hide it with levity, his voice was shot through with fear.

'Some other time, perhaps,' muttered Bloch, waiting for the order to charge.

'I'd like that.'

Then Kraus swung his sword wildly over his head.

'Men of the Empire!' he bellowed. 'Death to the enemy! Charge now, and Sigmar guide your blades!'

With a massed roar of their own, the halberdiers surged forwards. Behind them came the Averlanders, faces pale with terror, hands clasped tight on their weapons, sweat glistening on their brows.

At their head rode Schwarzhelm, sword blazing red against the flames, his throaty cries of defiance and hatred rising above the tumult. In his wake, desperate and valiant, five thousand infantry streamed into the well of fire and death.

HELBORG FELT THE ash-hot air stream past him as he spurred his horse into a gallop. Schwarzhelm had committed his troops, drawing attention away from the Reiksguard and leaving the field clear for the charge. The squadron comprised fewer than fifty horsemen, including himself and Leitdorf – a laughable force with which to threaten a host of thousands.

The wedge of riders around him tightened. Their massed hooves drummed on the packed earth as the knights swept towards their target. Half a mile to their left the walls of Averheim rose up into the storm-raked air, vast and dark. Ahead of them were file upon file of marching infantry, each clad in close-fitting plate armour and bearing a crystal halberd. Somewhere beyond them was Volkmar. The Theogonist's position had been obvious enough from the vantage of the rise, but was now lost in the smoke and confusion of the battlefield.

The success of the charge all depended on speed and power. The first blow would settle things.

'Karl Franz!' roared Helborg as the first lines of the enemy came into view. The dog-soldiers before him turned to face the onslaught. Too slowly. They'd be ripped aside.

'The Emperor!' replied the Reiksguard, crying aloud as one. Skarr was at the forefront of the charge, his ravaged face enclosed in steel and his blade flashing.

Rufus Leitdorf rode on his left shoulder, leaning forwards in the saddle and with the Wolfsklinge unsheathed at his side.

'For my father,' he murmured, too low for the others to hear.

The gap shrank, closed and disappeared. The wedge of cavalry, a steel-tipped spear of white and red, slammed into the defenders. Grosslich's infantry were ridden into the mire or cut down by the precision of the Reiksguard sword-work. Helborg kicked his horse onwards and it leapt into the press of Grosslich's rearguard, lashing out and kicking its hooves as it laboured through the mass of bodies.

Startled by the sudden onslaught, the resistance was weak. A group of heavily-armoured dog-soldiers attempted to form a line against the charge.

'Take them!' cried Helborg, pulling his horse's head round to meet the threat.

The Reiksguard wheeled, every horseman controlling his steed superbly. Without any drop in speed, the knights galloped at the wall of iron and steel. They crashed into the defence again at full tilt, breaking open the nascent line of shields and scattering the mutants. Some knights were knocked from the saddle or raked with a desperate halberd-stab from below, but the wedge remained intact, tearing forwards, heading ever further into the files of the corrupted troops.

'D'you see him?' shouted Skarr, crouching low in the saddle, his helmet drenched in blood and his sword still swinging.

'Not yet,' replied Helborg, impaling a dog-soldier with a downward plunge before bringing the Klingerach smartly back up for another victim.

Helborg felt stronger than he'd done since leaving Nuln. His shoulder spiked with pain, but he ignored it. Like Schwarzhelm, he lived for combat. Creeping around in the hinterland of Averland had been a drain on his soul. Now, surrounded by the filth he'd dedicated his life to eradicating, the tang of blood on his lips and the thunder of hooves in his ears, he was back where he belonged.

'Keep on this course!' he bellowed, directing his galloping steed towards a fresh attempt to halt them. 'Rally to the Theogonist when we see him. Until then, kill all who get in your way.'

With that, Helborg swerved to avoid a looming dog-soldier, carving a deep gash in the mutant's shoulder as he passed, before powering onwards to the line of mustering defenders.

His eyes narrowed under the visor and a warm smile creased his battle-scarred face. The hooves of his horse thudded as he hurtled towards his next target.

'Sigmar preserves those who fight,' he murmured to himself, licking his cracked lips with anticipation. '*Blessed* be the name of Sigmar.'

SCHWARZHELM STRODE FORWARDS and the Rechtstahl trailed a line of ripped-free gore behind it. He'd dismounted once the press around him had got too close and now went on foot amongst his troops, carving his way towards the sundered Imperial lines. Kraus was at his side, hammering away with his blade.

There seemed to be no end to the mutants, horrors and dead-eyed mortals looming up out of the dark, faces blank and blades swinging. The assault on Grosslich's flank had almost stalled. Bloch's men were capable of holding their own but the Averlanders were less accomplished. Schwarzhelm had seen dozens of them running from the field, crying with fear and leaving their weapons in the mud behind them. Those that remained were now surrounded, enveloped in the endless ranks of Grosslich's legions. The mutants exacted a heavy toll for any forward progress. Only Schwarzhelm kept the drive going, hauling his men forwards by the force of example.

'No mercy!' he roared, stabbing the Rechtstahl through the wheezing throat of a mutant and ripping it out. 'Keep your formation! Fear no traitor!'

He knew time was running out. They were too deep in to disengage.

'Where now?' panted Kraus, fresh from felling his man. His armour looked big on him, as if the weeks in the wild had physically shrunk the honour guard captain.

'This is the right course,' said Schwarzhelm, dragging a halberdier back out of harm's way before crushing the skull of his looming assailant. 'Unless the Empire army has fallen back to–'

With a scream, something dark and clawed flung itself from the enemy lines. It was cloaked in rags and had talons for fingers. The halberdiers shrank back, bewildered and terrified.

Schwarzhelm brought the Rechtstahl round quickly. Steel clashed against bone, and a flash of witch-light burst out from the impact. Kraus leapt forwards, blade at the ready.

'Get back!' roared Schwarzhelm, his sword dancing in the firelight, parrying and thrusting at the scuttling creature. 'Your blade will not bite this.'

Kraus fell away, blocking instead the advance of a slavering dog-soldier. Schwarzhelm worked his sword with speed, matching the spider-sharp movements of the horror. Every time the Rechtstahl hit, a blaze of sparks rained to the ground. The creature leapt at him, screaming with frustration, talons lashing.

Schwarzhelm ducked under the scything claws, shouldering his mighty pauldrons to the assault and swinging the blade fast and low across the earth. The horror reacted, spinning back on itself to evade the strike, but too late. The Sword of Justice sliced through sinew and iron, taking off the creature's legs and leaving it writhing in the blood-soaked mud.

Schwarzhelm rose to his full height, spun the sword round and plunged it down, pinning the horror's torso as he'd done with Tochfel in Averheim. It let out a final screech of pain and fury before the light in its eyes went out.

With the destruction of Natassja's pet, the dog-soldiers began to withdraw. None of them could stand against Schwarzhelm. In the shuffling confusion the halberdiers were finally able to push them back.

'Morr's blood,' spat Kraus, looking at the twisted carcass still twitching in the slime of the field. 'What *is* that?'

'Another one I failed to save,' replied Schwarzhelm grimly, stalking back to the front line. At his approach, the dog-soldiers fell back further. Soon his massive shoulders were busy again, hacking and parrying, driving the mutants inwards.

'Reikland!' came a voice then from further down the line of halberdiers. Schwarzhelm recognised it at once. Bloch. The halberdier commander was still unstoppable, as tough and enduring as old leather.

Schwarzhelm whirled round, hope rising in his breast. Drifts of smoke still obscured the battlefield beyond a few paces and the ash-choked darkness did the rest, but he could see the shadows of men running towards them.

'Hold your positions!' he bellowed, his gruff voice cracking under the strain. He couldn't afford for his troops to get strung out.

Then, suddenly, there were halberdiers around him. They weren't Bloch's men, but wore the grey and white of the Reikland. They looked exhausted, their faces streaked with blood and their breastplates dented.

'Against all hope...' one of them stammered, limping towards Schwarzhelm like he was some shade of Morr.

Bloch burst from the right flank after him, grinning like an idiot.

'We've broken through, my lord!' he cried, exposing the bloody hole in his smile where something had knocked half his teeth from his jaw. 'These are our men!'

Even as he announced the news, more Imperial troops emerged from the gloom. There were dozens, possibly hundreds.

'Maintain the assault!' growled Schwarzhelm, glowering at Bloch and pushing his way past the limping Reikland troops. 'You pox-ridden dogs, form up like you're in the army of the Emperor.'

Bloch's men immediately responded, swinging back to face the dog-soldiers and charging the disarrayed lines. Their commander disappeared with them, in the forefront as ever, hefting his halberd with brutal enjoyment.

Schwarzhelm turned on the nearest Empire halberdier. Everything was in flux. They were still heavily outnumbered, and their only hope lay in restoring discipline.

'Who's the senior officer here?' he demanded.

'I don't know, my lord. Kleister is dead, and Bogenhof is–'

'You'll do then. Get these men into detachments. Four deep, ten wide. Do it now. Follow my lead, and we'll clear some space around us. This isn't over yet.'

The halberdier looked back at him, first with surprise, then with a sudden, desperate hope.

'Yes, my lord!' he cried, before rushing to form his men up as ordered.

Schwarzhelm turned back to the fighting. If there were any more of those creatures, he knew he'd be the only one who could take them on.

'What now?' asked Kraus, hurrying back to his side.

'Get in amongst these men,' said Schwarzhelm, striding without break to catch up with Bloch's men. 'Get them organised and follow me. There'll be more of them as we go, and they all need leading.'

'So where are we taking them?'

Schwarzhelm turned back to shoot Kraus a murderous look.

'Grosslich must have seen us by now,' he said, his eyes narrowing under his helmet. 'He's here somewhere, and when I find him, he's my kill.'

Then Schwarzhelm stalked off, massive and threatening, his sword thirsting for the blood that followed it whenever it was drawn.

THE WALLS OF the city soared up into the sky, braced with iron and crested with thirty-foot-high sigils of Slaanesh. The curving symbols glowed red, throbbing in the darkness and spilling their unnatural light across the storm-born shadows.

Volkmar was close enough now. He could taste the tang of corruption streaming from Averheim, locked in the column of rumbling fire. There were presences in the aethyr, darting shapes swimming in the currents of translucent crimson. He could see their outlines, a twisted fusion of woman and Chaos-spawn.

'I am coming for you,' he growled, swinging his staff round to blast a lumbering mutant from his path.

Volkmar knew neither fatigue nor fear now. As truly as he knew his own name, he knew the Lord of End Times had come back to face him again. This time, the result would be different. He'd seen the other side of reality, had gazed across the planes of immortal existence and felt their cold embrace. Now enclosed in the sinews and blood of a man once more, he would not return there. Not until the Everchosen lay at his feet, drowning in his own betrayer's gore.

Volkmar felt a sudden hand on his shoulder, huge and heavy. He spun round, the Staff of Command responding instantly with a blaze of sparkling faith-fire.

'This is *enough*.'

Maljdir stood before him. The huge man was covered in sweat, blood and grime. The battle-standard at his shoulder was charred and ripped. The warrior priests surged onwards around the two of them, driving the enemy back further.

'What d'you mean?' hissed Volkmar, eager to return to the slaughter. 'He's *in* there. We're almost on him.'

Maljdir looked agonised. Perhaps it was fear. The old Ulrican had never displayed fear before. That was disappointing.

'Look around you.' Maljdir forcibly turned the Theogonist to face the following troops.

It took a moment for his eyes to clear, dazzled as they were by the splendour of his Staff.

'Where are my men?' he asked, suddenly filled with doubt.

There were fewer than three hundred left, all bunched together, fighting to keep up with the charge of their leader. Most of those that remained were warrior priests. The wizards were gone, and there was no sign of Roll. Even as Volkmar watched, a swordsman in the rear of his column was torn apart by a ragged thing with talons for hands, his flesh flung over the heads of his comrades as he screamed.

'They couldn't keep up!' cried Maljdir. 'You've dragged them to their deaths. We must pull back.'

Volkmar hesitated, and the light of his staff guttered like a candle-flame. He couldn't withdraw. Not now, not with the city so close.

'We're almost at the gates,' he insisted, shaking off the priest's hands. 'I can feel his presence in the city...'

'You're deluded!' roared Maljdir. 'Chaos is here, but not the one you seek.'

Even as he spoke, more mutants closed in around them. They sensed the end, and were no longer daunted by the Staff.

Volkmar reeled, feeling his visions lift from his eyes. The anger was still there, but the mania had gone, extinguished by revelation.

'We cannot...' he started, and never finished.

A snarling pack of dog-soldiers charged into the line of warrior priests ahead of them, knocking them back and hacking them down. Volkmar's forces had become a beleaguered island amid a swirling maelstrom of enemy troops. It was too late to go back, and hopeless to go on.

'I have doomed us,' said Volkmar, his eyes widening with horror.

Maljdir drew away then, hauled back into the fighting by the approaching mutants.

'You still have the Staff!' he roared, wading into action and wielding Bloodbringer like a great bell, swinging back and forth. 'Use it! Get us back!'

Then he was gone, ploughing into the attack, laying into the clutching fingers and stabbing blades of the dog-soldiers around him.

Volkmar looked up. The gates were at hand. They were open still, still choked with Grosslich's troops. Under the massive iron lintel, the fires raged out of control. Averheim was ablaze, and daemonic forces swam in the unlocked power of the aethyr. The scene looked just like another world he'd seen once, back when his soul had been unlocked. Now Averheim was just one of those slivers of eternity, a shard of ruin embedded in the world of men.

'No!' he roared, and his Staff rushed back into flame. 'No retreat. We end this here.'

He swung the staff round and sent a snarling bolt of fire at the talon-fingered horror still terrorising his men. The creature blew apart in a deluge of bone and dry flesh. Volkmar felt power well up within him again, fuelled by faith and fury. He span back, sending a flurry of spitting lightning into the pressing ranks of mutants. They fell back in disarray, their ranks broken by a power they had no defence against.

Volkmar himself began to shimmer with a golden corona. No Light magister's spell fuelled him now. A halo crested his brow, blazing into the unnatural night and challenging the fires of Slaanesh for mastery. He was Master of the Church of Sigmar, the mightiest of His servants, the head of His Cult on earth, and no power could stand against that secret knowledge.

He took his stand, cracking the earth as he trod it down, his cloak rippling with gold. The servants of Averheim fell back, daunted by the savage forces he'd unleashed. His surging luminescence rose up into the tortured air, defiant and isolated, a shaft of pure flame to challenge the vast pillar of fire ahead.

'Sigmar!' came a roar from his left, deep in the ranks of the enemy.

It wasn't Maljdir, or Roll, or any of his troops. Something had responded to the line of burning gold.

The press of dog-soldiers on his left flank suddenly broke apart, scattered by a new force emerging from beyond them. Volkmar whirled round, ready to face a new terror. Instead, a phalanx of horsemen burst from their midst, swords flashing, hooves churning. They swept aside all resistance, as powerful and pure as a storm.

As they came on, Volkmar's golden light surged to greet them, bathing the oncoming knights in a cloak of brilliance.

They were the Emperor's own, the Reiksguard, and at their head rode Kurt Helborg. The knights surged towards the surrounded Empire troops, careering around Volkmar's remaining men and enclosing them in a wall of steel. Caught between the onslaught of the Reiksguard and the dazzling power of the Theogonist, Grosslich's twisted soldiers fell back further. For the first time, their eyes wavered with fear. Even the most debased servants of the Dark Gods could recognise a runefang when it came among them.

Helborg thundered towards Volkmar, pulling up at the last minute. His charger reared, kicking its hooves high in the air. Helborg slammed open his visor, revealing the familiar hawk-nose and stiff moustache. He looked more magnificent than Volkmar had ever seen him, like a vision of Magnus the Pious reborn, severe and terrible.

'My lord Volkmar!' he cried, controlling his stamping, shivering mount with unconscious ease. 'I bring the rightful Elector of Averland to his throne. Will you join me in battle?'

Volkmar raised his staff high and the corona blazed ever more furiously, banishing the shadows and blinding the reeling, cowering mutants. No madness remained in him then, just the righteous fury of the battlefield.

'I will, my lord Marshal,' replied Volkmar, seeing the armoured figure of Rufus Leitdorf emerge into the light for the first time. The man looked far more commanding than he'd expected from his reputation. He rode his warhorse without fear, and the faith-fire rushed to greet him, dousing him in a cascade of gold.

Volkmar turned again to face the iron gates, still open, still wreathed in daemonic fire. This was a new task, one for which his burning faith was aptly suited. Even in the midst of ruin, there was always redemption.

'To the city, then,' he said, narrowing his eyes against the roaring flames, 'and judgement.'

## Chapter Eighteen

THE PLAINS WERE dark with men. Aside from the splinter force that had followed Volkmar towards the walls of the city, the Imperial troops still occupied a long line skirting around the north edge of the plain. They had made negligible progress towards their goal, frustrated by the sheer numbers of Grosslich's slave-army before them.

Losses had been heavy. Of the forty thousand soldiers committed to the field, less than half still stood to bear arms. The enemy had suffered too, though their capacity to absorb casualties was greater. The defenders had maintained their positions, grinding down the advancing Imperial infantry with remorseless efficiency. They never took a step back, never withdrew, just soaked up the increasingly desperate attacks, waiting for the Empire lines to break from exhaustion.

Along much of the Imperial battlefront, discipline had broken down. In the absence of a guiding hand at the centre, lines of communication broke. The system of supporting detachments, the pride of the Empire and its most lethal weapon, was hamstrung.

Companies found themselves suddenly isolated, ripe for flank attacks. Others assaulted the same point as their comrades further down the line, leading to confusion and a muddled retreat before priority could be established. Fighting even broke out within companies as the fear and fatigue got to them, divided between those who still had the will to fight and those who only wished to save their hides. Amidst all the uncertainty, demoralisation and misunderstanding, Grosslich's men advanced steadily, destroying those who no longer had the power to resist them and squaring up to those that did.

Only on the eastern flank was resistance still solid. Schwarzhelm's reinforcements had bolstered the line just as it was about to break. The men under his command were not the highest quality, but they were fresh to the field and led by the Emperor's Champion. Slowly, methodically, shattered companies were re-formed and given proper support. Assaults on Grosslich's forces were properly coordinated, and the ranks of the halberdier detachments were rotated in good order. Inspired by sudden hope, demoralised men stood up to be counted, and found their courage stronger than they'd thought.

Such resistance attracted attention. The heavier elements of Grosslich's forces began to shift across to the east of the battlefield, steadily increasing in number as the Imperial ranks staunched their horrific rate of losses.

Embedded in the midst of the renewed surge, Bloch pulled his halberd blade from the chest of a corrupted Averlander, watching with satisfaction as the man's eyes flickered and lost their lilac glow. In death, his victim looked just the same as any other battlefield corpse.

He withdrew from the front rank, letting the men around him take up the strain. Bloch had no idea how long he'd been fighting. An hour? Two? More? His arms throbbed with muscle-ache and his palms, each one as tough as horse-hide, were raw and bleeding.

'Where's Schwarzhelm?' he muttered, cursing the smog that obscured everything further than thirty paces away.

'With the Talabheim spearmen,' replied Verstohlen, emerging from the press of men to stand beside him. 'They're assaulting the trenches.'

Bloch rolled his eyes. Even in the middle of a bloody *battle*, the man was impossible to shake off.

'No damn use to us there,' he spat, getting ready to re-enter the front line. 'We can kill these scum, but if we get another one of those dagger-fingered freaks, we'll be in trouble.'

Verstohlen shuddered. His elegant face was bruised, and a long streak of someone's blood ran across his right cheek. Possibly his own, possibly his victim's. The spy had long since run out of shot and now did what he could with his long knife. He was out of place here, and it looked like he knew it.

'We're going to have to withdraw sooner or later,' Verstohlen said. 'We can't drive them back. Far too many.'

'You can tell the big man that,' said Bloch irritably. For a civilian, Verstohlen certainly liked to give his opinion on tactics. 'I was told to hold this front together, and that's what–'

Without warning, a huge explosion detonated from the press of troops before them. Men, both loyalist and traitor, were hurled into the air, spinning through the clouds of ash and soot like chaff.

Bloch was slammed to the ground, knocked clean off his feet by the blast. When he looked up, his vision shaky and ringed with black, a wide circle of devastation had been opened up. For thirty yards in every direction the earth had been flattened. Men lay across the scoured land, some dead, some moaning weakly in pain.

At the centre of the space stood a figure clad in crimson armour. The lightning from the Tower glinted from its glossy surface. He went on foot and carried a sword that dripped black liquid like an open wound. The man stood calmly, waiting for the battle to recover its shape around him.

A few yards ahead of Bloch, Verstohlen was getting to his feet. Somehow the blast had failed to throw him as far as the others. His weapon had been ripped from his fingers, and the gash on his cheek had opened up.

'Herr Verstohlen,' said Grosslich. The tone was resigned. 'I thought you'd had the sense to leave Averheim.'

Verstohlen stood shakily before the traitor elector, his tattered leather coat fluttering in the ash-heavy wind.

'Coming back wasn't exactly my idea.'

At the edge of the circle, Bloch spat a gobbet of blood onto the ground. He'd lost *another* tooth. That made him angry. He reached for his blade. Every part of him ached.

'Then it seems we're both the victim of the choices of others,' said Grosslich. 'I didn't want this either.'

'So give it up. Leitdorf still lives. He'll happily take the runefang back.'

It wasn't clear if Grosslich smiled at that. His helmet

obscured his entire face, and behind the eye-slit there was nothing but darkness.

'Your advice hasn't got any better, counsellor. There are other options for me. Though none left, I'm afraid, for you.'

Bloch staggered to his feet, feeling his boots slip against the mud as he scrabbled for purchase.

'Verstohlen!'

He was too slow. With a sickening inevitability, Grosslich drew his sword back. The counsellor stayed still, rooted to the ground, waiting for the strike. Even as Bloch lurched across the circle of devastation, crying out for Verstohlen to evade the blow, Grosslich swung the blade.

RUFUS LEITDORF LOOKED up at the gates. Grosslich had enlarged and changed them, replacing the stone blocks with iron columns and decorating the archway with a huge hammered 'G'. The mighty pillars on either side of them soared up nearly forty feet. Within the gaping chasm Natassja's bloodfire raged, filling the air with a surging, roaring sheet of flame. It looked like they were approaching some gigantic stained glass wall. Beyond the cordon, dark outlines of women flickered from roof to roof, swooping through the air like birds.

The legions still swarmed around them, but none could stand against Volkmar and Helborg together. The two men rode at the head of the vanguard, both wreathed in an aura of blazing gold. Any approaching dog-soldiers were cut down, either by the power of the Staff or the harrowing edge of the runefang. They were terrified of the sword. It seemed to have some hold over them, like a totem of their destruction.

Leitdorf took some heart from that, and was happy enough to ride in the lee of its protection. He'd felled a few of Grosslich's minions himself on the charge, but most of the deadly work was done by the Reiksguard. Fewer than thirty of the knights remained after their daring ride through the heart of Grosslich's legions, but they still fought with a zeal and skill that defied belief. They were nearing the site of their master's defeat on the Vormeisterplatz and the mood was one of cold vengeance. They would not leave Averheim again without exacting their toll.

'The blood of Sigmar!' roared Volkmar, riding ahead of Leitdorf, urging his troops on to greater feats. Every pace they took, every blood-drenched step, brought them nearer to the city.

A huge man bearing the Imperial standard marched beside the Theogonist, thundering out hymns of defiance even as he swung his warhammer.

'Despise the mutant!' he bellowed, smashing the skull of a growling dog-soldier with a grim relish. 'Purge the unclean!'

It was a brave show. For the time being, they were making progress. It had been a long time since Leitdorf had last been in Averheim. It looked like the place had changed quite a bit.

'You're troubled, elector.'

Leitdorf turned to see Skarr riding beside him, his visor raised and his broken-toothed mouth twisted in a wolfish grin. The preceptor was breathing heavily and his sword was streaked with gore.

'What are we doing here, preceptor?' replied Leitdorf. 'If we make the gates, then what? We'll never make it out again.'

Skarr shrugged.

'Helborg said he'd take you back to Averheim. He always keeps his word.'

The Reiksguard knight had a fey look about him. Leitdorf had seen it before from men in battle, particularly in the elite ranks of the Imperial army. This was euphoria to them, this killing. Fear meant nothing once that mood descended, just a semi-bestial love of the contest.

'Helborg has no idea of Natassja's power.'

'I'd say he does. You heard Schwarzhelm's testimony. She's at the heart of it.'

Leitdorf shook his head.

'Kill her,' he muttered. 'So simple.'

Skarr laughed, a grating sound like the rattling of old chains.

'I thought you'd be pleased to see her again,' he said, pulling his steed round. 'I've heard she's a beauty.'

And then he was gone, spurring his horse into the attack, his sword plunging into the wavering ranks of defenders.

The gates drew closer. As Helborg and Volkmar forged a path towards them, Grosslich's defenders dwindled. None retreated back through that archway. They seemed more scared of the city than of the attackers before them. Or perhaps there was some other reason why they wouldn't enter.

From within the mighty walls, the throbbing echo of power grew louder. Leitdorf could see the Tower properly now. The iron shell contained a heart of deepest vermillion, pulsing angrily like an artery. The clouds swirled still around its tip, dark and forbidding, and lightning lanced down its flanks.

It was vast.

Leitdorf let his fingers creep to the book at his belt,

though its presence gave him little comfort. He mouthed the last words recorded there, the ones he'd committed to memory.

*She comes for me in my sleep, walking in my mind like a nightmare. I cannot defeat her. None can defeat her. Even now, my mind breaks. There is nothing. No hope, only madness. Her name is agony. Her name is Natassja, and she will kill me.*

After that it was nonsense, a stream of half-syllables. Some poorly-remembered fragment of a dream, the final ravings of a great mind brought low by a woman.

'The gates!' cried Helborg, spurring his horse towards them.

The final push came. Volkmar, Skarr, the Reiksguard and the surviving Imperial troops pressed forwards, cutting their way towards the iron columns. Leitdorf, just as he had been at the Vormeisterplatz, was carried along in the midst of them, surrounded by knights and swept like flotsam on the tide.

The last of the defence fell under the onslaught of the Klingerach and the Staff of Command. Helborg rode under the iron portal, his steed stepping proudly. Volkmar followed him, and the golden aura of his passing lit up the agonised faces locked in the metal.

One by one, the surviving Empire troops stepped over the threshold, passing through the curtain of fire and into Averheim. The sounds of battle receded, replaced with the numb roar of the bloodfire.

Leitdorf took a look around him. The city he knew had gone. In its place was death. Nothing but death.

VERSTOHLEN SAW THE sword come at him. He couldn't move. His muscles were locked in place, held down by some weight. Even as the blade-edge swung at his neck, dripping with black fluid, his limbs remained frozen. He was going to die.

'Verstohlen!'

Bloch's voice, thick as a bull's, roared out from behind him. He was coming, tearing back into the line of danger, just as he always did.

Suddenly, from somewhere, the force clamping him in place lessened. Verstohlen jerked back. Grosslich adjusted too late and the tip of the blade missed its target, slicing across his chest. Verstohlen cried aloud as the metal cut through his leather jerkin and parted the flesh beneath. He fell to his knees, clutching at the wound. Blood, mingled with ink-black slurry, poured over his grasping fingers.

Then Bloch barrelled into Grosslich, knocking him sidelong with the force of the charge then landing a flurry of crushing blows on the traitor elector. He wielded his stave with a ferocious, controlled skill.

'I've marched halfway across this bloody province for this fight,' Bloch snarled through gritted teeth. 'Now you're getting one, you bastard.'

'Leave him!' cried Verstohlen, feeling his vision fade into dizziness. Something in his wound was poisoning him, rushing into his bloodstream and spreading toxins through his body. He tried to rise, but his legs gave out and he fell back to his knees. 'He's too strong.'

Recovering from his surprise, Grosslich began to meet Bloch's attack. His sword-edge whirled in tight arcs, picking out the weaknesses in the halberdier's technique. The twin blades still clashed together in unison. At the edges of the circle, other soldiers were beginning to find their feet.

'A man with the stomach to face me,' mused

Grosslich, hammering Bloch back two paces with a single swipe. 'A soldier after my own heart.'

'I'm nothing like you,' growled Bloch, pivoting the staff round and bringing the heel up for a jab.

'Maybe as I was, then,' said Grosslich, evading the blunt stave and switching his grip for a backhanded thrust. 'I'd have found a place for you here.'

'And I'd have died before taking it.'

Bloch jerked the blade back round and parried Grosslich's strike, giving ground with every exchange. Though his eyes glittered with determination, he was unequal to this foe. The battle had already been long, and Grosslich's muscles were animated with an unnatural strength.

Verstohlen clambered back to his feet, the world swaying around him. Stumbling drunkenly, he went for his dagger, thrown yards clear by Grosslich's theatrical arrival. His movements were clumsy and broken. Something virulent was worming its way within him. He grabbed the knife and whirled round, fighting the growing tide of nausea.

Bloch was fighting like a man possessed. Verstohlen had never seen a halberd wielded with such power and speed. Even the troops shuffling forwards on the far side of the circle seemed daunted by it. A dog-soldier made to leap into the fray, but Grosslich sent it back with a dismissive gesture.

'Get back, filth,' he spat.

'Want me for yourself?' jeered Bloch, seizing advantage of the diversion to launch a flurry of downward plunges.

Grosslich met them easily, adjusting his stance to absorb the blows. Verstohlen felt despair grow within him. Even if Bloch's blade connected, Grosslich's armour looked invulnerable. The counsellor limped back towards the duelling warriors too slowly, his dagger clutched in his clammy hands, sweat streaming from his brow. He felt useless, pathetic, wasted.

'A warrior's right,' replied Grosslich, planting his feet squarely and aiming a two-handed thrust at Bloch's chest.

Bloch swerved to avoid it, but the edge scraped along his breastplate, knocking him off balance. He regained his feet just in time to block the follow-up.

'You have no–'

He never finished. Grosslich's follow-up was a feint. His blade spun round in his hands as it dropped down and plunged deep into the flesh below Bloch's breastplate.

'Markus!' Verstohlen cried out as he struggled, mere feet away, his hand outstretched impotently.

Bloch's face contorted into a mask of agony. His halberd, the weapon that had taken him from Turgitz, to Black Fire Pass, and finally back to Averheim, thumped to the ground. The staff shivered as it rolled across the earth.

Grosslich shoved the blade in further, grasping the stricken halberdier by the shoulder and hauling him up along the impaling sword-edge.

Bloch gasped, choked, and a well of thick blood spilled from his throat. He clutched frantically at Grosslich's armour, scrabbling for some kind of purchase. Verstohlen crawled towards them both, nearly overwhelmed with black sickness.

'Markus...' he choked, watching the man die before him.

It was always the soldiers. First Grunwald, now Bloch. Verstohlen was consumed by a wave of self-loathing.

His charmed existence seemed like a curse to him then. This was his fault. Again.

Bloch looked at him. His eyes were glazing over. Blood bubbled from his mouth, running down his chest, streaked with black. From somewhere, he summoned the strength to grasp at Grosslich's armoured bulk. He grabbed the elector in a bear-hug. He could no longer speak, could barely stand, but the final look he shot Verstohlen was as clear as glass.

*Do it.*

Verstohlen's grief transmuted into fury. Thrusting aside his nausea, ignoring the pain streaming through his poisoned limbs, he leapt forwards, dagger in hand.

Grosslich sensed the danger and whirled round, trying to draw his weapon, but Bloch's dying body hampered his movements. His sword remained lodged, and for a second, a mere second, he was unprotected.

Verstohlen raised the dagger high over Grosslich and plunged it down with all his strength and skill. It went in between the rim of his breastplate and helmet, sliding through like a stick in water.

Grosslich screamed. He flung Bloch free. The halberdier's body swung into the air before crashing to the earth with a heavy, final thud.

Verstohlen staggered back, his veins thumping in his temples. His hands were shaking. Grosslich grabbed the dagger and hurled it from his neck. It spun through the air, spraying his own blood. Incredibly, he still stood.

Verstohlen began to back away, his dizziness returning, the blackness around his eyes closing in. Across his chest, the wound still leaked hot, pumping slurry.

'Damn you, counsellor,' Grosslich snarled, twisting

his helmet off and letting it fall to the ground. His face was drawn with pain. He strode towards Verstohlen, sword brandished in his hand, the dark light of hatred in his eyes. '*That* was the worst of your many errors.'

Verstohlen gazed up at the man's face in horror. It was a pale white, and the eyes were ringed with purple growths. The flesh was as glossy and rigid as his armour. Blood pumped from the wound at his neck, but it barely seemed to trouble him. It should have killed him.

'You could have *resisted* her,' said Verstohlen, feeling his consciousness weaken. He had no weapon. Even if he had, he was now too weak to use it.

Grosslich's face remained contorted with rage.

'Remember this, as I kill you,' he hissed. 'You were our *instrument*. Whatever choices I made, you made them happen. It's over now. The game is finished. You have no blade left that could hurt me.'

'But I do.'

It wasn't Verstohlen's voice. Both men snapped round.

Schwarzhelm was there, a giant amongst men, his armour encrusted with the patina of war, his eyes dark with betrayal. He raised the Rechtstahl, and the blade was as red as blood.

As Helborg rode through the barrier into Averheim he felt the heat of it crush his lungs. He took shallow breaths, almost choking as the searing air filled his throat. Averheim was a furnace.

No dog-soldiers followed them in. Helborg looked over his shoulder. The clamour of battle came from behind the hindmost Imperial soldier like a muffled echo. The enemy troops beyond the gates had turned

away from them, back towards the greater mass of
Empire soldiers to the north. It was as if, by passing
across the portal, they'd ceased to exist.

His men paused, waiting for the next order. A profound sense of dread had come over all of them. Less
than three hundred, mostly halberdiers, warrior
priests or knights. They now clustered together, eyes
wide, bravado forgotten, faces pale.

The battle-fury had gone. The only sound was the
low roar of the bloodfire, lifting their hair and pressing against their armour. It was hot but it did not
burn. Its purpose was not to injure, but to preserve.
Other things, inhuman things, thrived in such rarefied
airs.

Helborg looked about him warily, keeping a tight
grip on the Klingerach. Everything was blackened by
the fire. The street ahead was charred and ruinous.
Nothing living stirred on the stone, and the windows
of the houses gaped like mouths. Far ahead, some
massive brazier sent billows of lilac smoke into the
fervid air. The ground thrummed incessantly, as if
machines ground away far beneath their feet.

Above it all, the Tower loomed, dark and terrible,
shimmering behind a haze of unrelenting heat. The
dread leaking from it was palpable, a tight, horrifying
cloud of fear. The structure was an aberration. It didn't
belong. No mortal could dwell in such a place. Then,
and only then, did Helborg understand its purpose. It
was no fortress or citadel. It was an instrument. A
device. A means of focussing something within the
city.

None of the men spoke. None of them moved. Leitdorf looked like he was trying to remember
something by mumbling words under his breath.

Volkmar had let his golden fire ebb. The madness had passed from his severe features, replaced by the grim determination that had given him his nickname.

Helborg's steed was skittish under him. All the other horses were the same. One of them kicked out in a panic, infecting the others. They were going mad.

'Dismount,' ordered Helborg, and his voice echoed strangely. 'Horses will be of no use to us in here.'

The knights did as they were bid, and the released horses galloped back through the gates, preferring a death on the plain to one in the city. All men stood shoulder to shoulder on the road, swords and halberds held ready.

'Stay close,' warned Helborg, turning to look each of them in the eye. 'Fear is your enemy. It will kill you if you let it. Trust to faith and to your blades. The Tower is our destination. Stay true, and we will destroy the architect of all this.'

He walked forwards. Even as he did so, there was a howling noise from the far end of the street. As if a mighty wind surged towards them from far away, the fire in the air rushed and swayed.

Helborg tensed. The Klingerach felt suddenly heavy in his hands. All around him, men took up defensive positions.

Something was coming. Something fast.

'Trust to faith,' he growled, standing his ground. Beside him, Volkmar's fire flared up again.

Then they came. From the far end of the street, shapes appeared in the air. They grew quickly, hurtling towards the Empire troops like storm-crows, flapping and shrieking. In their wake was pure terror, dripping from the air and pooling on the blasted stone.

They tore past the rows of houses. Their shapes grew

clearer. They were women, or parodies of women, impossibly lovely, impossibly terrible. Their flesh was lilac, and their exposed skin shimmered in the blood-fire. In place of hands they had rending claws and in place of feet they had talons like a bird's. Their bald heads were crowned with forbidden sigils, and their mouths were stretched open wide, lined with incisors and poised to bite.

Some of his troops broke then, dropping their weapons and racing back to face their end on the battlefield beyond the gates. Helborg hardly noticed them go. The remainder braced for the impact, fear marked on their ravaged faces. Even the Marshal, inured to fear by a lifetime of war, felt his heart hammering and sweat bursting out on his palms, slick against the grip of his sword.

'Trust to faith!' cried Helborg again, hefting the runefang and preparing to swing.

Faith seemed like little protection. As swift as death, as terrible as pain, Natassja's daemons screamed down the street towards them, eyes black with delicious fury, faces alive with the joyous malice of those about to feed.

# Chapter Nineteen

VERSTOHLEN WATCHED AS Schwarzhelm broke into a furious, heavy charge. Kraus was at his right hand, as were a whole company of swordsmen in the colours of Talabheim. Behind the sorcerer, a unit of dog-soldiers had formed up. The opening cleared by Grosslich's sorcery began to close back in on itself.

Verstohlen, his vision still cloudy, the sickness eating at his heart, could only watch as the Emperor's Champion swept across the broken earth, his battle-ravaged features blazing with fury. As Schwarzhelm tore towards Grosslich, Verstohlen saw the same dark expression on his face as when Grunwald had died. Though his grim demeanour didn't always make it obvious, Schwarzhelm cared about his men like few Imperial commanders. When one of them died, he *felt* it.

Grosslich took a step back. His hands kindled lilac energy, snapping and snaking around his gauntlets. Tendrils of oily matter strung out along his sword-blade, catching on the viscous fluid still dripping from the metal. As Schwarzhelm closed him down, Grosslich fired a spitting column of it outwards. The pure stuff of the aethyr surged across the narrow gap between the two men.

Schwarzhelm didn't so much as pause. Still charging, he swept the Sword of Justice into the path of the corrupted essence.

The matter exploded. Shards of it spun into the bodies around, burning through armour and cracking metal. Both men and dog-soldiers shrank back from the swarm of glowing embers. In the centre of it, vast and inexorable, Schwarzhelm ploughed onwards, shrugging slivers of sorcerous discharge from his rune-warded pauldrons.

Grosslich tried to blast at him again, but by then Schwarzhelm was in range. The Rechtstahl came across in a sweep of such staggering force that Verstohlen thought it would cleave the man in two. Somehow, Grosslich got his own twisted blade in the path of it. He was slammed back heavily, his legs bending under the impact. A filigree of cracks ran across the crimson armour.

'Faithless,' hissed Schwarzhelm, swinging his blade back for the next strike.

'You can talk,' gasped Grosslich, giving ground and frantically blocking the rain of blows that followed. His face had twisted into a mask of loathing – for Schwarzhelm, but also for himself. The handsome features that had once awed Averheim had gone forever, scarred by the mutating whim of his new master. 'You *made* me.'

'I'd have killed you for Grunwald's death alone,' Schwarzhelm growled, his blade working faster and heavier with every plunge, knocking Grosslich back steadily, stride by stride. 'You need not give me more reasons.'

Verstohlen found himself held rapt by the exchange, unable to intervene, clamped down by the poisons coursing through his body. Schwarzhelm fought like a warrior-god of old, shrugging off Grosslich's attempts to land a blow and raining strikes of crushing weight on the sorcerer's retreating frame. The traitor's armour, invulnerable to the bite of lesser weapons, began to fracture under the assault. Even Bloch, for all his skill, hadn't as much as dented it.

*Bloch.*

Verstohlen spun round. Where was he? The rush of bodies began to obscure the open space Grosslich had opened up. Dog-soldiers and swordsmen surged across it, a mass of sweat-draped limbs and blood-streaked faces.

Verstohlen staggered along, pushing his way through a press of straining swordsmen. He was unarmed, vulnerable. He didn't care. The battle roared on around him. The sounds of it were muffled, the stench of it muted. As if drunk, Verstohlen clumsily shoved and ducked his way to where Bloch had fallen.

'Merciful Verena,' he whispered, the words slurring from his sluggish mouth. 'As you have ever guided me...'

He didn't need to finish his prayer. A line of Empire swordsmen swept in front of him, driving a detachment of dog-soldiers back several paces. In their wake, a gap opened up. There, lying on the churned earth, lay the halberdier commander, forgotten by the fury that boiled around him. His blood had stopped flowing and his face was as pale as ivory. Somehow he'd regained hold of his halberd, and it lay across him like a monument of honour.

Verstohlen limped over to him, falling to his knees by

Bloch's corpse. The commander had fallen awkwardly, his legs twisted and broken under him. His face was fixed in a snarl of aggression. Belligerent to the end.

The virulence was now deep within Verstohlen's bones. Without treatment he knew he'd be dead soon. Then the two of them, scholar and soldier, would find their end together, as unlikely a pairing as a minstrel and a slayer.

He looked up. The swordsmen had maintained the assault but the right flank had been left exposed. More dog-soldiers crept forwards. There was nothing between Verstohlen and them. They advanced steadily, eyeing the vulnerable figure crouching down next to the body of their master's last victim.

For a moment, he thought his end had come. He was weak. Far too weak.

'No,' he breathed, gritting his teeth and getting to his feet with effort. 'You shall not despoil this.'

He picked up Bloch's halberd. It was heavy, far heavier than he'd imagined it would be. For the first time, he began to understand the scorn of fighting men for those they protected.

The dog-soldiers kept coming. Verstohlen could see the unnatural light within the helmets of the lead warriors. The stench was just as it had been in Hessler's townhouse so long ago, the first time he'd seen one of the creatures up close.

'Damn you,' he snarled, standing over Bloch's body and lowering the halberd blade awkwardly. 'This is *not* for you.'

If they understood the words, the dog-soldiers made no sign. They came on remorselessly. Empire troops, seeing the gap in the lines, came up to Verstohlen's side. He was not alone. Without speaking, needing no orders, they closed in around the body of the fallen commander.

All knew the score. This was ground that would not be yielded.

As the first of the dog-soldiers came into range, Verstohlen narrowed his eyes, swallowed the bile rising in his gorge, adjusted his grip on the wooden stave and braced to meet the charge.

HELBORG SWEPT UP the Klingerach, aiming at the screeching face of the nearest daemon. It swooped past him, swerving away from the steel and spinning back into the air. They would not take on a holy blade. He swept round, looking to catch another of them with its edge.

They were too fast. Like hawks above prey, they darted into the crowd of men, picking off the weak and hauling them into the fire-laced sky. Their victims screamed with horror as they were born aloft. Warrior priest or knight, it made no difference. These were foes beyond all of them.

Volkmar kindled his staff again and lightning spat along its full height. He whirled round, releasing a volley of twisting bolts. They streaked up at the circling daemons. One hit, dousing the creature in a ball of swirling immolation. It screamed in its turn, an echoing mockery of the cries of mortal men. Its companions merely laughed, and the sound was alive with joyous spite.

'The men cannot fight these,' muttered the Theogonist. 'The fire sustains them.'

'We won't go back,' said Helborg, watching as the daemons clustered for a second pass. 'Can you do nothing?'

'Hurt them, yes. Kill them, no.'

The daemons swooped back between the houses, their claws now dripping with blood. As they came, the wind howled around them.

Helborg watched them come again, keeping his sword poised to strike. One of them dropped down low, spinning as it dived towards the earth, its face lit with a malign grin of exuberance. It went for the Reiksguard on his left flank, ignoring the bearer of the runefang. The man stood his ground, his trembling hands holding his broadsword in place to ward the impact.

Fast as a stab, the daemon took him. Helborg sprang. Leaping up at the sinuous figure, he whirled the Klingerach down across its kicking legs. The sacred blade sank deep into the daemonic flesh, sinking deep and severing aethyric sinews.

The daemon wailed, dropping its quarry and twisting away from Helborg. The Marshal pursued it, spinning the sword into a two-handed grip and preparing to plunge. The creature spat at him and disappeared. It re-emerged twelve feet away, cradling its wounds and wailing in agony before kicking back into the air. It soared upwards, leaving a trail of purple blood in its wake.

In the meantime more men had been plucked from the midst of the dwindling band and carried up into the high places to be dismembered. A steady shower of blood and body parts rained down on the survivors, evidence of their comrades' fate.

'No more of this,' snarled Helborg, turning to Skarr. The preceptor looked scared. He never looked scared.

'What, then?'

'We run.'

'Where to?'

Helborg gestured to the Tower, still distant over the roofs of the houses. Lightning flickered across the devastated cityscape, picking out the ruined frames of the buildings, now squatted on by daemons licking their blood-soaked fingers.

'There.'

Without waiting for a response, Helborg broke into a sprint. Needing no orders, his men did likewise. Leitdorf and Skarr went alongside him. The preceptor loped like a wolf, though no longer grinning. Volkmar took up the rear, keeping his staff kindled and doing what he could to ward the attacks from above.

The ravaged company ran through the streets, assailed at every step. The daemons were in their element, sustained and buoyed by the bloodfire, impervious to mortal weapons. The warrior priests had the most success at fending them off, swinging their icon-studded warhammers and slamming the unwary creatures against the charred walls. The big man with the standard still roared out his hymns and hefted his mighty weapon. Bloodbringer, he called it. It was a good name.

Despite the fragmentary successes, the sprint was a nightmare. Knights and halberdiers, both with little defence against the monsters of the aethyr, were plucked from the midst of them almost at will, destined for an agonising death in the spires of the city. With each corner the company rounded, another dozen were taken, whittling them down further.

Helborg was torn between anger and horror. There was nothing worse than a foe that couldn't be fought. He did his best to interpose himself between the daemons and his men, but they slipped past his guard all too easily. He was forced to listen as dying men's screams rang out across the rooftops, accompanied by the echoing laughs of the killers.

'We'll all be dead before we get there,' panted Leitdorf, his cheeks red with the effort of running. He'd managed to cast off some of his armour, but he was making heavy work of the chase.

'Then go back,' spat Helborg, unwilling to indulge the man's fears. 'I *will* find the one who did this.'

A phalanx of daemons screamed low across the heads of the fleeing band, pursued by Volkmar's inaccurate castings. Three of them had struggling bodies locked in their talons, all enclosed in plate armour. They were picking off the Reiksguard first.

'You think you can kill her, if you can't kill these?'

Helborg ramped up the pace, driving his men harder.

'The runefang will finish her,' he growled, his breath ever more ragged. His shoulder wound had opened again and he could feel the hot stickiness under his jerkin. The Tower was still too far away. 'Count on it.'

As he spoke, a daemon tore into them from the roofs on their left, diving down into the press of bodies and scattering them. It had miscalculated, coming in too fast. It rolled across the cobbles with its prey, unable to leap back into the bloodfire quick enough.

Skarr, further back amid the men, was on her in an instant, hacking at her with his blade to free its prey.

'Skarr, no!' roared Helborg, shoving his way through the jostling bodies to reach him.

The preceptor's blade passed harmlessly through the daemon's flesh, biting into the stone beneath and kicking up sparks. The daemon hissed at him, dropped her intended quarry and coiled to leap.

'Get back!' roared Helborg, almost there, Klingerach in hand.

Then the daemon sprang, catching Skarr full in the chest and hurling them both free of the men around. They crashed into the nearest wall, shattering the stone. Helborg saw Skarr's helmet bounce jarringly from the impact and the knight's limbs go limp.

Helborg burst free and leapt after them. The daemon crouched again, ready to tear up into the skies with her latest morsel. The Klingerach was quicker, tearing deep into the lilac-fleshed back, runes blazing as it bit.

The creature screamed, arching back, limbs flailing, trying to turn round. Skarr fell from her grasp, sliding down the stone and leaving a slick of blood on the wall.

Helborg withdrew the blade and the daemon spun to face him. The Klingerach flashed again, carving through the daemon's neck and severing her head. A powerful snap rippled through the air, radiating out and knocking the airborne daemons back up into the heights. For a moment, the severed head of their fallen sister still breathed. It looked up at Helborg with a mix of fear and amazement, before finally rolling over listlessly, lifeless and empty.

Leitdorf rushed to Helborg's side, his own blade drawn, too late to intervene. The surviving troops gazed at the Marshal in awe.

'Nothing is immune from the Sword of Vengeance,' panted Helborg, gazing at Skarr's unmoving body. His voice shook with emotion. 'You ask me how I'll kill her? *This* is how.'

Then he turned on his heel and motioned for the race to the Tower to resume. Far above, the daemons began to circle again, gauging the moment to strike, wary of the blade that had the power to extinguish them.

Along the twisting streets, the stone blackened with ashes, Helborg's men sprinted into the heart of the city, half their number slain, the Tower still distant, and the scions of the Lord of Pain on their backs.

VOLKMAR RAN. HIS robes curled tight around his huge frame as he went, slowing him down. His bald head was glossy with sweat, both from the exertion and from the pressing heat. Every muscle in his body screamed at him to stop, to hold his ground, to face the creatures that swooped on them.

Perhaps, if he did, he'd take a couple of them down. Maybe half a dozen. He could flay their unsubstantial flesh from their unholy bones, rip them into their constituent parts.

He knew Helborg was right. They couldn't fight this foe, not for any length of time. The bloodfire sustained the daemons, filled their unholy bodies with energy and power. This was their place, a city of mortal men no longer.

The ragged band of soldiers, whittled down to little more than a hundred, kept going. Laggards had been left behind, easy picking for the rapacious daemons. Those that remained huddled close together, gaining what protection they could from Volkmar and Helborg.

They passed over the river. The water boiled black, choked with ash from the fires. The Averburg, the ancient seat of the electors, was an empty shell. Its stark, flame-blackened walls rose up into the raging maelstrom, broken silhouettes against the burning clouds of crimson.

The daemons came at them again and again, giving no respite. With every pass, another man was taken, swept up into the spires for an agonising end. As the cries rang out across the ruins, Volkmar felt hot tears of anger prick at his eyes.

He wanted to stop. He knew he couldn't.

'My lord,' came Maljdir's voice from his shoulder.

The priest still ran powerfully alongside him, despite carrying the standard in one hand and the warhammer in the other. Though his beard was lank with sweat and his face as red as the fires around them, he hadn't given up yet. Damned Ulrican intransigence.

'So you were right,' snarled Volkmar, hardly breaking stride.

Maljdir shook his head.

'No,' he said, his words coming in snatches between his laboured gasps. 'I was not.'

He looked up at the looming Tower, now dominating the sky above them.

'Your zeal led us here.' Though effort etched his every word, there was a kind of satisfaction in his voice. He looked back at Volkmar. 'I should have trusted you.'

Volkmar just kept going. There were no certainties any more. For a moment back there, he'd been close to losing his mind. Above them, the daemons were gathering for a final pounce. There were dozens of them. The portals of the Tower were visible, dark and gaping, but they'd be lucky to make the nearest of them.

'Save your energy for the daemons,' rasped Volkmar, watching as the first of them plunged downwards. 'You'll need it.'

THE DAEMON HURTLED towards Helborg, only turning out of the path of the Klingerach at the last moment. The Marshal ignored it. Unless they made a mistake, they were too fast to engage with. The curtains of fire in the air buoyed them. This was their element. More screams from behind him told him they'd found another victim.

He turned a final corner and ran down a long, straight street. At the end of it, the rows of shattered houses finally gave out, revealing a pair of enormous iron-rimmed gates. Two pillars flanked them, crowned with fire. Beyond the gates, a wide and featureless courtyard opened up. The Tower stood in the centre. Up close, its scale was even more daunting.

'Volkmar!' he shouted, keeping up the pace. 'The gates!'

The Theogonist responded instantly, summoning bolts of golden flame from his staff and hurling them at the iron. The gates shuddered from the first impact, broke on the second. The metal slammed back hard, bouncing from the stone pillars as the hinges strained. Then they were through, the ever-diminishing company tearing across the open courtyard, harried and pursued at every step.

'I can sense her,' said Leitdorf.

The man was suffering. His red face still carried too much fat, and the sweat was running in rivulets down his cheeks. Just as he'd predicted, though, the daemons ignored him. The Wolfsklinge had a heritage they feared. Or maybe it was something more.

'Then you'll be the guide,' said Helborg, gazing up at the column of ruin looming over him.

The Tower was massive, a soaring dark skeleton of iron over a throbbing core of magma-red. Above the pinnacle, the ring of clouds had broken, exposing Morrslieb again. The power that had drawn the storm in over Averheim was beginning to dissipate.

Volkmar felt it too.

'Weakness?' he asked.

Leitdorf shook his head.

'No,' he said. 'Its work is done.'

Helborg didn't ask how Leitdorf knew that. He risked a look over his shoulder. A few dozen men were left, all haggard and panting from the sprint across the ruined city. No regular troops had made it. The remainder were warrior priests and a scattering of Reiksguard, the only ones with the stomach to endure the horrors of the air. The Tower would be no kinder to them.

'Once we're in, which way?' he asked Leitdorf, watching as the massive Tower gates loomed up out of the fire-flecked dark.

'Down,' replied the elector tersely. 'She's beneath the earth.'

Volkmar shook his head. 'There's nothing human in there.'

Helborg said nothing, but forced the pace once more. The gates drew close. Pillars of adamant framed the huge curved doors, glinting in the firelight. Sigils of Slaanesh adorned the iron, sunk deep into the metal in a sweeping pattern of silver. The vast bole of the Tower rose up into the night, soaring three hundred feet to the summit. The base of it was mighty, bound by pillars of obsidian and engraved bands of iron. The rumble of machines working in the deeps crept across the stone, and bloodfire rushed up the flanks of the enormous structure, washing over the colonnades and parapets as it raced to the apex.

The daemons came for them again, swooping down the sheer sides of the Tower, arms outstretched and ready for more feeding. There were dozens of them now. They'd been waiting for this, their last chance to pick them off in the open.

'Get those doors open,' snapped Helborg, but Volkmar was already working.

The Theogonist swung his staff round and hurled a stream of leaping fire at the barred doors. They shivered, but remained closed.

Then the daemons landed, crashing to earth and sinking their talons deep into the unprotected mortals below.

'Sigmar!' roared Helborg, tearing into them with the Sword of Vengeance. They darted away from the blade, cowed by the rune-wound power of the steel.

'Averland!' cried Leitdorf, though his meagre voice was carried away by the roar of the furnaces. He swiped wildly at the spinning creatures, and they evaded his blows easily.

Volkmar unleashed another volley, and the gap between the doors fractured.

The daemons kept coming, sweeping more troops up in their terrible embrace and tearing them apart in mid-air. One of them came for the big warrior priest with the standard. He stood his ground and brought his heavy warhammer round with incredible speed. The faith-strengthened head of it slammed into the oncoming daemon. Bright light blazed from the impact, knocking the creature back yards. It hovered for a moment, dazed.

The priest roared his defiance, keeping the standard aloft, whirling the warhammer over his head in triumph.

'Smite the mutant!' he bellowed. 'Purge the–'

A claw punched through his back and out through his chest. He coughed up blood in gouts as he was lifted from the ground. More daemons flocked to him, snapping at his flailing limbs and biting deep into his flesh. Too quick for Helborg to reach him, they dragged the heavy figure into the air.

'Fight the darkness!' Maljdir roared through his blood-clogged throat, still crying aloud as half a dozen daemons struggled to bear him aloft. He dropped the standard but kept swinging his warhammer, slamming more of them aside even as he was taken beyond the reach of help. 'Dawn will come again! Trust to faith!'

Then he was gone, hauled up the flanks of the Tower, his increasingly weak cries of denunciation and defiance echoing down from above before they were silenced forever.

Volkmar summoned fire a third time and the gates blew inwards, crashing back on their enormous hinges. A sickly jasmine stench rolled out to greet them. Beyond the portal, a corridor stretched away, dark and forbidding.

'Inside!' roared Helborg, pushing his men across the threshold, doing what he could to protect the swooping daemons from their backs. They hurried in, those that were left. Leitdorf was at the rear, followed last of all by Volkmar. As the Theogonist passed under the dark lintel, he turned and smashed his staff on the ground. A ball of force raced outwards, a shimmer in the air like the backwash from a massive explosion.

The daemons were hurled away, wheeling into the high airs and screaming with frustration.

'Close the gates!' Helborg shouted, seizing a door and pushing against it.

There were fewer than twenty of them left. The priests and Volkmar took one door, the Reiksguard and Leitdorf joined Helborg. Slowly, agonisingly slowly, the gates began to grind shut. Outside, quickly recovered from Volkmar's casting, the daemons rushed back, screaming for more blood. Helborg saw the foremost tearing towards him, her eyes alive with bloodlust.

'Harder!' he roared, straining every muscle. The gap closed too slowly. The daemons hurtled towards it, reaching for the diminishing space. If they got in, then they were all dead men.

At last, groaning and creaking, the mighty iron doors slammed into place. There were heavy thuds from the outside as the daemons crunched into them, followed by howls of petulant anguish. The iron doors buckled but did not break.

'There are wards here,' panted Volkmar, leaning on his knees.

'That won't hold them,' said Leitdorf, drawing huge, shuddering breaths.

All around, the surviving troops slumped to the polished marble. Helborg felt impatience prick at him. They needed to keep moving.

'How long have we got?'

Leitdorf shrugged, his shoulders shivering with fatigue.

'They know this place better than we do,' he said without conviction. 'Not long.'

Helborg looked over his shoulder. The corridor

yawned away into the dark, lit only by faint blushes of lilac. The walls were dark and smooth, polished to a high sheen. The muted thunder of the bloodfire still thrummed throughout the walls. The interior of the Tower was filled with strange, echoing sounds. The immense superstructure of iron creaked. From far below, unearthly noises rose up, warped and distorted by their passage through the catacombs. The stain of corruption was everywhere, thick and cloying.

At the far end of the corridor there was a huge spiral stairway leading both up and down. Flickering light, bright and unnaturally blue, came from below.

'Time to move again,' Helborg said. His voice was harsh, his expression unforgiving. 'And I hate to keep a lady waiting.'

# Chapter Twenty

SCHWARZHELM KEPT HIS weight perfectly balanced, watching for the counter-thrust. The raw power of his anger flowed freely, but it did not master him. The duel was too evenly poised for recklessness, and Grosslich was too strong. His natural skill as a soldier had been magnified by his corruption, and he matched Schwarzhelm's blistering assault stroke for stroke.

All around them, the battle was similarly poised. Schwarzhelm's men, a mix of the many companies Volkmar had brought into battle, were locked in combat with the dog-soldiers. Neither side had the mastery, and the line of grappling men stayed static, locked over the same patch of blood-soaked land.

As for the remainder of the army, Schwarzhelm could only hope they were holding together. He'd worked hard to restore some kind of shape to the Imperial lines, but the numbers were still against them. Killing Grosslich might bring some respite, but it wouldn't win the day. Whatever happened between the two of them, there were long hours of fighting ahead.

Grosslich pressed the attack, his sword crackling with lilac energy. As he did so, the clouds fractured over the summit of the Tower. Starlight shone through the gap, exposing the deep of the night above. Then, slipping into vision as the clouds sheared away, Morrslieb spilled its putrid light across the battlefield. Firelight mingled with the yellowish stain of corruption, making even the Empire troops look as ravaged as corpses.

Grosslich risked a glance upwards before meeting Schwarzhelm's challenge again. The swords crunched together, splattering the viscous slurry from Grosslich's sword in a wide circle.

'The Deathmoon,' he said, dodging a vicious swipe at his flanks and twisting Schwarzhelm's blade back at him. 'Sign of your defeat.'

'*My* defeat?' growled Schwarzhelm, letting his sword come back and seizing the grip with both hands. 'I remember you as you were. There's no victory for you here.'

He flung Grosslich's blade up out of position and stabbed at the traitor's midriff.

'Your death will be victory enough,' hissed Grosslich, sidestepping the strike and getting his sword back down into guard. His voice was ragged with effort.

'Tell yourself that, if you need to.'

Grosslich snarled and surged forwards. His sword spun round, spraying black fluid over Schwarzhelm's armour.

'You know nothing of my choices!' he spat, thrusting at Schwarzhelm's guard with renewed vigour. 'Dominion was denied me, though I was twice the man Leitdorf was.'

Schwarzhelm let the flurry of blows come to him, stepping into them, bringing his enormous strength to bear on the parries, engaging the peerless swordsmanship that had made his reputation on the battlefields of the Empire.

'Maybe once. Now you have diminished, and he has grown.'

'He lives?' Grosslich became agitated, and the disquiet fed itself into his sword-strokes.

'Even now he nears the Tower. Husband and wife are due a reunion.'

Grosslich's eyes filled with a mocking light. His face glowed sickeningly as his misshapen mouth cracked into a warped smile.

'She needs no husband,' he laughed, meeting a powerful thrust from Schwarzhelm and pushing it back. 'He can't destroy her. You can't. Only I have the power. Kill me, and you doom yourself.'

Schwarzhelm feinted to the left before bringing his edge back sharply, probing for the join in Grosslich's armour below the breastplate.

'You overestimate your power,' he said, his voice steely calm. 'Do you not recognise the Sword of Justice? It is a holy blade. It thirsts for your death, and you have nothing to answer it with.'

Grosslich laughed again. Quick as a snake, he pressed the attack, whirling his sword into Schwarzhelm's face. The strike was blocked, but the power behind it was sudden and massive. The locked blades fell back before Schwarzhelm's mighty arms halted the thrust. For a moment, the edge of the metal was close. Close enough for him to see the runes on Grosslich's sword-edge, half-obscured beneath the ever-flowing corruption across its surface.

'You don't recognise my blade either?' Grosslich crowed. 'You gave it to me. The runefang of Averland. The Sword of Ruin. All of this, you gave to me. I have bent it to my will, just as I have this province. It can hurt you, Schwarzhelm. Oh, this can *hurt* you.'

The two men broke apart again. For a moment, Schwarzhelm's eyes still rested on his enemy's sword. A flicker of doubt passed across his face. Above them, the Deathmoon spread its sickening sheen across the mass of struggling men. In every direction, thousands struggled, all lit by the fires of Averheim. All around him, his troops were pitted against a foe they couldn't hope to best. They would die, one by one, even if he halted Grosslich.

Schwarzhelm brought the Rechtstahl into guard, feeling the solid weight of it in his hands. The light of Morrslieb glinted from the steel, transmuted into pure silver by the holy metal. Grosslich waited for him, gathering his strength.

Doubt drained away. All that remained was combat, the purity of the test. It was one he had never failed, not even against Helborg. He wouldn't do now.

'Pain is fleeting, Grosslich,' he said, poised for the strike. 'Damnation is eternal. Let me show you the difference.'

'I'LL GO FIRST,' said Helborg. His voice resounded from the marble walls of the Tower. 'Leitdorf behind, Volkmar last.'

The men silently fell into their positions. None of them, even the warrior priests, looked sure of themselves. There was something sickening about the Tower. The long nights of agony had left their imprint in the structure, staining it as surely as a birthmark. A man didn't need Volkmar's skills to detect the perversion humming in the air.

'Remember yourselves,' the Marshal warned, peering ahead to the stairwell. Despite himself, his heart beat faster in his chest. After the terrible sprint to the Tower, the sudden eerie quiet was hard to deal with. Something awful lurked here, something ancient and suffused with malignance. 'Death in His service is glorious. Only the traitor fears destruction.'

He crept forwards, and the spurs on his boots clicked against the marble. The paltry band of men, now just eighteen strong, stayed close, eyes wide, knuckles white on the grips of their weapons. At the rear, Volkmar kindled a warm glow from the tip of his staff. It was scant consolation, and did little more than pick out the horrific images engraved on the walls.

They went down the stairs swiftly, hurrying round the broad sweep of the spiral and avoiding the twisted shapes embedded into the iron banister rail. As they descended, it got hotter. Breathing became more difficult and the growl of the hidden engines echoed more loudly. From far in the deeps, there came the sound of clanging, as if vast chains swung together. A muted howling resonated from far above.

'Daemons,' muttered Leitdorf, clutching at the book at his belt.

'Volkmar can handle them,' said Helborg. Terror seemed to invest the air itself, and he was not immune from it. 'Keep your mind clear. We'll be busy with your Natassja.'

'She was never mine.'

'Enough. We're closing.'

They reached the base of the stairs. A long vaulted passageway led directly ahead. The walls were richly decorated with sculptures, all carved with assorted scenes of creative agony. Limbs and faces were contorted across stone friezes, locked in impossible positions of excruciation. Helborg let his gaze alight on the face of a young woman. The carving was artful, despite the debauchery. Bathed in the light of Volkmar's staff, the subject still retained a warped kind of beauty.

Her eyes flickered open.

'Help me!' she gasped, muffled by the iron clamping her lips together.

Helborg recoiled in shock, bringing his blade up in a flash. The woman struggled against her sorcerous bonds, weeping with terror and misery. All along the corridor, other eyes opened. There were still people alive in there, locked in agony.

'You can't help them!' cried Volkmar, calling to a priest who had swung his hammer back, ready to smash them free. 'They are one with the Tower. Leave them.'

The band pressed on, walking a little faster, avoiding the piteous wails from the walls, hastening to avoid the fingers that somehow managed to clutch at them as they passed.

It kept getting hotter. The roar of the bloodfire became more complete. A doorway loomed up at them from the shadows, high and ornately carved. The corruption came from within it.

As they approached, a cloaked figure burst through the doors, screaming with fury. It might have been a man once, but it had been terribly transformed. Its spine curved over, forcing it to scuttle like an insect. Its flesh was ivory-white, though the eyes were ringed with black. One hand was chronically distorted, now little more than a collection of flesh-ribbons. The other was curled tight into a fist.

'Blasphemy!' it screamed, hurling itself at Helborg.

The Marshal caught it in mid-air with the edge of the Klingerach, hurling it back against the wall. The creature hit the iron with a crack, and slid down to the floor. For a moment it looked like it might get up again.

'Blasphemy...' it croaked. Its mouth filled with purple blood and its eyes glazed over. 'She will punish...'

Then it locked into a spasm, choking and gagging. Helborg advanced to finish it off, but it expired. It slumped, twisted and broken against the iron wall.

Leitdorf gazed at it with horrified recognition.

'Achendorfer,' he breathed, unable to look away from the man's distorted features.

'Not any more,' said Helborg grimly, resuming the march towards the doorway.

Volkmar and Leitdorf joined him. Together with the warrior priests and Reiksguard, they clustered at the portal to the chamber beyond.

Something vast was in there. The sound of a giant heart beating came from beyond the obsidian doors. The sigil of Slaanesh was engraved on each one, burning with the sweet stench of ruin. As Helborg's eyes swept over them, pain lodged behind his eyes.

'Trust to faith,' he said for a final time.

Then he pushed the doors open, and they swung wide. Beyond was a Stone. It was massive, rearing up from the floor like a leviathan emerging from the deeps.

They entered the chamber. Helborg looked up. Natassja was there.

And then, only then, did he truly understand what had happened in Averheim.

SCHWARZHELM PRESSED THE attack, whirling the Recht-stahl round hard, knocking Grosslich back with the force of the blow. From the corner of his vision he could see his men locked in battles of their own. They couldn't fight their way through Grosslich's men, but neither were they being driven back in their turn. Everything hinged on the duel.

Grosslich's armour was gouged with many rents, all inflicted by the Sword of Justice. Still he stayed on his feet. The wound in his neck had closed, and a ring of solid black blood formed a torc beneath his chin. His skills were impressive, no doubt augmented by the latent power in his sword.

It would do him no good. Schwarzhelm spun his blade at the traitor, pulling back at the last moment and flickering the tip above Grosslich's guard. The sor-cerer switched position, but too clumsily. Schwarzhelm stabbed forwards, aiming for a gaping crack in the breastplate.

The aim was good. Grosslich roared with pain a sec-ond time. He punched out with his gauntlet, aiming for Schwarzhelm's head. The big man reared back, keeping the sword in place, then plunged it in deeper.

Grosslich's face bloomed with blood like a translu-cent sac. He staggered, impaled on the sword edge. Schwarzhelm grabbed the man's pauldron with his free hand and hauled him further up the blade.

The two of them came together, their faces only inches apart. Grosslich's eyes went wide with shock and pain. The mutations on his face began to shrink away. The Dark Prince's gifts were being withdrawn.

'So you have sown,' hissed Schwarzhelm, twisting the blade, feeling the holy metal sear the tainted flesh, 'so shall you reap.'

Blood bubbled up in Grosslich's mouth, hot and black. The Averland runefang fell from his grasp. For a moment, his face looked almost normal. It was the face of a mortal man, the one who had inspired a thousand peasants to march under his banner. Before Natassja had twisted those aims, they had been noble enough.

'Dominion,' he drawled, blood spilling from his lips. *'Dominion...'*

His eyes went glassy, and his body went limp.

Schwarzhelm wrenched the Sword of Justice free and Grosslich fell to his knees. For a heartbeat he stayed there, struggling against the inevitable. He looked up at Schwarzhelm pleadingly. The mutations around his face shrank back into nothing. He was as he had been before, a son of Averland.

There was no hesitation. Schwarzhelm drew the Rechtstahl back and swung heavily. Grosslich's head came off in a single sweeping movement. It spun into the air and rolled across the mud, coming to rest amidst a detachment of halberdiers rushing into assault. The men trampled it into the mire, hardly noticing it amongst the horrors of the war around them. Soon it was lost, the skull cracked and smeared with blood and grime, gone amid the detritus of the battle.

The headless corpse teetered for a moment before thudding to the ground. Heinz-Mark's rule as elector was over, ended by the man who had crowned him.

Schwarzhelm bent down and retrieved the runefang from the mire. The black slurry had stopped dripping from the blade and the steel glinted from under the crust of corruption. He wiped it clean on his cloak, then took it up in his left hand. Just as he had done on the journey from Altdorf, Schwarzhelm carried two swords, one the Sword of Justice, the other a runefang.

He turned to face the dog-soldiers already clustering around him. They weren't daunted by the death of their commander, and the battle still surged unabated. Grosslich had never truly commanded them. He'd been a puppet to the last, a tool for the use of subtler powers.

Schwarzhelm narrowed his eyes. He could see Kraus leading the charge on his left flank. There were Imperial troops everywhere, all lost in close-packed fighting. The situation was still desperate, and Grosslich's death hadn't changed it.

He was about to plunge into the ranks of dog-soldiers ahead when he caught a glimpse of something out of the corner of his eye. A long, leather coat, flapping in the ash-flecked wind, worn by a man who had no business being on a battlefield at all.

'The last of the family,' said Schwarzhelm to himself, filled with renewed purpose and hefting his twin blades. 'I swear it now. Death will not find *you* this day.'

NATASSJA HAD GROWN. The last elements of her humanity had been shed, and she now towered ten feet above a mortal span. Her flesh was as black as jet, tinged with a faint outline of blue fire. Her eyes, still pupilless, blazed an icy sapphire.

Her human raiment was gone. Her flesh was clad in shifting strips of blackened silk, rippling around her and curling over the onyx skin. Her hair raged around her face like a furnace, caught up in the throbbing bloodfire as it whipped across her naked shoulders. The tattoos that had scored her skin for so long were gone, replaced by a single burning mark of Slaanesh at her breast.

Though still achingly beautiful, her features had already been twisted with mutation. Her feet were gone, replaced with cloven hooves. Her fingers ended in talons such as her handmaidens wore. They were sheer points of ebony, slender and curved. She moved impossibly quickly, as if there were no intermediate stage between her being in one location and at the next. Even when her mouth moved to speak, the pattern of her lips was eerie and unsettling. A long, lizard-like tongue flickered between glittering fangs.

Natassja now resembled the daemons that had served her, though it was she who was the greater and more steeped in corruption. For Natassja was no true-born denizen of the aethyr, but that most terrible and despised of creations, a daemon prince, a mortal ascended to the level of a demigod. She had exchanged a finite soul for an infinity of damnation, and the terms of the bargain were daunting. Her power was near-limitless, her invulnerability near-complete, her malice absolute. In exchange for that, thousands had died in terror.

Mortal weapons now had no purchase on her, death little meaning. The world of the five senses, so long her prison, was now fleshed out with a thousand shades of emotion. Her eyes were no longer bound by the trammels of matter but by the possibilities of a profound and piercing sentience. Where a mortal saw appearances, she saw realities, stretching away over a whole range of future states towards an impossible horizon. Men appeared before her as burning souls wrapped in a frail gauze, ready to be plucked out and consumed as a lesser being might select sweetmeats from a tray.

For so long, the Vision had been so beautiful. It did not compare to the reality.

Behind her, the Stone still throbbed with energy. It had been enough to complete her transformation, magnified by the Tower, called into being by the sacrifices of the humans who had died. Averheim was her altar, the stone across which the lambs had been slaughtered. Slaanesh was pleased. The Lord of Pain smiled on her now, gifting her with the merest sliver of His own consciousness. Though her flesh was real, rooted in the world like that of the lowliest creature of the earth, her soul was an inferno, a blaze of coruscation beside which those of mortals were mere candles.

'The Sword of Vengeance,' she said, recognising its pattern within the world.

Her voice was astonishing, even to her. All those who had died to bring her into being shared a part of it. Just as with the true daemons, many tongues echoed throughout her speech. Men, women and children all spoke through her, and the sound echoed from the walls like a massed chorus. As sharp as a scream, as deep and resounding as a sob, Natassja let her new vocal cords play across their full range. It delighted her. Everything delighted her.

From down below, the one called Helborg still stood defiant. He raised the blade she'd named, as if that little spike could hurt her now. Beside him, the worm who had once been her husband did likewise. There was a third man with them who mattered, a disciple of the boy-god. She could see his soul hammering at the bonds of flesh that enclosed it. He was no stranger to the realm of Chaos, that one. He'd been into it once, and come back out again. Intriguing. That shouldn't have been possible.

'The Staff of Command,' she said, recognising its name from the profile in the aethyr. It was ancient by the standards of the Empire, paltry by the standards of her master. It was capable of causing her some pain, but little more. 'You are the Grand Theogonist of the boy-god.'

She expected the man to rave at her then, to scream some screed about her being corrupted filth that would be driven from the face of the world by the righteous hosts of Sigmar.

He didn't. He stood his ground, and a grey, stinking cloud of dirty smog flared up at the end of his miserable staff. To him, no doubt, it was as beautiful as the rising sun.

'We recognise each other, then,' Volkmar replied. His voice came from far away. Natassja had to concentrate to hear it properly over the choir of psychic voices blaring at her. The world of the daemon was strange, far richer than that of a mortal, but confusing and hard to make sense of. It would take some time to get used to. 'If you claim to know me, then you know that you will not be suffered to live.'

Natassja didn't laugh at that brand of folly. The effrontery insulted her. She knew more about him than he could have guessed. Just by watching his soul writhe in its temporal bonds, she could feel his anguish. This one knew, deep down, the futility of what he did. He'd *seen* the end of the world. He'd been *shown* it. And still he failed to seize the truth in both hands. What the mortals called faith she knew as fear. An inability to see the full picture, a reluctance to receive what was out there to be given. There was nothing laudable in that. It was pathetic. Small-minded. Timorous.

As he spoke, the images swirling across her field of vision began to make more sense. She saw the origin of the materials that surrounded her, the age of the metals and the stories behind them. Such stories were imprinted into the matter of them, scored across the face of the world and stained in time. The iron in the shaft above her had come from a mine deep under the Worlds Edge Mountains. Even now, it screamed at the perversion around it. The world itself resisted her, knowing her for what she was. The world, however, was old and tired, and she was as young and vital as a flame.

Everything had a story imprinted on it. That was the ultimate truth. There was nothing in the cosmos *but* stories, some given form, some just fleeting shadows. The men before her were stories, unfolding through time, weaving in and out of possibilities like carp amongst weeds.

She gazed down at Helborg again. He'd had many choices. He could have killed Schwarzhelm. She saw that possibility twisting away into a distant future. If he had done, the Empire would have split, wracked by civil war for a generation of men until the hurt could be undone. Helborg had no idea of that. He'd been motivated by pity. So touchingly weak, so endearingly stupid.

'Nothing you can do or know can harm me, priest,' she said coolly, feeling the pangs of her birth still resonating throughout her pristine body. 'Coming here only hastens your second death.'

'So thought Be'lakor,' said Volkmar, his voice holding steady. His staff was beginning to bleed its dark grey sludge profusely, polluting the symphony of colours before her and ruining the glorious harmonics of the Stone. 'So thought many of your kind. You don't know as much as you think you do. I have the power to harm you.'

This was getting tedious. Concentrating on the mortals for long enough to hear their words was frustrating. There were more important, more uplifting things to devote herself to. As a mortal she'd only been able to experience sensation across four dimensions. Now there were twelve to wallow in, and wasting time in chatter was a poor way to begin her new life of wonder.

'Then put it to the test, little man,' said Natassja, looking directly at the shifting figures below her and preparing to use the powers that were curled tight within her. 'Do your best to wound me. Then, when all is done, I shall introduce you to pain of such perfection that the gods themselves will weep to hear you scream.'

# Chapter Twenty-One

VOLKMAR FED POWER to his staff and the tip burst into golden illumination. The nimbus filled the chamber, reflecting back from the utter dark of the Stone and banishing the shadows around the sculpted iron walls. The fury of the bloodfire roared back, swirling around the Staff of Command like a swarm of enraged hornets.

On either side of him, warrior priests surged forwards, all eager to land the first blow on the towering figure before them. With a pang of regret, Volkmar watched as the foremost were reduced to weeping, shuddering wrecks.

The daemon's power was a subtle one. Natassja had been elegant as a mortal and daemonhood had not changed her. There were no sudden bursts of flame or crackling discharges of aethyr-spawned lightning. Her powers were those of the mind, of sensation, of fear and pain.

The first warrior priest to get near her exploded into a ball of blood at a flick from her shapely finger. The Reiksguard at his side was next. She shot a cool glance from her smooth eyes and his armour shattered.

Beneath it, his body was transmuted into a writhing, hermaphroditic mess. Fleshy growths wrapped themselves around what was left of his throat and strangled the life out of him.

With every fresh death an echoing boom rushed up the shaft of the Stone. Volkmar could sense the enormous power contained there. It had been enough to grant Natassja her elevation into immortality and it had still been hardly tapped. With a dreadful realisation, he knew that there was nothing he could do to dent it. He might have had a thousand warrior priests with him and the result would have been the same. There was no hope left, not for them, not for Averheim.

'The blood of Sigmar!' he bellowed, defiant to the end.

He whirled the staff around and sent a stream of blazing fire at the daemon. It impacted directly on the sigil of Slaanesh at her breast and exploded, showering the chamber with spinning points of light.

Natassja took a step back, entirely unharmed. She bared her fangs and fixed Volkmar with a withering look of contempt.

He screamed, and staggered to his knees. Something vast and malice-drenched entered his soul. He could feel his essence being ripped away from within, dragged from his mortal frame on barbs of steel. She was destroying him.

His staff fell to the floor as he withdrew his power from it. Resisting the crushing influence of the daemon took all his residual art. He screwed his eyes closed, grimacing with pain. He was being dragged back to the hells he had escaped before. There, in the darkness, he could see the androgynous form of his nemesis. The Dark Prince had been waiting there since his last death, happy to welcome him back.

'Not...' he gasped, digging deep, drawing on every last shred of strength left in his battered body. 'Not *now*...'

Dimly, he was aware of more men rushing past him. There was a flash of light, and the crushing sensation eased.

Volkmar edged his eyes open, gasping for breath. Helborg had engaged the daemon. The notched rune-fang danced as the Marshal pressed towards the abomination.

Natassja evaded his blows easily. She shifted with incredible speed, darting from one place to another as if the steps in between positions had become completely unnecessary. Helborg's attack had at least diverted the terrifying power of her will, and Volkmar climbed back to his feet, picking up the staff again and preparing himself to use it.

'This is hopeless,' came a voice from his right.

Leitdorf was standing there, sword trembling in his hands, staring at the abomination with horror. His face was grey with fear.

'Stand your ground!' snarled Volkmar. 'Damn you, Rufus, stand your ground!'

Even as he spoke, another warrior priest was ripped apart by Natassja's malign will. She nodded curtly and the man's flesh was turned inside out, spilling his entrails across the Stone in glistening rings. Six men had already died without so much as making contact with her. Helborg fought on, roaring with defiance and frustration as she evaded his attacks.

'What good will it do?' Leitdorf wailed. All trace of his self-assurance on the battlefield had drained away, and he looked half-mad with fear. 'She's untouchable.'

Volkmar knew he was right. That didn't change a thing.

'This is your city,' he growled, preparing to kindle the staff again. 'Stand up for it.'

Then he strode back towards the daemon, and golden flame flared up along the shaft of his weapon.

'Scion of darkness!' he roared, sending a spitting column of lightning screaming towards the abomination. 'You will *not* prevail here!'

HELBORG LEAPT FORWARDS, trying to find purchase with the Klingerach. He knew the runefang would bite deep if it connected, but making contact with the flesh of the daemon was impossible. With a twist of his stomach, he saw more of his men being cut down, one by one. Natassja seemed to be picking off the lesser warriors first, toying with them all like a cat with its prey.

He stabbed at her massive thigh, whirling the blade around with blistering speed and force. At the very last moment, she shifted position, appearing a yard away, still in the same pose. She winked at him, flicked her fingers, and the last Reiksguard standing lost his skin. The man collapsed in a screaming, writhing pool of blood, held together by his armour and nothing else.

'Damned witch!' Helborg hissed, keeping his sword in guard and searching for some kind of opening.

Volkmar had got back to his feet by then, and sent a fresh stream of spitting golden fire straight at the daemon. His staff was the only weapon that seemed able to harm her daemonic flesh. Irritated by the interruption in her killing, she turned her attention back to the raging cleric.

Helborg tensed, ready to plunge back into the attack, but then caught sight of Leitdorf. The man had frozen. The Wolfsklinge was in his hands, but only just.

'Your blade, Leitdorf!' bellowed Helborg, rushing to the elector's side. As he did so, he saw Volkmar being beaten back, just as before. 'Remember Drakenmoor!'

Leitdorf shot him a panic-stricken look.

'I *can't...*' he began, but then Helborg was dragging him to face Natassja.

'We attack together!' he cried, pushing him forwards. 'Just as before!'

The Marshal hurled himself at the daemon. Somehow Leitdorf summoned the courage to join him, and the two men charged the monstrous figure.

Then, and for the first time, Helborg almost wounded her. Distracted by Volkmar's attack and faced with the onslaught of two ancient blades, Natassja faltered for just an instant. She pulled back from Helborg's blow, but failed to withdraw from Leitdorf's attack. The Wolfsklinge passed through her flesh without biting and came clean out the other side.

Off-balance, Leitdorf stumbled to his knees. As quick as a whip, Natassja kicked out with a hoof and sent him flying across the chamber floor. He hit the far wall hard. His sword spun from his grasp, coming to rest by the eviscerated body of a fallen Reiksguard knight.

Isolated and unable to land a blow, Helborg fell back.

Two of the surviving warrior priests charged at the daemon then, their warhammers swinging heavily. Natassja turned to face them and bared her fangs again. One priest simply exploded, his breastplate spinning across the floor and spraying blood. The other seized up, his face marked with agony. He shuddered, and his bones burst out through his flesh, lengthening with frightening speed, tearing the muscles as they came. The priest collapsed to the ground and dissolved into a mess of ripped flesh and still-extending skeleton.

By then there were only six priests left, all cowed by the daemon's contemptuous response to their attacks. Helborg looked over at Volkmar. The Theogonist was preparing for a third attack, but Natassja had badly hurt him. Leitdorf lived too, but he looked dazed and shaky on his feet.

'We can't do this,' breathed Helborg, aghast at the sudden awareness of his weakness. He took up the Klingerach again and prepared for another charge. Duty demanded no less, but he held no hope for it. 'We have come too late. The bitch will kill us all.'

LEITDORF GASPED FOR breath. The merest touch of Natassja's flesh had been enough to send a searing chill through his body. He'd felt the vast power coiled up within her then, and it dwarfed anything he'd ever felt before.

He gazed up at her, watching as she pulled the limbs from another warrior priest. Natassja looked almost bored, as if this were a mild distraction before the real entertainment began. Next to her, Helborg and Volkmar, two of the mightiest warriors in the Empire, looked more ineffectual than children playing at combat.

Determined as ever, Helborg charged back into contact, spinning the Sword of Vengeance around him, trying to land a blow on Natassja's shifting, ephemeral body.

As he did so, Volkmar sent a third barrage of faith-fire at her. The Theogonist aimed at her face and the swirling column of lightning impacted directly. She was knocked back against the Stone. The impact didn't do any real damage, but the interruption seemed to infuriate her.

She extended her palm and Helborg was flung back through the air, his limbs flailing as the unseen thrust slammed him aside. Then she clenched her fist and Volkmar doubled over. The light streaming from his staff dimmed, and he fell to his knees in pain.

Ignoring his own wounds, Leitdorf limped to Volkmar's side. He clutched at the Theogonist's shoulders as the man toppled to one side. The remaining warrior priests charged heroically at the daemon, drawing her attention away from Volkmar. Their six lives bought nothing but a few moments of respite.

'My lord!' Leitdorf cried, helping the man to the floor.

The Theogonist's eyes were filmy. It looked like he wasn't seeing very much.

'Too... *powerful*...' he gasped, and his fingers clutched at his staff feebly.

Leitdorf felt his despair turn to a desperate, frustrated anger. He looked up. The roof of the chamber was open, and a vast shaft of fire soared away into the distance. This had been Natassja's birth-chamber. The entire structure above was nothing more than an amplifier for the energies needed to bring her into being. That was why she'd needed Averheim. It was nothing to do with temporal power or riches. For her, the city had been a *machine*.

He looked at Natassja. She killed two more men then, flaying them alive with a twist of her fingers. The remaining quartet still came on, still trying to find a way to harm her. Helborg too had staggered back into range. Their bravery was phenomenal, but it would do little to save them.

'Can you ignite the staff again?' asked Leitdorf, a note of desperation in his voice.

Volkmar shook his head.

'Look around you,' he panted. 'This has been centuries in the making. We cannot hurt her.'

Leitdorf slammed his fist against the marble floor. He was no longer afraid, just furious. After all the pain, all the bloodshed, it had come to this at last. His inheritance, turned to ashes before his eyes, destroyed in order to bring a new horror into the world.

'There must be *something*.'

Volkmar shook his head. 'Her daemonhood is complete. Without knowledge of her true name, she is invulnerable to us.'

The last of the warrior priests was riven where he stood, his body torn into ribbons. Only Helborg, Volkmar and Leitdorf remained. The last ones to die, locked beneath the earth under a tower of iron.

From above, the distant howling grew louder. The lesser daemons were still looking for a way in. The bloodfire bloomed anew, roaring and thundering against the iron. The Stone could sense victory, and gloried in it.

'Her *name*?' asked Leitdorf, suddenly feeling a sliver of hope. 'What power would that give you?'

Volkmar looked up at him. There was a grim smile on his face, the resigned look of a man who knows death is upon him.

'I could hurt her then,' he growled. 'By Sigmar, I would *hurt* her.'

Leitdorf began to fumble at his belt.

'Find the power,' he ordered, his voice suddenly resonant again. 'Find it from somewhere. This isn't over yet.'

HELBORG PULLED THE body of the warrior priest back, but too late. The man's skin hung in strips from his frame. For a last few agonised moments, the priest still lived. He fixed Helborg with piteous eyes, blood and tears mingling across his destroyed face. Then he collapsed, just another corpse on the floor of the chamber.

Helborg withdrew a pace, keeping his blue eyes locked on the figure looming over him. Natassja smiled at him and flexed her talons.

'Shall I preserve you?' she mused, looking at the Marshal as if he were a morsel of food at the end of a banquet. 'These ones have died in an instant. Your death will last for an eternity.'

Helborg smiled wolfishly, keeping the runefang between him and the daemon.

'I am sustained by faith,' he said.

Natassja raised an amused eyebrow.

'You believe that *still*? Do you not think these priests had faith?'

'Their deaths were glorious. Their souls are with Sigmar.'

Natassja shook her head with disbelief.

'You mystify me, human,' she said. 'You all mystify me. You are shown the illusion, and still you refuse to see through it.'

Helborg circled round the daemon carefully, looking for any sign of weakness.

'I see enough.'

'Evidently not.'

She moved, quicker than thought, reaching out with a taloned hand to grab him by the throat. At the same time, Volkmar roared into life for a final time. A beam of gold lanced out from his staff and slammed Natassja backwards, dousing her in a cascade of golden shards.

She spun to face the Theogonist. The cool irritation had vanished from her features to be replaced by exasperation.

'Still not dead?' she spat. 'You're beginning to annoy me, disciple.'

She coiled to strike, curling her talons into a fist. Volkmar shrank back, his bloodied figure standing defiant against the coming onslaught.

'*Bedarruzibarr!*' came a voice from the edge of the chamber.

Natassja whirled round, amazement and horror suddenly rippling across her features.

Leitdorf stood before her. He held the book in his trembling hands. He kept reading. Just as it had done for her birth, the bloodfire in the chamber flared up at the sound. '*Bedarruzibarr'zagarratumnan'akz'akz'berau!*'

'Cease speaking, worm!' screamed Natassja, and her hands burst into blue flame.

'*Bedarruzibarr!*' thundered Volkmar, echoing Leitdorf's cry.

The Theogonist raised his staff and sent a flurry of crackling bolts into Natassja's torso. They impacted heavily. This time they seemed to damage her, and she staggered back towards the Stone.

'Cease!' she cried, still wreathed in bands of shimmering golden flame. 'This is forbidden knowledge!'

'*Abbadonnodo'neherata'gradarruminam!*' shouted Leit-dorf, his voice growing in confidence, tracing the words from the pages of his father's diary. With every syllable, Natassja seemed to recoil further.

Volkmar sent fresh volleys of faith-fire at her, his face alight with furious relish.

'Hear your name, spawn of Slaanesh!' he roared in triumph. 'Feel the powers at your command unravel!'

Buffeted by a wall of spitting fire, Natassja rocked back. The calm assurance of her superiority was gone. The syllables of her true name echoed around the chamber, fuelling Volkmar's torrent of righteous fire. She reeled under the onslaught, screaming as the fire tore at her.

Then Helborg was on her too, no longer seeming so diminutive. He hauled his blade round in a mighty arc, scything at Natassja's legs. The runefang connected, and a blaze of pure white light leapt up. Blood sprayed through the air, as black as the Stone behind it, sparkling like beads of onyx.

Natassja screamed again, her voice now filled with pain and frustration. She lashed out with her left fist, catching Helborg on his breastplate and sending him lurching backwards. She opened her other hand and let loose the full power within her.

The chamber shuddered, rocked to its foundations by the blast. The bloodfire blazed purple, roaring into a frenzy. Volkmar was knocked from his feet, and the Staff spun from his grasp. Cracks ran up the walls and the iron bands around them broke open. Wards were shattered, and the howling of the lesser daemons boomed down the shaft.

Leitdorf jumped aside just as the floor disintegrated under him. The marble rippled like a wave and cracked open. From below, the thunderous roar of the deep engines rolled upwards.

Natassja staggered towards Leitdorf, the last of Volkmar's golden fire streaming from her shoulders. She was badly wounded, and great gashes had opened on her flanks. They wept black essence, as dark and pure as jet.

'Worm!' she rasped, and her voice was fractured with hatred. The choir within her had begun to come apart. 'Utter not words beyond your comprehension.'

Leitdorf scrambled away from her, stumbling around the edge of chamber.

'*Malamanuar'neramumo'klza'jhehennum!*' he shouted, keeping up the recital even as he fled from Natassja's wrath. The very sound of it seemed to wound her.

He couldn't escape forever. The chamber held no hiding places, and Natassja still had the power to move quickly. She stood over the elector, towering above his paltry frame, poised to silence the words that cut through her power so completely.

Leitdorf kept shouting the words out, right until the end. Natassja pulled her hand back, wailing in agony as each syllable resounded around the chamber. A curved dagger unrolled into existence, extending from her flesh like smoke and firming into a wicked, twin-bladed instrument.

Helborg clambered to his feet and charged towards her. Volkmar hauled the Staff back into position. It was far too late. The dagger plunged down, seeming to cleave the very air around it. It lodged deep in Leitdorf's chest, pinning him to the stone beneath.

The elector screamed, and his body arched in agony. The book fell from his hands. As it hit the ground, Natassja glared at it and the parchment burst into green-tinged flame, shrivelling and curling into nothing.

But then Helborg was close enough. With the last echoes of the daemon's name still lingering in the shaft above them, he raised the Sword of Vengeance high above his head. The runes blazed in the blood-fire, reflecting the fury of the Stone, bending the rays of contamination back at it.

Natassja whirled to face the new threat, but her aura of invincibility had gone. She bared her fangs again, fixing Helborg with a look of such malice and terror that a lesser man would have crumbled under it.

Helborg's shoulder wound burst open, drenching his chest with blood. For a moment, Natassja's face rippled into Schwarzhelm's, and a bizarre mix of dae-mon and man screamed its hatred at him.

He didn't flinch. The blade came down in a mighty, crushing sweep. The edge bit true, carving through aethyr-wound sinews as readily as real flesh. A ball of brilliant light radiated from the impact, rushing across the chamber and swirling into the heights of the shaft. The bloodfire guttered in its wake. Fresh cracks radiated from the Stone, rippling across the floor and releasing gouts of smog from the furnaces below.

Natassja cried out with agony, and her many voices rebounded from the iron walls around her. Her face returned to its normal shape, transfixed in pain and fury. She twisted away from the runefang, exposing the huge, jagged wound in her torso. It gushed a tor-rent of bile, foaming and fizzing as it poured out into the world.

Helborg ducked under a vicious swipe from her

dagger hand and swung the Klingerach back at her. The blade sunk deep, cleaving Natassja's stomach open and jarring on the bones beyond.

The daemon fell to her knees, weeping blood. The bloodfire shuddered and veered away from her, suddenly averse to the failing presence in its midst. She dropped down further, bracing herself with a blood-streaked arm.

Natassja looked at Helborg, her face now level with his. Her expression was a mix of scorn, fury and astonishment.

'You have no idea what you've done, mortal,' she rasped, her voices jarring as they overlapped. 'You have *no idea...*'

Helborg didn't listen. The Sword of Vengeance rose high, glimmering in the firelight.

'I see enough,' he snarled, and brought the blade down.

FOR A MOMENT, nothing happened. Natassja's severed head rolled from her body, coming to rest close to the stricken form of Leitdorf. The bloodfire continued to roar, the engines continued to grind, the wind continued to howl.

Then the daemons came, tearing down the shaft, screaming like vengeful harpies. Helborg stood up to them, and the runefang blazed with a holy fire. All weariness had fallen from his shoulders. Just as before, he looked like one of the heroes of old, clad in sacred armour and wearing the hawk-wing helm of the Reiksmarshal. He waited for them to come to him, his cloak rippling in the bloodfire, still bearing the Sword of Vengeance in both hands.

The first of them hurtled down from the pinnacle,

teeth bared, arms outstretched. A second later, she lay on the floor next to her mistress, her body broken by Helborg. Another fell to the same blade, carved in two by the holy metal. The rest of them halted in their onslaught, suddenly looking with horrified eyes at the ruined body of their mistress. They hovered in the air above the Stone, frozen in terrible doubt.

As they surveyed the scene, Volkmar recovered his footing.

'The tide has turned, whores of Slaanesh,' he cried, reaching for his staff and fixing them with a vengeful glare. 'Leave while you can, or the Sword of Vengeance will tear every one of you apart.'

They looked at him, then at Helborg. The Reiksmarshal stared back, grim-faced and resolute. The blade in his hands glowed with residual energy, and the runes resonated. The sword was back with its master, and its thirst for killing was not yet sated.

Then they fled, screeching as they went, buoyed aloft by the surging bloodfire. The shaft echoed from their screeches, dying into nothing as they spiralled towards the distant pinnacle.

The Tower creaked ominously. Pieces of iron and stone detached from the walls and trails of dust ran down from the high places.

Helborg watched the daemons go, then stumbled across to Leitdorf. Volkmar joined him, limping heavily. As they went, the floor cracked further. Great booms rang out from far below, muffled by the layers of rock beneath them.

Leitdorf's face was pale. Natassja's dagger had dissolved into nothingness with the demise of its mistress, but the wound was ugly and hadn't closed. There was no blood, just a dark-edged hole. Leitdorf struggled to breathe. As Helborg approached, he tried to push himself up on to his elbows.

'Remain still,' said Helborg, coming to his side and looking anxiously at his wound. 'Can you do anything, Theogonist?'

Volkmar crouched down next to the Marshal. He placed his calloused hands on the incision, and Leitdorf recoiled in pain. The Theogonist closed his eyes, probing for aethyric residue. When he opened them again, his expression was grave.

'No lies between us, Rufus Leitdorf,' he said. 'This wound is mortal.'

Leitdorf smiled thinly.

'How stupid do you think I am?' Then he broke into coughing. There was blood in his throat, flecked on his armour.

'You have triumphed, elector,' said Helborg, his severe face drawn with pain. 'Do you remember your words in Drakenmoor? You have proved the bane of her.'

Leitdorf cast his weakening gaze over to the broken body of the daemon prince. It lay just a few feet away, huge, ravaged, and yet for all that still perversely alluring.

'I truly believed that I loved her,' he croaked. His face went from grey to white, and a slick of sweat broke out over his forehead. 'Can you believe that?'

Helborg and Volkmar said nothing. The sound of stone and iron grinding against each other grew from below. More debris showered down from the shaft and the roar of the bloodfire became intermittent. The Tower, bereft of its guiding will, was cracking.

'I thought she would deliver more than Averland to me,' said Leitdorf, his breath ragged, still gazing at

Natassja. 'I thought she would give me what I wanted. A *son*, Lord Helborg. Blame that desire, if you still need blame. My line dies with me here. I am the last.'

Helborg grasped the dying man's hand.

'You have saved the city,' he said. 'Your deeds will be remembered.'

'No,' Leitdorf replied, and blood ran from his cracked lips. His voice shrank to barely a whisper. 'Tell them what my father did. He discovered her name. Tell them–'

Leitdorf broke into coughing again, and black fluid bubbled up his throat. His hand clenched Helborg's tightly as he recovered himself. In his last moments alive, his face was a mask of pure determination.

'Tell them he wasn't mad,' he said.

Then Leitdorf's eyes went blank. He stiffened, and the fingers of his free hand clutched at the air wildly. He took one last shuddering breath, and then fell still. His pudgy face, speckled with blood and ash, relaxed. In the shifting firelight, the resemblance to Marius was striking.

More debris began to fall from above. A great iron spar tumbled down the shaft, clanging from the walls as it spiralled before crashing to the earth on the far side of the chamber. Flames, real flames, began to lick up from the cracks in the floor.

'We need to go,' said Volkmar.

'I will take the body,' said Helborg, reaching for Leitdorf's prone corpse.

'Leave it.' Volkmar stood up. 'It will slow you. This is his victory, and his realm. No tomb in Altdorf would be finer.'

Helborg hesitated, then ran a hand up to his bleeding shoulder. More cracks ran up the walls, lifting the plates of iron and exposing raw, pulsing aethyric matter beneath. The Tower was suffused with it, a conduit of baleful energies.

He rose, stooping only to retrieve Leitdorf's sword from where it had fallen.

'A pup no longer,' he said, looking bitterly at Leitdorf's body. 'You should have lived to wield this.'

Then Helborg and Volkmar left the chamber, hurrying under the doorway as the Tower began to fall apart. Behind them, the room was marked only by the corpses on the floor and the sinister presence of the Stone in their midst. It glowed in the darkness for a while, as if revelling in one last lingering expression of power.

Then it died, failing back to dull grey. The bloodfire flared around it, swirling in one last angry eddy, and went out.

THE BODIES WERE slumped on the earth as if sleep had stolen upon them all. Bloch was dead, and his muscles had grown cold. Verstohlen still lived, but his pulse was shallow and his flesh pale. He lay next to his comrade, insensible to the thunder of battle around him, lost in a private struggle against the poison within.

Standing over them, holding the line against the ravening horde beyond, Schwarzhelm heaved his sword back, dismembering a dog-soldier with the trailing edge of the Rechtstahl. All around him, his men fought on. The line was intact but thinning. Any pretence at an advance had long been given up. The Imperial forces were exhausted, driven to the utter reaches of fatigue by the unending masses of enemy troops before them. The walls of the city were no closer than they had been hours earlier, and the plain still swarmed with lilac-eyed soldiers. Averheim would not be taken by force. The best they could hope for was to hold for the dawn and organise some kind of withdrawal. In the face of the surviving war engines, the retreat would be ruinously blood-soaked.

'We're losing this fight!' came a familiar voice.

Kraus fought his way to Schwarzhelm's side. He'd lost his helmet in the melee and his forehead was shiny with blood. A hasty battlefield tourniquet had been wrapped around it, but it didn't do much to staunch the bleeding.

'You forget Helborg.'

Kraus snorted, and launched into the enemy troops before him. The wound didn't seem to have slowed him down much.

'He's one more sword,' he spat, his arms working hard. 'Just one more sword.'

Even as he finished speaking, though, something changed. A vast, rumbling boom resounded from the city, still half a mile distant and shrouded in smoke.

All felt it. Some stumbled as the earth reeled, their tired limbs no longer able to absorb the shock. The dog-soldiers halted in their tracks. The cultists around them went limp. Weapons fell from their slack hands.

Another boom. The bloodfire, that vast column of thundering, writhing flame, shuddered. The massive pillar of aethyric matter wavered like a waterfall cut off at its source. More crashes resounded out from the city walls. Above them all, the Tower loomed darkly, still wreathed in its corona of fire.

'Stand fast, men of the Empire!' roared Schwarzhelm, raising both swords above his head.

All down the exhausted lines, halberdiers and

swordsmen looked up in sudden amazement. The enemy had stopped attacking. Grosslich's mortal troops stood immobile and listless. In the heavens, the circles of cloud broke open, exposing the dark blue of the sky beyond.

There were more distant rumbles, and a cloud of ash and dust rose up from beyond the city walls. The lesser towers crumbled, one by one, falling back in on themselves with stately majesty.

'What is this?' asked Kraus. His face betrayed his hope. Before them, the dog-soldiers fell to their knees and began to claw at their faces. The dread power that had animated them had been withdrawn, and the agony of their twisted bodies now flooded into them. All across the plain, the Army of the Stone descended into a frenzy of pain and self-destruction.

Schwarzhelm didn't smile. He spun round, looking east. The night sky was stained with a faint blush of grey.

'This is the dawn,' he said. His raised blades caught the first glimmers of light.

The Iron Tower, huge and dominating, began to shed its high spars. Cracks ran up its massive flanks, stained red like the wounds of a living thing. Plumes of black soot rolled up from its foundations, effluent from the mighty machines still turning in the deep catacombs. As vast as it was, the withdrawal of the malign intelligence that had built it was too great a strain to bear. It was falling apart.

Men, freed from the incessant fight for survival, gaped up at the sight, their jaws hanging open. Some wept with relief, falling to their knees and crying praises to Sigmar and Ulric. Others vented their pent-up rage, wading into the supine rows of the enemy, laying waste to the defenceless thousands who still stood on the plain.

Kraus sheathed his sword, watching with dismay as the dog-soldiers in front of him clutched at their ruined bodies. Some ripped off their iron masks, revealing their horribly stretched faces. The Empire soldiers around him looked up at him uncertainly, caught between their hatred and confusion.

'What are your orders, my lord?' asked Kraus, looking as torn between instincts as they were.

Schwarzhelm sheathed the Averland runefang, keeping the Rechtstahl naked in his right hand.

'Keep the men together,' he said. 'The bodies of Verstohlen and Bloch are to be taken from here and preserved. If any apothecaries still live, tell them to minister to the counsellor. I would not see him die. Not now, not after all has been accomplished.'

'And what of you?'

Schwarzhelm began to stride through the writhing mass of dog-soldiers towards the city. None hindered his passage.

'The field is yours, captain,' he said, and his voice was free of the anguish that had marked it since the Vormeisterplatz. 'My brother-in-arms has been victorious, and homage is due.'

Ahead of him, the titanic pillar of flame faded and flickered out. The thrum of its burning died away, exposing the charred and crumbling spires of Averheim beneath. Free of the crushing, oppressive weight in the air, a cleansing wind tore across the battlefield. Tattered standards rippled back into life. Shattered detachments of soldiers regained their feet.

With an ominous creak, the Tower listed to one side. More spars fell from it, raining down on the shattered cityscape below. More cracks raced up its sides, breaking open the sigils of Chaos and cracking their symmetry. Real fire flared up from the dungeons beneath the base of the mighty columns, licking at the buckling iron, replacing the sorcerous flames that had wreathed the metal for so long.

There was a final rolling clap of thunder, born deep in the heart of ravaged Averheim and sweeping up into the soot-clogged air. The Tower reeled, shedding spiked buttresses and crossbeams. Its jagged crown tumbled, disintegrating as it spun from the pinnacle, and crashed to earth in a surging cloud of ash and fire.

With terrible slowness, the gigantic framework of Natassja's citadel crumbled in on itself. Iron ground against iron, throwing sparks high into the air. Like a landslip of the high peaks, the abomination slid gracefully into ruin.

A vast cloud of smoke and smog rose up in its wake, huge and threatening. Then it too was borne away by the wind from the east, ripped into nothingness and dispersed as the dreams of those that had made it had been dispersed.

The Tower was gone. The battle for Averheim was over.

# Chapter Twenty-Two

IN THE ANNALS of Imperial history, the victory at Averheim would be recorded as a triumph for the Grand Theogonist Volkmar. Honourable mentions would be given to the Lords Helborg and Schwarzhelm, as well as glowing tributes to the heroism of the martyred Rufus Leitdorf. The loremasters would record in exhaustive detail the tactical genius of the Empire commanders and the craven collapse of the forces of the great enemy. As ever, they would use the example of Grosslich's defeat as evidence of the futility of opposing the all-conquering Empire of mankind.

The archivists would not mention the destruction of the city. They would remain silent on the deaths of Averheim's entire population, either killed in battle or during the construction of the Tower. None of them would mention that, out of Volkmar's army of forty thousand, less than a quarter survived to return to Altdorf. Nor would they see fit to record the litany of mistakes and treachery that had led Grosslich to be crowned elector instead of Leitdorf. Confident in the faulty memories of those they wrote for, they knew the passing of time would erase such inconveniences.

The important thing was that the enemy had been defeated and the rule of Karl Franz reimposed.

The physical devastation, however, could not be hidden. Averheim was in ruins, scorched by fire and reeking with the residue of corrosion. The river was clogged with ash and the streets wine-red with blood-stains. Though the daemons had disappeared with the passing of the bloodfire, their spoor of madness still hung in the shadows.

It took months to cleanse the place. Hundreds of witch hunters were summoned from surrounding cities. Volkmar himself presided over the ritual exorcism and stayed in the heart of the shattered city for several weeks. His army remained too, though their swords were swiftly replaced with picks and shovels. The task of demolishing the remains of the Tower and restoring what was left of old Averheim was long and arduous.

In the days after the battle ended, there were many, Helborg among them, who counselled that Averheim should be abandoned. The stain of Chaos ran too deep, and the losses had been too grievous. It was Volkmar who overruled them. The greater war still ground on in the north, soaking up resources and manpower, sapping the will of the Empire. The populace needed a sign of victory. They needed to be shown that the lost ground could be recovered.

So he ordered the city to be reclaimed. Broken houses and streets were repaired with the labour of his men. Merchants, soldiers and families were enticed from the nearby towns with the promise of property and wealth. Grosslich's treasuries were discovered and the gold used for the work of reconstruction. Only the iron of the Tower was not reused. The ruins were cordoned off for weeks as a phalanx of priests ritually destroyed the foundations. The reek of molten metal hung over the city in a pall of bitterness long after the last of the iron had been turned into ingots and shipped away.

Beneath it all was the Stone. Only Volkmar descended back down to the hidden chamber during the long months of recovery, and he never said what work was done there. As the autumn faded into winter, the wide courtyard of the Tower was finally paved over again, and the last of Grosslich's gold used to sponsor the construction of a cathedral on the site. In later years, the Church of Sigmar the Destroyer of Heresy rose up in place of the Tower, vast and opulent, a counterpart to the restored Averburg across the river. It would become a centre of pilgrimage as the years wore on, drawing supplicants from across the southern provinces of the Empire. Few priests wished to serve in its incense-soaked naves, however. It swiftly developed an evil reputation for ill-luck, and the clerics were prone to bad dreams.

Though it took many more years, Averland recovered much of its prosperity. The people of the province were fertile, the land was still good, and memories were quick to dim. The destruction of Averheim was the making of some families, just as it was the doom of others. Trade resumed along the Aver, and the last of Grosslich's edicts were repealed.

A new Steward was appointed. Klaus Meuningen was a surprise choice, taken from provincial obscurity in Grenzstadt and given command of the capital. He proved capable enough, however, and loyal to the Emperor in most things. Under his rule, the clamour for a new elector faded again. Whenever the issue was raised, some excuse was found to shelve it. All knew that the matter would have to be returned to at some point in the future, but all also knew that it would be long before Averland was ready again.

In the immediate aftermath of the great battle, none of these things were obvious. Volkmar's troops were mostly just glad to be alive. Under Kraus's leadership, they gradually went about the grim business of finishing off Grosslich's will-bereft forces. When Volkmar returned from the city to resume command, huge pyres were constructed for the dead. As at Turgitz, one was raised for the corrupted, another for the uncorrupted. The latter burned with a pure, angry flame. The former would smoulder for weeks, tinged with lilac.

All knew that the vista would never be the same again. The old fertile soil had been ruined by Natassja's poisons, and the Averpeak now slumped into ruin where the war engines had demolished it.

Even there, though, the grass would grow again. It just took time, the great healer of all wounds.

VERSTOHLEN LAY ON a pallet and gazed at the roof of his tent. Despite the blankets and cloak that covered him, he shivered. The wind from the east was bitter, and the last shreds of summer had been driven away. Four days since the battle, and he had barely slept. Worse than that, the poisons still worked within him. Thanks to the expert attentions of one of Volkmar's apothecaries, he had survived the worst of it. He was enough of an alchemist to know that the damage done to him was severe, though. He still couldn't walk, and his vision was cloudy. Perhaps that would improve in time. Perhaps it wouldn't.

The flaps of the tent entrance opened, and Schwarzhelm ducked down through the gap. He was ludicrously outsized for the cramped space, and stooped within like a giant trying to squeeze into the hovel of a peasant.

'How do you feel?' he asked.

'Better,' he lied.

'There are rooms being made ready in the city. You should move to them.'

'I don't think so,' said Verstohlen, shuddering under his blankets. 'Here is fine. I never want to see Averheim again.'

Schwarzhelm shrugged.

'So be it, but I'll be gone soon. The Emperor has demanded my presence.'

'I'm glad of it. He's forgiven you?'

'I doubt it. There'll be penance for this. The north.'

'More fighting? How dreadful for you.'

Schwarzhelm didn't smile, but nor did he scowl. A cloud of bitterness seemed to have lifted from him.

'I could use a spy up there,' he said.

Verstohlen shook his head.

'I think my prowess on a battlefield has been demonstrated,' he said. 'In any case, the days of the family are over.'

He looked up at Schwarzhelm.

'I'm sorry, my lord,' he said. 'There'll be no more of this for me.'

Schwarzhelm raised an eyebrow.

'You're ill, Pieter. Make no hasty choices.'

Verstohlen smiled sadly.

'When Leonora died, all I wanted was a way to fight the enemy. You gave me that. We've done much good together, and I'm proud of it.'

He shook his head, thinking back over the past months.

'Not now. My usefulness is over. Perhaps there'll be some other way to continue in service. Or maybe my time has ended.'

Schwarzhelm pursed his lips thoughtfully. He gave Verstohlen a long, searching look.

'We'll speak on this again,' he said at last. 'There are many ways a man can serve the Emperor, and your gifts are unique. Think on it anew when your wounds are recovered.'

Verstohlen winced at the mention of his wounds. He knew that some of them would never be made whole.

'As you wish,' he said, suddenly wanting to change the subject. 'And what of you, my lord? This has been a trial for all of us.'

'So it has,' said the Emperor's Champion. 'And there will be more trials to come. But we have prevailed here, and that is all that matters.'

He rose awkwardly, hampered by the canvas above him.

'I'm glad to see you recovering,' he said gruffly. 'Remember what I said – make no hasty choices. Inform me of your progress when you can. I've lost many friends here, Pieter. I do not wish to lose another.'

*Friends.* That was not a word he'd heard Schwarzhelm use before.

'I will,' was all he said.

Schwarzhelm nodded, then turned clumsily and pushed his way from the tent.

Verstohlen lay back on his pallet, worn out by the exertion of conversation. Already he could feel the poisons within him boiling for a fresh assault. There would be no easy recovery from this, no simple road back to redemption.

'*Leonora...*' he breathed, and closed his eyes.

At the least, some good had been achieved. He saw her face clearly now. There were no more masks looming up in his dreams. The pain would endure, he knew, but the nightmares were over.

ON THE RUINED slopes of the Averpeak, Helborg and Volkmar surveyed the work below. Two miles distant, the ruins of Averheim smouldered. The day had dawned cold, and the smoke of many fires drifted across the wide plain. The stench of burning flesh and molten metal hung heavy in the air despite the sharp breeze still coming from the east.

'You've had word from the Emperor?' asked the Reiksmarshal, gazing over the scene of destruction impassively. His wound had been re-stitched, and he looked fully restored to health. His armour glinted in the pale daylight, and his heavy cloak lifted in the breeze.

Volkmar nodded.

'He's summoned Schwarzhelm back to Altdorf. I'm to remain until the city is secure.'

'Anything else?'

Volkmar smiled grimly.

'He sent his congratulations. I think he wants you back in the north soon.'

Helborg nodded curtly. That was to be expected. He was already itching to leave, eager to find the next battlefield. He'd return to Nuln, then to Altdorf, then onwards to wherever Karl Franz deployed him. Such was his life in the service of the Empire, and he'd have it no other way.

'This was too close, Theogonist,' he mused, looking over at the remains of the Tower. The shards of iron stuck up into the air like bones. 'If Leitdorf hadn't had the name of–'

'He did,' said Volkmar sharply. 'Providence willed it, and faith was repaid.'

Helborg nodded slowly.

'So it was,' he said. 'All the same.'

He turned away from the scene.

'Will there be a cenotaph for Leitdorf?'

'In time. He'll be remembered as a hero.'

'And his last wish?'

'History will not be rewritten. The cause of Marius's madness will not be disclosed.'

Helborg nodded again. He regretted that, but knew the reasons for it.

'Leitdorf thought he was immune to Chaos,' he said. 'I didn't believe it when he told me. Tell me Volkmar, are there bloodlines where corruption cannot hold?'

Volkmar shrugged.

'Perhaps,' he said. 'It matters not. His line is ended, and speculation wins no wars.'

'His words still trouble me. We could have learned much, had he lived.'

'Do not delve too deeply. The ways of the enemy are subtle. Only faith and steel endure.'

'For how long, Theogonist?' asked Helborg, looking at him bleakly. Both men knew what he meant. The war in the north would churn onwards indefinitely. With every victory there came ruinous cost. Averheim was just the latest in the litany of wounds suffered by the Empire. It couldn't last forever.

'Until the last of us falls,' replied Volkmar, and there was no comfort in his voice.

They were interrupted then. A heavy figure clambered up the slope towards them, sinking deep into the churned-up soil in his plate armour. A longsword hung by his side, and a pendant in the form of Ghal Maraz swung from his neck.

Volkmar bowed to Helborg.

'I have much to detain me,' he said, preparing to head back to the city. 'We'll speak again this evening. The dawn may bring fresh counsel.'

'Sigmar be with you, Theogonist.'

'Oh, I'm sure He will be.'

The man limped down the slope, nodding in greeting to Schwarzhelm as the men passed one another.

Then there were only two of them on the ridge, Helborg and Schwarzhelm, the masters of the Emperor's armies.

They both stood in silence, looking back over the city. A fresh column of troops from Streissen had arrived and was making its way across the pitted, trench-laced battlefield. Even from such a distance, both Helborg and Schwarzhelm could see the amazement and horror on the men's faces.

'I hear you're being taken from us,' said the Marshal at last, keeping his eyes fixed on Averheim.

'Soon,' replied Schwarzhelm, his voice rumbling from deep within his barrel chest. 'Karl Franz wishes to hear my penance.'

'Then be sure to tell him everything,' said Helborg.

'I will.'

More silence. Even after the reconciliation on the moors, there had been few enough occasions for the two old warriors to converse. In the aftermath of the battle, they'd found ways of avoiding one another, dancing around the issue between them like old lovers reunited by chance. They were death-dealers, not wordsmiths, and expression did not come easily to either.

'I'm glad you came back, Ludwig,' said Helborg at last. The words were clipped and awkward.

'Duty demanded it.'

'Even so. A lesser man would have kept his distance.' He turned to Schwarzhelm, and a wry smile broke across his face. 'I was ready to kill you.'

'You'd have been within your rights.'

Helborg waved his hand dismissively.

'The great enemy was at work. We both know that.'

'They played on my resentment, Kurt. That was real enough.'

Helborg looked at Schwarzhelm carefully.

'Then maybe you were within your rights too.'

Schwarzhelm said nothing. Helborg turned back to the vista below and drew in a long, cleansing breath. High up the Averpeak, the air was less caustic than on the plain.

'This must never happen again,' he said. 'We will always be rivals, you and I, but we must never be enemies.'

'Never,' agreed Schwarzhelm.

'Will you swear it?' asked Helborg. 'The swords are holy enough. They will witness an oath.'

He drew the Klingerach, and the blade glistened in the cold light. The notch was still present, halfway along the length of the blade. It would be forged anew when time allowed.

'I will swear it,' said Schwarzhelm, and drew the Rechtstahl.

The blades crossed, meeting at the hilt. Both men faced one another, divided by the locked steel.

'For the Empire,' said the Emperor's Champion, gripping the Sword of Justice tightly. 'No division between us.'

'For the Empire,' replied the Reiksmarshal, holding the Sword of Vengeance two-handed. 'No division.'

They stood in that position for many heartbeats, letting the spirits of their weapons hear the words, keeping the blades in place while the oath still echoed. Below them, the fields of death stretched away, a monument to the folly and avarice of treachery. The blackened stones still smoked from the fires of war, and the river remained clogged and choking.

Beyond them, though, on the horizon, fields of grass remained as lush as before. Mankind remained the master of Averland. In the distance, the cloud cover broke, exposing shafts of sunlight on the far hills. There was still beauty in the world, still riches worth fighting for.

At length, the swords were unlocked and sheathed. The two men said nothing more, but turned to walk down the slope of the Averpeak and back to the city. Behind them, the wind moaned across the grasses of the ridge, tousling the tufts and running down the far side to where the honoured dead had been buried.

There lay Skarr, and Bloch, and Gruppen, and others who had perished in the final battle for Averheim. No headstone marked their resting places, nor monument recorded their endeavours. Their deeds had been enough, and they were heroes just as much as those that still lived, a part of the tapestry of actions that had shaped the Empire since the days of Sigmar, a fleeting echo amid the clamour of the war that would never end, the war that would give birth to fresh heroes with every sword-thrust and spear-plunge, that would spawn treachery and deceit anew from the halls of madness at the roof of the world, and that would drench the lands of men in blood and valour until the End Times came and the long-honed mettle of humanity was put to the ultimate test at last.

Until then, their trials were over.

## Epilogue

IT WAS FAR into the east of Averland, far from the worst of the fighting. A mean place, just a few houses clustered inside a low stone wall. Chickens rooted through the straw and rubble of the only street, and old puddles of grimy water sat under the eaves of the dwellings.

So small it barely merited a name, the settlement had played no part in any of the great events of the province. It sat on the very edge of Marius Leitdorf's old domains, forgotten by all, cherished by none. In the five months since the recovery of Averheim, the new owners hadn't even bothered to organise a tax collection, and it remained as isolated as it had ever been.

At the far end of the village, one house maintained a burning hearth even in the middle of the day. Dirty smoke poured from the unseasoned wood, rolling into the grey sky. There were screams from the house within. Women came and went, some carrying pails of water, others with blood-soaked rags.

There was a girl inside. Maybe seventeen summers. Her cheeks were red with pain and effort, and her skin was glossy with sweat.

'Shallya,' cursed the wisewoman, throwing down another drenched rag and reaching for another. 'We'll lose both of them.'

The mother of the girl, cradling her head in her lap, stroked her daughter's hair.

'Strength to you, my child,' she whispered. Her anxiety made her words tremble.

The girl gritted her teeth for another contraction. Her screams echoed all round the village, shaming the men who stood at the filthy tavern bar. None of them was the father. They all knew who the father had been. They ground their teeth and knocked back the ale, trying to forget the ignominy. They'd done nothing to prevent it.

When the child was born at last, all three women were at the end of their strength. Against all predictions, the girl survived it, though her cheeks were rosy with fever and her eyes strayed out of focus.

The wisewoman wrapped up the baby in a dirty bundle of rags and made the sign of the comet over it. It was bawling with confused rage, fists clenched tight, eyes screwed closed.

'What is it?' demanded the girl's mother, peering at the wisewoman's bundle.

'A man-child,' said the wisewoman, handing the baby to its mother.

The girl took it and looked into the bawling infant's face. It had pudgy features. Not attractive, but redolent enough of the father.

'You must name him,' urged the mother. The anxiety in her voice had been replaced by excitement.

'He will take his father's name,' she murmured, lost in awe at the screaming ball of life in her arms.

'Insolence!' hissed the wisewoman. 'Choose another.'

The girl glared defiantly at her.

'I will name him as I please,' she said.

The wisewoman glared back.

'Choose carefully, girl,' she warned. 'You are favoured, but do not anger the gods. This is a child of the wyrdblood.'

She reached over to the baby and pulled the rags away from its face. It stopped crying and returned her glance. It shouldn't have been able to focus at all.

'Blessed Sigmar,' she whispered, taken aback. 'Keep him hidden, and guard him well. There is a destiny on this one. Just as there was on the father.'

The girl looked down at her child. Her defiance faded as the baby looked back at her. Its brown eyes were steady, and there was no fear in them.

'Siggurd, I will call you,' she said. 'Siggurd, son of Rufus, son of Marius.'

She smiled, and the pain of labour seemed to fall from her features.

'You will be mighty,' she cooed. 'Mightiest of them all. And when the time is ripe, the runefang will be yours.'

The wisewoman looked at her carefully. The girl was already feverish. Her eyes were lit with a strange light. She'd be lucky to survive the night.

'Siggurd, my son,' she whispered, falling into an exhausted slumber even as she held him tight to her breast. 'The runefang *will* be yours.'

# Appendix

My dear Erich,

As requested, please find enclosed the documents pertaining to the Averheim affair for deposit in the Palace Archives. Regrettably, the journals of the late Elector Marius Leitdorf did not survive the destruction of the city, though I have succeeded in retrieving some related papers from His Lordship's retreat at Drakenmoor. These will prove of limited interest, being mostly routine matters of state, but are included for completeness.

The correspondence between Heinrich Lassus and Natassja Heiss-Leitdorf is of more enduring importance. Though much of the communication between the pair will now never be found, the letters the Lord Schwarzhelm recovered from Lassus's office comprise a reasonably thorough account of their intentions.

Regrettably, my somewhat hasty deciphers did not survive the unpleasantness at Averheim, and in any case I would not wish to vouch for their total reliability – you'll understand that I was working under rather unusual circumstances. Since I have now left my previous employment, I judged that the best course of action would be to send you the originals, together with a summary of the means to their deciphering. It is simple enough – suprisingly so, perhaps, given the nature of what was discussed: an orthodox implementation of a Vignius polyalphabetic cipher with a substitution key of 'Wenenlich'. For convenience, I have reproduced the table here:

```
  A B C D E F G H I J K L M N O P Q R S T U V W X Y Z
A A B C D E F G H I J K L M N O P Q R S T U V W X Y Z
B B C D E F G H I J K L M N O P Q R S T U V W X Y Z A
C C D E F G H I J K L M N O P Q R S T U V W X Y Z A B
D D E F G H I J K L M N O P Q R S T U V W X Y Z A B C
E E F G H I J K L M N O P Q R S T U V W X Y Z A B C D
F F G H I J K L M N O P Q R S T U V W X Y Z A B C D E
G G H I J K L M N O P Q R S T U V W X Y Z A B C D E F
H H I J K L M N O P Q R S T U V W X Y Z A B C D E F G
I I J K L M N O P Q R S T U V W X Y Z A B C D E F G H
J J K L M N O P Q R S T U V W X Y Z A B C D E F G H I
K K L M N O P Q R S T U V W X Y Z A B C D E F G H I J
L L M N O P Q R S T U V W X Y Z A B C D E F G H I J K
M M N O P Q R S T U V W X Y Z A B C D E F G H I J K L
N N O P Q R S T U V W X Y Z A B C D E F G H I J K L M
O O P Q R S T U V W X Y Z A B C D E F G H I J K L M N
P P Q R S T U V W X Y Z A B C D E F G H I J K L M N O
Q Q R S T U V W X Y Z A B C D E F G H I J K L M N O P
R R S T U V W X Y Z A B C D E F G H I J K L M N O P Q
S S T U V W X Y Z A B C D E F G H I J K L M N O P Q R
T T U V W X Y Z A B C D E F G H I J K L M N O P Q R S
U U V W X Y Z A B C D E F G H I J K L M N O P Q R S T
V V W X Y Z A B C D E F G H I J K L M N O P Q R S T U
W W X Y Z A B C D E F G H I J K L M N O P Q R S T U V
X X Y Z A B C D E F G H I J K L M N O P Q R S T U V W
Y Y Z A B C D E F G H I J K L M N O P Q R S T U V W X
Z Z A B C D E F G H I J K L M N O P Q R S T U V W X Y
```

To decipher the texts in your possession, move to the row indicated by the first letter of the key, then along to the cell containing the corresponding letter in the ciphered text. The character at the head of the column will yield the deciphered character. Then move to the next letter of the key and ciphered text, and repeat. Be aware that the original text has been highly truncated, and that even after decoding it will require further work to render fully legible.

I need not remind you of the sensitive nature of the material, and recommend complete discretion in its handling. The Palace Archivists will be able to advise further, though be sure to seek guidance from one of the more enlightened, and one you can trust. Sadly, one can never be too careful in these straitened times.

I trust this finds you well, and please send my best regards to Alicia and the boys. I had no idea Rikard was in the pistolier corps – how time flies! Before long we will be old men, and such things as these will be long forgotten. As for me, I am uncertain where life will lead me next. I will depart Altdorf soon, perhaps for a long time. If you have some pressing need to contact me, the Shrine of Verena behind the court-rooms on the Salzenstadt may be able to assist, though I place no assurance on it.

I hope we may meet again at some point to discuss these and other matters. Until then, may all harm be warded from you, now and forever.

P. E. Verstohlen
Altdorf, Kaldezeit 2523.

## ABOUT THE AUTHOR

**Chris Wraight** is a writer of fantasy and science fiction, whose first novel was published in 2008. Since then, he's published books set in the Warhammer Fantasy, Warhammer 40K and Stargate: Atlantis universes. He doesn't own a cat, dog, or augmented hamster (which technically disqualifies him from writing for Black Library), but would quite like to own a tortoise one day. He's based in a leafy bit of south-west England, and when not struggling to meet deadlines enjoys running through scenic parts of it.

Read more about his upcoming projects at
*www.chriswraight.wordpress.com*

SIGVALD ~ DARIUS HINKS

WARHAMMER HEROES

# Sigvald

*Read this exclusive extract from the fourth Warhammer Heroes novel,* Sigvald, *by Darius Hinks, released July 2011*

'THE DECADENT HOST,' cried Sigvald. 'My beautiful children!' He kept his sword aloft as he surveyed the odd assortment of creatures arrayed before him. Knights clad in baroque, purple armour stood side by side with jet-eyed women, whose alabaster limbs ended in cruel, serrated talons. Looming behind them were pink, hairless horses, whose heads where shrouded in nests of writhing tentacles and whose tails arched up into the venomous spikes of scorpions. Above this forest of insectoid limbs and pulsing flesh, another collection of creatures fluttered and swooped around the pillars of the throne room. Some were no bigger than bats, but others were the size of men, and all of them had vibrant, purple skin, black leathery wings, and the leering faces of gargoyles. At the sound of Sigvald's praise, the creatures raised their voices again in an ecstatic, wordless scream.

The deafening cry was even louder than the first, and Sigvald finally allowed himself to smile. 'We have idled long enough,' he cried, rushing to the edge of the dais, as though he were about to dive amongst his adoring followers. Instead of leaping, however, he waved his sword at them in a decorous flourish and began to laugh. 'Between us we have created an idyll the like of which the world has never seen. Whole nations of men have come and gone, never dreaming that such pleasures were possible.' His face flushed with colour and he rushed across the dais, leaning out towards his army as he warmed to his theme. 'No one has experience the things we have. No one has done the things we have.' As he grew more impassioned, his face began to turn purple and he stumbled to a halt, shaking his head violently from side to side.

The crowd fell silent as Sigvald seemed to be consumed by some kind of fit.

Baron Schüler frowned. As Sigvald shook his head faster, it looked for a moment that the prince was about to fall over.

Then as quickly as it had started, the fit passed and Sigvald began rushing back and forwards again, a little less steady on his feet, but no less excited.

'The world is peopled with witless, passionless cowards,' he cried, sending a trail of spit out across the figures at the foot of the dais. 'None of them have the imagination to understand what we have created here.' He raised his hand and clutched at the air. 'But they would take it nonetheless.'

The army let out another roar, but his time it was a cry of furious denial.

'Yes, my children, they would take it from us. Even now, Mord Huk and his meat-headed butchers are marching brazenly across our borders, edging ever closer to the Gilded Palace. They want to crush this beautiful paradise beneath their clumsy hooves.'

The crowd roared again and several of the creatures began to thrash their claws and wings against the soldiers that surrounded them, itching to tear something apart.

From the bottom of the dais, Víga-Barói singled out Baron Schüler in the front row. His grey eyes burned with hatred as he glared at the bearded knight. As the crowd's frenzy grew in volume and violence, Víga-Barói remained stock-still. His only movement was to fold his hands firmly across his plum-coloured armour. He clutched his chest so tightly that some of the hooks embedded in his skin punctured the palms of his hands, and thin trails of blood began to trickle around the serpentine designs of his cuirass.

Baron Schüler was as oblivious to the knight's glare as he was everything else. As Sigvald continued his impassioned speech, the baron kept his gaze fixed on the princess. He cursed under his breath as Freydís strained to free herself from the chain that linked her to her guardian.

'We must put aside our games and stop this abomination,' cried Sigvald, shaking his sword again. 'Although it's beneath us, we must ride out and defeat them. I will not abandon you to such joyless dullards. Not after all that we have achieved together.' He waved to a tall figure, swaying in the shadows at the back of the hall. Oddrún was clutching the brass casket that contained Doctor Schliemann's head. 'My advisors have shown me a way to enter the home of these slavering dogs. I've learnt the secrets of Ör. Are you ready to sate your desires in the citadel of the Blood God? My children, will you join me?'

As one, Sigvald's warriors raised their weapons aloft, screaming in ecstasy and howling in tribute to their glorious prince.